I0613891

By Mortal Slain

by

E. R. Dillon

Deputy Kyle Shaw Mysteries, Book 4

By Mortal Slain

Contact Information: info@thewildrosepress.com

Cover Art by *Jennifer Greeff*

The Wild Rose Press, Inc.
PO Box 708
Adams Basin, NY 14410-0708
Visit us at www.thewildrosepress.com

Publishing History
First Edition, 2021
Trade Paperback ISBN 978-1-5092-3901-6
Digital ISBN 978-1-5092-3902-3

Deputy Kyle Shaw Mysteries, Book 4
Published in the United States of America

Kyle walked outside in time to see John's wagon rumble through the open gates with the three retainers riding escort behind the body of their master. A roan stallion with an empty saddle on its back trotted along with them on a lead rope tied to the wagon bed.

"Leave the gates open," he said to Vinewood, who was about to close them. "We're done here now."

He crossed over to the stable to retrieve his gelding. The groom met him at the entryway and handed the reins to him.

"Another Southron dead," the Scots groom said, holding the bridle while Kyle mounted his horse. "That can't be all bad."

"I wouldn't say that too loud, if I were you," Kyle said. "The English are a mite twitchy about such talk these days."

"I wish they'd twitch themselves back to where they came from and leave us in peace," the groom said with a fierce scowl.

Acknowledgment

My thanks and appreciation to Paul J. Tuger and Barbara D. Ragona, both of whom contributed their time and effort to the historical and grammatical accuracy of this story.

Historical Notes

Reginald de Crawford (Crauford) of Loudoun, Sheriff of Ayrshire (son of Reginald de Crawford who died in 1297). Relative of William Wallace (Scottish patriot). During the reign of Scottish King William the Lion, the hereditary title of Sheriff of Ayr was bestowed upon the Crawfords.

Prior Drumlay served at the religious house of St. John's Church in Ayrshire in thirteenth-century Scotland. He was a contemporary of William Wallace, the Scottish patriot who revolted against English oppression during the Scottish Wars.

Edward I, King of England (1239–1307) a/k/a Edward Longshanks (meaning "long legs") and Hammer of the Scots. Edward spent much of his reign reforming royal administration and common law. After brutally subjugating Wales, Edward turned his attention to the north to claim feudal suzerainty over Scotland. He met with both lay and ecclesiastical opposition during his military campaigns there. His deliberate destruction of Berwick, which was meant to terrorize the Scottish people into subjection, was the worst atrocity ever to stain the pages of English history.

Shortly after the Berwick incident, Edward confiscated the Stone of Destiny, which was the Scottish coronation stone, and brought it to Westminster. Edward died in 1307, before the issue of overlordship of Scotland was settled.

Edward of Caernarfon (future King Edward II of England) (1284–1327). Edward II was the fourth son of Edward I, whom he succeeded to the throne in 1307. His close and controversial relationship with Piers Gaveston provoked discontent among the English barons and eventually brought about Gaveston's execution in 1312. Edward II lost the decisive Battle of Bannockburn in 1314 to Robert the Bruce. After much internal strife over his failures in Scotland and the oppressive regime of his later years, Edward II was forced to relinquish the crown in 1327 in favor of his 14-year-old son, Edward III. Edward II died in Berkeley Castle on September 21, 1327, likely murdered on the orders of the new regime.

Sir Henry de Percy, 8th Baron Percy (1273–1314). Sir Percy fought under King Edward I of England in Wales and Scotland and was granted extensive estates in Scotland, which were later retaken by the Scots under Robert Bruce. Edward I appointed Sir Percy as Castellan of Ayr and Warden of Galloway, circa 1296. Sir Percy died at the age of forty-one, of unknown causes.

All other characters in this novel are fictitious. Any similarity to actual persons is entirely coincidental.

Foreword

Toward the end of the thirteenth century, Sir Thomas Rhymour's reputation as a soothsayer was well established in Ayrshire and the surrounding shires of Scotland. Tales of his prophecies, embellished and enlarged with each retelling, reached even beyond the lowlands into England and as far south as Cornwall.

In his twilight years, it was Sir Thomas's habit to visit the homes of nobles, whose invitations were undoubtedly issued in the hope of receiving an early warning of any turn of fortune.

When Sir Thomas grew tired of such venal attentions, he made a circuit of the local monasteries, enjoying a well-earned respite from those seeking his advice as a clairvoyant.

Among Sir Thomas's many predictions, one in particular foreshadowed the advent of a bane who would be instrumental in preserving the integrity of those in line for the English throne. It also foretold the consequences that would befall the bane should he fail to accomplish the task. The prophecy, which is relevant to this story, is as follows:

Debase ye not the sovereign line,
Those born to reign by right divine,
Else face ye must the grievous bane,
Who cannot be by mortal slain;
Lest stain he will the base of stone,
With blood from wounds that be his own.

Chapter 1

Ayrshire, Scotland
July 1298

Kyle Shaw, deputy to the sheriff of Ayrshire, sat at a table in a dark corner of the Bull and Bear Tavern. Beads of perspiration stood out on his forehead and formed on his upper lip. Although the windows along the side wall were open, there was no cross breeze to temper the warmth in the public house on that early evening in mid-July.

Kyle lifted a mug to his lips and swallowed a mouthful of watered-down ale. The amber brew was tepid and bland, yet it served to wash down the stale barley bread that came with his supper—a thick mutton stew with more turnips and onions in it than meat.

He closed his eyes and leaned his head against the wall behind him, ignoring the drone of conversation punctuated with raucous laughter. At that time of day, the tavern was filled to capacity with travelers seeking shelter for the night, burghers from town eating their last meal of the day, and English soldiers from the nearby garrison relaxing after the changing of the guard.

After listening to Sir Percy—the castellan of Ayr Garrison—rant for the past hour about an incursion into the north of England by Scottish rebels who left a trail of wanton destruction in their wake, Kyle was glad to have a moment to himself, undisturbed by the demands of his office as deputy. Sir Percy had made it sound like a full-fledged invasion into England, whereas in reality it was an ill-organized sortie by a ragtag bunch of rebels of Scottish descent attempting to throw off the oppressive yoke of English domination.

A loud voice from somewhere off to the left intruded into Kyle's quietude.

"You, there," said a man in a commanding tone. "Get up from that table. Make way for your betters."

Kyle opened his eyes to gaze in that direction through the haze of smoke from lighted oil lanterns, mildly curious as to the cause of the outburst and immensely hopeful the disturber of his peace would settle the matter quickly.

The man who spoke so boldly, a portly fellow in his forties, was evidently confident of his status, for he loomed over the recipient of his demand—a vagabond by the look of him—who sat alone at the table nearest to the tavern entryway. Even without three armed retainers standing behind him, ostensibly ready to carry out their master's will, the portly man gave the impression of being someone used to getting his way.

"You, sir, are interrupting my meal," the vagabond replied with sufficient volume to be heard over the hum of voices and the clank of pewter mugs. He spoke with a slight French accent, yet he used the proper English of an educated man, which seemed out of character with his impoverished appearance.

The voluble exchange between the pair of them apparently drew the notice of every person in the room, for the babble of conversation ceased abruptly. The only sound heard was the snuffle of dogs rooting for scraps of food in the dirty straw on the wooden floor.

The two men involved in the dispute were complete opposites in rank and appearance. One was arrogant, imperious, and comported himself as a man of means. He certainly looked the part in fitted green leggings and a tan linen shirt under a soft doeskin jerkin. A green hunting cap sat on his head at a jaunty angle. His plump face was shaved clean, and his hair, which was as black as his eyes, was cropped short in the Norman fashion. The large buckle that fastened his tooled leather sword belt was silver, as was the hilt of the sword at his hip.

By contrast, the vagabond was a lean man in his late twenties, clad in a short belted tunic of dun-colored homespun. The garment was patched in places and frayed at the hem, yet it fit him well. His face was handsome, with sharp features and a three-day stubble on his square jaw. His eyes were a curious shade of amber, and his long brown hair, veined with blond streaks from exposure to the sun, was clubbed back and tied at the nape of his neck with a leather thong. The stained home-tanned cowhide sheath on his belt was empty, for he was using his dagger—a small double-edged blade with a plain wooden handle—as a utensil with which to eat.

On hearing the vagabond's retort, the portly man's face flushed with anger, and blue veins began to throb in his temples. "How dare you speak to me like that," he barked. "I'll teach you manners, you lout." He reached for the silver hilt of his sword and drew forth the weapon.

The scrape of steel against the metal lip of the

scabbard reached Kyle's ears where he sat halfway across the room. He heaved himself to his feet, his brief reprieve from the cares of the constabulary plainly at an end. He started forward, ready to intervene between the two men, should it become necessary. Some of the English soldiers he passed along the way appeared hopeful that the dispute over the occupancy of the table would escalate into a brawl, which would brighten an otherwise uneventful evening.

The vagabond laid his dagger on the table and wiped his fingers on the front of his tunic. His countenance was neither compliant nor defiant. He just sat there waiting, as though to see what the portly man would do next. Even so, there was a wary vigilance about him, like a coiled spring ready to leap into action if pushed too far.

Kyle walked up at that moment and identified himself, including both men in the introduction. "What seems to be the problem?" he said, looking from one to the other.

"The fellow wants my table." The vagabond glanced down at the glob of thick stew clinging to a small slab of bread. "As you can see, I have not yet finished my supper."

Kyle's gaze shifted to the portly man. "He'll be done in a minute," he said in the most reasonable tone he could muster. He tilted his head at the drawn sword. "No need to shed blood over something so trivial."

The vagabond picked up his dagger and went back to eating his food.

"I will decide what is trivial and what is not," the portly man said. "Just do your duty and remove that man at once."

"What for?" Kyle said. "He is causing no mischief. In truth, you are the only one waving a sword about."

The portly man's face went from red to purple at the pointed remark. "I will not be contradicted," he blustered. "Do you know who I am?"

"You have me at a disadvantage, m'lord, for I cannot claim the honor of your acquaintance," Kyle said with a disarming smile meant to forestall the man's rancor. Otherwise, it might prove difficult to explain to Sir Percy why he—a deputy hired to keep civil order—engaged in a sword fight with an Englishman over a tavern table.

"I am Sir Guy de Forz of the House of Lancaster, Peer of the Realm." He lifted his chin as he spoke, clearly proud of his heritage.

"Welcome to the port town of Ayr, m'lord," Kyle said with a slight inclination of his head.

Sir Guy's measuring glance swept the tall Scots deputy in the prime of life from head to toe, taking in the tawny hair that fell in waves to his broad shoulders, the pale blue eyes as transparent as ice, and the well-muscled body under a belted brown linen tunic that reached his bare knees. The black eyes came to rest on the only blemish that marred the lean and finely chiseled features—a white seam of a scar that ran from temple to jaw on the left side of his clean-shaven face.

"A souvenir from a Flemish halberd on the field of battle," Kyle said in response to the portly man's questioning gaze. "Unfortunately for the halberdier, he did not live long enough to brag about it."

"I can tell you are a man of action," Sir Guy said. "I will take it, then, that you are capable of dealing with the barbarians that infest this land."

"Which barbarians are you referring to, m'lord?" Kyle said.

"The Scotch and the French, of course," Sir Guy said, glancing meaningfully at the vagabond.

"Perhaps you are not aware that I am a Scotsman, born and bred," Kyle said, just to be perverse.

"I am astonished to hear it." Sir Guy looked genuinely taken aback. "You do not converse in the unintelligible gibberish of the locals."

"I blame that on the years I spent in France," Kyle said. "I served in the French king's army as liaison between the provost marshal and mercenaries accused of criminal offenses."

"I see," Sir Guy said, apparently at a loss of words.

About that time, the vagabond cleaned both sides of his dagger on a bit of leftover bread and returned the blade to the sheath at his waist. He rose to his feet and slung a cloth sack over his shoulder. "Your table awaits, m'lord," he said to Sir Guy with an exaggerated bow. He retrieved his quarterstaff from where it lay on the floor under the bench, turned on his heel, and headed for the tavern door.

"It's about time," Sir Guy grumbled. He placed the tip of his sword against the lip of his scabbard and rammed it in. "Do not think you will get away with your effrontery," he said in a loud voice directed at the departing vagabond.

Without a backward glance, the young man opened the door and went out into the twilight beyond.

Sir Guy glanced over at Kyle. "As for you, I shall not overlook your dereliction of duty. Sir Percy will hear about this before I leave in the morning." He seated himself at the now-vacant table and gestured for his retainers to settle on the bench across from him.

****

"Pompous arse," the vagabond muttered under his breath as he stepped from the tavern with his staff in his hand. He carried his travel bag with care, for in it was the precious cargo with which he'd been entrusted.

He stood there for a long moment, gazing out into the empty courtyard, fully expecting Sir Guy's retainers to follow him outside to "teach him manners." While he waited, a fine mild dusk settled around him, washing the stable and the dwellings on either side of the public house into muted shades of gray.

The only people who came out the tavern door were burghers and other townsfolk. After a while, he decided to move on. His options of where to go were rather limited in light of the fact that he had but half a penny to his name.

There would be no options at all if he continued to dawdle in front of the tavern, so he started across the small open area, headed for the open gates.

Townsfolk in the street beyond hurried about their business, lest darkness overtake them. How ironic, he reflected, that man by nature feared the gloom of night, yet to him, it provided a sense of anonymity. A weighty task had been assigned to him, one that he must carry out at all costs, no matter the obstacles he encountered in the path before him.

On leaving the courtyard, he crossed Harbour Street to the river bank on the far side. There was still light enough at the end of the day to find a grassy place on the sloped embankment. He lowered himself onto the flowering clover and leaned back against his travel bag, using it to cushion his head.

The yellow reflection of the newly risen moon shimmered on the surface of the river. The flickering light on the water had a hypnotic effect on him. His eyelids soon grew heavy, and he drifted off to sleep.

An hour later, he awoke with a start. The moon, now high in the starlit sky, shed a silvery radiance on the trees along the river bank, carving out each branch laden with leaves.

He turned to glance at the empty street behind him. Now that folks had settled in for the night, perhaps this would be a good time see to the business at hand.

He climbed to his feet and headed back to the tavern courtyard across Harbour Street.

****

Uninterrupted slumber was a rare thing in Kyle's house these days for two reasons: his son—a four-week-old infant with a lusty pair of lungs—and his stepson—an energetic fifteen-month-old toddler who put everything into his mouth from pebbles to bugs and anything else that he could get his chubby little hands on. Both children lay in the bed snuggled between him and his wife, Joneta.

That was why the insistent knocking on his front door, which robbed him of the last few minutes of precious sleep, elicited a despairing groan that came from the depths of his soul.

Joneta opened one hazel eye to peer at him. "Do ye want me to get that, my love?" she said in a voice furred with sleep. Tumbled locks of light auburn hair spread out around her head on the pillow.

"Nay, dearest, you stay put so as not to wake the bairns." He tried not to shake the bed as he rose from it, lest the hue and cry of the never-ending feeding cycle start up again. By some miracle, the children slept on, their breathing even and regular as to suggest his effort to leave them undisturbed had met with success.

He snatched his brown tunic from the back of a chair and slipped it over his head as he hastened into the front room. He jerked open the door to stop the noisy pounding on the wooden jamb.

Bright sunlight flooded into the room, nearly blinding him after the gloom inside. He lifted a hand to shade his eyes and found an English soldier in light armor waiting outside, holding the reins of a couple of horses, one of which was his own sorrel gelding.

It was Sergeant Vinewood, a comely young man of middle height, well put together with wide shoulders and a narrow waist. Women liked him for his engaging smile and seductive brown eyes. Kyle liked him because he was dependable, trustworthy, and more tolerant of Scottish folk than most Englishmen.

On a Sunday morning, however, his sergeant was the last person he wanted to see. "What is it?" he said, unable to keep the edge from his voice.

A smile tugged at Vinewood's lips. He was clearly amused at the sight of his immediate superior standing there, barefooted with rumpled hair and his tunic on inside out. "Did I wake you?"

Kyle drew in a deep breath and let it out in a single blast. "What do you think?" he said with a pained expression on his face.

"Sorry to disturb," Vinewood said, his countenance now grave with the weight of his message. "It's one of the guests at the Bull and Bear. He's dead. I suspect foul play was involved, otherwise they would have sent for Prior Drumlay to collect the body."

That chased the cobwebs from Kyle's mind. "Fetch John Logan," he said, referring to the apothecary whose knowledge of herbs and simples was well known throughout the shire, as was his expertise in the post-mortem examination of victims to determine the cause of death.

"I already dispatched someone to inform Master John of the incident," Vinewood said.

"Good lad," Kyle said. "Have you notified the sheriff? You know how he hates to be left out."

The sheriff of whom he spoke was Reginald de Crawford, the late sheriff's eldest son who had recently returned from duties in the north of Scotland to carry on in his father's place as sheriff of Ayrshire, a hereditary title held by the Crawfords for generations.

"Not yet," Vinewood said. "He's attending Mass at Saint John's. I thought it best not to disturb him."

"I will fill him in later, then," Kyle said.

He ducked inside to splash water on his face. After drying off, he righted his clothing, pulled on his boots, and buckled on his sword belt. He raked a hand through his hair to tame his unruly locks and headed out the front door, closing it softly behind him.

****

The vagabond smiled to himself as he used the hoe in his hands to uproot an especially tenacious weed. What a good idea it was to come to the priory yesterday evening to seek shelter for the night. His stomach was full, a rare occurrence during the last few months spent living off the land. He felt well rested, too, thanks to sleeping on a soft pallet under a roof that did not leak, rather than lying on lumpy ground under the stars, where he was subject to the capricious whims of the weather.

Before the midmorning sun topped yonder wall, he would be on his way with food in his pouch and ale in his goatskin bottle.

He turned his attention to the garden plot. If he expected to finish on time, he would have to put his back into it. With the smell of freshly turned earth in his nostrils, he continued to chop at errant weeds that had sprouted up between the neat rows of bean plants.

****

Kyle and Vinewood rode up Harbour Street in the early morning light. When they reached the gates of the Bull and Bear Tavern, they turned into the small courtyard in front of the public house where travelers could debark safely within the enclosed area.

The tavern was a plain two-story, wood-framed structure that hunched like an eyesore among the fine stone houses built by prosperous burghers along the south side of Harbour Street. On the north side of the street, sunlight glittered on the surface of the water as the River Ayr flowed westward toward the Firth of Clyde a short distance away. An alley on either side of the public house separated it from its well-to-do neighbors. A bull and a bear—the creatures depicting the tavern's namesake—had been artfully carved into a weathered signpost above the gated entryway.

"Shut the gates," Kyle said to his sergeant. "Except for the apothecary, don't let anybody in or out until I finish up."

Vinewood dismounted to do as he was bidden.

Kyle nudged the gelding toward the stable that closed in one side of the tavern courtyard.

The groom, a grizzled man of indeterminate age,

came out to hold the gelding's bridle.

"What's going on here?" Kyle said as he swung down from the saddle.

"I were about to ask ye the same," the groom said with the soft burr of a lowlander. "I heard loud voices inside the tavern earlier. Then, a man come out and told me to call the sheriff. I sent a boy along to the garrison to fetch ye. That's all I know. The man locked the tavern door, so I couldn't get in to see what the ruckus was about."

"Besides the boy, did anybody leave the premises this morning, either before or after you heard the voices?"

"Nay," the groom said. "I were here the whole time. All the horses stabled here last night are still in their stalls, too."

"Let's keep it that way unless you clear it with me first," Kyle said. "Understood?"

"Aye," the groom said with a nod.

The crunch of wooden wheels on the gravel driveway brought Kyle's head around.

Vinewood opened the gates to let John Logan, a staid Scotsman on the downhill side of fifty, drive his wagon into the tavern courtyard.

"Good morrow," Kyle said as the apothecary hauled on the reins to bring the old brown mule to a halt.

"Good morrow to ye," John said, climbing down from the high seat. His gray hair glinted like polished silver in the sunlight. "So, who died?"

"Don't know yet," Kyle said with a shake of his head. "I just got here myself."

John plucked his leather medicament bag from the

wagon bed, and the two of them walked up to the front door of the public house.

Kyle tried the latch, but it was locked. He lifted a hand and rapped on the jamb.

The sound brought forth a leathery middle-aged man with a hatchet nose who peered at them through the gap in the half-opened door.

Kyle recognized him as one of Sir Guy's retainers.

The man evidently recognized Kyle, too, for he opened the door wide to let him and John gain admittance.

The front room of the tavern, which was filled with tables in no particular order, looked the same as any other day. There were no occupants at those tables, though, and that made the room seem larger and emptier.

"I received word that someone here has died," Kyle said.

"It's my master," the retainer said in a flat voice. It was hard to tell whether he was glad or sad, for his weathered face remained impassive. "I took it upon myself to send for you."

Kyle frowned at the news of Sir Guy's demise. The man was an overbearing English nobleman, proud of his title and status, yet no more so than most men of rank and position. Should the circumstances surrounding Sir Guy's death prove to be suspicious, it would only confirm that the man had enemies, as did most men of wealth and power. "And you are…?" he said to the retainer.

"Dooley, chief of the guard. I have been in Sir Guy's employ for more than ten years."

"Where is his body?"

"Last room on the second floor," Dooley said.

"Who found him?"

"I did."

"Did anyone besides you go into his room?"

"I didn't go into the room," Dooley said. "I saw enough from the doorway to know he was quite dead."

Kyle exchanged a glance with John.

About that time, the tavern keeper, a short heavyset man with a tan apron over a wrinkled black tunic, came out of the back room and scurried over to where Kyle stood near the entryway.

"It's about time ye got here," the tavern keeper said with reproach in his voice. "That man"—he stabbed a blunt finger at Dooley—"is determined to run me out of business. He banished the guests to their rooms and refused to let them come down to break their fast."

"And rightly so," Kyle said. "I don't want anybody underfoot while I look into this matter. That includes you, too."

"Why, oh, why did the fellow have to die in my tavern," the tavern keeper lamented, wringing his pudgy hands in evident distress. "Why couldn't he depart this life somewhere else?"

"Keep the front door locked for now," Kyle said to the taverner. He swung around and headed across the room, with John and Dooley at his heels. He mounted the steep wooden stairs against the back wall and stepped onto the landing on the second floor.

A tiny window at the top of the stairs shed sufficient light to dispel the gloom in the long hallway ahead of him.

The hollow clump of boots on the wooden floor brought a dozen guests from their rooms. They crowded into the hallway behind Kyle, John, and Dooley and followed the three of them to the far end, where the two other retainers in Sir Guy's employ stood in front the last doorway, effectively barring entry to the room.

"What happened to the man in there?" said one of the guests.

"Is it true he's dead?" said a second guest.

"You cannot keep me here," said a third guest. "I have pressing business in Carlisle. I must get on with my journey right away."

"Go back to your rooms for now," Kyle said to them. "I will speak to each one of you in turn. After that, you will be free to go."

That seemed to mollify them for the moment, for they turned to shuffle back down the hallway, murmuring to one another on the way to their respective rooms.

Kyle went on to the end of the hall. The retainers stepped aside to let him approach the door. When he opened it, the nauseating smell of vomit assaulted his nostrils. He crossed the floor to the long narrow window and flung open the shutters to let in fresh air and light. He turned and swept the room with his gaze.

The furnishings consisted of a bed with a thin blanket on it. A pitcher and bowl sat on a small table beside the bed.

A green hunting cap and a sheathed sword lay discarded on the floor, as though they had been dropped in haste.

Sir Guy reclined on his side on the bed, fully dressed and curled in the fetal position with his arms pressed against his midsection, as though hugging himself. His waxen features were frozen in a grimace of pain, and the foaming spittle around his slack mouth was flecked with blood. A puddle of pink-tinged vomit befouled the floor beside the bed, and streaks of vomit stained the blanket near his mouth.

"What do you think?" Kyle said to John, who squatted by the bed to get a closer look at the body.

"My first guess would be poison," John said, rising to his feet.

"Mine, too." Kyle glanced up at the trio of retainers who watched in silence from the open doorway. None of them as much as blinked an eye at the news.

John leaned over to grasp a limb. "He's still stiff."

"How long do you reckon he's been dead?" Kyle said.

"From before midnight, for sure," John said.

Kyle looked on while John conducted a cursory examination of the body. When finished, he wiped his hands on an unsoiled portion of the blanket and reached for his medicament bag.

"Any signs of violence on him?" Kyle said.

"None that I can readily see," John said. "I will know more when he's laid out in the mortuary chapel."

Kyle beckoned to the retainers. "As you heard," he said when they ambled into the room, "there is a possibility that Sir Guy died from ingesting poison. None of you seemed shaken at the news. Why is that?"

The three men exchanged glances and shrugged their shoulders.

"It is unfitting," Dooley said, taking the lead in speaking for his comrades, "for hirelings like us to meddle in the affairs of kings and nobles."

"I see." Kyle expected an evasive answer, and he got one. It did tell him, though, that Sir Guy inspired loyalty in his men, and that was good to know. "I take it Sir Guy kept his own counsel in his dealings with others."

"He did," Dooley said. "Hence, only he would know why anyone would want to take his life."

"Well, then," Kyle said. "I still need an accounting from each of you as to your whereabouts last night."

"Do you really believe one of us murdered the master?" Dooley seemed unperturbed at the notion, which spoke volumes about his own innocence and that of his companions.

"Everyone is a suspect until the issue of Sir Guy's death is resolved," Kyle said.

"Since you put it like that, I'll tell you," Dooley said. "We all slept in the room next door."

The other two retainers nodded their accord.

"What took you so long to attend to him this morning?" Kyle said.

"I didn't hear him moving about in his room," Dooley said. "If I had, I would have gone in to him immediately. This being Sunday, I thought he decided to sleep in after a hard day on the road yesterday."

"Did any one of you leave the room at any time during the night?" Kyle said, scrutinizing their faces for signs of deceit.

They all shook their heads in denial.

"All right, then," Kyle said, satisfied they were telling the truth. "You may go, although I would appreciate if you would help John carry the body down to the wagon outside for transport to Saint John's Priory."

"No need for that," Dooley said. "We will take Sir Guy to Penrith for burial. His family would want him interred in the de Forz ancestral tomb."

"So you shall," Kyle said, "but only after a more thorough examination of his body. After that, I will release his remains into your care."

"Very well." Dooley bent down to retrieve Sir Guy's cap and sword from the floor and placed them on top of the body. The three retainers and John each gathered up a corner of the blanket and lifted the dead weight clear of the bed.

While they carried the body out the room and along the hallway, Kyle knocked on the first door to interview the occupants.

It took him less than an hour to question all twelve guests to determine where they had been between dusk and midnight. Each shared a room with at least three other men, so nobody could open the door or even move about the room without somebody being aware of it. Fortunately for them, each one corroborated the others' story.

Now that the guests were allowed to leave, they did so with alacrity, not even pausing for a bite to eat on their way out the front door of the tavern.

Kyle descended the stairs at a more sedate pace and walked over to where the tavern keeper stood by the entryway, watching his guests depart in haste.

"I'm glad the matter is settled," the tavern keeper said. "Now I can get back to business as usual."

"The matter is far from settled," Kyle said. "Sir Guy died from something he ate here."

"The new cook is not as experienced as the last one, but his cooking isn't that bad."

"It wasn't the food that killed Sir Guy. It was the poison in it."

"Poison?" the tavern keeper said, aghast. "That cannot be so. I served everyone out of the same pot. Ye ate some of it, too."

"Are you sure Sir Guy didn't receive extras, like sauce for his meat or pastry for dessert?"

The tavern keeper shook his head emphatically. "He ate bread and stew, like everybody else. After that, he and his men retired to their rooms for the night."

Kyle recalled the underlying sour odor of the vomit and its pinkish color. "Did Sir Guy perhaps take a flask of wine up to his room?"

"If he did, he didn't get it from me," the tavern keeper said.

"Let me know if you recall anything more from last night. Even if it seems insignificant, it might have a bearing on this matter."

"I know nothing except what I already told you. However, I will do as ye ask."

"Thanks," Kyle said.

He walked outside in time to see John's wagon rumble through the open gates with the three retainers riding escort behind the body of their master. A roan stallion with an empty saddle on its back trotted along with them on a lead rope tied to the wagon bed.

"Leave the gates open," he said to Vinewood, who was about to close them. "We're done here now."

He crossed over to the stable to retrieve his gelding. The groom met him at the entryway and handed the reins to him.

"Another Southron dead," the Scots groom said, holding the bridle while Kyle mounted his horse. "That can't be all bad."

"I wouldn't say that too loud, if I were you," Kyle

said. "The English are a mite twitchy about such talk these days."

"I wish they'd twitch themselves back to where they came from and leave us in peace," the groom said with a fierce scowl.

Kyle thought nothing of the groom's remark. The man merely gave voice to the hostility most Scots felt toward the English, whose unwanted occupation of their homeland for ten long years had brought them nothing but hardship and privation. With no king on the Scottish throne and Edward of England camped on their doorstep in his eagerness to claim feudal overlordship of Scotland to enrich his coffers, it was no surprise that the Scottish populace was primed and ready to rebel against the English boot on their necks.

Chapter 2

Later that same morning, Kyle headed down Harbour Street to Ayr Garrison. Warm sunlight caressed his back and the top of his head as he rode past the market grounds.

As usual, the marketplace was astir with burghers from town, along with farmers and shepherds from nearby villages, all meandering along the rows between colorful merchant stalls and food carts, sheep pens and chicken cages.

At the end of the street, Kyle turned north to enter the walled garrison. He crossed the wooden drawbridge with the hollow clop of the gelding's hooves in his ears. After passing under the iron teeth of the raised portcullis, he rode into the open courtyard and headed for the sheriff's office against the curtain wall, where he dismounted and tied his horse to the rail out front. Now that Reginald was sheriff, it was his—Kyle's—duty to report to him, rather than directly to Sir Percy, as was his custom prior to Reginald's return.

The door to the small wooden office was propped open to let in a cooling breeze. Kyle went inside and, not finding Reginald in the front room, he drew aside the privacy curtain to see if the man was in the back room, which he was not.

Being unacquainted with the newly arrived sheriff's habits, he did not know where else to look for him. Thus, he thought it best give an account of the morning's investigation to Sir Percy and fill in Reginald later.

He set out on foot for the main hall on the far side of the courtyard. Along the way, he passed archers honing their skill by shooting arrows at bales of straw. Off-duty soldiers stood around in twos and threes, laughing and talking among themselves, while others sat on the long bench in front of the barracks in the shadow of the overhang, cleaning their gear or sharpening their weapons.

On entering the main hall, Kyle walked through the neat rows of tables to the back of the cavernous room and mounted the stairs to the administrative offices on the second floor. He went down the long hallway to the office at the end. His wide-shouldered frame filled the open doorway as he paused to knock lightly on the doorjamb.

Nicholas the clerk, a man in his fifties with ginger hair going gray at the temples, looked up from making an entry on the parchment scroll spread out on the desk before him. His craggy face broke into a smile when he saw the deputy standing there. "Come to see Himself, have you?" he said with a Cornish accent.

"Aye," Kyle said with a nod.

The black skullcap and long black robe that the clerk usually wore lay folded on a low stool beside his desk in the anteroom. He now had on a belted tunic made of thin black linen, in which he looked more comfortable, given the level of heat in the windowless room.

"Is he free?" Kyle said.

"Let me check." Nicholas rose with the quill pen

still in his hand and went into Sir Percy's office. "They will see you now," he said upon his return.

" 'They'?" Kyle said.

"Sheriff Crawford is in there, too," Nicholas said.

"Good," Kyle said. "Now I won't have to report on this twice." He strode past the clerk's desk and entered the office beyond.

The room was spacious, with a marble-topped oak desk in the center of the floor area. There was a washstand near the open window overlooking the courtyard, a large storage trunk in the corner, and a side table littered with scraps of parchment, discarded quills, and various other writing oddments.

Sir Henry de Percy, who sat at the desk with his back to the window, was a man in his mid-twenties, with soft brown eyes and cherubic features. His blue jacket-like cotte was fashioned from the finest linen and stylishly cut. He wore no jewelry, other than a large gold signet ring on the middle finger of his right hand. His bearing was that of a man aware of his responsibilities, as was expected of an English nobleman appointed to the exalted position of Castellan of Ayr and Warden of Galloway by King Edward of England.

Sheriff Reginald de Crawford occupied one of the two carved chairs in front of Sir Percy's desk. He was a lean grim-faced man in his thirties, blue-eyed with long brown hair and a drooping mustache that framed thin unsmiling lips. His gray tunic was made of coarse linen, with a sleeveless black leather jerkin over it. A sword and a dagger hung from the leather belt around his waist.

Color burned high on Reginald's narrow face at the

sight of his deputy. "I'll thank ye to remember that I am sheriff here," he said to Kyle, disapproval evident in the downward turn of the corners of his mouth. "I should be the one to look into Sir Guy's death. Why did ye not send for me?"

Sir Percy lifted a hand to silence him. "You can take that up with him later. At this moment, your time would be better spent hunting for the man who murdered a peer of the realm practically under your nose." To Kyle he said, "Tell me what you know thus far."

Kyle related the details of his investigation earlier that morning. "John Logan will conduct a comprehensive examination of the body this afternoon."

"That should have been done already," Sir Percy said.

"The delay is necessary to allow rigor to pass," Kyle said. "That way, a more accurate assessment can be made."

"Oh, I see," Sir Percy said, although he looked no wiser for having learned that fact.

Reginald stirred in his chair. "I will make sure things are done in proper order, m'lord. No need for a deputy to involve himself in this inquiry. I can take it from here." His gaze shifted to Kyle, as though daring him to object.

"This matter is too important to entrust to either of you alone," Sir Percy said. "I want both of you on the case, so that one might see what the other misses."

"But I am the sheriff here—" Reginald said, his tone indignant.

"So you are," Sir Percy said, cutting him off with

an impatient wave of his hand. "And as such, you will answer to me for every step you take in locating and catching the killer. Therefore, I suggest you work hand in glove with your subordinates to solve this murder."

Reginald rose slowly to his feet, his expression sullen. "As ye wish, m'lord," he said with a slight bow. "Should ye need me, I shall be in the mortuary chapel overseeing Master John's examination of the body." He withdrew in silence.

Kyle was about to follow the sheriff out when Sir Percy bade him to stay. "What is it, m'lord?"

Sir Percy got up from his chair and walked over to the window, where he stood looking down into the courtyard below. "Sheriff Crawford is not the easiest man to get along with," he said. "Unlike his father," he added in a wistful tone. He turned and met the deputy's pale blue eyes. "Be that as it may, his connection with the de Forz family might prove useful."

"How so?" Kyle said.

"While Crawford was stationed up north, he formed an acquaintance with certain barons and landed gentry who are kin to Sir Guy. Should they require updates on the progress made in this matter, Crawford will be the most suitable fellow to handle it."

"Indeed."

Sir Percy crossed over to his chair and settled on the cushioned seat. "Being newly returned, Crawford has not yet proven his ability to apprehend villains and perform other such duties required of the constabulary. On the other hand, you have successfully resolved difficult cases in the past. Thus, I am counting on you and you alone to ferret out Sir Guy's killer."

"That may not be so easy. Reginald and I tend to

butt heads on every little thing."

"Why is that?"

"I think he is afraid I might usurp his power and take over his position as sheriff."

"That is ridiculous," Sir Percy said. "Does he not know that I have the final word with regard to such matters? Work around him, then. One more thing: I expect to be apprised of all new developments as they occur. Is that clear?"

"Even before Reginald?"

"Especially before him."

"As you say, m'lord," Kyle said.

"Now for the particulars," Sir Percy said. "In case you were not aware, Sir Guy's older brother, Charles, passed away several months ago. With Sir Guy now dead, that makes the youngest of the three brothers the only living male heir in the de Forz line."

"How did Charles die?" Kyle said, curious by nature and suspicious by trade as a man of law.

"While hunting deer. He was deep in the woods when he caught an errant arrow full in the chest. He subsequently died of his wound."

"Who shot the arrow?"

"To this day, no one knows. It hardly matters anyway, for it was ruled an accident."

The thought crossed Kyle's mind that Sir Guy, as a second son who by law inherited nothing, could have orchestrated his elder brother's death to claim all rights and title to the de Forz fortune. "Was Sir Guy a member of the hunting party?"

"I see where you are going with this," Sir Percy said. "Sir Guy was, indeed, on the scene. However, he was surrounded by witnesses who claimed they were with him the whole time. Hence, he could not have taken the shot that killed Sir Charles."

Kyle cocked a skeptical eyebrow. Apparently, no one considered the fact that Sir Guy could have hired someone to do the deed for him. Still, the death of Sir Charles de Forz in some obscure forest in England should be of no concern to him, seeing as how the matter was now closed. He took a tentative step toward the doorway. "If that is all, I will be on my way."

"I wish that *were* all," Sir Percy said with a sigh. He ran a hand through his hair, leaving the neatly arranged brown locks in disarray.

"Is something troubling you, m'lord?" Kyle hoped the man would not take that as an invitation to launch into another diatribe against Scottish rebels.

"The Northumberland invasion weighs heavily on my mind these days," Sir Percy said. "I am sure I told you about that raid."

"You did," Kyle said. "In tedious detail," he added under his breath.

"I fear the same thing will happen here in Ayr."

"Given the increase of civil unrest in the shire, there is a good chance it will."

"Is there nothing that can be done to stop it?" Sir Percy said.

"There is," Kyle said. "Pull all English troops out of Scotland and send them back to England."

"That will never happen," Sir Percy said, clearly incensed at the suggestion.

"Then, prepare for the worst."

"It sounds like you are siding with the rebels, Master Shaw. Have you finally stepped across that line?"

"You asked for my opinion, and I gave it to you. Would you prefer that I tickle your ears with empty words and hollow promises?"

"I suppose not." Sir Percy looked unsure of himself, a state in which he rarely let anyone see him. He leaned back in his chair, his eyes fixed on nothing in particular, as though pondering the truth of Kyle's words.

Sir Percy was silent for so long, Kyle took that as his cue to withdraw, which he did.

"Do you think we'll be safe here in the garrison?" Nicholas said as Kyle walked into the anteroom. Due to the proximity of his desk to Sir Percy's office, he was in a position to overhear every word spoken in there. Being English, he evidently shared the same concerns as the castellan.

"If there is a rising," Kyle said, "this is the first place insurgents will torch."

Nicholas stroked his chin in thought. "This might be a good time to send my wife and child back to Cornwall."

"It would, indeed," Kyle said. "When men wage war against each other, it is the women, the children, the old, and the infirm who suffer the most."

Five minutes later, Kyle rode from the garrison. As he turned onto Harbour Street, the insistent growling in his stomach reminded him that his last meal had been yesterday evening. Determined to remedy that situation before going to the mortuary chapel, he headed for the marketplace.

Even the heat from the noonday sun did not deter peddlers on the market grounds from hawking their wares or burghers from haggling with vendors over the price of their goods. There were rows of merchant stalls with everything from weapons to household goods on display. A juggler entertained onlookers by keeping four balls aloft at the same time, while a troubadour's lively song added to the din.

On spying a cluster of vendors with pushcarts selling cooked food in the shade of an oak tree, Kyle nudged the gelding in that direction. He dismounted in front of a cart with hot fried pasties laid out on a wooden rack to cool. He paid the pie man for two pasties filled with spiced mutton and consumed the crusty morsels on the spot.

He led his horse back along the crowded walkway, taking in the sights and sounds around him as he made his way back to Harbour Street, where he climbed into the saddle and continued on to the priory next door.

As it was Sunday, the iron gates were open to allow parishioners access to Mass at Saint John's Church—a large red sandstone edifice with a lofty bell tower that dominated the priory grounds.

Kyle rode through the gates, nodding a silent greeting to the brown-robed porter looking out from the gatehouse. He followed the curved driveway around to the mortuary chapel built against the back wall of the church.

The small stone chapel huddled in the shadows behind the church building, its exterior stained green with lichens. The only way in was through a single door with a pointed arch. A thick layer of sod covered its sloping roof. It had no windows or other apertures, which by design kept the interior cool even in the heat of summer.

Kyle dismounted beside John's wagon, which was

parked in the shade of a beech tree.

Reginald was evidently in the chapel, too, for his rawboned bay was tethered to a low-hanging branch near the wagon.

Kyle tied the gelding's reins to the same sturdy branch as the sheriff's horse and went over to open the arched door. He ducked to avoid cracking his head on the low lintel, after which he stood erect inside.

The air within the square chamber felt cool after the summer heat outside. The odor of stale incense mingled with the dank smell of earth. A narrow door on the far wall provided access to the vestry of the church beyond. A granite altar of modest proportions abutted a side wall, with a perpetual sanctuary light on it and a wooden cross affixed to the mortared stones above it. The only other furnishings were a table-like slab of granite in the middle of the floor and a single iron lampstand with a lighted clay cresset suspended from it by a thin chain.

John and Reginald stood close to the granite table, with the lampstand positioned at one end so as to illuminate the naked body lying on the cold stone surface.

A spasm of irritation crossed Reginald's face at Kyle's approach. "Ye are late."

"He's just in time, actually," John said, wiping his hands on a scrap of cloth. "My examination is now complete." He gave Kyle a brief smile, which caused a dimple to flash in his left cheek. "Except for old scars, I found no marks on Sir Guy to indicate an attack with a weapon of any kind. Nonetheless, he did suffer an untimely death."

"Have you determined the kind of poison used to

kill him?" Kyle said.

Reginald glowered at Kyle, apparently for asking the question he was about to present to John.

"It was either mandrake or wolfsbane," John said.

"How can ye be sure?" Reginald said, joining the conversation.

"The symptoms are similar for both," John said. "Burning in the abdomen, vomiting, loss of bowel control. Such a death would have been slow and painful."

"Yet he did not cry out," Kyle said. "His men slept in the next room. They would have heard him if he had raised his voice. That makes me wonder if there was someone in the room with him keeping him quiet."

"Considering the nature of both poisons, that may not necessarily have been the case," John said. "There is a certain seizing of the muscles, especially those around the throat, common to each of those poisons. Such paralysis would have prohibited Sir Guy from calling for help or even rising to his feet to seek assistance."

"Can either poison be detected in food?" Kyle said.

"Wolfsbane has a bitter taste," John said. "It can be masked, though, with strong spices. On the other hand, mandrake has an apple-like flavor, which is why it is sometimes called 'the devil's apple.' As for putting it in food, it would take no effort at all to conceal the taste. If someone made an infusion by boiling the skin or bark of the mandrake root, and then added it to food or drink, the result would be quite palatable, although extremely deadly."

Reginald listened in silence, apparently more interested in John's learned discourse than in asserting his seniority as sheriff over the investigation.

"Sir Guy's vomit had an odd pink color to it," Kyle said. "That could be the result of drinking wine, could it not?"

"Quite possibly," John said.

"So when added to wine," Kyle said, "wolfsbane would noticeably taint it, whereas mandrake root would enhance the taste. Is that right?"

"That sounds logical," John said. "Mandrake has been used medicinally to loosen stiff joints and heal ulcers. Unfortunately, it is better known for its magical properties. Because of that, the root is thought to be a key ingredient in witches' brews and potions. Some claim it induces fantastical visions. Others believe the plant emits a terrible scream that kills anyone who tries to pull it from the ground. Even after it has been safely harvested by tethering a dog to the root, just cutting into it can be deadly."

"A dog?" Kyle said.

"Aye," John said. "Unlike humans, dogs are pure of heart. Thus, they are not affected by the mandrake. If a rope is tied around a dog's neck with the other end attached to the mandrake plant, the dog can extract it from the soil without harm to itself. Even then, the root is still dangerous. According to ancient tradition, the proper ritual must be performed over the plant before one can safely cut into it."

"What sort of ritual? Kyle said.

"Three circles must be drawn in the ground around the mandrake with a sword," John said. "Then, the person making the first cut must be facing west as he slices into the root. Before making the second cut, one must dance round the plant, taking care not to step on the drawn circles, all the while proclaiming aloud the mysteries of love."

Reginald made a strangled sound deep in his throat.

When Kyle glanced over at him, he got the distinct impression the man was trying his best not to laugh out loud. He looked away quickly in order to retain control over his own countenance, for that, too, was his initial reaction to the nonsense coming out of John's mouth. "You don't really believe that, do you?"

John shrugged his shoulders. "Who am I to dispute the wisdom of the ancients? Granted, many of the legends surrounding the mandrake do sound ridiculous. Yet there must be a grain of truth to them. Otherwise, how would such tales come about in the first place?"

"Do you have any mandrake root at your shop?" Kyle said.

"I do not," John said adamantly. "Nor will I stock it in the foreseeable future. Neither would any other reputable apothecary. Not in this part of the world, anyway."

Chapter 3

"In summary, then," Kyle said, "the killer likely used mandrake root, yet he would have had to go to great lengths to procure it."

"Something like that," John said with a nod.

"So the culprit might well have been among those lodging in the tavern," Reginald said to Kyle.

"Not likely," Kyle said. "Each had the other as witness to his whereabouts before, during, and after the commission of the crime."

"Did ye find out where each of them came from?" Reginald said. "Maybe they brought it in from afar."

"Unfortunately," Kyle said, "I did not think to ask that at the time I interviewed them. Nevertheless, even if one of them carried with him a sack full of mandrake roots, the question is how did he manage to poison Sir Guy without being seen doing it?"

"And why did he do it?" Reginald said.

"Exactly," Kyle said. A glimmer of hope flashed in his mind that the sheriff may yet prove to be an asset in this investigation, rather than the liability he purported to be from the start.

"Well, I'm done for the day," John said as he shook the folds from a black pall cloth.

"As am I." Kyle walked around to the other side of the granite table and grasped a corner of the thin black cloth to help John cover the body with it.

Reginald left the chapel without a word.

Kyle snuffed the burning wick in the clay cresset and went outside. John followed on his heels and closed the chapel door behind him.

Kyle set out for the beech tree where the gelding stood dozing in the shade with its muzzle close to the ground. He was about halfway there when he spotted the vagabond from the tavern walking across the driveway with a long-handled hoe slung over his shoulder.

"You, there," Kyle said in a voice loud enough for the man to hear. He started toward him at a brisk pace.

The vagabond stopped in the middle of the driveway. While waiting for Kyle catch up with him, he dug in the pouch at his side and pulled out a small square of linen, which he used to mop the sweat from his brow. "We meet again, Master Deputy."

"I should have gotten your name last night," Kyle said. "Perhaps you can now tell me what it is."

"Armand de Boulogne."

"What is your business here, Armand?"

A ghost of a smile touched the vagabond's lips at hearing the deputy pronounce his name as would a native of France. "Are you conversant in French?"

"I will ask the questions, if you don't mind," Kyle said. "We were discussing why you are here on the priory grounds."

"The good brothers kindly gave me shelter for the night. In return, I worked in the garden all morning to earn my keep."

"Are you aware that Sir Guy is dead?" Kyle said.

"I saw his body earlier when they brought it in on the wagon," Armand said. "How did he die?"

"I could ask you the same question."

"Why is that?" Armand said. "Is it because we exchanged heated words over the occupancy of a tavern table?" His amber eyes, shrewd and bright, narrowed on the deputy's face. "I gather that Sir Guy did not go willingly into the next world. Otherwise, you would not take it upon yourself to interrogate me."

About that time, the sheriff walked up with his horse in tow. There was a cleric beside him in a long black robe belted at the waist with a length of hemp rope.

Kyle recognized the cleric as a member of a mendicant order of monks known as black friars for the color of their robes. They sojourned from town to town and shrine to shrine, preaching the gospel message and ministering to the poor. They eschewed the daily routine and safety of the monastery for an itinerant life on the road. They were always welcome wherever they went, not only for their benevolent work, but also for the news they carried from one village to the next. Bound by the Rule of Saint Dominic to a vow of poverty, chastity, and obedience, they practiced mendicancy—or begging—and relied exclusively on charitable donations to survive.

This particular black friar was a man in his early thirties, with straight brown hair cropped short around the tonsured crown of his head. His sandals showed signs of wear, as would those of someone who covered many miles on foot. Of medium height, his wiry body was spare of flesh and his cheeks hollow beneath thrusting bones, as though given to frequent bouts of fasting. There was a certain beauty about his gaunt face, so full of passion and resolve, yet it was his eyes that drew notice. They were an odd shade of bluish-gray that looked violet in the sunlight.

"Brother Luke," Reginald said. "Is that the man ye saw?"

"It is," Brother Luke said, his violet gaze fixed on Armand.

"What is this about?" Kyle said.

"It is about apprehending a cold-blooded killer," Reginald said. To Armand, he said, "By the authority conferred upon me by the king of England, I hereby place ye under arrest for the murder of Sir Guy de Forz. Do ye have anything to say for yerself?"

"I had nothing to do with it," Armand said.

Reginald heaved a sigh and shook his head. "That's what they all say. Thrust out yer hands." He removed a rope from his pouch and held it up before him.

Armand's body went completely still. Only his eyes moved as his calculating gaze shifted from the sheriff to the friar and back again. For several heartbeats, it seemed as though he might bolt and run. He evidently decided against it, for he presented his wrists and watched impassively as the sheriff bound them together.

"Come along," Reginald said, tugging on the end of the rope. He swung up into the saddle and nudged his mount forward at a slow pace to enable his prisoner to keep up on foot.

The black friar turned to leave.

"Brother Luke," Kyle said. "A word, if you please."

The friar swung back around to face him.

"I would like to know what you told the sheriff to bring about Armand's arrest," Kyle said after he'd identified himself.

"I saw the man you call Armand loitering in the tavern courtyard last night," Brother Luke said in the sing-song cadence of a Yorkshireman.

"It is no crime to stand about, even there."

"Ordinarily, I would have paid no attention to the fellow. What caught my notice is that he kept to the shadows, as though he did not wish to be seen. When I later heard about Sir Guy's demise, I felt it was my duty to inform the sheriff."

"What were you doing at the tavern last night?"

"I did not actually go into the tavern," Brother Luke said. "I went around to the kitchen to beg for bread. A stale barley loaf would have sufficed, but the cook, generous man that he is, gave me two freshly baked ones. I was crossing the courtyard on my way to the street when I saw Armand lurking in the darkness of the stable wall, as still and silent as the timber planks behind him, which may be why no one but me marked his presence there."

"Why did you not come here to the priory for supper? You would have been welcomed as a brother in Christ."

"While on the road," Brother Luke said, "I kept the company of a man named Silas on his way back home after looking for work in Paisley. Alas for him, there was no work to be found there. We said our good-byes and parted ways. However, after I received such a bounteous allotment of bread from the tavern cook, I went to Silas's house to share the loaves with him and his family. They are quite poor, you see. In return, they offered me shelter for the night. I agreed to stay, of course, so as not to insult them by refusing their hospitality. I only came to Saint John's this morning to pay my respects to Priory Drumlay before continuing on with my journey south."

"I see," Kyle said. "Well, thank you for your time."

Brother Luke took his leave and set out across the grassy yard in the direction of the chapter house.

So, Kyle reflected, Armand's only crime, which was no crime at all in his opinion, was hanging about the tavern stable prior to Sir Guy's death. The problem was that Reginald, upon his return to take his deceased father's place as sheriff of Ayrshire, clearly wanted to make a good impression on Sir Percy, and his making a quick arrest was certainly the way to do it. Even though the evidence against Armand was circumstantial at best, allegations made by an eyewitness, especially a man of God, would carry weight in the eyes of the law. If Armand were truly innocent, he would now have to prove it beyond a doubt, whereas the sheriff's only duty was to establish the prisoner's guilt.

The crunch of wagon wheels on the gravel behind him prompted him to turn around.

John drew back on the reins to stop the mule. "Ye look worried," he said from his perch on the high seat of his wagon.

"I am." Kyle related the gist of his conversation with Armand the vagabond and his subsequent arrest for murder based on the black friar's assertions.

"Do ye really think Armand did it?" John said.

"I'm not sure," Kyle said with a furrowed brow. "And that's what bothers me." He stroked the stubble on his chin in thought. "When Reginald hauled him away, he did not have his travel bag with him. This might be a good time to see what is in it."

"He could have hidden it anywhere. Do ye want me to stay and help ye search for it?"

"Nay," Kyle said. "Go on home. Somebody here will know where it is."

The two of them parted company. John continued along the driveway toward the gates, while Kyle retrieved the gelding and headed for the prior's hall at the rear of the grounds.

He dismounted before a gray stone house set apart from the other buildings and tied his horse to the rail out front. He knocked on the oak door and stepped back half a pace to wait for someone to respond.

A young monk in a brown robe opened the door and peered at Kyle expectantly.

"I would like to see the prior," Kyle said.

"Come in," the monk said, stepping back to let him into the small receiving room. He withdrew without a word and closed the inner door softly behind him.

Prior Drumlay, a dour Scotsman in his late forties, came through the inner door a moment later. His gray hair was disheveled, as though blown by the wind, and his brown robe rumpled and frayed at the hem. Despite his untidy appearance, he was a competent administrator of Saint John's Priory and a good shepherd to the monks in his charge.

The two of them exchanged a greeting. The prior sat at the small table on one side of the room and gestured for Kyle to join him.

"What can I do for ye, Master Deputy?" the prior said, lacing his fingers on the wooden surface before him.

"I understand that a traveler of little means by the name of Armand de Boulogne slept on the premises last night."

"That is correct. I remember him well because he offered to work in the kitchen. Not many men would do that. Of course, Brother Mathew received him warmly, being glad to have another pair of hands to stir the pot and help clean up after everyone ate."

"Sheriff Crawford just arrested Armand for the murder of Sir Guy de Forz."

"So I heard," the prior said. He looked unperturbed.

"It seems as though news travels fast around here."

"Bad news travels even faster," the prior said. "I don't believe Armand did it. He didn't look like a killer to me."

"You would be amazed what some men are capable of when provoked," Kyle said. "As to the reason for my visit, Armand carried a travel bag when I first saw him at the tavern. He did not have it with him when the sheriff took him away. My guess is that it must still be here."

"Are ye thinking of sorting through his belongings?"

"I am, with your permission, of course. Who knows but that the contents may serve to clear his name?"

"Or establish his guilt, as the case may be."

"There is that, too," Kyle said with a noncommittal shrug.

"Since ye represent the law," the prior said, "I have no objection to giving ye access to his property. Ye will find the bag ye seek at the hospice. Ask for Brother Gabriel. He oversees accommodations for travelers and guests alike."

"Thank you," Kyle said, rising to his feet. "You are most kind." He took his leave and left the prior's hall.

It was a short ride across the grounds to the hospice, which was a long one-room wooden house situated on low pilings and set well apart from the monk's dormitory. Travelers of little means who sought shelter for the night could stay there for a tiny stipend, which included a hearty breakfast of bread and cheese the next morning.

The guest house, on the other hand, was a stone building built especially to accommodate important guests. It had five private rooms, each of which had a raised bed with a feather mattress on it. It was situated beside the monks' dormitory to ensure that clean towels and other amenities would be available at all times for the comfort and convenience of exalted visitors.

Kyle sought out Brother Gabriel and explained his purpose in calling upon him.

It took the director of hospitality several minutes to locate Armand's travel bag and quarterstaff, both of which he handed over to the deputy for his inspection.

Kyle hefted the hickory staff in his hand to ascertain why it was so top-heavy. The imbalance of weight was obviously due to the brass cross-like ornament, which resembled the hilt of a sword, affixed to the upper end of the thick rod. It looked like something a devotee would carry with him on a pilgrimage to sacred places. The rod itself was nearly six feet long, stripped of bark and worn smooth from handling. There was a seam on each side that ran the length of the staff, as though it had been split in two, the center whittled out, and the equal halves lashed back together with leather strips to anchor the long thin base of the brass ornament that had been placed within it.

He propped the quarterstaff against the wall and used both hands to loosen the drawstring at the mouth of the cloth travel bag. He subsequently removed a bulging goatskin that sloshed with the liquid contained therein and three tiny barley flatbreads, which he laid on the long bench against the wall. The bread was still soft—an indication that it was fresh. Evidently, Armand had stocked his bag in preparation for his departure. That might suggest an intention to flee, except for the fact that a guilty man would have taken to the road far sooner and under the cover of darkness. As it was, Armand hung around to work in the priory kitchen on the night of the murder and stayed well into the morning of the next day to weed a garden.

He upended the sack and dumped the remaining contents onto the bench. Out fell a thin folded blanket, a frayed off-white shirt, and a small linen cloth rolled into a tight bundle that was bound with a string. There was also a pair of flints for lighting a fire and a small crude wood carving recognizable as a horse, evidently a work in progress by a whittler with a measure of skill.

He picked up the small bundle, and with deft fingers, he untied the knot that secured it. He laid back the corners of the linen cloth to expose a jagged shard yellowed with age that looked like it had broken off a larger piece of the same hard substance. "What is that?" he said, puzzled.

Brother Gabriel squinted down at the fragment. "A rock, maybe? Or it could be a piece of bone. I've heard tales of peddlers who foist the skeletal remains of animals onto unsuspecting pilgrims, claiming the bones are holy relics of long-dead saints."

"Armand does not strike me as a gullible man," Kyle said. "But then, when it comes to religion, even sensible folks sometimes adhere to strange customs."

Brother Gabriel apparently took the remark as a personal affront to his religious beliefs, for he launched a censorious glance in the deputy's direction.

Oblivious to the monk's reaction to his comment, Kyle rolled up the cloth with the shard inside and tied the string around it. He returned it and Armand's other belongings to the sack. "Thank you for your help," he said as he handed the bag and the wooden staff to the monk.

He took his leave and left the hospice to mount the gelding tied to the rail outside. There was but one more person to question before he returned to the garrison to interrogate Armand.

"Brother Porter," he said when he reached the priory gates. "A word, if I may."

The porter stepped out of the gatehouse with a smile. Being gregarious by nature, he looked immensely pleased at the prospect of chatting with a visitor, even if it was a man of law. "At yer service, Master Deputy."

"Did anybody leave the grounds last night?"

"Nay," the porter said with a shake of his head. "Prior Drumlay chose me for this post because I am a light sleeper. Had anyone attempted to lift the bar on the gates, I would have heard him."

Kyle's gaze shifted to the ten-foot stone wall surrounding the priory grounds. "The gate is not the only way out."

"A fellow would have to sprout wings to get over

that wall," the porter said. "Although it was built to keep outsiders out, it does a good job of keeping insiders in."

Chapter 4

There was no dungeon *per se* at Ayr Garrison, for the sandy ground under Ayr Castle was unsuitable for excavation. Thus, all prisoners at the garrison were kept in a windowless dungeon-like outbuilding set against the curtain wall beside the stable. Gaps where the timber walls met the rafters let in air and light, and a latched door barred the only way in or out.

The wooden structure was of a size to hold upward of twenty prisoners, although at that moment, there were only five, including Armand de Boulogne. The only amenities were two chamber pots and sufficient straw to insulate the occupants from the dampness of the earthen floor. Because it was Sunday, the chamber pots had been emptied and the dirty straw replaced with clean.

Kyle walked across the courtyard, carrying in his hand written permission from Sir Percy to enter the dungeon. That was the only way he could get inside to talk to Armand, for such was the security within the garrison walls to prevent the escape of individuals held in custody.

He showed the official-looking missive to the guard, who then unlocked the door to let him enter.

Armand sat on the ground in a dark corner with his elbows propped on his knees and his head resting on his crossed arms. Another prisoner sprawled in the straw, snoring loudly, while three others sat cross-legged in a circle talking in low voices.

Armand lifted his head at Kyle's approach. "What brings you to this dreary place, Master Deputy?"

"You do, actually," Kyle said. With his booted foot, he scraped together a small pile of straw and sat down on it. "I have a question to put to you."

"I didn't kill that fellow, if that's what you want to know."

"Tell me why you hung around the tavern yard last night."

"I was waiting for the groom," Armand said. "I wanted to catch him when he wasn't busy."

"Why?"

"To see if he would let me pass the night in an empty stall. As it turned out, every one of them was occupied. He suggested I go along to the priory, which I did. He saw me to the gate and watched while I walked down the road. Ask him about it. He will vouch for the truth of what I say."

"I will talk with him because it is my job to do so. However, just so you know, I don't believe you had anything to do with Sir Guy's murder."

"Then set me free."

"It's not that simple now that you have been officially charged with murder," Kyle said. "There must first be a hearing, at which Sir Percy will sit in judgment. Based on the evidence presented to him, he will then make a determination of your innocence or guilt."

"When is the hearing?"

"Thursday morning," Kyle said. "That gives me three days to prepare your defense."

"If you should fail to convince Sir Percy of my innocence, what then?"

"I won't."

"You cannot know that for sure." Armand rose to his feet and began to walk back and forth like a caged lion, his smooth brow furrowed in thought. "Nay, this won't do," he said after a moment. "I must speak with Sir Percy now."

"I can ask him to grant an audience to you. Be advised, though, that it is unlikely he will see you before the hearing without good cause."

Armand ceased his restless pacing. "Then I shall write a note to him. Can I count on you to pass it along?"

"I can do that much for you," Kyle said.

****

Fifteen minutes later, Kyle stood in Sir Percy's office in front of the marble-topped desk, mystified at the castellan's reaction to Armand's written message.

After being supplied with a parchment scrap, a quill pen, and a tiny pot of ink, Armand wrote three Latin words in bold black letters: *omne datum optimum*.

Kyle knew enough Latin to read the words, which translated into English as "every perfect gift." He had no idea what the phrase signified or how it could possibly secure Armand's release.

But it did.

Without delay.

And with no questions asked.

Sir Percy sat at his desk, staring at the words on the rough-edged piece of parchment. His hand shook as he laid it with reverent care on the polished marble surface. "Bring me the prisoner who wrote this."

Though his voice was calm, his flushed features betrayed his extreme vexation.

"At once, do you hear?" he added, his volume a notch higher than before.

"And tell that lame excuse of a sheriff to get his arse in here right now," he shouted at the top of his voice, his face now a dangerous shade of purple.

Ten minutes later, two armed English soldiers escorted Armand into Sir Percy's office. The chains that bound the prisoner hand and foot clanked with each step he took.

Reginald followed behind with a scowling countenance as black as the leather jerkin he wore.

"Whose idea was it to restrain this man?" Sir Percy said in a controlled voice that boded ill for the person responsible.

The older of the two soldiers took an involuntary step back. "It was m-mine, m'lord," he stuttered. "As a precaution, for fear he would escape."

"Unshackle him this instant," Sir Percy said.

Both soldiers bent to the task of removing the iron cuffs from Armand's wrists and ankles.

"What is this about, m'lord?" Reginald said, clearly confounded at the castellan's behavior.

"You arrested the wrong man," Sir Percy barked.

"There must be some mistake," Reginald said.

"There is," Sir Percy ground out between his teeth. "And you made it."

"But he *is* guilty," Reginald said. "A holy friar will testify—"

"Enough, Master Sheriff," Sir Percy said, interrupting him with a sharp edge to his voice, his brown eyes fierce. "We will discuss it later." His gaze softened as he looked over at Armand. "Please sit down," he said with a sweep of his hand toward the nearest of the two chairs in front of his desk. He turned his head toward the open doorway and called out in a loud voice, "Nicholas."

Kyle exchanged a glance with Reginald, who looked even more confused than ever.

****

As Armand settled on the chair, he repressed a smile, not for the discomfiture he caused the sheriff, but because of the fact that Sir Percy actually grasped the meaning of the words he'd penned. It was a long shot on his part that the castellan would know what it meant. Yet, if he had not taken the chance, he just might end up languishing in prison or worse, facing the hangman.

Nicholas the clerk hurried into Sir Percy's office with a sheet of vellum and a small box in his hand. He sat in the vacant chair and spread the vellum across a corner of Sir Percy's desk. From the box he removed an inkwell, a shaker of fine sand, and a quill pen. He uncorked the inkwell, dipped the point of the quill in the black ink, and waited for Sir Percy to speak.

Sir Percy leaned back in his cushioned chair and rested his elbows on the wooden arms. "To whom it may concern," he began. "I, Henry de Percy, Eighth Baron Percy, Knight of the Realm, do hereby grant and guaranty safe passage to the bearer of this letter on and across the lands in my care as Castellan of Ayr and Warden of Galloway, which power and authority was bestowed upon me by His Royal Highness, Edward, King of England."

Sir Percy sat in silence while Nicholas added the usual closing language, along with the date.

The clerk picked up the shaker and shook fine sand across the black lettering to hasten the drying process. He then tilted the vellum and tapped the edge to knock off the loose sand before he handed the letter to Sir Percy for his review.

After a brief scan of the contents, Sir Percy seemed satisfied with the wording. He dipped his own quill pen in the clerk's inkwell and signed his name with a flourish.

By that time, the clerk had used the flints in his box to light the wick of a red beeswax candle taken from the same box. He dribbled melted wax onto the bottom of the sheet to form a tiny puddle beside Sir Percy's signature. He rotated the vellum half a turn so that the castellan could press his signet ring into the wax while it was still soft.

The clerk then gathered up his writing accoutrements and put them back into the box before he withdrew to the anteroom.

Sir Percy rolled up the letter and tied a narrow red ribbon around it. He rose from his chair and reached across the expanse of his desk to offer the scroll to Armand. "This will see you safely to the northern border of England. I can arrange an escort to accompany you, if you so desire."

Armand got up from the chair and took the scroll from Sir Percy's hand. "No need for that. If that is all, I shall be on my way." He glanced at each man in the room in turn, including the soldiers, to give them an opportunity to object. When no one did, he started for the doorway with the scroll clutched in his hand, lighter of heart than he'd been when he first entered the room.

****

No one moved or spoke for a long moment. The only sound heard was the clump of Armand's boots as he walked across the wooden floor on his way out through the clerk's office.

Sir Percy collapsed into his chair as Armand's footsteps faded down the hallway. "Ballocks!" he said with a sigh of relief. "That was close." His gaze then settled on Reginald. "What were you thinking when you arrested that man?"

"I had good reason to believe he was the murderer," Reginald said.

"Sir Percy," Kyle said with the purpose of distracting the castellan before the man could launch into a lengthy and wearisome tirade aimed at the constabulary in general and the sheriff in particular. His own past infractions would hardly be overlooked, either. "I have a question, if I may be so bold to ask."

"What do you want to know?" Sir Percy said, duly sidetracked.

"What is the significance of the phrase 'every perfect gift'?" Kyle said.

"So, you speak Latin, do you?" Sir Percy said.

"Very little and very badly," Kyle said.

"Ah, well." Sir Percy looked pleased at a chance to demonstrate his superior knowledge of the subject at hand. "The phrase is a quotation from the epistle written by the Apostle James. A papal bull of the same title—in Latin, of course—officially approved and ensured papal protection for all members, past and present, of the Order of the Knights of Christ and the Temple of Solomon, more commonly referred to as Knights Templar."

"Is Armand a Templar Knight?" Kyle said,

incredulous.

"He is but a servant of an exalted member of that Order."

"Did he tell you that?"

"Not in so many words," Sir Percy said. "In case you are not aware, Templar Knights rarely undertake clandestine missions of a religious nature on their own. I gather that Armand is on such a mission. Thus, he is entitled to the same papal protection as his master." He turned his head to fix a withering stare on Reginald. "That means he is untouchable."

"Even in the case of murder?" Reginald said.

"If I was convinced that Armand had done it," Sir Percy said, "I would write the bishop, in which case he would investigate the matter to determine the extent of the fellow's involvement and mete out punishment, if appropriate. As it is, there is no solid evidence linking Armand to Sir Guy's death. If just being seen in the vicinity was enough to convict a man, then everybody in the tavern would be at risk, including Master Shaw, for he too was there last night."

"Fair enough," Reginald said, his eyes now bright with understanding. As quickly as his countenance cleared, uncertainty and consternation clouded it once again. "That means Sir Guy's killer is still at large."

"So it does." Sir Percy glanced at the two English soldiers standing on either side of the doorway. "You may go," he said to them.

He waited while they filed out through the anteroom and tramped down the hallway. He gestured for Kyle and Reginald to sit in the empty chairs across from his desk. "As you are surely aware, a rising is imminent in this part of the shire. Ayr Garrison must be defended at all costs, so I cannot spare a troop, not even a small one, to deliver this packet"—he patted the envelope-like leather pouch on the side of his desk—"to His Majesty in London."

He glanced from Kyle to Reginald and back again. "I want the two of you to escort Sir Guy's body to Penrith. From there, you will proceed south without delay. Any questions?"

"Why do I have to go?" Reginald said. "My time would be better spent here hunting for Sir Guy's killer."

"Being Scottish," Sir Percy said, "both of you can travel through rebel territory without hindrance. Two stand a better chance of getting through to London, rather than if one went alone. As for finding the killer, the marshal of this garrison will undertake that task in your absence."

Kyle shot a glance at Reginald seated beside him, not sure he could tolerate the man's company for the duration of a long journey. He was not at all surprised to see the same sentiment reflected back at him. "When do we leave, m'lord?" he said with a sigh of resignation.

"First thing Monday morning," Sir Percy said. "That will allow the prior time to prepare the body." He slid the packet toward Reginald. "Guard this with your life."

"There will be expenses," he continued. He rose from his chair behind the desk and walked over to the trunk in a corner of the room. He lifted the lid and removed from it a small leather cinch purse, which he handed to Kyle upon resuming his seat. "This should be enough to cover the cost of your journey to London and back."

****

Kyle left the garrison and rode straight to John's shop on Tradesmen's Row. After tying his mount to the rail out front, he opened the door and walked into the white-washed stone building.

The heady scent of aromatic spices filled the air in the front room. Bunches of dried herbs hung from the low rafters overhead, and pots and jars of every size lined the shelves built along the side walls. A brazier stood in the corner with an iron grill across the top.

John sat at the table near the open window, pounding green leaves to a pulp in a stone mortar. He looked up at Kyle's approach and smiled. "Good morrow once again." His welcoming smile faded when he caught the worried expression on his friend's face. "What has happened?" he said, setting the stone pestle aside.

"Not an hour past," Kyle said, "Sir Percy commissioned me and Reginald to deliver important letters to London. We must depart early tomorrow morning and will be away for some weeks. Considering the inflammatory situation here in the shire, I fear that trouble might break out sooner than later. May I impose on our friendship to leave Joneta and the bairns in your and your lady wife's care while I am gone?"

"Of course," John said. "Colina will love having another lady to talk to. It would also afford Joneta an opportunity to rest, seeing as how she will have help looking after the wee ones."

"Thank you," Kyle said. "That's a load off my mind. If I can borrow your wagon, I will bring them over later today."

"Why don't Colina and I pick them up instead?

That will give you more time to prepare for your journey."

Kyle took out his own coin purse. Before he could open it, John held up a hand to stop him.

"No need for that," John said. "I'm glad to do it for you and your family."

"You're a good friend, John," Kyle said. "If anything should happen to them…" He could not finish the sentence for the suffocating pressure that close around his heart.

"I will keep them safe for ye," John said, "even if I must book passage to Belfast to do so."

Chapter 5

Monday morning dawned clear and bright, without a cloud in the sky. The air was still cool at that hour, considering that the temperature would rise significantly as the summer day wore on.

Concern for his family's welfare weighed heavily on Kyle's mind as he trod the short distance from his house to the garrison. Under his arm, he carried a saddle roll with a change of clothes, a sheepskin full of water, and a small sack of food for the journey ahead. Even though he'd left Joneta and the children in good hands, he would not rest easy until he was reunited with them upon his return to Ayr.

Beneath his leather scale armor, sweat trickled down his back between his shoulder blades. The sword at his hip clanked with every step. When he reached the garrison, he walked across the wooden drawbridge and started toward the stable to saddle the gelding. On the way, he passed a number of soldiers headed for the main hall to break their fast, while others were coming out of the same building to go about their regular duties.

Nicholas stood in front of the barracks, looking out over the soldiers in the courtyard, as though waiting for someone. On spotting the deputy, he set out across the open area at an angle so as to intercept him before he reached the garrison stable. "A word, Master Shaw, if I may," he said, falling in step beside him.

"Certainly." Kyle slowed his pace in deference to the older man's shorter stride.

"I heard Sir Percy charge you with the delivery of his letters."

"He did."

"What about your family?"

"What about them?"

"Will they be all right while you are gone?"

"I've made arrangements for their care while I am away."

"That's a relief."

Kyle halted and turned to face the clerk. "What do you mean by that? Is there something I should know about?"

Nicholas paused, blinking several times, as though trying to make up his mind. Evidently, he came to a decision, for he said, "A black friar recently come from the north brought news that, after the rebel victory at Sterling Bridge, one garrison after another has fallen into rebel hands. Among the documents in the packet entrusted to your care, there is a letter with an urgent plea for King Edward to send reinforcements here."

"Are you sure about that?"

"I penned the letter myself for Sir Percy's signature."

Kyle frowned at the implications of increasing the number of troops at Ayr Garrison. "That is sure to stir up trouble."

"It will that."

"Why are you telling me this?"

"I thought you should be made aware that delivery of that letter will mean more soldiers on hand to fight against your countrymen."

Kyle fell silent to ponder the gravity of the situation. It was now clear why Sir Percy did not want the packet to fall into rebel hands. Still, did the castellan really believe his king would comply with a request for additional soldiers, especially while disgruntled Scots chafing under English domination fomented rebellion in larger, more important towns and cities in other parts of Scotland? "Thanks for the warning. However, it is my duty as deputy to carry out all assignments entrusted to me. That includes this one."

"I was hoping you would say that." Nicholas clapped a hand fondly on Kyle's shoulder. "God speed on the road."

Kyle bade the clerk good-bye and continued on his way to the stable to saddle his mount. The thought crossed his mind that he would have been better off not knowing the contents of Sir Percy's letter. Nevertheless, he would do his best to see that it was delivered into the hands of the designated recipient, come what may.

****

An hour later, Kyle, Reginald, and Sir Guy's three retainers rode behind a young monk who drove a mule-drawn wagon through the open gates of Saint John's Priory. The young monk turned onto Harbour Street and set out for the eastern edge of town.

The mortal remains of Sir Guy de Forz lay coffined in the back of the wagon. Because he was a nobleman with royal connections, it was expected that his body would be sent home for burial in the family crypt. In order to delay decomposition during the 120-mile trek from Ayr to Penrith in the sultry heat of mid-July, his corpse had been embalmed.

Unlike the funerary custom of dismembering the body of a dignitary who died far from home and boiling the pieces until only the bones remained for ease of transport—an impious practice opposed by the Church—a rudimentary embalming process entailed only those steps necessary to forestall the progression of decay that occurred naturally between death and burial.

First, the internal organs were removed and washed with rosewater. The viscera were then placed in a pottery jar, which was filled with wine and sealed with wax. Next, the empty cavity was sluiced with brine and sprinkled liberally with rosemary, crushed cloves, and other aromatic herbs and spices. After that, the cadaver was wrapped in layers of fine linen cloth and covered with melted beeswax to seal it in on all sides. The body and the jar of viscera were then encased in a wooden coffin sheathed with lead to make it airtight.

Sir Guy's personal effects, which included a silver-studded bridle and a tooled leather saddle, filled a corner of the wooden bed beside the coffin. His horse trotted along behind the wagon on a lead rope. Kyle, Reginald, and the retainers brought up the rear.

Brother Luke sat in the high seat next to the driver. The nomadic black friar was there at the behest of Prior Drumlay to accompany the hearse-like wagon as far as Penrith, after which he would be free to continue his travels on his own.

Upon reaching the outskirts of town, the cleric handling the reins continued on an easterly course.

Kyle shaded his eyes against the glare of the sun. The inland road stretched out before him like a narrow white ribbon through a grassy tableland of rolling hills and shallow dales. Distant peaks along the eastern horizon took on a purple cast in the morning haze. The farther they got from town, the greater the risk of attack by bandits. The only advantage to open country was that they could see trouble coming from a long way off.

They soon entered hill country. The peaks there were higher and the slope of the ground more defined. They rode through great swathes of wooded uplands and circumvented yawning ravines and deep gullies. Danger lurked behind every large boulder or hairpin turn, where outlaws could lie in wait to ambush them. In anticipation of that possibility, they each took turns scouting the road ahead.

Whenever they came to a stream that cut across their path, they paused to water the horses and refill their sheepskin vessels. Otherwise, they kept to a steady pace.

It was late in the day by the time they skirted the village of Ochiltree and rode on to Cumnock, where they passed the night in a villager's house.

They set out early the next morning, this time in a southeasterly direction. They kept to the Roman road that tracked the course of the River Nith through the barren hills and dales of Dumfriesshire. Stunted shrubs and wild gorse studded the vast wilderness around them, broken now and again by a shepherd's hut or a flock of sheep grazing on hardy tufts of summer grass.

As Kyle rode along, he kept a wary eye on the hills on either side, for he could not shake the feeling of being watched. They were now traversing the inhospitable terrain of the wilds, where brigands and bandits were known to flee to escape the hangman's noose.

Such lawless men could be hiding just beyond the crest of any one of those hills, able to see without being seen all who passed below, ready to waylay foolish folk who traveled alone and unwary sojourners who made themselves an easy target by sleeping out in the open. He could only hope that the presence of the monks and the sight of the coffin would enable them to remain unmolested.

They met few people along the road, and those whom they did overtake gave them a wide berth before hurrying on their way.

During the heat of the day, they stopped often to rest the mule, for the weight of the lead-lined coffin was excessive. In addition, the cobbles in certain stretches of the road were broken and uneven, which forced them to slow their pace to avoid damaging the wheels of the wagon.

At night, they always managed to find a barn or a shed in which to sleep, once the owner learned the purpose of their journey. The silver coins the owner received for showing such hospitality didn't hurt their cause, either.

About the fifth day, they reached the Solway Plain—a wide flat stretch of verdant lowlands that extended from Gretna in southern Scotland on into Cumbria in the northwest corner of England. The fertile grasslands were well suited for farming and grazing livestock, which accounted for an increase in the number of cottages in that vicinity on both sides of the border. Some homesteads stood isolated and alone amid green fields and plowed land, while clusters of houses along the road formed small villages here and there.

Kyle tilted his head at the burned-out hulk of a stone house on the English side of the border. "It looks like Scottish rebels left their mark here," he said to Dooley who rode beside him.

"That is more likely the handiwork of border reivers," Dooley said. "While kings and nobles dispute the ownership of border lands, reivers take advantage of the confusion to line their own pockets. They loot neighboring farms and drive off the livestock to sell at the marketplace. In the meantime, the enemy gets the blame for the theft."

"Sounds like they are quite a nuisance," Kyle said.

"They are worse than that. Reiving is so rampant in these parts that anyone caught looting can be hanged on the spot."

"And that doesn't slow them down?"

"It only makes them more cautious as to where they strike next," Dooley said.

Their journey came to an abrupt halt on the marshy bank of the River Esk. The water was deep and the current swift as it flowed into Solway Firth a short distance to the west. They turned upstream to follow a beaten track for half a mile before they found a suitable ford where the wagon could cross without bogging down or worse, being swept away. Once they safely negotiated the sandy shallows, they continued south for another ten miles.

Before long, the lofty keep of Carlisle Castle hove into view in the distance. The stone tower jutted above the formidable wall that encircled the city nestled on the southward side of the castle.

Since it was late in the day and since Penrith was some twenty miles distant, they entered Carlisle through the east gate and sought out the nearest inn at which to spend the night.

They resumed their journey early the next morning and followed the road through Eden Valley for the last leg of the trip. Dense woods and thick undergrowth crowded both sides of the well-used track. It was an ideal setting for a surprise attack, which prompted Kyle and the other horsemen to keep a ready hand on the hilt of their sword, just in case.

It was late afternoon by the time they reached Penrith. The trees fell back from the road as they approached the market town. Penrith Beacon rose majestically from the heart of the forest on the left, and the setting sun shone on a collection of red sandstone houses that lined the main street. Saint Andrew's Church—a tall edifice made of red sandstone blocks—stood like a lone sentinel at the far end of town.

They rode on to the de Forz manor to hand over Sir Guy's remains. Kyle and Reginald requested a private audience with the immediate family.

Dooley led them to a small receiving chamber with a large mullioned window that let in the light. On the far wall, a rectangular tapestry depicted the family crest of three gold lions passant guardant on a scarlet field. He bade them to wait before withdrawing from the room.

Half an hour later, Sir Kenneth, the youngest of the de Forz brothers, entered the receiving room dressed in somber garb appropriate for mourning. A man in his thirties, he was a more handsome version of Sir Guy, with the same black hair and shrewd ebony eyes. "Do sit down," he said with a wave of his hand that took in the hard-backed chairs facing the empty fireplace.

Kyle and Reginald did as they were bidden.

Sir Kenneth settled on the nearest chair and listened in silence while the sheriff explained the circumstances under which Sir Guy died.

"Do ye know of anyone who bore such a grudge against yer brother as to want him dead?" Reginald said.

"Nay," Sir Kenneth said without hesitation.

The fact that Sir Kenneth did not pause to reflect on the facts in order to present an accurate response piqued Kyle's interest. "Could Sir Guy's death be in any way connected with the hunting accident in which your eldest brother lost his life?" he said, joining the conversation.

The question apparently caught the younger de Forz off guard, for he shifted in his chair, as though more uncomfortable with the query than the hard wooden surface on which he sat. "I don't know what you mean," he said at last.

Reginald shot an inquiring glance at Kyle, but he remained silent.

"Come now, Sir Kenneth," Kyle said. "You cannot really believe Sir Charles died by accident."

Sir Kenneth leaned back in his chair and folded his arms across his chest. "Are you implying that Guy had a hand in it?" he said, his eyes narrowed in speculation.

"He stood to gain the most from his older brother's death," Kyle said.

"And I gain the most from Guy's death," Sir Kenneth said. "Yet I had nothing to do with that."

"You must forgive my delving into such matters," Kyle said with a smile. "As a lawman, it is my habit to question everything and everyone."

Sir Kenneth scowled at the deputy for a long moment.

Kyle wondered whether he had probed too far and too deep, and now because of it, he and the sheriff might be forcibly evicted from the premises. To his surprise, their host spoke up in a reasonable tone.

"It is true that Guy never liked coming in second to anyone," Sir Kenneth said. "Not to speak ill of the dead, but it did rankle him that Charles inherited everything, while he got one paltry castle in the Lake District and the small allotment of land on which it sat."

"I take it there was sibling rivalry between those two," Kyle said.

"They tolerated each other well enough," Sir Kenneth said. "It was their retainers that caused problems. The two factions got along like cats and dogs, always trying to best one another in every little matter. The one thing they *did* agree on after the hunting accident was if they ever found out who shot the arrow, that person would pay dearly for it."

Sir Kenneth ended the audience, but not before he invited them and the two clerics to stay at de Forz manor for the night so that they all might attend the funeral service at Saint Andrew's Church in the morning.

****

The next day, when the requiem mass was over and Sir Guy finally laid to rest, Kyle and Reginald took their leave of the de Forz family. They were about to mount their horses when the black friar hurried over to speak with them.

"May I go with you?" Brother Luke said. "With border reivers afoot, I would feel safer if I could travel in your company."

"Where are you headed?" Kyle said.

"South, the same as you," Brother Luke said.

Kyle and Reginald exchanged a glance.

"I can pay my way, if that is what worries you," Brother Luke said. "Prior Drumlay gifted me with five pennies in the king's silver in case of need."

"That's not the problem," Kyle said. "The thing is, we can get to where we're going faster on horseback."

"Rather than traveling over land," Brother Luke said, "you may want to consider going east along the Tyne Valley to Newcastle. Any merchant vessel in port there can take you down the coast to the Thames, where you can hire a barge to bring you upriver to London. Such a route will cut a full ten days off the journey."

Kyle and Reginald exchanged another glance.

"That's actually a good idea," Reginald said.

"It is," Kyle said. "And it clearly shows how little we know about the layout of this land." His gaze shifted to the black friar. "How did you find out about Tyne Valley?"

"The canon at Saint Andrew's mentioned it to me yesterday evening," Brother Luke said.

"Did he also mention how to get there?" Kyle said.

"He did," Brother Luke said.

"Well, then," Kyle said to Reginald. "Rather than blunder about the countryside, it would be in our best interest to take him along."

"I agree." Reginald looked over at Brother Luke. "Ye are welcome to come with us. I hope ye don't mind riding double."

"Not at all," Brother Luke said with a smile that brightened his gaunt face. "God bless you."

"Well, then," Kyle said. "If we leave now, we should be able to cover quite a bit of ground before sundown."

"What about the holy brother who drove the wagon?" Reginald said with a worried frown. "Are we just going to abandon him?"

"I spoke to him earlier in the day," Kyle said. "Prior Drumlay tasked him with certain duties that will keep him here for quite a while."

A thoughtful expression crept across Brother Luke's countenance. "Can you spare a few more minutes?" he said, glancing from one to the other. "There is one more thing I must do."

"Certainly," the lawmen said in unison.

Ten minutes later, Brother Luke came back leading the brown mule that had been hitched to the funeral wagon. He bent down to grasp the back hem of his robe, which he brought up between his knees and tucked under his rope belt. With his lower limbs now free from the confines of his long garment, he threw a leg over the creature's bare back and scrambled aboard. "I'm ready to go now," he said as he gathered up the reins attached to a simple bridle on the animal's head.

"How did you get the monk to part with the mule?" Kyle said.

"It was not that difficult," Brother Luke said. "Both he and I are bound by a vow of poverty. Hence, we can own nothing. Neither can we buy or sell for personal gain. So, in exchange for a small donation to the church, he allowed me the use of this beast."

"Well done," Kyle said with admiration. He swung up into the saddle, as did the sheriff.

The three of them nudged their mounts forward

and set out up the road that would take them back through Eden Valley and on to where the River Tyne meandered through the formidable mountain range to the east.

Chapter 6

Twilight was well on its way to becoming night by the time Kyle, Reginald, and Brother Luke made it back to the walled city of Carlisle. They rode through the east gate and headed for the inn at which they had stayed on their previous visit. After a meager supper, they retired to their room to sleep.

Reginald spent a restless night thrashing from side to side on his pallet. Early the next morning, he woke with chills and fever. His face looked pale and drawn under his summer tan.

The sheriff's malady grew worse as the day wore on, with vomiting and diarrhea that lasted until well into the late afternoon. He ate very little, and what he did swallow came back up, even the thin soup that Kyle brought to him.

Toward evening, Reginald's symptoms abated and his color returned to normal. He clearly felt better, for he got up from his pallet and went with Kyle and Brother Luke to a nearby tavern to eat a light supper. The three of them returned to the inn for a night's sleep before continuing their journey.

At first light, they walked up the lane to the tavern to break their fast. They had just sat down to eat when someone came up to their table.

"Good morrow to you," said a familiar voice with a slight French accent.

Kyle looked up into the amber eyes of Armand de Boulogne, who stood there with his staff in one hand and his travel sack in the other.

Reginald hardly spared the man a glance. Apparently at that moment, he was more interested in his bowl of oatmeal porridge, which he consumed with the enthusiasm of a hungry man.

On the other hand, Brother Luke seemed quite perturbed by Armand's sudden appearance, as evidenced by his lowered brow and the downward turn at the corners of his mouth.

"What brings you here?" Kyle said after returning the man's greeting.

"The insistent growling of my stomach," Armand said. "And you?"

"The same," Kyle said. "Won't you join us?"

Armand's gaze shifted to the black friar's disapproving countenance. "Another time, perhaps."

"Take care, then," Kyle said with a nod.

Armand sought out an empty table against the side wall, where he sat down and signaled for the server to attend to him.

Kyle gazed at the black friar in expectation of an explanation for such obvious censure.

"That fellow broke the Fifth Commandment," Brother Luke said. "He is an unrepentant sinner who must be shunned."

"There is no proof that links Armand to Sir Guy's death," Kyle said. "Beware of unfounded accusations. Otherwise, the accuser himself would be guilty of violating the Eighth Commandment, would he not?"

"Are you implying that I bore false witness against my neighbor?" Brother Luke said.

"Not initially," Kyle said. "But now that Armand's name has been cleared, that would surely be the case this time around."

Apparently unwilling to belabor the issue, Brother Luke picked up his wooden spoon without another word and concentrated on eating his porridge.

When they finished their meal, they left the tavern and walked back to the inn to pack their gear. After saddling their mounts, they rode up the street toward the east gate. On leaving the city, they set out on the eastward road at a steady canter.

They covered several miles before Kyle happened to glance over his shoulder.

There was a man on a pale steed trailing half a mile behind them. The distance was too great to make out who it was. Although they all rode in the same direction, the rider appeared disinclined to catch up with them.

"Hold up a moment," Kyle said, drawing back on the reins.

"What's wrong?" Reginald said as he brought his rawboned bay to a halt alongside the gelding.

"We have company," Kyle said, tilting his head the distant horseman.

Reginald trained his eyes on the oncoming rider, his hand raised to shade his eyes against the sun. "I doubt it's a reiver. From what I heard, they travel in packs."

"It could be one of their scouts looking for easy pickings," Kyle said, squinting in the glare of the morning sun.

"Well, then," Reginald said, drawing forth his sword with a slick whisper of steel. "Let's give him a hearty welcome, shall we?"

"Why don't we see who it is first?" Kyle said. "It may simply be somebody going the same way as us."

Reginald looked unconvinced. Even so, he acquiesced to the wisdom of his companion's words by returning his sword to its sheath.

The three of them waited in silence, watchful and wary as horse and rider advanced on them.

When the horseman drew within a hundred feet, Kyle recognized him as Armand on a small but sturdy dappled gray mare. "Ho, there. Where are you bound?"

"That way," Armand said, pointing to the east.

Kyle was unsure whether the answer he received was purposely evasive or merely literal. Because he liked the man, he gave him the benefit of the doubt. "We are all going in that direction. Why don't you travel along with us, for safety, if for no other reason?"

When no one, including Brother Luke, voiced an objection to the deputy's offer, Armand consented to join them. The four of them then continued on their way.

The road soon narrowed to a rough track. Unlike the peaceful countryside of Eden Valley, they were now in a region of ruggedness and solitude, with yawning chasms and tumbling streams. They followed the trail ever eastward between soaring peaks and sheer cliffs. The only thing that saved the area from being a complete wilderness was the occasional homestead that dotted the landscape.

Dusk came early to valley country nestled between towering mountains. At the close of the first day, they sought shelter for the night in a deserted cottage quite a way off the beaten path. There were holes in the sod roof, yet it kept the rain off their heads during the steady drizzle that had started with the onset of darkness. They ate a cold supper of bread and cheese before turning in for the night.

****

Armand found a suitable place to recline on the dirt floor of the cottage. He removed a thin blanket from his travel bag and wrapped himself in it against the coolness in the night air. Using his bent arm as a pillow, he lay down on his side and composed himself for slumber. In the hush that followed, he heard the scuffle of tiny feet moving about the shadowed corners of the cottage. Evidently, he and his companions were not the only occupants of the abandoned dwelling.

With a shiver of repugnance, he pulled the corner of the blanket up over his head and positioned it in such a way as to cover his face. It was only a matter of time, though, before he dozed off, at which time his grip would relax. He should light a fire to keep vermin away. Unfortunately, with only damp tinder and soggy wood to be had, that was not feasible. He turned onto his other side, shifting around to find a comfortable position on the hard-packed earthen floor. After a while, he gave it up with a sigh.

"Can't sleep?" said Kyle who lay beside him.

"It's the rats," Armand said. "Can't stand the little buggers."

"There is something I've been meaning to ask you."

Armand rolled onto his back. "What is it?" he said into the darkness.

"How did you come to be involved with the Knights Templar?"

"Why do you ask?"

"Just curious."

"What do you know about them?"

"They are a rich and powerful organization which enjoys the pope's protection."

"True, but that is not all," Armand said. "They started out as a military order whose sole purpose was to protect Christian pilgrims sojourning in the Holy Land. They succeeded so well that Pope Innocent the Second issued a papal bull giving them special rights and privileges. That brought great wealth and status to the order, and most of its members still adhere to an austere code of conduct and style of dress. Regrettably, some have fallen prey to greed and a lust for power."

"Are the Knights Templar a religious order, then?"

"Not really," Armand said. "The members are not officially ordained. They do, however, consider themselves defenders of the Faith who especially revere the Virgin Mary. They are renowned as highly skilled warriors whose fearless style of fighting long ago became the model for other military orders."

"No wonder Sir Percy was so impressed with you," Kyle said. "Tell me, are you on a secret mission for the order?"

"If I told you," Armand said, "it would no longer be a secret, would it?"

"Fair enough," Kyle said. "I shall leave you to rest in peace, then."

****

The next day dawned dreary and overcast. A ceiling of gray clouds hung low, cutting off the tops of the mountains on either side. After a bite to eat, they saddled the horses and made their way back to the muddy track.

Kyle rode behind Armand, mulling over the conversation they'd had on the prior evening. He now knew more about the Knights Templar than he had before. Still, Armand had once again managed to evade a direct question put to him. This time, it was about his mission, which was evidently important enough to keep the man's lips sealed. All he could do was wait and see how things unfolded.

They continued on for about half a day before they reached the place where two narrow streams, one from the north and the other from the south, converged to form a river.

Brother Luke pointed to the wider watercourse. "According to the canon at Saint Andrew's, that is the River Tyne."

"What else did the canon tell you?" Kyle said.

"To keep a sharp eye out for bandits," Brother Luke said.

"Good advice, that," Kyle said.

The four of them splashed across the nearest tributary and rode beside the river that snaked through the dense woodland carpeting the valley below.

It was late afternoon when they spotted a thread of smoke rising from amidst the trees some distance ahead of them.

"Might that be bandits?" Brother Luke said, his eyes wide with nervous apprehension.

Kyle gazed thoughtfully at the thin gray column ascending to the leaden sky overhead. "Could be."

"It may be a cottar," Reginald said.

"I hope so," Armand said. "I'm not too keen on bedding down with rodents again tonight."

"And I'm not fond of sleeping out in the rain," Reginald said. "Why don't we go take a look?"

"I'm all for it," Kyle said. "However, I suggest we proceed with caution, just in case it *is* bandits." He urged his mount forward, while the others trailed behind him.

Half an hour later, they crested a ridge and rode down the slope toward what looked like a homestead in a small clearing. As they drew near, they saw that the smoke came from a wooden barn, most of which had been reduced to ashes. Only a side wall and part of the roof remained intact.

The cottage appeared to be undamaged by the fire, for it was made of stone with a sod roof. The front yard looked clean and tidy. There was a small garden around the side of the dwelling with leafy cabbage plants and turnip greens laid out in neat rows.

Kyle rode into the open yard ahead of the others and cast a wide measuring glance around him. The ground, which was still soft from the recent rain, was crisscrossed with prints, both animal and human. Yet the place seemed deserted, without a visible sign of life. No chickens. No stock. Not even the usual dog to alert the owner to the presence of trespassers. No one would willingly abandon such a well-kept homestead without good cause.

As Kyle approached the cottage, he noticed that the front door stood slightly ajar. There was also an unbroken procession of ants entering the house through the gap between the threshold and the bottom of the door.

He got off the gelding and approached the entryway. "Anybody home?" he called out in a loud voice.

When no one responded, he pushed on the door to open it wide.

The stench of rotting flesh assaulted his nostrils. From what he could see in the subdued light within the cottage, crude circles and angles had been drawn on all four walls with a wet substance that left long vertical dribble lines beneath each one. He stepped inside to get a closer look at the symbols, only to discover that the medium used to paint them onto the stone surface appeared to be blood.

With his eyes, he followed the line of ants that cut across the center of the floor and ascended the leg of a table near the hearth.

On reaching the top, the ants proceeded directly to a lump of flesh the size of a man's fist situated in the middle of a circle of burned-out candles, each of which had melted down to a greasy stub.

The small mound of flesh appeared to be the source of the smell that befouled the air.

Brother Luke walked into the cottage and stopped short at the sight of the symbols on the walls. "Is that blood?" he said, aghast.

"Looks like it." Kyle peered closely at the drawings. "What do you make of those marks?"

"It's devilry," Brother Luke said, making the sign of the cross on himself.

"It is that," said Armand's voice behind them. "More specifically, they are ritualistic symbols used in a conjuring spell."

"The church forbids dabbling in the dark arts," Brother Luke said, his tone dogmatic.

Kyle turned to look at Armand. "How would you

know about conjuring spells?"

"I have seen depictions like those before." Armand plucked a slender stick of kindling from the wood box by the hearth and walked over to the table to poke at the lump of flesh, which caused the ants to disperse in every direction in a flurry of frantic activity. "Just as I thought."

"It's a heart," Brother Luke said, drawing back in disgust.

Kyle leaned close to inspect it. "From an animal?"

"I hope so," Armand said. "That's likely where the blood on the walls came from."

At that moment, Reginald appeared in the doorway. "Ye need to take a look at what I found in the ashes."

The four of them tramped outside and crossed the small yard to the smoldering ruins of the barn.

When they rounded what was left of the side wall, Reginald pointed to the charred remains of two human forms lying among the burned carcasses of a dozen sheep and a couple of cows.

One of the soot-blackened bodies was slightly larger than the other. Both were stiff and brittle, the burnt flesh shriveled against the bones, mouths agape and arms behind them, as though their hands had been tied before they perished in the flames. The alignment of their legs and feet was such that it appeared their ankles had also been bound together.

"What do ye think?" Reginald said. "A man and a woman?"

"More than likely," Kyle said.

"How long ago, would ye say?"

"Seeing as how the ashes are still warm," Kyle

said, "my guess is either late yesterday or early this morning."

Brother Luke fell to his knees and began to mumble under his breath, his head bowed and his hands joined in prayer.

"So whoever did this is less than a day ahead of us," Reginald said. "We need to alert the local constabulary."

"If you tell the village bailie about this," Armand said, "are you not afraid he will arrest the lot of us for murder?"

"We didn't do it," Reginald said.

"Neither did I kill Sir Guy," Armand said. "Still, I ended up in the dungeon."

"I see yer point," Reginald said, rubbing a thoughtful finger along the stubble on his jaw.

Brother Luke concluded his prayer and climbed to his feet. "We have to tell someone about this," he said as he swatted bits of dirt and grass from the front of his robe. "The bandits who did it must be punished for their crime."

"Bandits didn't do this," Kyle said.

"How can you be sure?" Brother Luke said.

"They would have driven off the stock to either eat it or sell it," Kyle said.

"Maybe we should just go on our way," Reginald said. "If *we* found these poor souls, someone else will, too." He looked from one to the other. "What do ye think?"

"We can't just leave them like that," Brother Luke said. "They deserve a decent burial."

"We dare not disturb anything," Kyle said. "The bailie must see things exactly as they are, without alteration or interference from any of us, no matter how well meant our intentions are."

"Are you not concerned that the heart may have come from one of them?" Brother Luke said with a glance at the human remains, his eyes shadowed with revulsion.

"Of course I am," Kyle said. "Be that as it may, this shire, in fact, this entire country, is out of our jurisdiction. Reginald and I have no authority here."

Armand gazed at the sheriff. "I am with you. I think we should move on, and quickly, too."

"As do I," Kyle said. "We are foreigners, and as such, we wouldn't stand a chance in an English court of law if charged with murder, not to mention witchcraft and destruction of property."

"How so?" Brother Luke said. "Are the English not civilized enough for you?"

"A rapacious band of Scotsmen passed through here burning and pillaging not six months ago," Kyle said.

"What has that to do with the matter at hand?" Brother Luke said.

"In case you haven't noticed, I am Scottish," Kyle said. "So is he," he added, cocking a thumb at Reginald. "That alone puts us at a disadvantage, no matter what we claim to the contrary. What is worse, should we happen to run into the kinfolk of that unfortunate couple, we will likely be hanged on the spot, without even the hope of a trial."

"If you want the law involved so badly," Armand said to the black friar, "go fetch the bailie in the nearest village on your own."

"Why should I?" Brother Luke said.

"To give the rest of us a head start," Armand said. "We will need it in case of pursuit."

"Oh, very well," Brother Luke said, ill concealing his aggravation. "Let us be on our way, then."

The four of them went over to where their steeds were grazing on tender cabbage leaves in the garden.

Kyle mounted his horse, and the others followed suit. "We should stay off the main track for a bit. At least until we put some distance between us and this place."

"I'm inclined to agree with ye," Reginald said. "If the locals discover that we were here, it will be hard to explain why we left in a hurry."

They set their faces toward the east and rode into the forest, following a deer trail through the undergrowth.

A cooling breeze sprang up from the east. Gray clouds overhead scudded westward, exposing a great expanse of open sky tinged with shades of orange and pink from the late afternoon sun. The soft light spread a golden sheen across the tops of the trees above them.

They had gone several miles when they came to a split in the deer track. They reined in to decide which fork they should take.

"I say we go that way," Reginald said, pointing to the left.

Kyle sniffed the air. "Do you smell smoke?"

"I do," Reginald said.

"That means there are people nearby," Kyle said.

"Bandits?" Brother Luke said, glancing over his shoulder.

"It might be that lot who murdered the homesteaders," Armand said. "I would hate to stumble upon them by chance. Maybe we should see where they are so that we may circumvent their camp."

"Good idea." Kyle looked over at Reginald. "Care to come along?"

"I'll stay here and keep the horses quiet," Reginald said.

"Me, too," Brother Luke said.

Kyle slid to the ground and handed the reins to Reginald. Armand did the same, leaving his staff in the sheriff's keeping.

The two of them set out in single file through a tangle of vines and underbrush. Briars tore at their clothing and prickled exposed skin. As the hot summer day faded into early evening, the sing-song stridulating of cicadas filled the air, as did the cloying scent of honeysuckle. They had gone about three hundred yards when a soft breeze carried the smell of roasted meat to them.

Kyle paused to inhale the tantalizing aroma with appreciation. "We're getting close," he murmured.

"We are that," Armand whispered. "I can hear voices, too."

They crept forward in the cool green dusk under the trees, stepping with care over fallen limbs, lest the sound of a snapped twig give them away. When they'd drawn as close as they dared, they crouched behind the huge trunk of a downed oak to survey the encampment beyond.

Twenty yards ahead of them, a dozen flatbed wagons formed a loose circle in the center of a grassy meadow. A black goatskin tent had been set up on the inward side of each wagon. Most of the grass in the clearing had been trampled flat. In some places, it was worn away completely. Small children laughed and played within the enclosed area. Women in long skirts with colorful scarves on their heads tended to cooking pots suspended over small campfires in front of their respective tents.

There were also a number of men in the clearing. Some sat on chunks of logs close to where the women were cooking. Others stood about in groups of twos and threes talking and laughing. Most wore baggy pants gathered at the ankle or stuffed into knee-high boots. All wore either a sleeveless vest or a loose-fitting shirt bound at the waist with a leather belt. Just beyond the ring of wagons, a dozen ponies and a small herd of goats grazed on lush green summer grass under the watchful eye of a couple of adolescent boys in similar garb.

"Romany," Armand said softly.

"Who?" Kyle said.

"Folks who wander from place to place," Armand said. "They never stay long in any one location. I wonder what they are doing this far north."

"Are they friendly?"

"They can be. I am not sure about this lot, though."

"Perhaps we can ask for a hot meal and a place to bed down for the night."

"I don't recommend it."

"Why not?"

"Because they will want something in return."

"Like money?"

"Like our horses."

"And if we don't give them up?" Kyle said.

"They might just take them by force," Armand said. "What would stop them from slitting our throats while we slept?"

"I see your point," Kyle said.

"I hope you do," Armand said. "We should leave before they catch us skulking around their campsite. From what I can tell from here, they outnumber us five to one."

Kyle was about to retreat from his place of concealment behind the fallen tree trunk when cold steel touched the side of his neck. He glanced over at Armand, only to see a blade at his companion's throat as well. "Now, what?"

Chapter 7

"Hands up," said a man's voice behind them.

Kyle stood up slowly, lifting his arms high. From the corner of his eye, he glimpsed Armand doing the same.

"Are you Englander?" said a high, almost girlish voice with a foreign intonation.

Kyle tried to place the accent, for he'd never heard anything like it before. "Nay, I'm Scottish, from across the border to the north." With a jerk of his thumb at Armand, he added, "He's French." He started to turn around, but he froze when the edge of the blade bit into his bare skin. He felt a slight tug on the sheath at his side as his captor confiscated his dirk.

"Are you sure about this, Conri?" said the one with the high voice.

"I know what I'm doing, Eri," Conri said in a condescending tone. He repositioned the blade, placing the point against the back of Kyle's neck. "Drop your sword belt."

Kyle weighed his options before complying with his captor's demand. There were at least two men behind him. There could be others, which would complicate matters. Another problem was his uncertainty of Armand's skill, or lack thereof, to help him fight their way out of the tight spot they were in.

Kyle's hesitation prompted Conri to press the sharp

tip of the dagger deeper into his skin, causing blood to ooze from the puncture wound on the back of his neck. "Do it," he commanded.

Since the chance to take action had now passed, Kyle lowered one hand to unfasten the buckle and let his sword belt fall to the ground.

"Put your hands behind you," Conri said.

The captives did as they were bidden, at which time their wrists were secured with rope.

Conri slipped a noose over Kyle's head, drawing the rope tight enough to choke him if he resisted, yet with enough slack to let him breathe. After doing the same to Armand, he allowed both of them to turn around.

Kyle exchanged a glance with Armand at the sight of their captors.

There were only two of them, neither of whom looked a day over sixteen years of age. From their mode of dress, they appeared to be from the Romany encampment. Their shirts and baggy pants were dark brown, and their faces and forearms well tanned from hours spent in the sun. Had they not stepped out into the open, both would have been hard to spot against the trunks of the trees behind them.

One was tall and lanky, with sharp features in a lean face, high cheekbones, and a nose curved like the beak of a hawk. His eyes were as black as obsidian, as were the tumbled locks of hair on his head. His complexion was darker than his companion's, as though he'd spent more time out of doors.

The other was short and slight of build, with a tangle of dark curls that covered half of a youthful face streaked with grime. The lack of peach fuzz above the full lips marked him as an adolescent, yet there was a shrewd intelligence in his light brown eyes. An unstrung bow hung from his left shoulder. Feathered arrows in the quiver across his back stuck up over his right shoulder. His gaze flicked from Armand to Kyle and back again. “We may have made a mistake, Conri. They don’t look like bandits to me.”

Conri tucked Kyle’s dirk under his belt. “Then why were they scoping out the camp?”

“I thought it was a bandit campsite,” Kyle said.

“I did, too,” Armand said with a nod.

Eri gazed from one to the other. “They might be telling the truth,” he said to his companion. “Maybe we should let them go on their way.”

“I don’t agree.” Conri bent down to retrieve the sword belt on the ground and proceeded to buckle it around his own narrow hips.

“That doesn’t belong to you,” Eri said.

“It does now,” Conri said.

“Unbelievable,” Eri said with a shake of his head.

“Let’s go,” Conri said to his captives. He pointed toward the encampment with the dagger in his hand. “That way.”

They set out through the woods in the encroaching gloom with Kyle and Armand in the lead. As they crashed through the undergrowth, birds fluttered away in alarm. Squirrels fussed and chattered from the safety of the treetops.

When they came to the edge of the forest, they stepped out into the open meadow. By that time, dusk had faded into a fine neutral twilight. The smell of cooking food grew stronger, and the shrill cries of children at play got louder as they approached the circle of wagons.

With a wave of his hand, Conri indicated for Kyle and Armand to pass through the gap between two of the wagons.

As the four of them walked into the clearing, a hush fell over those in the camp. Every eye turned in their direction. Women paused at their chores to peer at the outsiders. Children stopped playing to stare openly.

An older man rose from a low stool and came forward to meet both captors and captives alike. He was a dark leathery fellow in his fifties, with close-trimmed gray hair and a magnificent salt-and-pepper mustache that curled up at the edges. He was built like a wrestler, with a barrel chest and muscular arms. He carried his head low on his brawny shoulders, like a bull ready to charge. His clothing—a belted shirt with baggy pants tucked into his boots—was a deep green color that would camouflage him well in the forest.

"Greetings, Ordog," Conri said with a slight bow.

"What have you there?" Ordog said.

"We caught them spying on the camp," Conri said.

"Did you, now?" Ordog's gaze roved over the captives. "What is your name?" he said to Kyle, possibly taking him as the leader because he was bigger and taller than Armand.

"Kyle Shaw." He thought it prudent not to mention that he was a man of law.

"What is your business here, Kyle Shaw?"

"No business at all. We smelled smoke and stopped to see where it came from."

"Is that so?"

"It is."

"Where are you bound?"

"East coast."

"Just you and your companion?"

"There are a couple of others in our party. They are waiting for us in the woods."

"Is that them?" Ordog said, pointing at Reginald and Brother Luke, who at that moment stepped into view from between the wagons to enter the clearing. The sheriff's hands were tied behind him. The black friar was unconstrained, perhaps due to the fact that he was a man of God.

"Aye," Kyle said, his brow puckered with concern, for the possibility of rescue just got slimmer.

The man who brought the latest captives into camp prodded the sheriff with the butt end of his spear, thus urging him to walk over to where Kyle and Armand stood bound hand and neck. Brother Luke followed on his own.

"Anybody hurt?" Kyle said as Reginald drew near.

"Nay."

"What happened?"

"They caught me off guard. There was nothing for it but to go with them."

"And the horses?"

"They took them, too."

Kyle fell silent to reflect on whether the theft of their horses was the sole purpose for their capture. If that were so, there might be room to negotiate their release. On the other hand, he and Armand were afoot at the time, which meant there might be some other reason they were being held.

Romany men, women, and children began to gather around. Some held resinous torches aloft to illuminate the encroaching darkness, while others crowded close to see what was going on. Their expressions ranged from curiosity to suspicion.

Light from the torches cast Ordog's face in shadow as he strode up and down before those looking on. "These men claim they are just passing through," he said in a voice loud enough for all to hear. "Should we take them at their word?"

"Let them be tested," shouted one man.

"Aye," yelled another. "Put them to the test."

Those gathered murmured to one another, nodding their heads in agreement.

Ordog glanced from one captive to the next. "So, excluding the holy brother, which of you will stand up for his companions, then?"

Before Kyle could open his mouth, Armand stepped forward. "I will."

"You don't know what you're letting yourself in for," Kyle said to him in a low voice.

"Do you?"

"Not really."

"It can't be any worse than being trussed up like an animal for who knows how long."

Ordog looked Armand over from head to toe. "Untie him," he said to Eri. Apparently, he was satisfied that this particular captive was a suitable candidate for what lay ahead.

Before Eri did as he was bidden, he dug a coin from the pouch at his side and handed it to a Romany man who was taking bets on the outcome of the match. He then came forward to loosen the knot binding Armand's hands.

Kyle looked on with trepidation, unsure whether Armand was up to the task. Although a servant of a

Templar Knight, such association did not imbue the man with fighting skills. Thus, a successful outcome was questionable at best. Judging from the solemn countenance of both Reginald and Brother Luke, it was clear that they, too, shared the same sentiment.

****

Armand rubbed his wrists where the rope had burned his skin. "What is the test the big fellow spoke of?" he said to Eri, who was lifting the noose over his head.

"It is like a rite of passage," Eri said. "If you pass the test, it means the gods favor you. Thus, you are worthy of trust."

Ordog removed the long leather belt from around his waist and wrapped one end about his hand to secure his grasp on it. He let the other end dangle from his fingers.

That seemed to be the signal for those looking on to form a loose circle around Ordog and Armand. The Romany bearing torches held them high to shed light on the entire open area.

Armand gazed at the somber faces of the Romany surrounding him. "Exactly what does this test involve?"

"All you have to do is hold onto your end of that strap," Eri said.

"That doesn't sound so difficult," Armand said. A frown darkened his features, though, when he saw another Romany man hand a lighted torch to Ordog.

Eri took the torch from the nearest man and pressed the wooden shaft into Armand's hand. "Here, you'll need this."

"Is there anything else I should know?"

"Whatever you do, don't let go of the strap."

"What happens if I do?"

"You'll fail the test." Eri leaned close to speak in a low voice. "Try not to catch fire. The first one who does loses the match. I put hard-earned money down on you. If you win, I win. If you lose…" He let the words hang in the air between them.

Armand ambled over to where Ordog waited in the center of the circle, taking the man's measure on the way. The fellow towered head and shoulders above him. His body was well muscled and powerfully built. Without a doubt, he was a formidable foe at first glance. Yet his movements were slow and ponderous, and he appeared to favor his right leg.

Now that he—Armand—had committed to pitting his skill against his opponent, he had no qualms about winning the fight. Though he bore the man no malice, he would do what was necessary to ensure that he prevailed in the end.

Just as Armand seized the loose end of the belt, Ordog gave it a sharp tug to jerk it from his grasp.

Armand barely managed to hold onto it.

As Ordog adjusted his stance to contend with the younger man, the strap went slack for a split second.

That was long enough for Armand wrap his end of the belt around his hand with a twist of his wrist to secure his grip on it, even as he made a mental note to be on guard against other tricks from his opponent.

With a span of only twenty-four inches between them, Armand and Ordog circled each other, their torches held ready.

Ordog feinted with his torch, poking it at his adversary while onlookers cheered him on.

The Romany man taking bets scribbled frantically

on a smooth piece of slate with a sliver of charcoal to keep track of wagers flung at him from all sides.

Armand ignored the goings-on around him, focusing instead on the big man on the other end of the short tether. Wary and alert, he watched for a blink or a twitch that would give away his opponent's next move.

Suddenly, the corded muscles in Ordog's neck tightened.

Armand heeded the subtle warning by bracing his booted feet in anticipation of the impending strike.

Sure enough, Ordog yanked on the leather belt again.

Armand let the force of the tug pull him forward. This time, he shuffled to the right, all the while keeping the leather strap taut.

The maneuver forced Ordog into the awkward position of reaching across his own left arm to hit his opponent with the torch. He pivoted a quarter turn to face his foe squarely. The muscles in his arm bunched as he tightened his grip on the belt in anticipation of his next move.

Armand once again braced himself, ready for action.

Ordog wrenched mightily on the belt to drag Armand within reach.

For the second time, Armand bore to the right, making Ordog swing around in place to confront him. The two circled each other warily, both looking for an opening to strike.

Heat from exertion brought beads of moisture to Ordog's forehead. Soon, rivulets of sweat streamed down the sides of his face and ran into his eyes. He blinked hard to clear his vision, even as he tugged hard on the belt to bring Armand close. Though he struck out with the torch at the speed of a serpent, he missed his opponent completely.

Before Ordog could draw back his arm to strike again, Armand delivered a hard kick to the inside of the man's right knee.

Ordog's leg buckled at the unexpected blow on such a tender spot. He toppled to the right, dropping the torch to throw out his hand to break his fall. His other hand convulsed on the leather strap, pulling against it in a futile effort to catch his balance.

Before Ordog hit the ground, Armand discarded his torch and stepped around behind him to bring the leather strap up under his opponent's chin.

The instant Ordog relaxed his grip on the strap, Armand seized it with his left hand and wrenched it from the downed man's grasp. He placed his knee in the middle of the fellow's broad back and hauled on both ends to choke him with his own belt.

Now pinned to the ground, Ordog flailed the air with his arms in an effort to reach the smaller man behind him. After several vain attempts, he gave it up to claw at the leather strap cutting into his throat. His dark eyes bulged, from alarm as well as from the throttling pressure against his windpipe. His face turned bright red, and his features contorted in a grimace of agony. His mouth opened and closed like a fish out of water.

Romany onlookers gaped in amazement at the outsider who had subdued their champion without singeing a hair on his head or scorching a thread of his garment. In the hush that followed, the only sound heard was that of Ordog choking.

"Do you give over?" Armand demanded, keeping

the leather strap tight against Ordog's throat.

A couple of men on the sidelines started forward to intervene, but a tall lean man with an air of authority lifted his hand to stop them.

Ordog's face went from brick red to purple before he finally nodded his head.

Armand released both ends of the belt at the same time and stepped back out of reach.

Ordog sucked in great breaths of air. He rubbed his throat as he clambered to his feet, favoring his right leg as he did so. After a moment, his coloring returned to normal. "The gods truly favor you," he croaked. He then held out his hand in an overt gesture of peace.

Armand clasped the bear-like paw in his own hand. "They had to for me to get the better of you."

"You have earned your freedom."

"What about my fellow travelers? Will you free them, too?"

Ordog threw back his head and gave a single bark of laughter, which ended in a short bout of coughing. "Bold as brass, you are." He clapped the smaller man on the shoulder. "I like you."

Eri collected his winnings from the man tallying wagers and dropped half of the coins into the pouch at his side. He then hurried over to join Ordog and Armand. "Here, you earned this," he said, pressing five silver pennies into Armand's hand. "I knew you could do it."

Armand tucked the coins into the front of his tunic.

"I can't believe you bet against me," Ordog said to Eri.

"The newcomer is younger than you, Uncle," Eri said. "And faster."

"Are you implying I'm old and slow?" Ordog said. He looked hurt.

"I merely took advantage of an opportunity to double my money," Eri said. "You taught me that, Uncle."

"So I did," Ordog said with a chuckle.

"Will there be any more testing?" Armand said to Eri. "If so, I would like to know about it ahead of time."

"That's pretty much it," Eri said. "You have proven yourself worthy of trust."

Now that the match was over, most of the Romany lost interest and began drifting toward their wagons.

The tall lean man who'd stopped his cohorts from interrupting the match drew near to where Armand stood with Ordog and Eri. He walked with the sinuous grace of a cat. A drooping black mustache dominated a face that looked like burnished bronze in the yellow light from the torches. His eyes were black, as was his long straight hair, which was pulled back and bound with a leather thong at the nape of his neck. He would have been handsome but for a thin-lipped mouth set in an uncompromising line.

"Greetings, Kedah," Ordog and Eri said in unison.

Kedah acknowledged their salutation with a nod. To Armand, he said, "By besting your opponent, you proved your courage and your strength. By sparing his life, you proved your wisdom. For that, you have my respect."

"I was brought here against my will," Armand said. "It was neither my wish nor my intention to kill anyone. Do not mistake me, though. If I must, I will not hesitate to do so."

"It was a necessary precaution to ensure the safety

of my people," Kedah said. To Ordog, he said, "Release them and return their possessions to them."

"The horses, too?" Ordog said.

"Especially the horses," Kedah said.

Ordog limped away to do as he was bidden.

"Go with him," Kedah said to Eri who stood gazing at Armand with open admiration.

Eri set out behind Ordog without haste, as though reluctant to miss out on the conversation.

Kedah turned back to Armand. "I understand you and your party are bound for the east coast."

"That is correct," Armand said.

"Interesting," Kedah said with a tight smile. "In case you are not aware, this camp is situated well to the south of the eastward road." He met and held Armand's gaze. "So, tell me, what really brings you here?"

About that time, Kyle, Reginald, and Brother Luke walked up to join Armand, who glanced at each one in turn, uncertain whether he should speak up or remain silent.

"Tell him," Kyle said. "He's bound to find out sooner or later. Better sooner than later."

"All right, then," Armand said.

"Well?" Kedah said, eyeing him with keen expectation. "What prompted you to come out this way?"

"Murder," Armand said. "More accurately, two of them."

Chapter 8

Kedah's dark eyes glittered in the torchlight. "So you are fugitives from the law." It was more of a statement than a question.

"Not yet," Kyle said. "At least, not until the local constabulary tracks us down." He proceeded to relate how they came across the bodies in the ashes of the barn.

"I see." Kedah looked at Kyle with deep reserve in his gaze, as though he did not believe a word of it.

At that moment, Eri and Conri walked over to join them.

"The bailie will likely scour the countryside once he discovers the bodies," Kyle said. "Since he knows his way around better than we do, he will surely overtake us."

"What's going on?" Conri whispered to Eri.

"Apparently, they killed some people and left the bodies lying about," Eri murmured.

"Really?" Conri said with a grin that exposed strong white teeth. He seemed extremely gratified that his former prisoners were felons on the run. Evidently, such a prospect increased the element of danger in capturing them, which in turn made him appear all the more courageous for successfully doing so.

Kyle's casual glance in Conri's direction sharpened at the sight of his sword belt buckled around the young man's waist.

Kedah followed Kyle's gaze with his eyes. He cocked an expectant eyebrow at Conri, who immediately unbuckled the leather belt.

"Sorry," Conri said, handing both the sword belt and the dirk to Kyle. "I forgot about them."

"No problem," Kyle said as he buckled on the belt.

A frown crossed Conri's youthful face, as though he suddenly remembered why he was there. He leaned close to whisper something in Kedah's ear.

Kedah's gaze shifted from Kyle to Reginald and back again. "I was just informed that you are envoys on the king's business. I hope you will forgive me for detaining you and your companions."

Reginald exchanged a nervous glance with Kyle. "The letters…"

"Untouched, after noting the royal seal on them," Kedah said.

Kyle called to mind the image impressed into the wax that sealed the letters. The imprint came from Sir Percy's signet ring. Though it was not an imperial seal by any stretch of the imagination, it looked rather imposing to the untrained eye.

Perhaps this would be a good time to leave the Romany camp. All of their property had been restored to them, except for the horses, which he was confident would be returned as well. Kedah had given his word before witnesses that he would do so, and he struck Kyle as an honorable man. "We should be on our way now."

Reginald, Armand, and Brother Luke were clearly ready to depart, too, for they nodded their heads with enthusiasm.

"I cannot allow you to go," Kedah said.

Kyle froze into wary stillness, unsure whether that meant they were even now considered prisoners. They were outnumbered, yet this time around he would not hesitate to fight his way to freedom.

"It is more dangerous out there than you think," Kedah said. "Rather than stumbling about in the dark, why don't you stay here and break bread with us this evening. Then, after a good night's sleep, you can set out at first light."

The tense muscles in Kyle's shoulders relaxed upon hearing the man's explanation. It certainly sounded more appealing than stepping off the edge of a cliff in the dead of night and tumbling to their death into a yawning abyss. In addition, their weapons had been given back to them, which would not have been done if they were still regarded as captives. Thus, he could discern no ulterior motive behind the offer to stay the night. "It *has* been a long day, and I *am* weary." He turned to his companions. "What about you?"

The three of them exchanged a thoughtful glance, one with the other, after which they voiced their concurrence to remain until morning.

"It is settled then," Kedah said. "Come with me." He led the way over to a goatskin tent indistinguishable in the torchlight from others of its kind that had been set up within the circle of wagons.

"This is Illiana," Kedah said, indicating a plump woman with pleasant features seated on a low stool beside the campfire.

Illiana ceased stirring the contents of a soot-blackened cooking pot to rise to her feet. "Welcome," she said with a friendly smile. She appeared to be in her thirties, though in the darkness it was hard to tell her true age. A beaded scarf on her head covered most of her dark hair, and like other women in camp, she wore a loose blouse and a long skirt bound at the waist with a sash.

"She is an excellent cook," Kedah said. "If you stay here long enough, you will grow fat on her cooking."

Illiana's smile grew wider, as though pleased at hearing such high praise. Her dark eyes lingered on Kyle, giving him a sweeping glance from his handsome face to his dusty boots and back again. She tore her gaze from him to bid them all to sit.

Kedah, Brother Luke, and Reginald settled on a log close to the entrance flap of the tent. Armand, Eri, and Conri sat cross-legged on the ground nearby.

Illiana picked up the low stool by the campfire and placed it beside the log on which the others sat. "Sit," she said to Kyle.

She took a single piece of flat bread the size of a large pancake from the warming basket by the fire, folded it in half, and filled the crease with thin slices of mutton from the pot. She handed that one to Kedah, after which she made another with more meat in it for Kyle. She fixed smaller ones for the others and set one aside for herself. She filled tarred leather cups with mead and passed them around in the same order.

Kyle followed Kedah's example of tucking in the ends of the folded bread to keep the contents from spilling out while he bit into it. The stewed meat was tender and tasty. He was so hungry that he would have eaten it even if it had been tough and stringy.

With the onset of darkness, a huge orange moon

had risen in the sky, shining through the tops of the trees to the east. Almost everyone in camp sat in front of their own tents, eating their evening meal and talking among themselves. Despite the peace and isolation of their surroundings, a pair of armed guards had apparently been assigned to patrol the perimeter of the campsite outside the circle of wagons.

Illiana kept pressing food on Kyle until he could eat no more. Between a full stomach and the warm sweet mead, he could barely keep his eyes open. "You are right," he said to Kedah. "Your wife's cooking is the best."

Illiana stared openly at Kyle, while Eri and Conri paused in the middle of their conversation to glance from him to Kedah and back again. The abrupt hush that befell the Romany gathered there made him wonder if he'd violated some sacred tribal custom.

Kedah gazed into the flickering blaze, absently fingering the small gold ring in his earlobe. Light from the fire illuminated the stark expression on his face. The corners of his mouth turned down, as though in sadness. After a long moment, he cleared his throat, as if to signal an end to the uncomfortable silence. "My wife is dead," he said in a flat voice. "Illiana is my niece."

"I beg your pardon," Kyle said. "I meant no offence."

Kedah's somber demeanor softened somewhat. "You could not know of it." He got up from the log. "You must be tired. Get some rest." He ducked into the tent and vanished into the gloom within.

Conri climbed to his feet, thanked Illiana for supper, and strolled away, apparently to bed down for the night with his own family.

About that time, the youths tending the animals herded them into the open area inside the circle of wagons. They threaded a long rope through the bridles of the horses and tied the loose ends of the rope to a stake in the ground to keep the animals from wandering away during the night. They did the same for the goats, slipping the rope under the loose collar around each creature's neck to secure them.

Kyle and his companions went over to unsaddle their mounts and carry their gear back to Kedah's tent, where they sought a place on the ground near the campfire to pass the night.

Kyle leaned back on his saddle and covered himself with his blanket. He wasn't expecting trouble. Still, he kept his sword by his side, ready to use if he needed it.

Illiana placed a thin quilt on the ground beside him. She reclined on it near the edge and drew the other half over her body.

Reginald, Armand, and Brother Luke spread their blankets on the far side of the fire.

Eri went into the tent, only to come out a moment later with a straw mat, which he set on the ground beside Armand. After unrolling it, he stretched out on it.

Kyle tucked his hands behind his head and gazed up at the night sky. The stars looked like brilliant pinpoints of light against a black velvet canopy overhead. As the Romany camp settled down for the night, a wolf howled in the distance. It was a long, lonely wail that raised the hair on the back of his neck. An owl hooted nearby, a night hunter that drifted on wings as silent as a wraith. The chirp of crickets around him lulled and soothed him. The effects of the mead made his eyelids heavy. The instant he closed his eyes, he sank into oblivion.

****

Armand lay on his back with his head resting on his cloth travel bag. He was drifting toward peaceful slumber when a hoarse whisper in his ear startled him to wakefulness.

"Are you asleep?"

It was Eri.

"Not anymore," Armand said, his voice low so as not to disturb the others.

"I think my aunt is taken with your handsome friend."

Armand grunted by way of a response.

"He wears no token from a wife. Is he married?"

"Don't know," Armand said, stifling a yawn. "I never asked."

"What about you?"

"What about me?"

"Do you have a wife?"

"Nay," Armand said, shifting slightly to the left to avoid an annoying lump on the ground. "Do you?"

"As a matter of fact, I've been thinking a lot about that lately."

"About what?"

"Taking a mate."

"Aren't you a tad young for that?"

"Years mean nothing in matters of the heart."

"That's an astute observation for somebody your age."

" 'My age'? I'm older than I look."

"Really?" Armand said, smiling into the darkness.

"How old are you, then?"

"Old enough to know what I want."

"I am, too," Armand said. "Would you like to know what I want?"

"I would."

"I want a good night's sleep, starting right now." Armand turned onto his side and pulled the blanket up around his shoulders.

****

Kyle woke with a start shortly before dawn. He lay there for a long moment listening for any sound that may have disturbed his slumber. The camp around him was quiet, except for the restless stamping and shifting of the horses.

He lifted his head to glance over at Reginald, Brother Luke, and Armand reclining on the other side of the campfire, which by that time had burned down to glowing embers. They were still asleep, as was Eri who lay sprawled across his mat beside Armand.

He was about to turn over and go back to sleep when a high-pitched squeal rent the air.

It was an animalistic sound, the kind that struck terror into the heart, for it came from a wild boar—an ill-tempered beast with four-inch tusks that protruded from the sides of its lower jaw. Those tusks, which were actually overgrown teeth, were razor sharp and capable of disemboweling any creature that strayed into its path.

Kyle thrust his blanket aside and leapt to his feet as the campsite exploded in a flurry of activity. Men and women scurried about, shouting to one another. Children cried out in fear. Horses neighed in fright. Goats broke loose from the picket line to scamper in all directions, adding their frantic bleating to the din.

A number of Romany men lit pitch torches from the smoldering remains of their campfires and raised them aloft to illuminate the gloom in the open area. Once it was confirmed that the boar was not inside the circle of wagons, the initial panic of those in the campsite settled into a cautious quietude. In a matter of minutes, a semblance of order returned to the camp.

A couple of men, apparently the guards assigned to make the rounds outside the encampment, staggered through a narrow gap between the wagons. The younger of the two appeared to be seriously injured, while the older one looked unscathed.

"Zoli's hurt," cried the older guard. "Give me a hand here." With the young guard's arm over his shoulder, he half carried, half dragged him into the camp.

His shout for help brought a dozen men running toward him.

Kyle heard it, too, which prompted him to hasten in that direction to render assistance, if he could. His companions followed on his heels. They arrived on the scene behind others who had rushed over to rally round the injured man.

By the look of him, Zoli was in bad shape. The left side of his pants had been slashed open from waist to ankle. Torn flesh, red and raw, on his thigh was visible through the long slit in the fabric. The lower portion of the garment was soaked with blood that dripped to the ground with every step.

Kedah and Ordog took charge of the situation. They joined hands and scooped the young guard onto a makeshift seat in their arms. Together, they carried him to Illiana's tent, where she directed them to deposit him gently on Eri's straw mat near the fire.

After a cursory examination of Zoli's wound, Illiana ducked into the tent and came out seconds later with a pan of water, two blankets, and a leather medicament pouch. Those carrying torches crowded close and held them high to provide sufficient light for her to minister to the injured man.

Practically everyone in the camp gathered there, some to lend silent support, others in a show of concern.

Kyle stood among them, both concerned and troubled, for Zoli's survival depended on Illiana's skill and competence. As with any wound, there was always the possibility of infection. If gangrene set in, death would be slow and painful. He hoped for the young man's sake she knew what to do and how to do it.

Zoli appeared to be about twenty years of age. He was clearly in intense pain, though he tried not to show it. Despite the predawn coolness in the air, sweat slicked his brow and beaded above his upper lip. He just sat there, staring sightlessly before him without moving a muscle, as though frozen in shock from his harrowing experience.

The other guard, evidently Zoli's father from the similarity of their features, squatted beside him. Only when the older man placed a comforting hand on his shoulder did Zoli stir out of his daze.

Zoli watched impassively as Illiana used a razor to cut away the garment three inches above the wound. He inhaled sharply and held his breath as she washed away the blood to expose a ragged six-inch gash in his flesh. He looked on, pale and anxious, as she threaded a fine bone needle with a thin strand of homespun thread soaked in wine. He gritted his teeth as she stitched together the torn edges of his skin.

When she finished, she knotted the thread and nipped it off short with her dagger. She rummaged around the medicament pouch for a corked jar of white powder, a portion of which she shook onto the palm of her hand. She mixed in several drops of oil to make an unguent, which she spread along the sewn incision before binding the wound with a long narrow strip of cloth.

By that time, Zoli's face was ashen, and he was shivering uncontrollably.

She then took a tiny phial from the pouch and poured a single drop into a full cup of mead.

"This will help with the pain," she said, giving it to him to drink, which he did without hesitation. She bade him to lie back, after which she covered him with one blanket and slipped the other one, folded like a pillow, under his head.

Meanwhile, the grudging pallor in the eastern sky had lightened to a dove gray. No longer smothered by darkness, the wagons and tents around the campsite slowly took on shape and color in the first light of dawn. A thick vaporous mist crept along the ground, veiling the grass and everything below the height of a man's knee. The air was fresh and cool, tinged with the smell of damp earth and the pungent scent of evergreens from the forest beyond.

Since there was no longer a need for lighted torches, those who had them snuffed the flames in the dirt and set them aside.

Now that Zoli had fallen asleep, his father seemed

ready to talk. “That boar came out of nowhere,” he said, laying a hand on his son’s chest, as though to reassure himself of the steady heartbeat beneath his fingers.

Everyone crowded close to hear the tale.

“We were making the rounds as usual outside the camp,” said the older man. “All was quiet around us. The moon had long since slipped behind the trees. It was still dark, so we stayed out in the open field, about fifty paces from the forest and the same from camp.

“We were walking along when I heard something moving about the undergrowth in the forest to the left. Zoli told me I was hearing things. I stopped to listen anyway. I thought it might be more intruders, like them.” He tilted his head at Kyle and his companions who stood among the Romany.

“After a minute or two of silence,” he continued, “I began to think maybe I had imagined it. Then, I heard it again. This time, it was louder, like something crashing through the brush. Zoli heard it, too. He said it was a deer, but I knew better. Deer don’t make that much noise unless somebody’s chasing them, and it was still too dark for a hunt. Then all went quiet again.

“We waited for the sound to start up again, but it stayed quiet for so long, we gave it up. We were about to walk on when we heard it squeal. That’s when I knew it was a boar.

“It was close. Too close. Maybe five paces away. Our daggers were useless against such a beast. We started running toward camp. There was no way we could reach the wagons if it came after us, but we had to try.

“It caught up with Zoli first. I saw him go down. I stopped to help him. By that time, the boar had circled around ahead of us. It was now between us and the wagons. It just stood there, a dark blot against the light color of the grass. I hauled Zoli to his feet. There was nowhere to go and nothing we could do except wait for it to charge at us again. If we were going to die, we would do it on our feet, like men.

"Then, for no reason, it ran off. Something must have scared it away. I thank the goddess for that, else it would have been the end for the two of us.

"I helped Zoli hobble back to camp. If I didn't get him patched up quick, he would bleed to death."

He gazed down at his son. The only sound in the hush around him was the soft rasp of the young man's breathing.

"Zoli will be fine," Illiana said, laying a gentle hand on the older man's arm.

Her words seemed to soothe him, for the tension in his body relaxed noticeably.

"That critter is a menace," Ordog said to those gathered there. "Before it attacks anyone else, I say we track it down."

"I agree," Kedah said.

The Romany in attendance nodded their accord, after which most headed for their dwellings to get ready for the hunt.

"Illiana will prepare something for you to eat before you depart," Kedah said to Kyle and his companions. "I will bid you farewell now, for I plan to join the hunt."

Kyle turned to Reginald. "I think we should stay and help. What do you say?"

"Why should we?" Reginald said. "We're already two days behind as it is."

"If we don't catch that boar now, there's a good chance we just might run into it on the way to the road."

"Oh," Reginald said. "When ye put it like that, I reckon half a day won't make that much difference."

"How about you?" Kyle said to Brother Luke.

"I'm not much of a hunter," the black friar said. "I would only get in the way if I went."

"And you?" Kyle said to Armand.

"That boar presents more of a danger to the women and children here," Armand said. "I say we stay for the hunt."

Eri gazed at him with approval, as though pleased to hear an expression of concern for his people.

"If you have room for three more," Kyle said to Kedah, "we'd like to go with you."

"Have any of you ever hunted boar?" Kedah said.

Kyle shook his head, as did Reginald and Armand.

"It's a dangerous enterprise even for a man with experience," Kedah said. "The boar is a wily creature with a keen sense of smell. It may attack you from behind or charge at you head on. Either way, its tusks can gore you to death. Zoli is lucky to get away alive." He looked at each one in turn. "It would be no reflection on you if you chose to remain in camp during the hunt."

Kyle exchanged a fleeting glance with Reginald and Armand to confirm their tacit concurrence. "I speak for the three of us when I say the offer to join you still stands."

Chapter 9

Kyle stood among a group of nine men waiting to leave for the hunt. Like the others, he was armed with the boar-hunting spear that Kedah had given to him. Like other spears, the shaft was eight feet long and made from the sturdy wood of a rowan tree. The flared iron head on the business end tapered to a point sharp enough to pierce the tough hide of a large animal. Unlike other spears, this one had a metal crossbar about ten inches down from the tip designed to prevent an enraged boar from pushing its way down the wooden shaft to gore the hunter.

Out of habit, Kyle reached down to rest his left hand on the hilt of his sword. Then, he remembered it wasn't there. Such a weapon would be useless on a boar hunt, which is the only reason he agreed to leave it behind. Though he wore his dirk on his belt, he still felt naked without a sword at his hip.

The buzz of conversation ceased among those gathered as Ordog walked over to join them. The newly honed metal tip of his spear gleamed in the first rays of the rising sun.

At Kedah's signal, they set out in single file, silent and with purpose, headed for the woodland to the east. The air was fresh and cool under a canopy of branches overhead.

As they wended their way through the trees, a hush

fell over the forest around them, broken only by the occasional twitter of a bird. They moved like wraiths through the morning mist that hovered just above the ground. Their boots made no sound as they trod on the soft rot of leaves and pine needles on the forest track. Each took care to follow in the footsteps of the man ahead of him.

After a while, they came to a place where the strong smell of urine hung in the air.

Ordog pointed to a decayed log on the ground that had been ripped open along its length. "See that?" he said to Kyle. "Boars do that to root for grubs. They also tear up the soil in search of earthworms and insects. That's how you can tell where they've been. That stench means the critter we're after has been here recently."

They split into twos and threes to find places to take cover among the trees on the downwind side of the site. Eri paired up with Armand and went to the left, while Ordog went to the right, taking Kyle with him.

Kyle followed Ordog to a secluded glade. Straggly tufts of summer grass quivered in the faint breeze that swept across the small open area. Sporadic bursts of sunlight broke through the leafy branches above them. The last vestiges of mist clung to the ground in the shadow of the trees.

Ordog walked up to a stately beech tree and looked at the ground around it with approval. "No man can stop a charging boar."

"Then, how do you kill it?" Kyle said.

"Like this." Ordog stabbed the blunt end of his spear into a network of roots a couple of paces from the base of the beech. With both hands about midway along the shaft, he lowered the metal tip until it hung about fifteen inches above the ground. "Now, you wait for the critter to come to you," he said as he squatted down to sit on his heels.

"That seems simple enough," Kyle said. The resigned expression on Ordog's face prompted him to ask, "Is there anything else I should know?"

"Boar hunting is more about nerve than skill. An experienced man knows where to set the back end of his spear so as to impale a boar on the tip. Only a man with steady nerves can hold his spear without wavering so as to catch a charging beast square in the chest."

"I see," Kyle said, and he really did. Normally, a hunter tracked his prey to kill it. Apparently, that was not the case for boar. According to Ordog, this particular critter hunted the hunter.

Kyle glanced around to find a suitable tree, which came in the form of an ancient oak with a wide girth located seven paces to the left of Ordog's beech. On the ground under thick spreading branches were acorns aplenty, which would surely attract the greedy beast. He placed the butt of his spear at the bottom of the gnarled trunk and hunkered down to wait.

"I wouldn't do it like that, if I were you," Ordog said.

"Like what?" Kyle said, looking around to see what he'd done wrong.

"I wouldn't prop the end against a tree. If a charging boar skewers itself on the point, the wooden shaft will likely snap like a dry twig. It needs room to skid back a little to lessen the shock of impact. Should the shaft break while you're holding it, the beast will run you over and kill you outright, or worse, mangle you badly enough to make you wish you were dead."

Kyle needed no further urging to transfer the butt of his spear from the tree trunk to the ground, where a tangle of slender roots bulged from the soil.

Now, there was nothing more to do than wait.

Butterflies fluttered aimlessly across the glade. Honeybees flitted from flower to flower, their drone soothing and hypnotic. In the tranquility of the forest around him, his thoughts wandered over the things that weighed heavily on his mind: Joneta and the children, the escalating civil unrest in Ayrshire, and possible motives behind Sir Guy's death.

****

Armand found a secluded spot to hide in the underbrush. He sat on his right heel and propped his elbow on his bent left knee to keep his spear level.

Eri squatted down beside him. "Set the base in the ground like this." He placed a hand on Armand's hand to steady the shaft while he reached around Armand's body to grasp the lower half of the spear. With a sharp jab, he drove the blunt end into the earth behind them.

"Thanks." Armand turned his head to glance at his companion who was close enough for him to feel hot breath on his neck. That was when he noticed flecks of gold in the light brown eyes gazing back at him. He stared at the youthful face only inches from his own, intrigued by the flawless complexion and the delicate curves of cheek and chin. To his dismay, his heart pounded against his breastbone at such unwonted nearness. He shook off the hand still resting on his own and leaned away to distance himself from the curiously disturbing intimacy of Eri's semi-embrace.

Eri released his grip on the spear. "Is something

amiss?"

"Not at all," Armand said quickly.

Too quickly, even to his own ears. He fervently hoped his denial sounded convincing.

Eri appeared not to notice Armand's discomfiture. "Have you ever thought about taking a mate?"

"What?" Armand said, looking askance at his companion. It was not a topic he cared to discuss at that particular moment.

"I said, have you ever—"

"I heard you the first time," Armand said, cutting him off. "This is neither the time nor the place to talk about that."

"Why not?"

"For fear we might spook the boar, should it hear our voices," Armand said in an effort to change the subject.

"On the contrary," Eri said. "It will serve to drive the critter over to where Ordog and your handsome friend lie in wait in yon glade."

"We still ought to keep it down, just in case."

"As you wish," Eri said, his tone a notch lower than before. "I've been on hunts in the past, you know. It's going to be a while before the boar actually shows up. So, have you ever thought about it? Taking a mate, I mean."

Armand shook his head over the fellow's persistence. He had nothing shameful to hide, so perhaps he should just answer the question and be done with it. "It crossed my mind once."

"Was she pretty?"

"Why are you so interested?"

"I'll take that to mean she was ugly."

“Not at all,” Armand said, his tone wistful. “She was quite beautiful, in fact.”

Dead silence.

“Is that not what you expected to hear?” Armand said, suppressing a smile.

“Why didn’t you marry her?”

“I was too poor at the time to support a wife.”

“And now?”

“I’m still poor.”

“That wouldn’t matter if you truly loved each other.”

“What’s with all the questions?” Armand said.

“Just curious,” Eri said.

“There is a fine line, you know, between curiosity and prying.”

“Would it be prying to ask whether you plan to seek out the lady once you’ve made your fortune?”

Armand chuckled. “You don’t give up, do you?”

“Persistence is a virtue.”

“I give up,” Armand said.

“Well, would you?”

“It’s been years since we last met. She’s probably married with five children by now.”

The snap of a brittle stick nearby brought an abrupt end to their conversation. The two of them bent low over their respective weapons, their eyes on the dense foliage across the way.

****

A soft rustle in the undergrowth off to the right drew Kyle’s notice.

He listened intently, every sense alert to danger. When he heard the sound again, he wondered whether it might be something other than a boar. The movement was furtive and deliberate, more like a lynx. Although wild cats preferred the rough terrain of hill country, it was common enough for a solitary male to take to the woods to hunt for smaller prey. He remained motionless, ready for whatever was about to make its appearance in the glade.

The leaves twitched and shook as something pushed through them. With a final shudder, the branches parted.

To Kyle's surprise, two Romany men broke from the cover of the forest to enter the secluded glade.

"Malcus," Ordog said in a low voice to the lean man with a narrow face. "Take that side." He waved a hand to indicate the trees on his right.

The two men trod silently in that direction. In less than half a minute, each of them had chosen a fitting place to wait for the boar to show itself.

Before long, something large crashed through the underbrush a short distance away. The noise grew louder and closer with each passing moment.

Kyle suspected it was the boar this time. He cast a questioning glance at Ordog, who confirmed it with a nod. He tightened his grip on the spear, holding the butt end firmly against the ground. He kept the tip low and pointed directly toward the source of the sound.

The others in the glade crouched over their spears, eyes forward and watchful.

As Kyle looked on, the bushes on the far side of the glade thrashed violently. Suddenly, the long-awaited beast erupted into the small clearing in a swirl of mist.

The boar was huge and black. Its head was massive, set low on narrow shoulders. Stiff bristle-like hair covered its pot-bellied body down to its cloven hooves. Long yellow tusks jutted from its lower jaw. The wily creature halted and threw up its head. Flared nostrils in its flat snout twitched as it sniffed the air. Tiny black eyes glared at the intruders across the glade.

Kyle went utterly still, every sinew in his body drawn tight. He kept his gaze focused on the boar, hardly daring to breathe, lest the slightest sound attract its notice. Being unpredictable like most creatures of the wild, it might charge at him or turn tail to vanish into the forest. If it charged, he must hold the spear steady in order to pierce its heart. Otherwise, those curved tusks would rip his flesh like a hot blade through butter.

While waiting to see what the boar would do, he caught a slight movement out of the corner of his eye. He took his gaze off the creature to cast a fleeting glance in that direction.

Ordog had abandoned his crouched position to kneel in the mud, his body upright and rigid. His mouth was twisted in agony, and his face was as white as chalk. In the next heartbeat, he dropped his spear to clutch at his chest with both hands.

Kyle's gaze flicked back to the boar in time to see it lower its head, its beady eyes fixed on the incapacitated man. He sprang to his feet with his spear in hand and covered the short distance to Ordog's side in three bounding leaps.

The sudden movement distracted the creature for a split second before it launched itself at both men.

With the furious pounding of hooves in his ears, Kyle squatted beside Ordog and thrust the butt end of his own spear into the same hole where Ordog's spear had been set in the earth. He bore down on the back half of the shaft to keep it in place.

The huge boar galloped across the glade, headed straight at him. He lowered the tip of the spear and held the shaft parallel to the ground, braced and ready for contact.

The beast was nearly upon him when he realized its lowered head would interfere with a clean frontal kill, a crucial detail Ordog had failed to mention to him. With his heart in his throat and an expletive on his lips, he shifted the point of spear ever so slightly to the left at the last instant.

The metal tip grazed the right side of the boar's thick skull before piercing its body. As the sharp point sank into gristle and flesh, the enraged creature let out an ear-splitting shriek of agony.

The jarring impact taxed every muscle in Kyle's body. Only with great effort did he retain his grip on the shaft.

The terrific weight of the boar caused the butt of the spear to skid back along the ground for nearly two yards, tearing a deep groove in the turf along the way. Kyle slid back with it until the blunt end hit a large root.

The spear stopped abruptly.

The boar did not.

Momentum carried the beast forward in slow motion along the iron spearhead until the crossbar brought it to a halt. It squealed in rage and anguish all the while. Its stumpy legs scrabbled in the dirt, tearing up clumps of grass as it strained to reach Kyle's unprotected throat with its wicked tusks.

Blood seeped from the wound in its chest and

spattered onto the ground below. It oozed down the length of the spear to puddle against Kyle's hands, making the wood slick and difficult to hold onto. Yet hold it he did, for the maddened creature was far from dead. He leaned his full weight against the lower portion of the shaft to anchor the back end against the root. His very life depended on keeping it there.

About that time, Malcus ran over to thrust his spear into the boar's side. His attempt to kill it only infuriated the creature further. It thrashed its head from side to side in an effort to snag Malcus with its razor-sharp tusks.

Malcus backed away and kept a respectful distance after that.

The boar's ear-splitting squeals continued as its pumping legs tried to propel its body farther along the shaft of the spear. The only thing that kept the beast from doing so was the metal crosspiece at the base of the spearhead.

Then suddenly all went quiet in the glade.

The light of life faded from the boar's eyes. Its bristly body slumped forward with its head resting on the wooden shaft of the spear.

The yellowed tusks were so close that Kyle could reach out and touch them. Still shaking from the adrenaline surging through his veins, he pried his stiff fingers from around the shaft of the spear and drew his dirk. He leaned forward to plunge the blade into the boar's neck and slit its throat to let the blood drain from the gash.

After that, he rose to his feet and hurried over to check on Ordog, who lay unmoving on the ground only inches from the strip of churned earth that marked the boar's frenzied passage. To his relief, there was no blood on the older man to indicate the tusks had injured him in passing.

He picked up Ordog's spear and went back to plunge the metal tip into the boar directly behind its shoulder in order to pierce its heart. Only then was he satisfied that the beast was truly dead. Wounded animals had been known to rise up and maim careless hunters who failed to take such a precaution.

Just as he went over to minister to the fallen man, others from the hunting party burst into the glade, evidently drawn by the boar's squeals.

Kedah hurried over to where Kyle bent over Ordog's body. "What happened to him?" he demanded, frowning in concern.

Kyle gazed down at Ordog's weathered face, now pale and drawn in the midmorning light. "I don't know."

Chapter 10

Kyle went down on one knee to press his fingers into the flesh on the left side of Ordog's windpipe. "He's alive," he said on detecting a steady throb under his fingertips.

Just then, Eri entered the glade with Armand a step behind him. When the young man saw Ordog on the ground, he ran over to join those gathered around him. "Did the boar do this?" he said, looking from Kyle to Kedah and back again.

"The beast didn't touch him," Malcus said, walking up at that moment. "He fell down on his own."

Eri dropped to his knees beside the prone man and placed a hand on his shoulder. "Uncle," he said, shaking him gently. "Wake up."

Kyle got to his feet and brushed away the bits of grass that clung to his knee. "I saw that happen to a fellow once."

"And?" Kedah said.

"Unfortunately, he died," Kyle said.

Ordog's eyes snapped open. "Died?"

"How do you feel, Uncle?" Eri said. "Are you all right?"

"Quit fussing over me, child." Ordog stuck out his hand for Eri to help him to his feet. "I'm fine, as you can see."

Eri peered at him closely. "You look a mite peaky,

Uncle. I'll bet you haven't been taking the brew Illiana made for you."

Ordog stood straight and tall, as though to give the impression that he'd completely recovered from his earlier episode. "You nag like an old woman," he said, blustering. Yet, he studiously avoided the young man's gaze.

"You'd better take it from now on," Eri said with a note of warning in his voice. "Otherwise, I'll tell her about this. You're my favorite uncle, and I don't want to lose you."

Ordog looked embarrassed at being scolded in front of the other men. His gaze then settled on Malcus who was making preparations to field dress the boar. He nudged Kyle in the ribs and pointed in that direction. "Ever skinned an animal that size before?"

"Can't say I have," Kyle said.

"How about you?" Ordog said to Armand and Reginald who stood nearby.

"Not me," Armand said with a shake of his head.

"Me, neither," Reginald said.

Apparently now recovered from whatever ailed him, Ordog walked over to extract his spear from the boar's side.

Kyle attempted to pull out his spear. Because it was too deeply embedded in the muscular chest, it would not budge. Armand came over to help him, and between the two of them, they managed to extricate it from the carcass.

Malcus took a skinning knife from the sheath at his side and proceeded to gut the boar. Coiled loops of purple intestines and foul-smelling liquids spilled out onto the earth below the long red gash in its underbelly.

Ordog drew his dagger and bent down to cut the tongue from the boar's mouth. He brought it over to where Kyle, Armand, and Reginald stood watching. "This is for you, in honor of your first boar hunt." He seized Kyle's hand and placed in it the slick appendage dripping with blood. "Eat."

For several heartbeats, Kyle peered down at the severed tongue in his grasp. The slimy wedge of raw flesh was encased in a warty membrane. Not only was it revolting in appearance but a disgusting odor emanated from it, too. The thought of sinking his teeth into it caused his stomach to churn. He seriously doubted whether he could swallow even the tiniest bite without gagging.

He glanced up to find the gaze of every Romany man in the glade upon him, as though waiting to see what he would do. At the risk of violating a sacred tribal custom, he turned to Armand. "Here," he said, thrusting the bloody tongue into his hand. "You eat it. It's your first boar hunt, too."

Armand passed the blob of flesh to Reginald so swiftly and smoothly that the sheriff hardly had time to react.

Unwilling recipient that he was, Reginald dropped the severed tongue like a hot potato. "I wouldn't eat that even if my own mother gave it to me," he said, glaring at everyone staring at him.

Kyle expected immediate censure. Instead, Ordog threw back his head and laughed out loud, as did the other Romany in the glade. Even Kedah grinned from where he stood looking on.

"I wanted to see if you would actually eat it," Ordog said, wiping tears of laughter from his eyes.

"You foreigners sometimes do the oddest things." He picked up the severed tongue and handed it to the man beside him who walked over to place it beside the heart and liver already in a woven straw basket.

Kyle wiped his hands on the grass to clean the sticky blood from them.

Malcus turned away to bind the boar's forefeet together with a strip of leather. After checking the knot to make sure it was secure, he did the same with the hind feet.

Another man brought over a long stout pole made from a freshly cut sapling cleaned of branches. He slid the pole through the boar's legs from back to front. He and Malcus then grasped one end of the pole, while two other men took hold of the opposite end. Together, the four of them lifted the dead weight of the carcass off the bloodstained ground and started back to camp.

The rest of the hunting party set out along the forest trail behind the men bearing the boar's carcass. Kedah, Ordog, and Kyle brought up the rear.

"Did you really think I would eat that tongue raw?" Kyle said to Ordog.

"Not really," Ordog said with a chuckle. "But if you did, it would have been amusing to watch."

"You almost caught me off guard that time," Kyle said, smiling. "You can be sure it won't happen twice. One good gibe deserves another, so now I owe you one."

Ordog's step slowed so as to fall behind Kedah and the others. "Actually, I owe you." His weathered countenance grew serious, as though from a troublous thought. "When the boar came at me, I was ready for it. Then all of a sudden, I could neither move nor speak.

Yet, I saw and heard everything that went on around me. If you hadn't stepped forward when you did…" He broke off in midsentence, as if he could not bear to finish the thought.

"Has that ever happened before?' Kyle said quietly.

Ordog hesitated for an instant before a cheerful expression replaced the brooding frown on his face. "Not to worry. I am convinced it had something to do with the boar's magic. Tonight, I shall eat its heart to take on its power."

"Will you cook it or eat it raw?" Kyle said dryly.

Ordog laughed. "I wish my dagger was as sharp as your wit," he said, slapping Kyle heartily on the back.

They walked along the forest path in companionable silence for a while.

"Do you have a lady?" Ordog said unexpectedly.

"I have a wife," Kyle said.

"Any children?"

"Two wee ones."

"I have something for you to give to your lady wife," Ordog said. "It's just a bauble, but ladies like baubles."

"Why not give it to your lady?"

"There is but a single bauble. If I give it to one, the others would be jealous."

" 'The others'?"

"Aye," Ordog said. "Ladies find me irresistible, don't you know?"

Kyle gazed in disbelief at the blunt-featured, barrel-chested older man beside him. "If you say so."

"Ask him," Ordog said, pointing at Kedah half a dozen steps ahead of him. "He'll tell you."

As if on cue, Kedah glanced back at Kyle. "It's true," he said with a nod.

After the incident with the boar's tongue, Kyle assumed this was another gibe and saw no harm in playing along. "I will accept your gift with thanks," he said with exaggerated graciousness.

"I shall give it to you when we get back to camp," Ordog said.

They walked on until they came to a fork in the trail. The hunting party bore to the right, while Kedah and Ordog went left to take the shorter but rougher way back to camp.

Kyle turned left to follow Kedah and Ordog.

It was darker in that part of the forest, where the trees crowded closer together. Dense underbrush intruded onto the track, barely standing aside to let them pass. Lacy ferns and coarse bracken covered the ground. Leafy vines hung down from moss-covered branches, blocking most of the sunlight overhead.

Before long, the three of them came to a creek at the bottom of a deep hollow.

Kyle skidded down the nearly vertical slope behind Kedah and leaped across the narrow span of water. He scrambled up the steep embankment on the other side, and when he reached the top, he paused to glance behind him.

Ordog had just crossed the creek and started up the sharp slope when his breathing became noticeably ragged.

"Need a hand?" Kyle said.

Ordog lowered himself onto a dry root protruding from the ground beside the creek. "Leave me," he said, blotting sweat from his brow with his sleeve. "I'll catch you up in a bit."

It didn't seem right to abandon the man, especially if he was ill. Unsure of whether to comply with his request, Kyle cast a questioning glance at Kedah who stood beside him.

"Let's go," Kedah said to Kyle. He turned away and continued along the forest path.

Kyle gave Ordog one last glance before he set out after Kedah. "Is it all right to leave him alone?" he said when they were out of range of Ordog's hearing. "He doesn't look so good."

"He looks awful," Kedah said.

Kyle slowed his pace. "I should go back. He may need help."

"What can you do but hold his hand?" Kedah said. "It would hurt his pride if you did that. When we get back to camp, I will send Eri with a horse to fetch him."

"It may be too late by then."

"If it is his time to meet the goddess, let him do so with dignity, not coddled like a feeble old man. He would hate that."

With a sigh of resignation, Kyle resumed the trek back to camp. Along the way, he cast frequent glances over his shoulder in the hope of catching sight of Ordog trailing after them.

****

Kyle and Kedah reached the Romany camp well ahead of the others in the hunting party.

Word of their success spread quickly. Women stoked their fires and put water on to boil in their cooking pots. The older children laid two straw mats on the ground to provide a clean place for the butcher to cut up the carcass.

About that time, Ordog meandered into camp, looking as though he had not a care in the world.

Because of his association with John the apothecary, Kyle recognized the symptoms of a man suffering from an ailment of the heart, which if left untreated could result in abrupt death. He also knew the boar had no magic to cause such a malady. It would be difficult, however, to explain that to folks who believed in those things. Although he and Ordog shared a measure of camaraderie, it was not his place to interfere in the man's life. Still, he felt compelled to point out, at some convenient time, that certain herbs, when used properly, could improve, if not cure, such a condition.

A short time later, the hunting party entered the camp. Everyone came over to see the boar. Once it had been deposited on the smaller of the two mats, Malcus set about removing the hide, which if left on too long would taint the meat.

A couple of men stepped forward to spread out the unwieldy skin, raw side up, on the other mat. The hide looked like a huge ragged-edged carpet with slabs of glistening yellow fat adhering to most of the irregular pink surface.

As chieftain, Kedah had the right to decide how the boar would be divided, so under his supervision, Malcus went to work carving up the carcass and doling out the meat in proportion to the number of individuals in each family.

Once the meat had been distributed, the women skewered the tender cuts on a spit and placed them over an open flame to roast. The remainder would later be sliced thinly and rubbed with salt before being hung on a smoke rack to preserve it. The leftovers, mostly bones and gristle, went into their cooking pots along with vegetables to make soup.

While the women prepared the food, the men sat on the ground in the center of camp to hear about the hunt. Even Zoli, leaning heavily on a stout cane, limped over to join them.

With all eyes upon him, Malcus stepped forward to recount the tale for his eager audience.

Kedah approached Kyle, Armand, Reginald, and Brother Luke where they stood apart from those assembled. Eri was there, too, hovering at Armand's elbow, as usual.

"I know you are anxious to continue your journey," Kedah said. "However, because of you"—here his gaze settled on Kyle—"we have the safe return of one of our own, along with meat in abundance. Grace us with your presence for this feast, after which we can send you on your way with provisions befitting honored guests."

"I accept your offer with thanks," Kyle said.

"I do, too," Reginald said. "I'm famished, not to mention bone weary after the hunt."

"You will stay, won't you?" Eri said to Armand.

"Of course I will," Armand said.

Kedah looked at Brother Luke. "And you?"

The black friar nodded his head in agreement.

"It is settled then," Kedah said with a smile.

Kyle was about to seek out a place to wash the grime from his face and hands when loud voices sharp with anger brought his head around.

Ordog and Malcus appeared to be engaged in a hot dispute in front of the other Romany gathered there.

Kyle followed Kedah over to where the two men stood toe to toe, glaring at each other.

"What seems to be the problem?" Kedah said, looking from Ordog to Malcus and back again.

"He claims the kill is his," Ordog said.

"It *is* mine." Malcus gave Kyle a look potent with threat, as though daring him to contradict his words. "The mark of my spear in the hide will prove it."

"The kill belongs to Kyle Shaw," Ordog said, pointing at the deputy.

"How do you know?" Malcus said, his upper lip curled with derision. "You were down—"

"Because I saw it," Ordog said, cutting him off.

"You lie. You were in a swoon."

"Then how would I know the boar lived on after you speared it? How, too, would I know you backed away in fear while Kyle Shaw continued wrestling with the beast on his own?"

Malcus shot a venomous glance at Kyle. "He must have told you that."

Ordog's dark brows folded together in a frown. "He did not, but that's beside the point. I personally witnessed Kyle Shaw impale the boar on his spear and then pierce its heart with my spear. The kill is his. Thus, he should get the hide." His gaze shifted to Kyle. "What do you say?"

Malcus cast an anxious glance at Kyle, for his credibility in the presence of his peers hung on Kyle's response.

A hush fell over those looking on as they waited to hear what the outsider had to say.

"The boar lived on for less than a dozen heartbeats after Malcus pierced its side," Kyle said, his voice raised for all to hear. "So, who is to say his spear thrust did not hasten its death? It is fair to conclude, then, that

Malcus and I killed the boar between us."

Malcus let out the breath he had apparently been holding.

Ordog's frowning countenance grew more forbidding. "The next time you call me a liar," he said to Malcus, "I will throttle you with my own hands."

Malcus eased away from him to stand nearer to Kedah.

"Since that is the case," Kedah said, "let the hide be divided so that each may receive half."

"I am grateful to be the recipient of such bounty," Kyle said. "However, I shall be leaving this camp soon and do not care to carry a raw hide with me. It is my wish, therefore, that my portion should go to the man most skilled in making boots. Those boots shall go to the children here to keep their feet warm during the cold season."

Onlookers murmured to one another and nodded their heads in approval. Those who had sons and daughters clearly appreciated the generosity of the gesture.

Malcus turned away, but not before Kyle caught the flush of anger on his face. Any protest Malcus made now to justify getting the entire hide would make him appear selfish and petty. He would have to accept the chieftain's decision whether he liked it or not. As indicated by his expression, he definitely did not like it.

Chapter 11

Kyle inhaled the aroma of roasting pork with appreciation. He sat in the shade of Kedah's tent with his companions. The goatskin sides had been lifted like awnings and propped up with poles to keep them open. The sun was high overhead, and a soft breeze stirred the air, somewhat tempering the midday heat of summer.

Eri squatted by the campfire, keeping a watchful eye on the spitted meat sizzling over the flames, while Illiana fried thin flat patties of barley dough on a greased metal disc nestled on the smoldering coals.

Ordog walked up with Conri who was carrying a pottery jug of ale under his arm. Conri placed the jug on the small low table near the campfire and went over to chat with Kedah.

Ordog beckoned to Kyle. "Come with me."

Kyle got to his feet and set out beside the older man, headed toward a tent farther along the way. That one looked similar to all the other tents, which prompted him to wonder in passing how the occupants could tell them apart at night.

When they came to Ordog's tent, the older man went inside to rummage around for a moment. He reappeared with something clutched in his fist. "This is what I promised you." He opened his hand to reveal a rectangular gold pendant on a fragile gold chain. The clear green emerald in the center of the pendant glimmered in the sunlight.

Kyle whistled in admiration. "It's beautiful."

"Do you think your wife will like it?"

"She will love it. However, she's never going to see it."

"Why not?" Ordog said, his dark brows furled.

"You said it was a bauble. That stone is worth a fortune."

"Is not your wife worth it?" Ordog said, his eyes bright with challenge.

"Of course she is," Kyle said. "But that's not the issue here. I simply cannot accept it."

"It isn't stolen, if that's what you're concerned about," Ordog said. "My father gave it to me after my mother passed away. It is mine to do with as I please." He took Kyle's hand and laid the delicate pendant across his palm. "And it pleases me to give it to you."

"When you put it like that," Kyle said, "how can I refuse?" He held it up to admire the emerald once more before tucking it into the pouch at his side. "Thank you. Joneta will love it."

The two of them started back toward Kedah's tent. On the way, they passed a young man scraping fat from the inside of the boar's hide to prepare it for tanning. Farther along, an old man sat at a grinding wheel sharpening a knife. Beyond that, another man worked on the broken spoke of a wagon wheel. Some of the younger girls helped with the cooking, while others spread newly washed garments along the slatted sides of their wagons to let the clothing dry in the sun.

"This camp is like a small village," Kyle said as he walked along.

"It *is* a small village," Ordog said. "As you can see,

everyone does their part. There is no king here."

"What about Kedah?"

"He is chieftain by agreement. If he should step down for any reason, another would be chosen in his place. That isn't his name, by the way. 'Kedah' means 'leader' in our tongue."

"Interesting." Kyle turned to the older man with a serious expression on his face. "There is but one thing I would like to know."

"What is that?" Ordog said, his countenance equally grave.

"When do we eat?" Kyle said.

Ordog chuckled. "I'm going to miss you when you leave."

"I shall miss you, too." Kyle liked the tranquil atmosphere among the nomadic Romany who were unconstrained by borders and boundaries. No enemy troops camped on their doorstep. Neither was there rebellion in their ranks, ready to flare up at the slightest provocation, like in his own country.

"Can you not stay a while longer?" Ordog said.

"I wish I could. However, I am bound by duty to carry out the task assigned to me as soon as may be."

"Be sure to pass through here on the way home, then."

"A request from a friend is virtually a command," Kyle said, gratified at receiving such an invitation. "God willing, I shall do just that." He especially meant the part about God's will, seeing as how it might take divine intervention for him and Reginald to avoid arrest and detainment in London.

Ever since he'd left Ayrshire, the thought of what might await them at the end of their journey gave him an uncomfortable feeling, like that of standing too close to the edge of a cliff. True, they had an obligation to deliver Sir Percy's letters. Yet that alone did not guarantee them a warm welcome in the English king's court. Should they be mistaken for Scottish rebels, they would likely face incarceration or worse, execution as traitors to the English cause.

By the time he and Ordog made it back to Kedah's tent, the meat was cooked and ready to eat. He found a place to sit with the others under the goatskin awning. Ordog settled on the ground beside him with a grunt.

Illiana handed Kedah a thin flatbread wrapped around a piece of roasted pork. She served Kyle next, and then the others. She passed out tarred leather cups of ale in the same order, after which she sought out a place to sit and eat in the shade of the awning.

****

Armand bit into the meat and found it quite flavorful. It was so moist that juice ran down his chin and dripped to the ground. He wiped his mouth with the back of his hand before consuming the rest of his meal with gusto.

Ordog cast a glance in Illiana's direction. "I used to be her favorite," he said around a mouthful of food. "She always gave me the largest portion."

"Are you jealous of the foreigners, Uncle?" Eri said with a mischievous grin.

"Absolutely not," Ordog retorted. "I was just making an observation."

"Not to worry, Uncle," Eri said. "Things will go back to normal once they leave."

Armand happened to look up just as Eri stole a sidelong glance at him. For a fleeting moment, he glimpsed the sadness that clouded the young man's countenance, as though downhearted over his—Armand's—imminent departure.

In the next instant, Eri's face cleared, prompting Armand to wonder if he'd simply imagined it.

Over the past couple of days, he'd grown fond of the young man as a comrade, and the thought of parting company left him feeling unsettled. But such was life on the road. There were new friends to meet and old ones to remember. For some reason, though, this friend would be more sorely missed than all others of his acquaintance.

Ordog tilted his head back and drained the contents of his cup. "Fetch the ale, will you?" he said to Illiana.

She rose to her feet and trudged over to the small table. The campfire was burning low, so instead of picking up the pottery jug, she reached into the wood box to gather up a handful of kindling. She tossed the sticks onto the flames, sending a flurry of red embers and gray ash soaring high into the air.

The swirl of glowing cinders seemed to mesmerize her. She stood there without moving, her eyes fixed and staring, her face devoid of expression. Orange and gold blazons burst forth to lick at the dry wood, casting an eerie radiance over her solemn features.

She began to speak in a singsong cadence: "Debase ye not the sovereign line, those born to reign by right divine. Else face ye must the grievous bane, who cannot be by mortal slain. Lest stain he will the base of stone, with blood from wounds that be his own."

Brother Luke sat up straight, as though in alarm. "Is she a seer?" he demanded of Ordog seated beside him.

"Be quiet," Ordog said with a wave of his hand. "Let's hear what she has to say."

"Soothsaying is an abomination—" Brother Luke said.

"Shut it," Ordog barked, cutting him off. "I want to hear this."

The black friar seemed taken aback at the older man's abrupt tone, but he held his peace after that.

With eyes glazed as though in a trance, Illiana turned toward those seated under the awning. She lifted her right arm at full stretch and pointed directly at Armand. "Behold!" she cried. "Steward of the gods."

Armand glanced at Eri, thoroughly mystified. He had no idea of the meaning behind the woman's words.

Eri lifted one shoulder in a small shrug, as if he, too, was baffled.

Still transfixed and staring, Illiana shifted her extended arm slightly to the left to single out Brother Luke. "Behold," she said in an ominously soft voice. "Servant of the gods."

The black friar squirmed, as though ill at ease as the center of unwanted attention.

Illiana's outstretched arm swung still farther to the left. "Behold," she said, her index finger aimed straight at Kyle. "Instrument of the gods."

Her arm now moved to the right until her pointed finger isolated Reginald from those around him. "Tribulation in the flesh," she said in a husky whisper. Tears welled up in her eyes and spilled onto her cheeks.

The color ebbed from Reginald's face, and his eyes grew wide with fear. "What does that mean?" he said, turning to the man beside him, who shook his head in response.

Those gathered under the awning exchanged puzzled glances in silence, as though each hoped the other could explain what the prophetic words portended.

A loud pop from the wood burning in the campfire broke the spell.

Illiana looked around in bewilderment, as if wondering why everyone was staring at her. She touched a hand to the tears on her cheek and blinked at the moisture on the tips of her fingers. “What just happened?” she said to no one in particular.

“My cup,” Ordog said, holding it out to her. “It’s empty.”

“Oh.” She picked up the jug of ale and brought it over to where he sat on the ground. As she poured the amber brew into his cup, her demeanor became calm and serene once again. Performing familiar duties seemed to alleviate her distress and set her mind at ease.

Brother Luke was the first to address the matter. “Does anyone have any idea what her words meant?”

“It has something to do with the kingly line,” Ordog said.

“What about the grievous bane?” Eri said. “Who might that be?”

“It could be a person,” Ordog said.

“Or an object,” Armand said, joining the conversation. “Like a sword or a lance.”

“A sword can’t be slain,” Eri said.

“Exactly,” Armand said. “So that must be it.”

“Then how are you the steward of it?” Eri said. “You don’t even have a sword.”

“Perhaps it comes into my possession,” Armand

said. “To keep it until it is needed.”

“If you are the one with the sword,” Eri said, “how does Kyle Shaw come to be the instrument of the gods?”

“Maybe his lot is to wield the blade,” Armand said.

“And him?” Eri said, gesturing toward Brother Luke.

“He is a friar,” Armand said. “As such, it is his calling to serve the gods.”

“I serve only one God in the heavens,” Brother Luke said.

“But you are still His servant, are you not?” Armand said.

“I am that,” Brother Luke conceded with a nod.

“What about me?” Reginald said, his face a mask of dread and trepidation at what the future may hold for him.

“Tribulation could mean any number of things,” Armand said. “Heavy debt, a grievous wound, loss of possessions, hunted by the law, and so on.”

“But not necessarily death, right?” Reginald said with a note of desperation in his voice, as though in need of reassurance.

“There would be no tribulation in the flesh if you were dead,” Armand said.

Reginald seemed less agitated after hearing that. “Ye are right, of course,” he said with a nervous laugh. “However, it looks like the bane might have more of a problem than me if he fails, seeing as how he is doomed to shed so much blood from his wounds that it will stain the stones.”

Ordog turned to Armand. “Do you think that is truly what the prophecy means?”

"Can you offer a better explanation?" Armand said.

Ordog frowned in thought for a moment. "Not really," he said at length.

"There is no need for undue concern over the woman's words," Brother Luke interjected.

"Why do you say that?" Ordog said.

"Because it is likely nothing more than superstitious nonsense," Brother Luke said with disdain.

"You believe in miracles, don't you?" Ordog said.

"Of course I do," Brother Luke said. "It is a proven fact that relics from saints of old possess the power to heal the sick."

"And that's not superstition?" Ordog said.

"Nay, brother," the black friar said. "That is faith."

"I see," Ordog said, clearly unconvinced.

"Be that as it may," Brother Luke said, "that so-called prediction can have nothing to do with me."

"Is that so?"

"Aye."

"That's too bad."

"Why?" Brother Luke said.

"Because Illiana singled you out from the rest of us," Ordog said. "So whether you like it or not, you're in it up to your ears."

Kedah, who had remained silent through the discussion, finally spoke up. "The timing of her pronouncement seems odd to me," he said, his brow puckered in thought. "Why now on the verge of their departure? Why not when they first came into camp?"

"I can't answer that." Ordog's gaze settled on Illiana, who was wrapping up the leftover meat and placing the extra flatbreads into a basket. "No use asking her about it, either. She never remembers what she does or says during those bouts. You know that."

"I wonder what prompted her to speak at this time," Kedah said.

"Maybe it was because she knew they were leaving and this would be her last chance to do it," Ordog said.

"That would require forethought and planning on her part," Kedah said, "when in fact these trances overcome her without prior warning. There must be some strong force at work here for her to prophesy about the foreigners."

That set off a round of murmurs that rippled through those gathered under the awning.

"Forgive me," Kedah said, turning to Kyle. "I trust my thoughtless ramblings have not unduly upset you. It is just that I find it more useful to think aloud."

"Not to worry," Kyle said. "Illiana's prediction was too vague to be a cause of concern. What does trouble me is what lies ahead. I sincerely hope we can reach our destination and return home without incident."

"Then go with the blessing of the goddess," Kedah said. "May you and your companions have a safe and uneventful journey. I have asked Illiana to set aside food for each of you. Give her a few more minutes to wrap it properly."

Armand turned to Eri beside him. "Well," he said with a sigh. "I suppose it is time to saddle the horses." He stood up to stretch his cramped muscles.

"You won't forget me, will you?" Eri said, rising to his feet.

Armand gazed down at the young man who stood close enough for him to detect the scent of wood smoke on his clothing. It was not the comeliness of the youthful face, but the rapt stare that Eri fixed upon him with those light brown eyes that caused his breath to quicken and his heart to thump in his chest.

"Of course not," he managed to choke out through a mouth that suddenly went dry. He averted his gaze to pick a shred of grass from the front of his own tunic.

For some inexplicable reason, he felt drawn to Eri, like a moth to the flames. What frightened him was the strength of that attraction. He'd never been so inclined before. Worse, he was unsure what to do about it. Perhaps it was best that he was leaving. Time and distance would surely help to diminish his perplexing fascination for the fellow.

"I shall never forget you," Eri said softly.

Armand glanced up to find Ordog's frowning gaze on him, which made him wonder whether the older man's acute attention stemmed from concern or disapproval.

At that moment, a Romany couple in their early twenties walked with grave dignity under the awning of Kedah's tent to seek an audience with their chieftain. Neither the man nor the woman looked like they were there to socialize.

One glance at their anxious faces brought Kedah to his feet. "What seems to be the problem?" he said, gazing from one to the other.

"It's Rudi," a woman said, wringing her hands. "He's gone. We can't find him anywhere."

Chapter 12

On hearing the woman's words, Kyle rose to his feet, as did those around him.

He recognized the man from the boar hunt. He was a tall slim fellow, with angular features in a beardless face. Unlike others of his kind, his skin was fair and his eyes were green. In contrast, the woman was small and dark, with long black hair and soft brown eyes.

"When did you first notice Rudi was missing?" Kedah said.

"A short while ago, when I called him to eat," she said, her hands clasped at her waist. "I went over to see the children he usually plays with, but he wasn't with them. Then I checked with the guards outside the camp, but they hadn't seen him either. I didn't know where else to look. That's when I told Baylor about it."

"He wanted to go with me to track down the boar," Baylor said. "I told him it was too dangerous for a boy his age." A look of apprehension crossed his face. "He's a headstrong child. I fear he might have sneaked out of camp anyway and followed us into the forest."

"How old is your son?" Kyle said, joining the conversation.

"Seven summers," Baylor said. "He knows his way around the woods, which is why I wasn't too concerned at first. But we've been back from the hunt for hours now, and he's still nowhere to be found."

"I think we ought to look for him," Ordog said.

"I do, too," Kedah said. To Baylor, he said, "Spread the word for everyone to meet here as soon as possible."

"Thank you," the woman said, her eyes bright with unshed tears.

Baylor put a comforting arm around her shoulders, and together, they headed back the way they came.

Reginald walked over to where Kedah stood gazing at the departing couple. "I hope ye understand that we cannot share in the search. It is important that we get back on the road." He glanced expectantly at Armand, Kyle, and Brother Luke.

"I'm staying to look for the boy," Armand said.

"As am I," Kyle said.

"Time is of the essence to deliver those letters," Reginald said with a scowl. "We've already lost two days. We have a duty—"

"As a parent," Kyle said, cutting him off, "I cannot turn my back on a child in peril, even if he is not my own. You can continue the journey on your own. I shall catch up with you after the boy is found."

Reginald's face flamed red up to his hairline. "Sir Percy will hear about this," he sputtered. To Brother Luke, he said, "Come on. Let us be on our way."

"I want to help with the search," the black friar said.

Kyle resisted the urge to smile. It was the first time since he'd met Brother Luke that he actually liked the man.

Reginald glared at the three of them, his face flushed and frowning, his arms at his sides with his hands knotted into fists.

Men and women from the camp, including the lost boy's parents, began to gather in front of Kedah's tent. Several older children came over to stand with them, adding to their number.

The high color on Reginald's face faded at the sight of the Romany who rallied to find the missing child. The pink blush that remained on his cheeks seemed to come more from embarrassment than from anger. "I reckon I can spare an hour or two to look for the wee lad," he said, shuffling his feet.

Kyle clapped the sheriff on the shoulder. "I knew I could count on you. Besides, the quicker we find him, the quicker we can be on our way."

Ordog led the group out of camp and into the woods, bound for the same forest track the boar hunters had taken earlier that morning. Kyle and his companions followed along behind them.

It was cool in the shade of the trees, where a canopy of branches blocked the early afternoon sun. Now and then, patches of blue sky peeked through the latticework of leaves overhead. A soft breeze stirred the air, bringing with it the musty smell of moist earth and the cloying scent of honeysuckle.

When they reached the trailhead, Ordog instructed the searchers to fan out on both sides. They were to walk on a course parallel with the pathway, each staying within ten paces of the other so as to make a thorough sweep of the area.

The terrain on either side of the main trail was rough, with deep ravines and sharp drop-offs that marked the abrupt end of a footpath. In places darkened by overhanging rock formations, lichens grew on jutting stones, making the surface slippery and the footing treacherous.

The searchers moved forward, slowly but surely, in a single ragged line, vanishing from sight behind trees and dense brush, only to reappear and vanish again.

Kyle prowled the ground with his eyes, looking for a footprint or a broken branch that would indicate the boy had passed that way. He poked and prodded mounds of earth with a knotty stick he'd found in the detritus on the forest floor. He inspected gnarled tree trunks for hollow cavities spacious enough to fit a child. He rummaged through heaps of leaves and piles of limbs to see what was under them. Those around him did the same.

Except for calling out the missing child's name, they carried on in silence, their mood somber, as though expecting to find a body rather than a living child.

For the next two hours, they scoured forest tracks and trails and everything in between. As the afternoon passed its peak, the shadows on the ground began to lengthen.

Kyle had just paused to take a swig of water from his skin bottle when a man somewhere off to the left raised a shout.

"It's Rudi!" the man cried. "I found him!"

From the jubilance in the man's voice, Kyle surmised the child was still alive. He broke rank with the others and hastened in that direction.

As the searchers converged on the scene, the man who had summoned them was helping a slim boy crawl out from under a tangle of fallen branches.

The child's face was streaked with dirt. There were grass stains on his shirt. His pants were crusted with mud and torn at the knee. Bits of broken twigs and dry leaves stuck out from the untidy mass of brown curls on his head. He wore a boot on one foot. The other foot was bare and bleeding from minor cuts and scratches.

When his mother arrived, she rushed up to him and fell to her knees to hug him tightly.

Baylor came running over to gather both mother and child into his arms, blinking hard as though to hold back tears.

Instead of joy at their reunion or even relief that he'd been rescued, the boy's countenance reflected fear and trepidation. Although safely ensconced in his mother's embrace, he kept glancing over his shoulder, as though looking for something or someone. After his mother rose to her feet, he clung to her hand, as if afraid to let her go.

"I wonder what frightened him so," Kyle said to Ordog in a low tone.

Ordog shot a speculative glance at the boy. "I do, too." He walked over to where the child stood with his parents and squatted down before him. "You're in safe hands, Rudi. You can rest easy now."

The boy peered at the older man, his gaze solemn and steady. Yet a shadow of doubt lurked in the depths of those immense hazel eyes.

"Ordog is right," Baylor said, ruffling his son's hair. "No need to worry about the boar any longer. It's dead."

The boy looked over his shoulder one more time before he lowered his gaze to stare at the boot on his left foot. "They put me in a sack," he said in a small voice. His chin quivered as he spoke.

The boy's remark sparked a dangerous glitter in Baylor's green eyes. "Who did that to you?" he demanded, his lips drawn tight.

Ordog glanced up at Baylor and lifted a hand for silence. He turned back to the boy. “Tell us what happened,” he said in a calm voice.

Baylor stood there fuming with his fists clenched. He remained quiet, though, apparently to hear what his son had to say.

“What was that about the sack, then?” Ordog said, gently prompting the boy.

Those looking on crowded close to hear what the boy had to say.

“I went into the woods this morning to track the boar on my own,” Rudi began, his speech halting. “I must have gone too far off the trail, because when I looked up, nothing around me looked familiar. That was when I saw something bright through the trees ahead. I crept closer to take a look.

“It was a tent like ours, only bigger. It had stripes, too. They were red and yellow, like the colors in the banner on top of it. There were four fine-looking horses and a mule staked in front of the tent. There were three men that I could see. One was sitting on a stump, sharpening a weapon. I could hear the scrape of the stone along the blade. Another was cooking meat on a spit over the campfire. Still another was brushing one of the horses.”

“Four horses mean four riders,” Ordog said. “Where was the fourth man?”

“He must have been the one who came up behind me and struck me on the head. That was all I remember until I woke up in a sack hanging in the air. The top was tied shut so I couldn’t climb out of it. I was afraid to move, lest they kill me. So I kept real still and listened while they talked among themselves."

"What did they say?" Ordog said.

"They were arguing about whether to do it tonight or not, seeing as how they now had a proper offering."

"How did you get loose?" Ordog said.

"I waited until all went quiet. I slit a tiny hole in the sack with the knife Pa gave me to keep in my boot. That way, I could see where I was, which was inside the tent. When I was sure I was alone, I cut the sacking and climbed down quiet-like. I could hear the men talking and laughing out front, so I slit the back of the tent and crawled outside. No one was looking in my direction, so I ran away as fast as I could." His face crumpled, as though he were about to cry from the strain of his horrific experience. "When I couldn't run anymore, I hid myself in case they came looking for me."

"That's enough for now," his mother said. She took him by the hand and led him over to a log on which she made him sit. She moistened a rag with water from her water bottle and wiped the blood from the cuts on his foot. She then tore a long strip of cloth from the hem of her skirt and wrapped his entire foot. Though a temporary fix, the cloth would protect the sole of his foot on the trek back to camp.

"It sounds like the boy ran into a small hunting party," Kyle said, musing aloud. "If they were flying a pennant, it was likely an English lord or some other nobleman of consequence."

"Englanders or not," Baylor said, "we must ferret them out and teach them a lesson. If we don't act quickly, they might soon be gone."

Ordog looked over at Kedah. "What do you think?"

“I think we should go back to camp and double the guard,” Kedah said. “Rudi is alive and well. That is all that matters at present.”

“But those men seized my son against his will and trussed him up like an animal,” Baylor said, scowling. “Who knows what harm they meant to inflict upon him?”

“Your boy was in the wrong place at the wrong time,” Kedah said. “He had no business even being there.”

“Are you saying it was his fault?” Baylor said from under lowered brows.

“Not entirely,” Kedah said. “Nevertheless, should you mete out punishment, however just in your view, to English nobles on English soil, we will be declared outlaw. Others of their kind will hunt us down and kill us without mercy. That includes our women and children, too. Need I remind you that we are interlopers in this land and that our remaining here depends on the sufferance of its inhabitants?”

“When you put it like that…” Baylor said, albeit grudgingly. He was clearly against letting the matter slide, but he evidently had sense enough to keep his opinion to himself.

Malcus and three other Romany men came over to stand with Baylor, as if to lend him tacit support by their presence.

“Let this serve as a warning for the rest of us,” Kedah said. “No child under twelve summers or any woman is to leave camp without a male escort, whether to hunt or tend the animals or draw water. We are not alone in these woods. Thus, we must take steps to prevent another incident like this from happening.”

The Romany gathered there nodded their heads and voiced their accord.

Ordog frowned, as though in puzzlement.

"Do you disagree?" Kedah said.

"Not at all," Ordog said. "I was just wondering what they meant by 'offering.' That makes it sound like they intended to use the boy as a blood sacrifice."

Brother Luke looked from Ordog to Kedah and back again, plainly appalled at the notion.

Kedah turned to Kyle, who stood beside him. "That cottage you mentioned when we first met," he said with a thoughtful look on his face. "The one you came across with the strange symbols on the walls."

"I shall never forget it," Kyle said. "What about it?"

"Could there be a connection between it and the Englanders who took Rudi?"

"If there is," Kyle said, "there's no way to prove it. Whoever murdered that man and woman left behind no evidence of their presence."

"That's too bad," Kedah said. To Ordog, he said, "We should head for camp."

"It's time to go back now," Ordog said in a voice loud enough for all to hear. "Follow me." He turned his face to the east. With the late afternoon sun on his shoulders, he set out toward the main trail.

The searchers followed on his heels. The mood among them was more cheerful than it had been earlier in the day. This time, they chatted and laughed as they walked.

Baylor stooped low to let Rudi climb onto his back.

The boy clung to his father like a burr, grinning with childish glee. His mother trod beside them with a smile on her face now that her lost child had been restored to her.

Kyle, Reginald, and Brother Luke brought up the rear, with Armand and Eri trailing after them.

"I'd sure like to see what's in that tent," Kyle said to Reginald beside him.

"For what purpose?" Reginald said.

"You heard Kedah," Kyle said. "They may be the ones who murdered those cottars."

"Even if ye could locate their camp, which is highly unlikely since we don't even know where to look, what makes ye think they would invite ye inside if there was something within that could implicate them?"

"That's where you come in," Kyle said, gazing pointedly at the sheriff.

"Uh-uh," Reginald said, holding up both hands and shaking his head. "Ye are not dragging me down that road."

"All you have to do is distract them long enough for me to take a proper look around inside."

"It will never work."

"Why not? Can you think of a better way to find evidence?"

"What if there is none? What then?"

"Then we leave, with no harm done."

"And if they catch us? They would hang us on the spot."

"They won't catch us if we're careful."

"I've heard that before," Reginald said. "I don't believe it this time, either."

****

Armand walked along the forest track beside Eri. Now that he was leaving, there was much he wanted to say. Yet, he was unsure whether he should say it. He would probably never see the young man again, so why hope for something that could not be.

Eri trudged along in pensive silence. He, too, seemed lost in thought, for his pace grew slower with each passing moment.

They soon fell far behind those ahead of them. Armand was about to suggest they catch up with the others when Eri stopped abruptly.

Armand shuffled to a halt. "What is it?" he said, glancing around to see if anything was amiss.

For several seconds, Eri stood there with his eyes squeezed shut, as though in pain, his breathing short and labored. Without warning, he fell to the ground like a shot bird, landing in an untidy heap in the middle of the pathway.

Eri's sudden collapse startled a muted yell out of Armand. He dropped to one knee and shook the young man's shoulder to rouse him, but to no avail. "What's wrong?" he said, between alarm and bewilderment.

Then something occurred to him that sent a stab of fear through him. What if the disgruntled Englishmen had tracked them down and shot at Eri out of spite? Being at the tail end of the group, they'd set themselves up as easy pickings. He leaned over his fallen companion to look for an arrow lodged in his back. To his relief, there was none.

His thoughts then turned to something less obvious but just as deadly. In his travels, he'd seen hearty men fall ill and die in a matter of hours. He rolled Eri onto his back and placed a hand on his forehead, only to find the skin beneath his fingers dry and hot to the touch. "He's burning up," he said to himself.

He gazed down at the young man, who lay there as still as death with a face as white as ash. There was no sign of life that he could readily see. Sickening dread fluttered in the pit of his stomach at the notion that Eri might be dead.

"*Mon Dieu!*" he cried, lapsing into French. "*Non!*"

He put a hand on Eri's chest to feel for the hammer of his heart.

In the next instant, he jerked his hand away, his mouth gaped open in shocked surprise.

Chapter 13

On hearing Armand's cry of distress, Kyle glanced over his shoulder. He and Reginald had lagged behind the main group, which was apparently too far ahead for any of them to hear it.

"I'd better go take a look," he said to the sheriff beside him.

"If there's trouble," Reginald said, "give a shout."

"Will do," Kyle said.

The sheriff continued on his way, while Kyle swung around and hurried back along the forest trail.

Within a minute or so, he met Armand carrying Eri, who lay unconscious in his arms. "What happened?" he said as he drew near.

"Eri collapsed for no reason," Armand said between breaths. "I think it might be a fever."

Kyle caught the note of desperation in Armand's voice, as if Eri was more to him than a casual acquaintance. One glance at the angst on the man's face confirmed that there was definitely something going on between those two. "What can I do?"

"Help me get her back to camp."

" 'Her'?"

"Eri is a maid," Armand said without emotion, as though merely stating a fact.

Kyle took the news in stride, although he did find it odd that the Romany went to so much trouble to hide

Eri's gender from them. There was no doubt in his mind that they knew she was a girl, especially after having lived with her for years. Needless to say, this was not the time to initiate a lengthy debate as to why they did it.

"She had me completely fooled," Armand said.

"I can say the same," Kyle said. "Why would she conceal her identity when none of the other women took the trouble to do it?"

"Her reason for doing so is of no consequence to me at this moment. She is gravely ill. I must take her to Illiana, to make her well again."

"I know a short cut," Kyle said. "It's a little rough, but we'll get there faster."

They headed down the forest track. By the time they reached the fork in the trail, Armand was breathing hard from the effort. Though Eri was smaller and lighter than a man, it was quite taxing to bear the dead weight of a limp body for an extended period of time.

Kyle lifted Eri from Armand's arms to let him catch his breath and recover his strength. After that, they took turns carrying her in order to cover the distance more quickly.

They followed narrow deer paths through dense undergrowth in the forest, traversed rocky slopes, and sloshed across shallow creeks.

When they reached the edge of the clearing around the circle of wagons, they heaved a dual sigh of relief. They trudged across the grassy open area and entered the campsite, dog-tired from the taxing trek through the woods.

"I'll tell Illiana you're coming." Kyle passed Eri over to Armand and hastened toward Kedah's tent. On the way, he flexed his shoulders to ease the ache in his muscles.

****

The sight of Eri lying motionless in Armand's arms brought forth the handful of Romany who had remained in camp during the search.

"What's wrong with Eri?" Zoli said, hobbling forward on his cane.

"Is Eri hurt?" said a woman with two small children peering out from behind at her skirts.

Armand plodded on in silence, his jaw set and his eyes fixed on Kedah's tent, clearly determined to reach his destination before his legs gave out under him.

Illiana sat in the shade of the awning with a basket of garments beside her, plying a needle to a tear in a shirt. At the sound of excited voices, she looked up from her sewing.

"Eri has taken ill," Kyle said as he approached.

Without a word, she set aside the shirt and went into the tent. Seconds later, she came out with her medicament pouch and a straw mat, which she spread on the ground in the shade. She took a shirt from the basket and rolled it up like a pillow.

"On here, if you please," she said to Armand, who had just arrived at the head of a small procession of curious Romany.

Armand went down on one knee to lay Eri gently on the mat. He took the pillow-like garment that Illiana handed to him and placed it under her head, after which he stood up and shuffled back a pace. It was far enough to be respectful, yet close enough for him to hover like an anxious parent over an ailing child.

About that time, the searchers straggled into camp.

News that Rudi had been found spread quickly among those who'd been left behind. Those who had gathered around Eri drifted away to greet the searchers and ply them for the details.

Only Zoli remained there under the awning. He leaned heavily on his cane, his face strained and pale, his mouth turned down at the edges.

Ordog had evidently heard the news about Eri, for he hurried over to Kedah's tent, his brow knitted in a frown. He strode up just as Zoli turned to Armand.

"So what happened to Eri?" Zoli said.

"We were on the way back to camp when she swooned for no apparent reason," Armand said. "Kyle Shaw and I carried her here as quickly as we could."

Illiana and Zoli exchanged a meaningful glance. She seemed amused. He looked worried.

"What is it that ails her?" Ordog said to Illiana.

Illiana crouched beside Eri and laid a hand on her forehead. At once, twin lines appeared between the older woman's dark brows. "It's definitely a fever."

A low moan from Eri brought Armand a step closer, his expression somber and wretched, as though fretting over his inability to render aid.

Eri opened her eyes and squinted against the reflected glare of the late afternoon sun. "Oh, my head," she said, lifting a hand to her temple. She glanced from Illiana to Armand and back again. "How did I get here?" When she attempted to rise, Illiana gently pushed her back down.

"Lie still," Illiana said. "I'll fix something to ease the pain." She stood up and walked over to where a pot of soup simmered over the open flames. She took an empty bowl from the low table by the campfire and dipped it into the water barrel situated under an outside corner of the tent where it could catch the runoff after a rain. She poured some of the water into a small pottery crock, which she set directly on the hot coals.

While waiting for the water to heat, she removed a tiny sack from her medicament pouch and dropped two pinches of a powdered substance into an empty cup. When the water in the crock began to steam, she poured a small amount into the cup and stirred in a bit of honey, evidently to mask the taste.

She brought the cup over to Eri and set it within her easy reach. "Let this steep for a few minutes before you drink it."

She turned away to rummage through the basket of garments until she found an old worn-out shirt that was ripe with age. The fabric tore easily when she ripped off a sleeve. She dropped the soft material in the bowl of cool water. When fully saturated, she wrung it out and folded it neatly. She settled on the mat next to Eri and laid the cloth on the reclining young woman's forehead.

"What can I do to help?" Armand said.

"Whatever there is to do, I will do it," Zoli said, his tone adamant.

Illiana looked pointedly at the large bandage around Zoli's bare thigh, the bottom half of which stuck out below the frayed hem of his tunic. Her gaze then shifted to his face. "You need to stay off that leg," she said in the mother-voice. "Otherwise, you'll pop your stitches. Once that wound opens up, there's a good chance gangrene will set in."

Zoli frowned at being admonished in front of an outsider, yet he didn't argue with the older woman. From the mulish expression on his face, he didn't seem quite ready to comply, either.

Illiana removed the rag from Eri's forehead and dipped it in the cool water. After wringing it out, she put it back on the young woman's brow.

"I'm fine," Eri said. "Really, I am."

"You will be when I'm done," Illiana said. "Now, stay put and behave." She turned to look up at Armand. "So you now know about Eri, do you?"

Eri sat up abruptly, her eyes on Armand's face. The rag on her forehead plopped unheeded onto her lap.

"Only by chance," Armand said, meeting Eri's steady gaze. "I must say, I was thoroughly deceived."

"Sorry," Eri said, watching him closely, as though for any sign of disapproval.

"It was done for the best of reasons," Illiana said. "And the oldest, too."

"And that is?" Armand said.

"To protect her virtue, of course," Illiana said. "It is an essential quality in an unmarried woman. Both a maiden and her family would suffer great humiliation if some man were to dally with her to satisfy selfish carnal desires. Unlike the other women in camp, Eri has no family to protect her. She must rely on such a ruse to keep outsiders at bay, should they take notice of her. She says she feels less vulnerable in the guise of a male." She retrieved the rag from Eri's lap and dropped it into the water bowl. "Did you mean it when you said you wanted to help?"

"Absolutely," Armand said, inching closer.

Zoli opened his mouth to protest.

Illiana raised a hand to forestall the young Romany's objection. She picked up the cup and climbed to her feet.

"See that Eri drinks all of this," she said, handing the cup to Armand. To Zoli, she said, "Come with me." Without a backward glance, she started toward the tent where the young man lived with his father.

Armand gazed down at Eri, at once thrilled that she was a woman and unaccountably apprehensive for the same reason. He longed to stay in camp to get better acquainted with her. Still, he had a duty to carry out his assigned task, which was the sole purpose of his journey. He could continue on to his destination by himself, but given the volatile political climate in England, it was safer to travel in the company of lawmen, even if they were Scots. Having a holy friar with them didn't hurt, either.

Since the others planned to depart first thing in the morning, his time with Eri was limited. After that, there was no telling when or if they would ever meet again.

He stood there in pensive silence for so long that she tapped his booted foot with her fingers to gain his attention from where she sat on the straw mat.

"Are you going to give that to me?" she said, indicating the cup in his hand.

Now roused from his reverie, he went down on one knee to be on eye level with her. "Forgive me. I have much on my mind."

"Is something troubling you?" she said.

"It is nothing," he said, presenting the cup to her.

She took it from his hand and brought it to her lips. "This is horrid," she said after taking a sip. She gazed at him with narrowed eyes, as though something just occurred to her. "Who told you that I am a maid?"

"Nobody said anything about it."

"Then how did you find out?"

Too late, he realized he'd walked into the jaws of a verbal trap, with no way out.

"I—um," he stammered, sinking fast in a mire of his own making.

He cleared his throat to stall for time to come up with a plausible explanation. One look at her unsmiling countenance persuaded him that it had better be good.

The heat of a guilty blush crept up his face all the way to his hairline. "I'd rather not say," he mumbled at last. At that instant, it was all he could think of, and it sounded lame, even to him.

"I'm disappointed," she said.

"Because I didn't answer your question?"

"Nay," she said. "Because it took you so long to figure it out."

"Oh," he said, glancing down at his hands. He prided himself on possessing a glib tongue, yet for the second time in less than half a minute, he was at a loss for words. He was convinced it had to do with her presence, for that was the only time he felt nervous and anxious. He looked up and met her gaze.

"I forgive you," she said.

She bestowed a dazzling smile upon him that took hold of his heart so suddenly, it left him breathless and unable to speak.

He gazed at her for a long moment, moved yet unmoving, clearly liking what he saw. Unless he was mistaken, it appeared she felt the same.

A movement at the corner of his eye reminded him that he and Eri were not alone under the awning of Kedah's tent. Ordog and Kyle were there, too. As might be expected, their close proximity put a damper on his fervor, since both men had unquestionably seen and heard every nuance of warmth and caring that had just passed between him and Eri. Conversely, he could not help but overhear their conversation, prompted no doubt by their unintentional yet astute observations.

Ordog turned to Kyle beside him. "It seems those two fancy each other."

"I'm afraid it may involve something more dangerous," Kyle said.

"Like what?"

"Love."

"I'm not sure I approve."

"It's a wee bit late for that," Kyle said.

Armand smiled to himself. Was that it? Was it love that made his heart soar every time he looked at her or even thought about her? Falling in love was the farthest thing from his mind. It must have crept up on him when he wasn't looking. Still, this was not the time for sentimental attachment. He must resist the urge to succumb to the thrall of love, and not just to lessen the pain of parting on the morrow. He prided himself on being a reasonable man, and if there was ever a time to listen to the voice of reason, this was surely it.

He glanced down at the cup in her hand, noting the amount of potion left in it. "You must drink that to get well."

"It's too bitter," she said, wrinkling her nose.

"It is supposed to taste like that. That's how you know it is medicine. Please drink it. If you don't, I shall worry about your health."

She gazed at him intently, as though trying to determine whether he meant it. She apparently made up her mind. "All right, but only because you insist." She upended the cup and gulped down the contents, gagging on the last mouthful.

He patted her on the back until she regained her composure. "Good girl." He took the empty cup from her hand and set it aside. "Now, you must rest."

She lay back down on the mat with her head on the makeshift pillow. "Will you stay here with me?" she said, gazing up at him.

"I am not going anywhere." He sat cross-legged on the mat beside her and wrung the water from the rag, which he placed on her forehead.

She closed her eyes. Within seconds, her breathing became regular and even.

He looked down at her face, so tranquil in slumber. It broke his heart to think that in a matter of hours, he would never see it again. Neither would he ever hear her voice.

He peered more closely at her, now that he could without her being aware of it. The signs were there the whole time, yet he had failed to see them: the delicate features, the small nose with a sprinkling of freckles, the sweep of long black lashes resting on smooth cheeks. Why had he not noticed them before?

Though stunned at first upon discovering her true gender, his attraction to her was real. It was like his body had sensed that she was a female, even if his mind was not yet aware of it. As for his growing affection for her, he never expected that to happen. Now that it had, what was he going to do about it? More to the point, what *could* he do about it?

Chapter 14

Kyle sat on the ground with the others in front of Kedah's tent. A cooling breeze tugged at his shirt and ruffled his hair.

Overhead, an avalanche of pink and orange clouds rolled toward the setting sun. Only the rim of the burnished copper orb was visible above the tops of the trees. A reddish glow bathed the western sky, while to the east, the azure vault of the heavens slowly melted into a pearly dusk.

Bone soup bubbled in a pot over the campfire. It had been hours since his last meal, yet Kyle's stomach rebelled at the smell of boiled pork. He clenched his teeth against the urge to vomit.

He felt hot and cold at the same time. His joints ached. He closed his eyes against the throbbing in his temples. Within seconds, the sounds of the camp receded into the distance. His nausea ebbed as he drifted in the twilight between wakefulness and slumber.

"Are you ill?" said a woman's voice, so far away, yet so familiar.

Startled awake, he opened his eyes to see Illiana standing before him. He nodded his head, which was easier than trying to speak with a throat as dry as parchment.

Illiana went into the tent for a moment and came

out with a mat and a blanket. She spread them on the ground beside him and bade him to lie down.

Reginald, who sat cross-legged nearby, peered closely at his deputy. “Ye don’t look so good.”

“You wouldn’t either if you were ailing,” Illiana said. “You might want to move along, lest you come down with it, too.”

The sheriff evidently took her words to heart, for he scrambled to his feet and departed in haste.

Kyle reclined on the mat and closed his eyes. That was all he remembered until he awoke to stars winking in the night sky. The moon, full and bright, shed its silvery luminescence upon a camp at peace.

He tried to sit up, but the spinning in his head prompted him to lie back down. It was difficult to focus both eyes at the same time, so he shut one and looked over at Armand with the other.

The young man sat beside the sleeping girl, plying the tip of his dagger to a small wooden object by the light of the campfire.

“How’s Eri?” Kyle said in a low voice so as not to disturb Illiana slumbering nearby.

“Still feverish,” Armand said, glancing up from his whittling. “And you?”

“Not so good.”

“There are others in the camp who have fallen ill, like you.”

“How many?”

“Four, at last count,” Armand said. “There may be more by morning.”

“What about you?”

“I feel fine.”

“Glad to hear it,” Kyle said, heaving a long drawn-out sigh. The effort to speak left him exhausted, minimal though the conversation had been. He gladly sank into the gloom that closed over him and held him tightly in its shadowed embrace.

Sometime later in the night, the touch of an arm lifting his head and shoulders brought him up from a dreamless sleep. He felt the hard rim of a cup against his lips. A lukewarm liquid flooded the recesses of his mouth. It tasted sweet on his tongue, yet there was an underlying bitterness to it. He swallowed to keep from choking. Then the arm and the cup were gone. Once again, he slipped into an abyss of darkness.

****

At first light the next morning, Armand opened his eyes to a thin mist that hung low on the ground within the campsite. A mellow haze in the eastern sky grew brighter with each passing moment.

He scrubbed a hand over the stubble on his cheeks and chin. Though he'd slept for several hours, it had been a restless slumber that left him drained and weary.

His thoughts turned to Eri on the straw mat an arm's length away. He lifted his head to glance at her, only to find her steady gaze upon him. As he stared into those mesmerizing light brown eyes, his pulse began to race.

"How do you feel?" he said, unable to look away even if he wanted to, which he did not.

"Sad," she said.

"I was referring to your health."

"I'm in pain."

"Where does it hurt?"

"Here," she said, placing a hand over her heart.

"I'm sorry." He too suffered from a similar

affliction at the thought of parting from her. Yet it was his own doing, since he was the one leaving. The fact that it was for the noble purpose of fulfilling a sacred trust did little to alleviate his emotional distress.

Resigned but wretched as a result of his chosen fate, he reached out a hand and laid it on her forehead. Her skin felt hot to the touch. "You are still not well."

"I'm thirsty."

"I will get you something to eat, too."

"The way I feel, it will likely come back up."

"Just a few bites, then. You must eat to keep up your strength."

"I'll give it a try."

"Good girl," he said.

He rose to his knees and helped her to a sitting position. He then got up and went over to the low table for a small wooden bowl, which he filled with broth from the pot over the campfire. He poured ale from the jug into a cup and took one of the stale flatbreads from under the cloth that covered the wicker basket. With the bowl and a spoon in one hand and the cup and the bread in the other, he walked back to Eri's mat.

He set the cup on the ground within her reach and sat on the mat across from her. He tore the stale bread into small pieces, which he dropped into the bowl to soak up the hot broth.

Apparently, the sounds of his moving about woke Illiana, for she got up and put away her bedding. After checking on both Eri and Kyle, who was still asleep, she left with her medicament pouch, evidently to tend those in the camp who had fallen ill.

Minutes after Illiana left, Ordog walked up to Kedah's tent. "How is Kyle Shaw?" he said to Armand.

"He's done nothing but sleep since yesterday evening," Armand said.

"I reckon that's a good thing." Ordog sat down on the edge of Eri's mat. "Are you feeling better now?" he said to her.

"Of course I am," she said. "Nothing keeps me down for long. You know that." She picked up the cup and sipped the ale in it.

After stirring the contents of the bowl to make sure all the bread was saturated, Armand scooped up the smallest piece with the wooden spoon and fed it to Eri, who ate it without enthusiasm.

When he offered another spoonful of broth-soaked bread to her, she declined with a shake of her head.

"You eat it," she said. "I've had enough." She took another sip of ale, which she seemed to tolerate better than solid food.

"Are you sure?" Armand said, holding the filled spoon out to her.

"Quite sure," she said.

"All right, then." He was about to thrust the spoon into his mouth when he noticed the strange expression on her face. He thought it might be because she still wanted the food he was about to eat, so he presented it to her again.

When she declined a second time, he helped himself. After the first bite, he realized how hungry he was. It took him but a moment to consume the rest of the broth-soaked bread, after which he helped himself to another bowl of the same.

"He certainly has a healthy appetite," Ordog said to her.

"He is hale and hearty, and I for one am glad of it,"

she said. "How else could he have stayed up half the night looking after me?"

"Up half the night, was he?" Ordog said, hurling a censorious glance in Armand's direction.

"Aye, half the night," she said, ignoring the reproach in the older man's voice. "I am now on the mend, thanks to his efforts."

Ordog drew in a long breath and let it out in a single blast, which was sufficient to convey his displeasure without saying a word.

Armand glanced from her to Ordog and back again, unsure whether he should stay or go. When he made a move to rise, she placed a hand on his arm to stop him.

"We've done nothing shameful, Uncle," she said. "I am disappointed that you think we did."

"That never crossed my mind," Ordog said, avoiding her gaze.

"Indeed," she retorted, clearly unconvinced.

"I am only concerned for your welfare."

"I can take care of myself," she said.

"It's not you I'm worried about," Ordog said with a fleeting glance at Armand.

The awkward silence that fell among them stretched out to a full minute.

Uncomfortable at being the cause of their disagreement, Armand felt like he should do something to smooth over the breach. He reached inside the front of his tunic and withdrew a wooden horse of a size to fit in the palm of his hand. "I finished this last night while you were sleeping," he said, offering it to her. "I want you to have it, so you don't forget me."

Her eyes lit up at the sight of the diminutive carving. She turned it over in her hands to admire the detailed workmanship on it. “I have something for you, too.”

She removed from her wrist a masculine-looking bracelet made of thin strips of red-stained leather plaited together. “So you don’t forget me, either,” she said as she tied it around his left wrist.

Ordog scowled at the pair of them.

“There,” she said to the older man. “It’s done.”

“Is he, too, so inclined?” Ordog said.

Armand glanced from one to the other, sure he missed something, but unsure what it was.

She turned to Armand. “Do you like my gift?”

“Very much,” he said, holding up his left arm to admire the plaited leather bracelet.

“And me?”

The question caught him off guard. He hesitated for several heartbeats, primarily because of how Ordog, in his current state of agitation, would react to the truth. When he caught the anxious yet hopeful expression on her face, he decided to speak up, despite the consequences. “Aye,” he said at last. “You, too.”

Though clearly relieved, she appeared reluctant to show it. “Satisfied?” she said, flashing an I-told-you-so look at the older man.

“With you, maybe.” Ordog tilted his head at Armand. “With him, I’m not so sure.” He clambered to his feet with a grunt. As he ambled away, the slanting rays of the rising sun gilded his face and cast an elongated shadow on the ground behind him.

“What was that about?” Armand said.

“I’m tired,” she said, rubbing her eyes. “Let me rest for a while.” She leaned back on the makeshift pillow, her gaze on his face. “I’ll explain later. I promise."

****

Kyle sat up and looked around him. Armand, Eri, and Illiana were asleep nearby. Reginald and Brother Luke were absent, likely bedded down elsewhere in the camp out of fear of contagion.

The darkness of night had given way to a pale glow in the eastern sky. The tents within the circle of wagons were but hunched shadows in the predawn light that marked the advent of a new day.

His stomach growled at the tantalizing aroma of boiled pork. He got up, only to find he was still weak, even though the symptoms of his earlier malady were gone. When he felt steadier on his feet, he went over to the small table for a wooden bowl and one of the stale flatbreads, after which he helped himself to the soup in the cooking pot suspended over banked coals in the fire pit. He sat on a chunk of wood and started in on the food. It was the best he'd ever tasted, or so it seemed after his long fast.

He'd just finished eating when Armand sat up and stretched.

The young man pressed a finger against his lips to urge Kyle to silence. He stood up and shook the dust from his blanket, after which he rolled it up and stuffed it into his cloth travel bag. "How do you feel?" he said in a hoarse whisper.

"Better, thanks," Kyle said in an undertone. "I don't feel as wobbly now that I've eaten."

"Are you up to going to the creek for a wash before the others rise?" Armand said in a low voice.

"I am," Kyle said softly.

Together, they left the campsite and made their

way to a narrow stream a short distance into the woods. When they found a suitable place clear of fallen logs, they shed their clothing and waded into the deeper water in the middle.

"I was worried about you," Armand said. "You've been laid low since the day before yesterday."

"I feel fine now," Kyle said, easing into the icy water. "How is Eri?"

"Back to normal, thank God."

"And the others who fell ill?"

"A few recovered quickly, but some are still ailing. Illiana is keeping a close eye on them. The friar made himself useful by helping her tend to them."

"How many sick altogether?"

"Eight."

"It could have been worse."

"There is a rumor going around that we brought bad luck to the camp."

"I'm afraid Malcus is right."

"How do you know he was the one who spread the tale?"

"Who else would go to such lengths to hasten our departure?"

"I should have known it was him, especially after witnessing the run-in he had with you over the boar's hide."

"Malcus is right, by the way," Kyle said. "Reginald suffered from the same malady during our stay in Carlyle a week ago."

"I didn't know that."

"Did I miss anything else while I slept?" Kyle said.

"Only Reginald's grousing about losing another two days."

"Is that all?"

"Pretty much," Armand said. "Oh, and just so you know, you are responsible for the smile on Illiana's face."

"What did I do?"

"She seemed really pleased to take care of you personally."

"I shall have to thank her for that." Kyle ducked under the surface to wet his hair and came up gasping. "That's really cold."

After a quick scrub from head to toe, they headed for the sandy bank to dry off.

The morning air, though cool at that early hour, felt warm on Kyle's skin. He slipped his tunic over his head and pulled on his boots.

They went back to camp and headed for Kedah's tent, where Illiana was frying thin barley flatbreads on a greased metal disc atop hot coals.

"Are you hungry?" she said to Kyle.

"Not anymore," Kyle said. "I ate some soup earlier."

"Hunger is a good sign," she said as she turned over the flatbreads to cook them on the other side.

"I appreciate your attending to me while I was ill."

"It was the least I could do for a guest in our camp."

"Could I trouble you further for some of that bread to take on our journey?" Kyle said. "I'll be glad to pay for it."

"No need for that," she said. "Give me a few minutes to finish up here. I'll let you know when it's ready."

With the rising of the sun, the Romany began to

stir within the campsite. Small children ran around and played, while women set about preparing the first meal of the day. A trio of older boys released the goats and the ponies and herded them out into the open field beyond the wagons.

While waiting for the flatbreads to fry, Kyle and his companions gathered their belongings, filled their water skins, and saddled their mounts.

Armand, Reginald, and Brother Luke went to get something to eat while Kyle sought out Kedah.

He found the chieftain chatting with Ordog, who was brushing the rough coat of a sturdy black and white pony in front of his tent.

"We'll be on our way shortly," Kyle said, addressing both men. "I want to thank you for your hospitality over the last few days. I hope our presence wasn't too much of an inconvenience."

"It has been interesting, to say the least," Kedah said with a nod of his head.

Ordog winked at Kyle. "What he means is we don't get visitors all that often, and he'd like to keep it that way."

"Ordinarily, that would be true," Kedah said. "But in your case, Kyle Shaw, I am grateful you came. Without your timely intervention on the boar hunt, my old friend here"—he tilted his head at Ordog—"might now be singing with the goddess."

Ordog patted the pony's shoulder affectionately, his gaze on Kyle. "Kedah is right," he said, setting the brush aside. "I am in your debt and will remain so until I return the favor in kind." He slipped a bridle over the creature's head, put a small rectangular blanket on its back, and placed a battered saddle on top of it. After tightening the cinch strap, he rolled an extra shirt and a couple of other items into a blanket, which he thrust into an oilskin sack and secured to the back of the saddle. He ducked into the tent for an old battle axe, which he slid into a thick leather loop on the saddle made for that purpose. "That is why I've decided to go with you."

Kyle exchanged a glance with Kedah, who shrugged his shoulders.

"I know you have concerns," Kedah said, "but it is something he must do. It would be useless to try to talk him out of it."

"I have no intention of talking him out of it," Kyle said. To Ordog, he said, "You are an honorable man, and I shall be glad of your company. I don't think the others will raise any objections to your coming along."

Ordog looked immensely pleased to hear it.

Kyle moved on to say his good-byes to the others he had come to know during his short stay in the camp. After he had made the rounds, he headed back to where Armand, Reginald, and Brother Luke waited with their mounts in the middle of the open area. Kedah was there, too, as was Ordog with his pony.

"Ordog will accompany us on our journey," Kyle said to his companions.

Armand and Brother Luke appeared to take the addition to their group in stride.

That was not the case with Reginald, who frowned at the announcement. "That means another mouth to feed," he grumbled.

"He is perfectly capable of fending for himself," Kyle said in the older man's defense. "What's more, we don't know what dangers await us on the open road.

With him along, we have one more man on our side."

Illiana walked up with two cloth bundles that smelled of freshly cooked flatbreads. She handed one to Kyle, who hung it from his saddle bow. Ordog took the other bundle from her and tied it to his saddle roll.

About that time, Eri arrived on the scene with a bow and quiver of arrows slung over one shoulder and a cloth travel bag over the other. Her loose clothing made it difficult to determine whether she was male or female, which was evidently by design since Reginald and Brother Luke were still unaware of her true gender.

Ordog gave her a sweeping glance from the dark curls on her head to the home-tanned brown leather boots on her feet. "What are you up to now?"

"I'm here to protect my interests," Eri said, tilting her head in Armand's direction. "When do we leave?"

" 'We'?" Reginald said, clearly taken aback. "What makes ye think *ye* are coming with us, too?"

"The farther south you venture, the more protection you'll need," Eri said. "I'm a dead shot with a bow and arrow. Besides that, I don't eat much."

"I'm a dead shot with a crossbow," Brother Luke said, joining the conversation, "but you don't hear me bragging about it." When they all turned to stare at him, he added, "I wasn't always a friar, you know. I served in the king's army before I took the cowl."

"I've never seen you shoot a crossbow," Eri said to him.

"Maybe you will someday," Brother Luke said.

"That is neither here nor there," Reginald said to Eri. "The point is: how do ye expect to keep up when ye don't even have a mount?" He glanced at his fellow travelers for corroboration. "I say we leave him here.

He will only slow us down."

"Eri can ride with me." Armand swung up into the saddle and held out his hand to pull her up onto the horse's rump behind him. "Will that do?" he added, looking pointedly at the sheriff.

Chapter 15

The sun had been up for a full hour by the time Kyle and those with him finally left the Romany camp. They rode along a pathway through the woods that would take them to the main road. Moss and decaying leaves under the hooves of their mounts muffled the sound of their passing.

Not a breath of air stirred the musty stillness of the forest. The delicate greens of new summer growth on deciduous trees around them contrasted with the dark green foliage of ancient oaks. Errant sunbeams that penetrated the leafy branches overhead threw a patchwork of light and shadow across the narrow track.

Before long, they emerged from the cool shade of the woods into the blazing heat of the sun. The main road lay just ahead, a hundred feet beyond the fringe of trees. There was no one in sight in either direction, as was expected for such an isolated region.

They rode across the open stretch of ground to the road, where they turned east and settled into an easy canter.

They had gone barely half a mile when a small group of horsemen rounded a bend in the road a short distance ahead of them. They reined in with their hands on their weapons, ready to defend themselves should the oncoming riders present a threat.

Reginald squinted at the horsemen through the

morning haze. "Do ye think they're border reivers?"

"We're a mite far south for them," Kyle said.

"What about bandits? I heard they roam these hills."

"Could be." Kyle lifted his hand to shade his eyes from the glare of the sun. "On the other hand, those steeds look too well fed for the likes of petty thieves and cutthroats."

"I count five horses," Reginald said. "Only three riders, though."

"One horse is loaded down like a pack animal."

"What's that on the other one?"

"A rug, maybe?" Kyle said, straining his eyes to make out what it was. "It looks more like a body, though."

"Out here?" Reginald said, turning to stare at the deputy. "Surely, ye must be mistaken."

"There's one way to find out," Kyle said. "They'll be here in a minute."

They sat in silence while waiting for the riders to approach.

As the horsemen drew closer, Kyle recognized them from an earlier encounter at the Bull and Bear Tavern. "Those are Sir Guy's retainers. The one in the lead is Dooley, chief of the guard."

"Sir Guy de Forz?" Reginald said. "The one who was poisoned?"

"How many Sir Guys do you know?"

"Only one, of course," Reginald said. "What, pray, are they doing out here in the middle of nowhere?"

"Let's find out, shall we?" Kyle lifted his arm in greeting as the riders came within hailing distance.

Dooley and the two men with him brought their

horses to a halt half a dozen paces away. The two animals on lead ropes swung wide at the end of their tethers before shuffling to a stop.

One was a brown mule laden with a large bundle tied securely to its back. The other was a tall black warhorse with a dead man slung across the saddle. The legs dangled on one side, while the head and arms hung down on the other.

"Well, well, if it isn't the deputy from Ayrshire," Dooley said with a humorless smile. "What brings you out this way?"

"I could ask you the same question." Kyle tilted his head at the body draped over the saddle. "What happened to him?"

"Isn't this a tad out of your jurisdiction?"

"A wee bit more than a tad, I'd say." Kyle leaned forward to rest his forearms on the saddle bow. "But you know how it goes: once a lawman, always a lawman." He met and held Dooley's eyes. "So what happened to him?"

The chief of the guard's surly demeanor vanished behind the shadow of fear that darkened his countenance. "That's just it," he said, licking his lips. He glanced at his companions, as though to bolster his courage. "I don't know."

Kyle sat up straight, his interest piqued at Dooley's odd behavior. "Then how did he die?"

"I don't know."

"Did you examine his body?"

"I did." Dooley looked over at the other two retainers. "We did."

"And?"

"There was not a mark on him."

"Where did you find him?"

"In his tent."

Kyle's eyes flicked to the mule carrying a bundle that looked like tightly folded sailcloth. It wasn't the size that held his attention but the red and yellow striping on it. Those were the colors of the tent Baylor's son had mentioned when relating the details of his capture by four men in the woods. "Who is he?" he said, casting a fleeting glance at the dead man.

"Sir Kenneth de Forz of the House of Lancaster," Dooley said.

Kyle's brows drew together at the mention of that name, for Sir Kenneth was Sir Guy's younger brother. There was no doubt in his mind that Sir Guy had been murdered. He'd witnessed the aftermath of that himself. The eldest brother, Sir Charles, had died in a hunting accident, or so he'd been told. The fact that each of the de Forz siblings had perished before their time suggested death by design for all three. The question at hand was what was the real cause of Sir Kenneth's demise?

In addition, there was Dooley's blasé attitude about Sir Kenneth's passing, as though he only attended to the man out of a sense of duty to the family, whereas he'd clearly respected Sir Guy and had served him loyally for years.

Another setback was the tent, for with its removal went any incriminating evidence that might have been found at the scene.

"My sympathy to the family on their loss," Kyle said. "Where are you taking him?"

"To the de Forz manor for burial," Dooley said.

"Should not the local constabulary be informed of

his passing?" Kyle said. "After all, he is, or rather was, a man of noble status."

"I prefer to let his family make that determination."

Kyle's eyes narrowed speculatively on the chief of the guard's face. "Sir Kenneth seemed well enough when I met him a week ago at Sir Guy's funeral. Don't you find it peculiar that he should expire so unexpectedly?"

"What are you suggesting?"

"I lack authority in this province, so far be it from me to suggest anything."

Dooley shifted uneasily in the saddle. "There is an explanation for his death, strange though it may sound."

"I'm listening," Kyle said.

"It was demons." Dooley looked dead serious, without a trace of humor on his face.

Kyle stared at the retainer in disbelief. He glanced at Reginald astride the rawboned bay beside him, not at all surprised that the sheriff had reacted in the same manner.

Dooley leaned forward, his voice low as though to impart a confidence. "Sir Kenneth feared the demons would come after him."

"Why?" Kyle said, more to humor the man than out of curiosity.

"Because they *were* after him, and last night, they finally got him."

Kyle snorted in derision. "You must think me a fool," he said, impaling the man with an icy stare.

Dooley squirmed in the saddle, as though unnerved by the dangerous light in the pale blue eyes fixed upon him. "On the contrary," he said with gravity. "My impression of you in Ayr was that of a meticulous but reasonable man."

"Then you should know that I only deal in facts, not fantastical tales of demons and such."

Dooley looked over at his cohorts, as though seeking their consent to speak.

"Tell him," said the retainer nearest to him.

The other man, who held the lead rope of the pack mule, shrugged and nodded his accord.

Dooley turned back to the deputy. "Sir Kenneth liked to dabble in the dark arts. It was a secret everyone knew about. His family disapproved, of course, but that didn't seem to bother him. He considered himself a mystic acquainted with the power of uncanny things."

"For argument's sake," Kyle said, "let us say he did in fact indulge in devilry. Would he not then be sufficiently familiar with the ways of demons to avoid falling prey to their traps?"

"So it would seem, except for one thing."

"Which is?"

"The death curse."

"What death curse?"

"The one the woman placed on him."

"What woman?"

"The one from the homestead farther up the road."

A mental image flashed into Kyle's mind of the man and the woman whom he and his companions had found burned beyond recognition. "How far up the road?"

"About half a day's journey."

"Why would the woman place a death curse on Sir Kenneth?"

"She only did it after he ran her through with his sword."

"And why did he run her through?" Kyle said, keeping a tight grip on his patience.

"To stop her from binding him with a spell."

"What possessed him to seek her out in the first place?"

"She summoned him by incantation, or so she claimed."

"For what purpose?"

"To make him renounce his right of succession to the throne," Dooley said. "According to her, he was unsuited for the kingly line. She and her minion tried to put a hex on him, but Sir Kenneth ran them through before they could complete the ritual. Unfortunately for Sir Kenneth, the woman placed a death curse on him with her dying breath."

"What happened after that?" Kyle said.

"Sir Kenneth burned the witch and her man to weaken their power. He slaughtered the animals and burned them, too. He claimed that spilling innocent blood would protect him until he found a way to break the curse." Dooley glanced over at Sir Kenneth's body lying across the saddle. "I guess he was wrong."

"I find it hard to believe that demons killed Sir Kenneth," Kyle said.

"Evil spirits are extremely powerful," Brother Luke said, joining the conversation. "Those who conjure them leave themselves open to demon attack. The church records contain numerous cases of demon possession."

"The holy man is right," Dooley said. "There is no other explanation for the suddenness of Sir Kenneth's death. He was fit when he went to sleep last night. This morning, he was dead for no discernable reason. His mouth was open and his eyes wide and staring, like he'd been frightened to death."

"There has to be a more earthly cause," Kyle said. "I recommend letting an expert examine his body when you return to the manor. I also suggest going over every inch of the tent cloth and the bedding. A thorough search may turn up something that was overlooked the first time around." He glanced up at the midmorning sun and then over at the body across the back of the black warhorse. "The day is wearing on, so I'll leave you to it."

"Right you are." Dooley shook the reins and urged his mount forward. His men followed on his heels, towing the mule and the warhorse behind them.

Reginald gazed after the departing riders. "That was quite a tale, farfetched though it was."

"It does explain one thing, however," Kyle said.

"What's that?"

"Why Baylor's son was captured."

"What do ye mean?"

"Dooley mentioned the spilling of innocent blood. I suspect Sir Kenneth meant to use the boy in some sort of protection ritual."

"How can you be sure it was Sir Kenneth who took the lad?"

"Because of the red and yellow stripes on the tent. How many of those would you find in the woods around here?"

"I see what you mean," Reginald said with a frown. "The lad escaped just in time."

"Ordog," Kyle said, turning to the older man. "Do you think Baylor might have paid Sir Kenneth a late-night visit for taking his son hostage?"

"Baylor can be hot-headed at times," Ordog said, "but he's not stupid. He wouldn't do anything that would bring retribution down on the camp. The fact that he got his son back would have been enough to cool his temper and soothe his rancor. Had he known about the death curse, though, he might not have been so quick to forgive."

"Now that I think on it," Reginald said, his eyes narrowed in thought, "Dooley and the other two retainers might have been in on catching the lad for Sir Kenneth." He gritted his teeth. "And we just let them get clean away."

"In keeping with the boy's story," Kyle said, "only one man actually captured him. That was likely Sir Kenneth himself. Dooley and his men might have gone along so as not to openly defy their lord, but none of them struck me as the kind to stand by and watch the wanton slaughter of an innocent child. I trust they would have looked for a way to help the boy escape. As it turned out, he got away on his own."

"I guess we'll never really know the truth of it," Reginald said with a sigh. "We'd best be on our way, then." He nudged his bay in the belly and started along the road.

With the jingle of harness in his ears, Kyle set out behind the sheriff. While he rode, he pondered all the ways to kill a man without leaving a telltale mark on his body.

Chapter 16

Kyle and those with him forded the shallows near Hexham and continued along the track on the south side of the River Tyne. As they rode on, the peaks and rocky terrain around them gave way to more open land suited for farming and grazing sheep. The river beside them grew deeper and wider with each passing mile.

Before long, they spied a walled town on the north side of the river. A stone castle sat on a hill inside the surrounding wall. The elevated ground allowed sentries on the battlement an unobstructed view of the countryside in all directions.

Crenellated watchtowers jutted up at set intervals along the entire length of the stone wall that encompassed both the town and the castle within.

There was a closed gate in the west wall, with a sprawl of houses on either side of the road leading up to it. The proximity of the village to the entryway would enable the villagers to take refuge inside the fortified town in the event of danger.

The southernmost portion of the wall fronted the river. There was but one way into town from the south, and that was through a waterfront gate, accessible only by a single bridge over purling water that rushed toward the North Sea ten miles to the east.

"That must be Newcastle," Kyle said as he reined in at the foot of the bridge. He glanced up at the gray clouds obscuring the late afternoon sun. “Perhaps we can pass the night there.”

Reginald brought his mount to a halt, as did the others. “How do we get inside? The gate is closed.”

“So it is,” Kyle said, eyeing the massive wooden door set deep within the stone archway at the far end of the bridge spanning the river.

A couple of helmeted guards peered out from the watchtower above the south gate, plainly watching the newcomers with interest.

There was a village on the south bank of the river comprised of rows of wooden dwellings, shed-like warehouses, and fenced holding pens for stock. The wharf east of the bridge stretched out for a hundred feet along the waterfront. Stout timbers had been used to build the landing dock, thus rendering it capable of harboring several low-draft barges at the same time.

Kyle turned down the main street that ran through the center of the village and rode past vacant warehouses and empty stock pens. Men, women, and children whom he’d seen walking about had vanished into their houses as he and the others approached. Only a handful of stray dogs remained, evidently too lazy to move from where they lay stretched out on the ground in the shade.

Kyle was about to turn around and go back to the river road when he spotted a burly man sitting on the steps in front of his house. “Good morrow,” he said as he halted the gelding.

The man glanced up from mending the seam of a leather pouch and nodded his head in greeting. “Same to ye, stranger,” he said in the soft burr of a Northumbrian. There was no mistaking the guarded expression on his face.

Kyle introduced himself and the sheriff of Ayrshire, then the others in turn.

The man seemed more relaxed after that, although he still kept a watchful eye on them. "What brings the lot of ye here?" he said, glancing from one to the other.

"Just passing through," Kyle said. "We could use a place to stay tonight." He tilted his head in the direction of the walled town. "In there, maybe."

"I doubt they'll let ye set foot inside, not after what happened round here."

"What happened?"

"Half a year gone now, the Scotch swept through this province looting and burning as they went, making a right mess of the countryside. Folks hereabouts live in fear of the buggers coming back. The raiders made it all the way to the North Sea, leaving nothing but scorched earth behind them. They torched the quay there, too, and all the boats and barges tied up at the wharf."

"Has the harbor at the mouth of the Tyne been repaired since then?" Kyle said.

"Nay," the man said. "Burned to ashes, it was. There's still no place for merchant vessels to dock and not a single barge left to tow trade goods up the river."

"We were hoping to board a southbound ship there," Kyle said.

"That's too bad," the man said with sympathy.

Kyle exchanged a brief glance with the others. "We still need somewhere to sleep tonight. What about one of the empty storage sheds here? We'll gladly pay for the use of it."

The man perked up at the mention of money. After a moment, he frowned and shook his head. "Once these folks discover that ye hail from north of the border, I cannot vouch for yer safety."

"All right, then," Kyle said. "How far is it to the next port?"

The man narrowed his eyes in thought. "That would be Stockton on Tees. It's not that far down the coast, but ye may have a bit of a wait for a vessel sturdy enough to put to sea."

"Why is that?"

"Stockton is but a small market town, suited best for local trade."

"What is the largest port beyond Stockton?" Kyle said.

"Hull on the Humber."

"How far away is that?"

"About a week's journey, depending on the weather."

"How do we get there?" Kyle said.

"Follow the Great North Road south until ye come to York. From there, the southeast road will take ye all the way to Hull. If you do not tarry, ye might could reach Durham before nightfall."

"Thanks for your time." Kyle turned the gelding and headed back the way he came, with the others trailing behind him.

When they reached the river road, they halted their mounts to decide what to do.

"I say we go on to Durham," Armand said. "There is light enough left in the day to travel there, and taverns to stay in once we arrive."

"I'm for that," Kyle said.

"At this rate," Reginald said with a fierce scowl, "it will take us weeks to get to London."

"Have you a better idea as to how to proceed?" Kyle said.

After a moment of thought, Reginald acquiesced, albeit reluctantly, with a shake of his head.

"To Durham, then." Kyle shook the reins and urged the gelding into a canter.

****

Armand pulled the saddle from the back of his dappled gray mare and heaved it up onto the wooden partition that separated one stall from another. He removed the saddle blanket and spread it out to dry beside the saddle on the dividing wall.

Water dripped from his hair, and his sopping tunic stuck to his chest and thighs after the downpour that had caught him and his fellow travelers two miles outside of Durham. It was full dark by the time they'd reached the outskirts of town, where they turned into the first tavern they found on the main road.

He opened his cloth travel bag and checked to make sure the contents remained undamaged after a thorough soaking in the rain. Now that he'd attended to his mount, he looked forward to a hot supper in the tavern.

"Ready?" he said to Eri, who stood inside the stall with him.

Her clothing and hair were as wet as his. She seemed not to notice, though, for she was occupied with peering out over the half door of the stall. "See that fellow over there?" she said, her eyes on the man tending to the horse in the stall directly across the aisle.

He followed the direction of her gaze. From what he could make out in the muted illumination within the stable, the man was tall and muscular, with wide shoulders and no neck at all. His nose jutted from his square face like the beak of a hawk, and light glistened on the oily surface of his bald head whenever he moved.

"Aye," he said, turning back to her. "What of it?"

"He's been watching us since we arrived."

"We probably look a sight, drenched to the skin as we are."

"It's more than that," she said with narrowed eyes. "I get the feeling he's up to no good."

"Let us take our stuff with us into the tavern so as not to tempt the fellow."

"Aye to that," she said as she gathered up her travel bag, along with her bow and quiver of arrows.

He opened the stall door and led the way out into the aisle. He glanced over at the man in the opposite stall to get a better look at him, but the fellow turned his back to them and busied himself with brushing his horse.

After securing the latch on the half door of his mare's stall, he and Eri walked up the aisle between the rows of stalls and out into the misting rain in the small courtyard beyond. The two of them hastened across the open area and into the tavern to look for Kyle and the others.

That public house in Durham was smaller than the Bull and Bear Tavern in Ayr, yet it smelled the same, sounded the same, and looked the same. The aroma of roasting meat mingled with the acrid smell of burning oil from lighted lanterns. A smoky haze hung in the air, and dirty straw covered the timber plank floor. Mongrel dogs lurked under the tables, growling and snapping at each other over discarded bones and table scraps.

Raucous laughter punctuated the hum of voices from patrons who occupied nearly every table.

Armand and Eri made their way to the back of the room where they joined Kyle, Reginald, Ordog, and Brother Luke already seated at a table in a far corner.

"I don't see why we have to sit back here," Reginald said, clearly disgruntled. "The server will surely overlook us."

"I ordered meat and ale for the lot of us when we first arrived," Kyle said. "The fellow will collect for it when he brings it."

"I could have ordered my own food," Reginald said.

"You could have," Kyle said, "but I thought it best to keep a low profile while we're here."

"Why should we?" Reginald said, indignant. "We've done nothing wrong."

"In case you forgot, we're the only two Scotsmen in a room full of English folk."

"Oh, that," Reginald said, after which he kept an eye out for the server in morose silence.

"I know it was dark when we got here," Eri said, "but from what I could see, Durham isn't that big. We could have passed it by without even noticing."

"It is a town like any other town, except for one thing that sets it apart from all others," Armand said.

"And what is that?" Eri said.

"Durham Cathedral," Armand said. "Holy relics from a bygone era are sheltered there. More importantly, it is the final resting place of Saint Cuthbert, whose shrine is situated behind the High Altar."

"He must have been an important person," Eri said.

"Saint Cuthbert was more than that," Brother Luke interjected. "Tales abound of his miraculous healings, both during his life and after his death, which is why he was sainted. It is said that pilgrims who visited his shrine were cured of all manner of diseases."

Eri looked at Armand for confirmation. "Really?"

"It's true," Armand said with a nod of his head. "Many years ago, long before the Normans invaded this land, the monks on Holy Island who were charged with the care and keeping of Saint Cuthbert's tomb came under attack by Vikings. The monks decided to move Saint Cuthbert's body to a safer location. When they opened his tomb to exhume his remains, instead of bones, they found his body intact, with no decomposition at all. It was in the same condition as it was at the time of his death hundreds of years earlier."

"I'd never seen Saint Cuthbert's body myself," Brother Luke said, "but many a pilgrim who went to his shrine testified as to the truth of that miracle."

"Anyway," Armand continued, "the monks set out from Holy Island with Saint Cuthbert's body on a rolling bier. While they wandered the countryside in search of a new home for their beloved saint, the wheels of the bier got stuck at the foot of a hill called Warden Law. Try as they might, they could not move the bier. Their bishop proclaimed a fast and prayed for three days for spiritual guidance. During that time, Saint Cuthbert appeared to one of the monks and instructed that his coffin be taken to Dun Holm. The monks could move the bier after that, but they did not know the way to Dun Holm."

"So, how did they get there?" Eri said.

"Legend has it," Armand said, "that a milkmaid

came along looking for her lost cow, a dun-colored cow, by the way, which was last seen at Dun Holm. The monks took that as a sign from Heaven and followed her to a wooded hill bordered on three sides by the River Wear. They erected a modest shelter there for the coffin, and the rest is history."

"You seem to know a lot about saints and such," she said.

"That is due to my spiritual training," Armand said.

"Spiritual training?"

"Aye."

"You're not a priest, are you?" she said with a worried frown. "I heard they are not allowed to marry."

"I'm no priest," Armand said. "I am merely an avid student who values sacred things and takes my religious beliefs seriously."

"I see." She looked relieved. "By the way, can we go into the cathedral while we're here?"

"Ye can do that on yer own time," Reginald said, intruding into the conversation. "The deputy and I must be on our way first thing in the morning."

"Perhaps you can make a visit on the way back," Armand said to her.

Eri looked disappointed, yet she acceded to his suggestion without a word.

****

Kyle stifled a yawn. Now that he'd eaten, he could hardly keep his eyes open. Of course, that could be the result of the two full mugs of ale he'd consumed with his meal. Food at this tavern was tasty, yet there was something to be said for English ale. It was much stronger than that served at the Bull and Bear in Ayr, maybe because the taverner here didn't water it down, like they did back home.

"We ought to turn in early," he said to those with him. "We have a long ride ahead of us on the morrow."

They gathered their belongings and trekked up the stairs to an empty room on the second floor. They shed their wet outer garments and spread them out to dry, after which they each found a spot on the floor to settle down for the night.

Eri placed her blanket on the floor in front of the door, as though with the intent of blocking the entryway. "Just a precaution," she said in response to Ordog's questioning gaze.

"Against what?" Ordog said.

Everyone in the room paused to listen as she related her suspicions about the man in the stable.

"Swap places with me, then," Ordog said. "I'm heavier than you. Should he attempt to creep in here tonight, he cannot shift me so easily."

Reginald placed a protective hand on his saddle roll. "He must be after the pouch."

"No doubt about it," Kyle said. "Because of the way you're guarding it, he likely got the impression it's gold coins you're carrying, rather than letters."

"Those letters are more important than gold," Reginald said.

"Aye," Ordog said, "but that fellow doesn't know it." He removed a dry blanket from his oilskin sack and wrapped himself in it before reclining on the floor with his back against the wooden door. "In any event, if he does come for the pouch tonight, I'll be ready for him."

Chapter 17

The night passed without incident, or so Ordog claimed upon rising the next morning. Eri seemed more at ease after hearing that no one had attempted to enter their room.

They donned their outer garments in the muted light of dawn and carried their belongings downstairs, where they broke their fast. After purchasing extra bread and cheese to take on their journey, they went out into the cool morning air and headed for the stable to saddle their mounts.

Despite Ordog's denial of any nocturnal disturbance, Kyle was certain he'd heard a furtive metallic click in the wee hours of the morning, as though someone had fiddled with the door latch from the outside. The first person who came to mind was the suspicious fellow whom Eri had described.

Of course, there were surely others of that ilk of whom he and his companions needed to be wary, since their journey would take them down an isolated road through unfamiliar territory. In addition, they were at a disadvantage in not knowing which locations presented the most danger to travelers. Therefore, it behooved them to pay more than the usual attention to their surroundings and proceed with caution.

They set out on a southward course with a mild north wind caressing their backs and the rising sun on their left. The weather was fair and warm, and the air clean and fresh after the night's rain. The sky above was an arch of vivid blue, without even a wisp of white cloud to mar its pristine beauty.

They followed the old Roman road through hill country. Hardy shrubs grew in cracks along ridges and outcrops of stone along the way. Coarse grass carpeted knolls and hollows around them. Here and there, patches of yellow wildflowers and red clover infused a splash of color into the remote midlands.

Soon, scattered stands of trees on either side of the road thickened into great swathes of woodland that clothed the slopes.

On reaching the top of a rise, Kyle spied four oncoming riders in the distance. He thought nothing of it, for the Great Northern Road upon which he and his companions rode was the most straightforward route available to both northbound and southbound travelers.

About a quarter of a mile down the road, a dozen horsemen burst from the cover of the forest on the right. They rode at a full gallop, swiftly crossing the three-hundred-foot stretch of open land between the road and the trees. Once they converged on the road, they came to a halt. Each of them took up a position that made it obvious they meant to block the passage of the approaching riders.

Kyle reined in, his hand raised to signal the others to stop. The five of them were less than a hundred yards behind the horsemen blocking the road. It was close enough to see what would happen, yet far enough away to remain unobtrusive.

Reginald squinted to peer through the settling dust. "What do ye suppose that lot is up to?"

"It looks like they mean to confront those men coming toward them," Armand said.

"That big fellow on the bay in the center of the road," Eri said, pointing at the bald man astride a brown warhorse with a cropped black mane. "He reminds me of that varlet from the tavern stable."

Ordog reached for the axe that hung from his saddle. "Does he now?"

"What are you doing?" Brother Luke said to the older man. "He might be part of a deputation sent to arrest dangerous felons."

The four riders advanced to within twenty feet of the band of horsemen before bringing their mounts to a stop.

"What nonsense is this?" shouted one of the four, a man in green finery and a black wide-brimmed hat. "Get out of the way."

Kyle nudged the gelding forward to better hear the exchange between the parties. Those with him did the same.

"Hand over yer purse or forfeit yer life," the bald man said in a commanding tone.

"You churl!" the man in green said. "How dare you accost a courier on the king's business."

"Deputation, my arse," Ordog said. "They're nothing but outlaws."

"We should stay out of this," Reginald said. "It is none of our concern."

"I agree," Brother Luke said.

"Twelve against four," Kyle said as he removed his battle axe from the leather loop on his saddle. "That's not what I call sporting. The least we can do is lower the odds."

"I'm with you." Ordog set out at a sprightly pace toward the horsemen in the road ahead, keeping to the grass beside the cobbled stones to muffle the sound of his pony's hooves.

"What are we waiting for?" Eri said to Armand. "Let's go." She lifted the bow from across her shoulders.

Before she could string it, Armand lifted a hand to stop her. "Put that away," he said. "I have something more effective at close range."

While she slipped the bow over her head and shoulder, he tugged on the ornamental crosspiece at the end of his staff and drew forth a long sword. "Here," he said, handing the wooden shaft to her. "Use this like a lance."

Eri tucked the staff under her arm and held it parallel to the ground. "What a clever place to conceal a weapon."

"So it is," Armand said to her over his shoulder. He urged the mare onto the grassy verge to follow after Ordog.

Kyle nudged the gelding into a trot to catch up with the three of them.

About that time, the bald man took out his sword and pointed it at the four riders. "I gave ye fools fair warning," he said. To his men, he shouted, "Take them down! Leave no witness standing!"

"Viper!" cried one of the bandits. "Look to the rear."

The bald man glanced behind him. His eyes flared in surprise at the sight of Kyle, Ordog, Armand, and Eri galloping toward him with weapons ready.

The four riders took advantage of Viper's

momentary inattention by pulling out their swords and spurring their mounts forward. The clang of metal rang out as they met the bandits head on. Steel flashed in the noonday sun, and shouts filled the air.

The man in green looked concerned as Kyle and those with him bore down upon him and his men.

"Stand down in the name of the law!" Kyle bellowed as he approached the bandits. He had no jurisdiction there, of course, but none of the bandits would know that.

The man in green's worried expression gave way to relief at the lawman's timely appearance.

On the other hand, Viper clearly took umbrage at the lawman's intrusion. His face flushed red with rage. Blue veins stood out on his temples. He jerked his horse's head around, radiating anger with every move. "I'll take care of this," he yelled to his men. "You see to those four."

Rather than waiting for Ordog, who was in the lead, to come to him, Viper spurred his mount forward to meet the older man.

As they thundered past each other, Viper swung his sword at Ordog with a vicious overhead chop meant to cleave his foe in two. If he expected an easy victory, he was mistaken, for the Romany raised his axe and deftly blocked the stroke.

The two of them turned their mounts and charged at each other once again.

Several seconds later, Armand and Eri arrived on the scene. He struck down a bandit who tried to bludgeon him with a mace.

She caught another bandit in the chest with the blunt end of her makeshift lance and sent him tumbling back over his horse's rump. The blow did not kill the man, but it put him out of commission during the ensuing fracas.

Kyle cut a swathe through Viper's men, hacking without mercy any bandit foolish enough to come within reach of his axe.

Within minutes, three bandits lay dead on the ground, while five others were bleeding badly from serious wounds.

One of the cohorts of the man in green was bent over the neck of his horse, as though he, too, had suffered a grievous injury.

Viper evidently noticed that the odds were no longer in his favor, for he whirled his mount and bellowed to his men, "To the forest, lads. Make haste!" With a snarled oath directed at Kyle and his companions, he started across the open space toward the trees.

The wounded bandits headed out after their leader, struggling to keep up with him as best they could.

Armand slid his sword inside the end of the wooden shaft and returned the staff to the holder on his saddle. "Hang on tight," he said to Eri as he took off like a shot to round up the riderless horses now on the loose.

The man in green rode over to his injured cohort and dismounted so that he could help the fellow down from his horse. The two others in his retinue came over to render aid to their wounded comrade, whose face looked strained and pallid.

Kyle swung down from the saddle and hurried over to where the injured man sat in the grass. "How badly is he hurt?"

"A flesh wound, I think," said the man in green. He stood up and doffed his wide-brimmed black felt hat. "Miles Aldensford, Knight of the Realm, at your service," he said with a courtly bow. He was a slender man in his late twenties, slightly above middle height, with ivory skin tanned gold by the summer sun. His face was clean shaven, with hollows below high cheekbones and a thin straight nose over full lips. His shoulder-length hair was dark brown, as were his agile brows. Wide-set gray eyes looked out from beneath long black lashes.

"Kyle Shaw, deputy to the sheriff of Ayrshire," he replied by way of introduction.

"Ayrshire," Sir Miles said, frowning thoughtfully. "That's north of the border, is it not?"

"It is," Kyle said.

"I guessed it from your speech," Sir Miles said. "However, where you hail from matters not a whit to me," he added with a dismissive wave of his hand. "Your intervention against those brigands was most welcome. Without it, I doubt I would be standing here before you. That goes for my men, too."

"Considering the number of your assailants," Kyle said, "it was the least we could do." Out of habit, he rested his hand on the hilt of his sword. "Speaking of assailants, have you any idea why they would attempt to waylay you in broad daylight?"

"This is an isolated strip of road," Sir Miles said. "There would be no better place to lift the purse of an unsuspecting traveler."

"That sounds reasonable," Kyle said with a nod. "Although I must confess," he continued, turning the full brunt of his pale blue stare on the young man, "the attack not only seemed planned, but personal, too."

"If I had any doubts that you were a man of law as you claim," Sir Miles said, "I would no longer have such misgivings."

"It was not my intention to interrogate you," Kyle said. "I was simply making an observation."

"An astute one, at that," Sir Miles said with a smile that lit up his whole face. "I pass through here regularly enough to become a target. It is not me those brigands wanted, though. It is the letters I carry. They can be sold for the information contained in them. That is why they had no qualms about striking me down, along with my men."

About that time, Reginald and Brother Luke rode up to join them, as did Armand and Eri with three riderless horses in tow.

The wounded man groaned aloud as his two comrades helped him to his feet. His color was better now that the long gash on his chest had been bound. His cotte was ripped across the front and stained with blood, yet he seemed more at ease now that the tattered remains of his garment had been laced up once again.

"Can you ride?" Sir Miles said to his injured cohort.

"Aye," the man said with a nod of his head. He gritted his teeth while his companions helped him up onto the saddle.

Sir Miles reached for the trailing reins of his own horse. "Where are you bound?" he said to Kyle.

"Why do you ask?" Kyle said, reluctant to reveal their destination, even to this harmless-looking man.

"Just curious," Sir Miles said. "These are dangerous times, even for a man of law. I fear that if you are bound for London, you may not get there at all."

"Why do you say that?"

"Alarming reports of Scottish rebels pillaging northern shires have spread throughout England like wildfire. These days, every foreigner is suspect. So, have a care, my dear fellow, with whom you speak and what you say, especially about revealing where you come from. There is no telling when you might stumble upon an overzealous bailie who thinks he is rendering a great service to king and country by chaining you to a wall to await trial as an insurgent against the crown."

"I appreciate the warning," Kyle said.

Sir Miles swung up into the saddle. "Well, then. We must be on our way." He removed a cloak clasp from the pouch on his saddle and held it out to Kyle. "Should you run into trouble, mention my name and present this as proof of our acquaintance. Anyone of consequence in this county who sees it should recognize it."

"Thanks," Kyle said, taking the clasp from the man's hand.

With a wave of farewell, Sir Miles turned his mount's head to the north and set out up the road with his cohorts trailing behind him.

Kyle looked down at the small metal object in his hand. It was similar to a ring-and-pin clasp commonly used to fasten the folds of a man's cloak at the neck. Rather than a closed ring, this clasp was more of a semicircle with an opening on one side, like a horse shoe. The curved part of the clasp was fashioned from artfully twisted bronze. There was a tiny ram's head with curled horns on each end of the open side, which by design kept the pin from slipping off.

"What have ye there?" Reginald said.

"Something I hope we never have to use," Kyle said as he tucked the cloak clasp into the pouch at his side.

Eri slid nimbly off the rump of Armand's mare and proceeded to examine each of the three horses that had belonged to the dead bandits. After a moment, she singled out a chestnut mare with four white stockings and a cream-colored mane and tail. "I like this one," she said as she scrambled up into the saddle. "Maybe we can sell the other two to help with travel expenses."

Armand glanced over at Brother Luke perched on the bare back of the brown mule. "Would you care to swap that mule for a horse with a saddle?"

"I would, indeed," Brother Luke said with a grateful smile. "I cannot sell the mule, however, because I do not own it. It must be donated to the next church or monastery we encounter down the road." He jumped to the ground and walked stiffly over to a dun-colored gelding that was nibbling at a tuft of grass growing between the cobbles.

Kyle's gaze settled on Ordog astride his black and white pony. "Would you like the other horse?" he said, indicating the remaining gray gelding.

"Not a chance." Ordog reached down to pat the pony's neck. "This fellow may be old, but he's still got a few good years left in him, like me."

"Now that we have that sorted," Reginald said, "what are we going to do with those bodies? We can't just leave them lying in the road."

At that moment, the clatter of hooves on cobblestones brought their heads around. Five horsemen were coming toward them at a rapid pace from the south.

"Bugger all," Eri said, peering into the distance. "It's the bandits coming back to finish us off." She slid the bow over her head and propped one end on her stirrup to string it. After taking an arrow from her quiver, she fitted the notched end on the string without drawing it back, as though waiting until the riders came into range.

"I think not," Kyle said. "If it were them, they would surely bring more reinforcements than that."

"Whoever it is," Reginald said, "they are bound to notice those dead men lying about."

"Then we shall tell them the truth of what happened," Brother Luke said.

"I think you should speak for us," Kyle said to Armand.

"Why him?" Reginald said, his tone petulant. "I bear the hereditary title of sheriff, not him. It is my duty to represent us."

"Any other time," Kyle said, "I would agree with you. At present, however, we are in a country that is openly hostile to anyone of Scottish descent. Since your accent will surely give you away and impugn the rest of us by association, it is more prudent to let Armand do the talking."

"All right, then," Reginald said with evident reluctance.

"Just say as little as possible by way of explanation," Kyle said to Armand. "And of course, don't mention where we came from under any circumstances."

"Got it," Armand said.

For the next few minutes, Kyle and the others waited in silence for the oncoming horsemen to approach.

When they came within hailing distance, they reined in. All five were armed with sword and dagger, and the countenance of each was closed and wary.

The man in the lead gave Kyle and those with him a measuring glance from head to toe. He was a stout fellow in his fifties, with blunt features in a round face and shrewd blue eyes that missed nothing. "What happened here?" he said in the drawl of a Yorkshireman as he tilted his head at the bodies sprawled on the ground.

"Who might you be?" Armand said, nudging his mare a pace closer.

"Jack Garvey, constable of Derlinton."

"What brings you out this way?"

"I'll ask the questions, if ye don't mind," Garvey said. "So, what happened here?"

"We came upon bandits besetting four travelers," Armand said. "We stepped in to help the travelers, which led to the death of those men, as you can see."

"How many bandits were there?"

"About a dozen."

"Anybody else hurt?"

"One of the travelers was injured pretty badly, as were several of the bandits."

Constable Garvey looked around him. "Where are they now?"

"The travelers went north, and the bandits fled into the forest." Armand pointed at the dense growth of trees on the right. "That way."

"There's not a scratch on any of ye that I can see."

"I guess we were lucky."

Constable Garvey fell silent, as though to ponder Armand's words. "That's quite a tale," he said after a moment.

"It's the truth."

"What's yer name?"

"Armand de Boulogne."

"Foreigner," Garvey said with a slight curl to his upper lip. "I think ye and yer friends should accompany me to Derlinton."

"For what purpose?"

"For further questioning."

"Why?"

"Because there are three dead men in the road, and I have only your word that it was they who attacked you."

"Then, why should I believe that you are the constable of Derlinton? I have only your word that you are who you claim to be."

"I see yer point," Garvey said. "However, you offer no proof that ye didn't rob those men and murder them to seal their lips. So, until I gather all the facts, I must detain the lot of ye until this matter is cleared up. Now drop yer weapons."

Kyle decided that it was time for him to join the conversation. "One of the travelers whom the bandits attacked was Sir Miles Aldensford," he said in his best English accent. He dug the cloak clasp from his pouch and held it up for the constable to see. "He left this with me as a token of safe passage."

"Never heard of him," Constable Garvey said. "Now, are ye coming peaceful-like, or must we use force?"

As though on cue, the sound of steel scraping against the metal lip of a scabbard filled the air as the constable's men took out their swords.

With a nocked arrow already in hand, Eri drew the bowstring all the way to her ear and took aim at Constable Garvey.

Her unexpected behavior elicited gasps of disbelief and voluble protests from Brother Luke and Reginald.

"Armand told you the truth of what happened," she said, narrowing her eyes at her chosen target. "We saw you coming from a long way off. We could have fled into the forest, but we didn't because we are innocent. It's your problem if you don't believe us. Now, tell your men to drop their weapons and get off their horses. That goes for you, too."

Constable Garvey sat without moving, holding his ground with an icy calm. "What makes ye think I will comply with yer threat?" he said in a voice as hard as steel.

Eri released the arrow with a snap of her fingers. The sharp metal head struck the hard leather cantle of his saddle with a hollow thump.

Constable Garvey's eyes flared at the sight of the arrow's tip protruding from the inner side of the cantle, only inches from his groin. His men looked as uneasy as he did.

Eri nocked another arrow and pulled the bowstring all the way back. "I could send the next shot through your left eyeball." She paused for a moment, as though to let her words sink in. "Or you could tell your men to throw down their weapons and alight from their steeds. That includes you, too, of course."

Chapter 18

Constable Garvey's only reaction to Eri's demand was a visible tightening of his thin lips. After a tense moment, he evidently made up his mind to acquiesce, for he signaled to his men to do as they were bidden.

Each of them dropped their weapons and dismounted.

"Fetch their horses," Eri said to Ordog and Armand. When neither man made a move to comply, she added, "Please. I know what I'm doing."

Armand and Ordog exchanged a glance before they nudged their mounts forward. They gathered up the reins of the five horses and led them away from the constable and his men.

"What is the name of the nearest village?" she said to the constable.

"Woodham."

"Where is it exactly?" she said.

"Three miles to the south. It sits off the road a mile or so to the west."

"That is where you will find your horses. I will send someone from there to pick you up in a wagon. That should give us enough of a head start in case you plan to pursue us. In my opinion, your time would be better spent searching for Viper and his band of cutthroats." She jerked her thumb at the dead men in the road. "Those are his men lying there."

She motioned for Ordog and Armand to start down the road with the constable's horses and the bandit's gray gelding in tow. Brother Luke set out after them on his newly acquired horse with the brown mule on a lead rope.

Only after she set out down the road behind the others did she relax the bowstring and return the arrow to the quiver, leaving the constable and his men standing in the road behind them.

Half an hour later, they turned off the cobbled road onto a dirt track that led them through the woods to a settlement of eight houses clustered around an open courtyard-like area.

Kyle sought out the village head—a middle-aged man with a drooping brown mustache who lived in a two-room wooden house with a well-kept garden patch beside it.

Others in the village gathered round to see who the strangers were and why they were there.

"What can I do for ye?" the headman said, glancing from Kyle to Reginald and back again.

"Have you heard of a bandit by the name of Viper?" Kyle said.

"Aye," the headman said. "I've heard of him. What about it?"

"He and his band beset some travelers up the road."

"Anybody hurt?"

"There were some casualties among the bandits. The constable of Derlinton is now on the scene. He needs a wagon to transport the bodies. Is there anybody here willing undertake that task? They will earn a penny in the king's silver for their trouble."

The headman's dark eyes brightened at the prospect of earning money. "I have a wagon. I can do it."

"Can you leave right away?"

"Aye, as soon as I hitch up the mule." The headman started to walk off, but he turned back after a couple of steps. "Those horses ye brought with ye. Are they yers?"

"Only the gray one," Kyle said. "The others belong to the constable and his men."

"How did ye come by them?"

"It's a long story," Kyle said. "You can ask the constable about it when you see him."

"All right, then," the headman said, although he made no attempt to move from where he stood.

"Is there anything further?"

The headman shifted from one foot to the other. "It's about payment."

"I think the sum is quite generous for the service to be rendered."

"It is that. I just wonder who will be paying it."

"That would be me." Kyle dug in his coin purse and pulled out a silver penny, which he gave to the man.

With the coin clutched in his hand, the headman hastened around the side of his house toward a shed in the rear.

After that, the villagers who had gathered there seemed to lose interest, for they drifted away one by one.

Reginald walked up to stand beside Kyle. "Should we not also be on our way?" He cast a disparaging glance in Eri's direction. "Now that we are fugitives from the law."

"Let us wait until the headman departs," Kyle said. "Otherwise, it may slip his mind that the constable is standing in the road waiting for him. Although he would then be one silver penny and five horses richer, there will be hell to pay once the constable learns of his perfidy and goes looking for him."

While the village head hitched the mule to a rickety wagon, Kyle and his companions sat in the shade and ate the food they'd brought with them. They were watering their horses when the headman's wagon finally rumbled up the rutted track, only to vanish into the trees beyond.

They hobbled the horses that belonged to the constable and his men, which would permit the animals to graze freely on lush summer grass without wandering too far from the village.

"Do you trust the headman to do as you ask?" Ordog said as he swung up into the saddle.

"Ordinarily, I would not," Kyle said, mounting the gelding. "Since the constable of Derlinton is involved, I think the fellow will do what he was paid to do, however reluctant he is to do it."

"Aye to that." Ordog rode over to the gray horse and took hold of its reins to draw the animal along behind him.

After climbing into the saddle, Brother Luke did the same with the mule.

When the others were mounted and ready, they all set out up the track, headed back to the old Roman road, where they would continue their journey south.

Green hills and vales soon gave way to the blue distances of the moors—a vast plateau of heather-darkened terrain, swept by the wind, bleak and treeless, with secluded valleys too steep-sided and narrow for human habitation. Here and there, a tiny village clustered around a clear cool stream, while higher up, a lone homestead nestled in the lee of a sandstone ridge along the moorland scarp.

The sun hung low in the western sky by the time they rode into Derlinton. Although there was no way they could run afoul of Constable Garvey because of the head start they had on him and his men, they hastened through the bustling market town anyway. Once they reached the outskirts, they breathed a communal sigh of relief.

Northallerton was the next town several miles down the way, with a modest sprawl of dwellings on either side of the road. Because it was situated on the moor in the middle of nowhere, the only thing it had going for it was its location, which was at a junction where the north-south road crossed an east-west road. Since it was less populous than Derlinton, it had fewer shops and tradesmen. It did, however, have a tavern that provided the amenities necessary for anyone passing through: food, drink, and lodging for the night.

In the falling dusk, they turned into the tavern courtyard and went on to the stable. After tending to their horses, they went into the public house and settled at a table against a side wall.

****

While waiting for the server to bring their food, Armand rose to his feet. "I shall be back in a moment. I want to take a look around outside."

He made his way through the tables and stepped out into the empty courtyard. The cerulean sky above was fading into a deep blue twilight.

It was inevitable that the constable of Derlinton would pursue them, especially after Eri had threatened him with bodily harm. Thus, it was to their advantage to have an exit plan in the event they needed it. They could have slept out on the open moor instead of spending the night in a tavern. That, however, would have exposed them to predators, the most insidious of which was the adder—a poisonous snake especially active during the summer months. There were also harmless-looking stretches of soft bog that could swallow a live horse in a matter of seconds, should an unwary rider dare to venture across it.

Armand walked around to the rear of the tavern and noticed an alleyway that led to the next street over. There was also a drop roof over the back door and a couple of windows above that. He would make sure the room they procured was one of the two overlooking that porch-like roof.

By the time he went back inside to join the others, the server had already brought bowls of stew and cups of ale. The food was bland and the ale lukewarm, yet he ate his fill without complaint. After a long day in the saddle, he was as hungry as he was weary.

Kyle stood up and stretched, after which he dug a coin from the pouch at his side.

"Is that for the room?" Armand said.

"Aye," Kyle said.

"I suggest we get one facing the rear of the tavern. There's a porch back there that will come in handy in the event of a hasty exit."

"Good idea," Kyle said before seeking out the taverner to procure such a room.

There was nothing to do after that except to go upstairs and bed down for the night.

On entering the small room, Armand crossed the timber plank floor and opened the shutters to let in the night breeze, which helped dissipate the stale air in the closed room. After spreading his blanket beside Eri, he made himself as comfortable as he could on the hard wooden surface.

"About the constable," he said to her in a low voice. "I fear we made an enemy of the man. Would it not have been better to convince him, rather than coerce him?"

"It would," she said, staring up at the ceiling, "if he'd been the sort of man who listened to reason."

"I thought he assessed the situation in a rational manner. Had I been in his position, I may have drawn the same conclusion."

"What conclusion? That we were desperate characters just for being there on the scene? I think not. I've met his kind before. They judge by sight, rather than insight. As a Romany, I am all too familiar with such treatment."

He smiled into the darkness. "At times, I too have been judged."

"You? For what?"

"For the patches on my garments. Poor people are looked down on simply because they are poor."

"Then you know how vexing narrow-minded folks can be. We Romany are a nomadic people by tradition. Honor and loyalty and devotion to family rank high among us. We live by a moral code enforced by the chieftain of each clan." She rolled onto her side to face him. "Did you know that if a Romany kills a fellow

Romany with iron, the punishment is death?"

"I didn't know that."

"If he takes a fellow Romany's wife, he is banished from the clan. He is also banished if he betrays a fellow Romany. To the world, though, we are nothing but thieves and swindlers, the dregs of society because we live in tents and survive by our wits. I've even heard it said we would sell our own women and children if there was enough money in it. That is not only untrue but insulting, too. It is the same no matter where we go."

He fell silent because he did not know what to say to console her. She'd put her finger on the pulse of the matter: that there were, indeed, those who considered themselves better than others based on wealth and connections. Sad to say, that would always be the case as long as the rich and the privileged continued to lord it over the poor and the powerless.

"Do you think I was wrong to draw on that constable?" she said after a long moment.

"I might have done the same in your place."

"But you didn't."

"Nay, I did not. Sometimes it is more prudent to wait and see what happens. He might have come around eventually."

"My only regret is that you and the others will be punished for something I alone did. If the constable catches up with us, I shall take full responsibility for my action."

"I would never let that happen," he said, his voice slightly furred with sleep. "Now, let's get some rest while we can. Who knows what tomorrow will bring."

It seemed that he had just closed his eyes when the twitter of a skylark out on the moor brought him up from the murky depths of slumber. He opened his eyes to the faint light of dawn coming in through the unshuttered window.

After a yawn and a stretch, he rose to his feet. Eri was already up and moving about the room. He was rolling up his blanket when the others began to stir.

"We'll meet you downstairs," he said to them.

He and Eri picked up their gear and started down the steps. When they reached the bottom, they wended their way through the empty tables, for there were no patrons at that hour of the day.

They were about halfway across the room when the front door of the tavern swung open.

The sight of Constable Garvey standing in the entryway brought Armand to an abrupt stop, which caused Eri to bump into his back. Though he put out a hand to keep her behind him, it was too late. Her sharp intake of breath told him she'd seen the constable.

From the look of smug satisfaction on the constable's face, it was clear that he'd seen her, too.

Chapter 19

Kyle clumped down the wooden stairs at the back of the tavern to the room below. He paused on the last step with his saddle roll under his arm, his gaze focused on the stout man standing in the front entryway. Even in the muted illumination, he recognized Constable Garvey.

The constable ambled into the public house, leaving the door open behind him to let in the morning light. "Well, well," he said to Armand and Eri who remained where they stood in the middle of the room. "Look who's here."

Eri stepped around Armand to confront the constable. "It's me you want," she said, setting her travel bag on the nearest table. "Leave the others be."

"That's right noble of ye," the constable said.

"It's me you came for, isn't it?" Eri said. "For taking a shot at you?"

"That's not the only reason why I'm here," the constable said with a tight smile.

Kyle walked over to hear what the man had to say.

"After ye left us stranded on the road," the constable said, "we followed the hoof prints that led into the woods. That's where we found a fellow propped against the trunk of a tree, too badly wounded to ride any farther."

"What did he have to say for himself?" Eri said.

"He wove some wild tale about how he and his cohorts were traveling on the road, minding their own business, when they were beset by brigands."

"That's a lie!" Eri cried with vehemence.

"I know."

Eri seemed taken aback upon hearing his words. "You do?"

"Aye."

"How so?"

"I recognized him."

"Who was he, then?" Eri said.

"Three-Fingered Pete, notorious thief, swindler, and murderer. You name it and he's wanted by the law for it. Though his injuries are serious, I think he'll live long enough to face the noose for his crimes."

"So you believe us now?" Eri said.

"I'm beginning to lean in that direction."

Kyle stepped forward to join the conversation. "It might interest you to know that Sir Henry de Percy, castellan of Ayr Garrison and warden of Galloway, has entrusted us with delivering letters to His Majesty in London."

"So ye say," Constable Garvey said, fixing him with a skeptical gaze.

"What would it take to convince you as to the truth of the matter?"

"I would like to see the letters for myself."

"You may look at them," Kyle said, "but you may not open them, for they are addressed to the king of England. To tamper with them would amount to treason." He signaled to Reginald, who had already walked up with Ordog and Brother Luke by that time.

Reginald removed the packet from his saddle roll

and handed it to the constable. He gave the impression of full cooperation with the constable's request, yet he never took his eyes from the letters. He also had the sense not to speak.

Constable Garvey opened the packet and examined the unbroken seals on the letters within. "Why did ye not mention this earlier?" he said, lifting his gaze to meet Kyle's pale blue eyes.

"It would have been folly on our part to assume you were who you claimed to be, since you offered no proof as to your identity. You will recall my earlier mention of Sir Miles Aldensford. Evidently, the bandits discovered that he is a royal courier, for they did their level best to murder him, no doubt to confiscate the dispatches in his possession, to be sold for the information contained in them, I imagine."

"This changes everything," the constable said as he returned the packet to Reginald. "Do forgive my impertinent behavior on the road yesterday. Let me make up for it by providing an escort for yer safe passage to London."

"A large troop might draw the attention of those with ill intent. For our own protection, it would be better to stay out of the public eye as much as possible. I trust you will take no offence at my refusal of your kind offer."

"None taken at all," the constable said.

"Well, then," Kyle said. "After we break our fast, we shall be on our way."

"Ye and the others may go, of course." Constable Garvey's gaze shifted to Eri. "That one, however, must stay behind."

"Why?" Kyle said.

"He must answer for the attempted murder of an officer of the law, theft of property, and obstruction of justice."

"By all means, arrest him as you see fit." Kyle raised a hand to forestall any heated objection that might come from Armand and Ordog. "Nevertheless, your name is bound to come up in my report to the king. He will surely want to know why you arrested a designated protector of imperial correspondence. Why, you may even be called before the throne to give an account of your actions."

The constable stood in contemplative silence for a long moment. He was evidently unaccustomed to opposition, as indicated by the color burning high on his cheeks. "Even so, the law is the law," he said at last. "Those who break it must face the consequences. The lad goes with me."

"Your decision grieves me," Kyle said. "By the way, that will go into my report, too."

"What, that I fulfilled my duty as a constable?"

"Nay, that you refused to listen to reason."

The constable cleared his throat. "Be that as it may, I stand my ground as an officer of the law. Since there is no more to be said, I shall now take my leave." He turned to Eri. "Surrender yer weapons and come with me."

Kyle flashed a warning glance at Armand and Ordog who both took a step toward the constable. "Since this involves letters to the king, I suggest we take the matter to His Majesty so that he may judge whether the criminal charges as alleged are justified."

A shadow of concern flitted across the constable's face. "There's no need for that. This can be handled through the local assize."

"Oh, but I insist," Kyle said with a dark smile. "Eri is practically a royal guard. Thus, I cannot leave his fate in the hands of just anyone." He nodded his head. "Aye, we shall settle this before the king." To Brother Luke, he said, "Kindly rouse the cook and ask him to prepare food for us." To the constable, he said, "Why don't you join us for a bite to eat? We have a hard ride ahead of us, and I would hate to see you grow faint from hunger along the way."

The constable looked like he was about to protest. He apparently thought better of it, for he went over and sat on the hard bench at the closest table, his brow furrowed in thought.

Brother Luke headed for the kitchen out back to do as he was bidden.

Both Armand and Ordog, their expressions grim, settled on the bench beside the constable.

Reginald seemed reluctant to go anywhere near the constable, so when Eri drew Kyle aside, he went over to stand with the two of them instead. "Must that man really come with us?" he said in a hoarse whisper to his deputy.

"I'm afraid so," Kyle said.

"But that means I shall have to remain silent till we reach London, lest my speech give me away."

"Look at the bright side," Kyle said. "You are no longer a fugitive from the law."

"Somehow, that doesn't help," Reginald said with a heavy sigh.

Kyle leaned close to the sheriff, his tone confiding. "We could put a sleeping draught in his ale and leave him here, snoring until nightfall. That would give us a good head start."

"If we did that," Reginald said, "we would become fugitives once again."

"Exactly," Kyle said. "Now you see why we must take him along."

"Bugger!" Reginald said under his breath. He turned on his heel and trudged over to the table to sit across from the others.

"Thank you for speaking up in my behalf," Eri whispered to Kyle. "But for your quick thinking, this would be the end of the journey for me."

"We are all in this together," Kyle said in a muted voice. "Now, we must find a way to convince Constable Garvey to drop the charges against you."

"Stubborn man that he is, he will be a hard one to persuade."

"Still, it must be done, and soon," Kyle said. "I certainly don't want him tagging along all the way to London."

"Perish the thought," she said with fervor.

Kyle led the way over to the table and slid onto the bench. Eri did the same.

Within a short time, the taverner—a stocky man with mild features and dark eyes below a balding pate—came over to their table with a platter of cold meat and bowls of hot soup with stale bread to soak up the broth. "Will that be all?" he said, wiping his pudgy hands on the front of his loose brown tunic.

"Where is the nearest church?" Brother Luke said.

"That would be at the crossroad," the taverner said. "Ye can't miss it."

"Is there a priest in residence there?" Brother Luke said.

"Sometimes," the taverner said.

"What does that mean?"

"Father Hugh is the only cleric to care for the flock in this district. Thus, it falls to him to make the rounds of every village chapel in the area."

"Is he in town now?"

"Nay," the taverner said with a shake of his head.

"I see," Brother Luke said, clearly disappointed.

"He may be back in a week or so, should ye care to wait for him."

"That won't be necessary. I just wanted to drop something off to him."

"The verger lives in the house behind the church. Maybe you can leave it with him."

"I might just do that," Brother Luke said. "Thank you."

After collecting the money for the food, the taverner went over to the sideboard, where he picked up a damp rag and set about wiping all the tables close to where Kyle and his companions sat eating. From the meticulous way he cleaned each table, it was obvious that his only purpose for doing so was to eavesdrop on them. Such a blatant invasion of privacy was not wholly unexpected from folks living in isolation on the moor, seeing as how a traveler passing through town was the only source of news for them.

They kept their conversation to a minimum throughout the meal until the taverner finally lost interest and drifted away to perform some other menial task.

"I really ought to go back to Derlinton," the constable said as he pushed away his empty bowl. "My sergeant might come looking for me if I fail to return soon."

"Then I suggest you send word to him that you will be on the road for quite some time," Kyle said.

"I suppose I could do that."

"And if you lack provisions for the journey," Kyle said, "you can pick some up along the way."

"I suppose I could do that, too."

"Then it is settled," Kyle said. It was clear to him that the constable did not really want to go to London, whether for fear of standing before the king to answer for his actions or because of unwillingness to embark on a dangerous and lengthy journey. Either way, the man's reluctance might make it easier to extricate Eri from his clutches. Having encountered such single-minded men in the past, he figured this would be a good time to set some ground rules. "You mentioned that Eri should give up his weapons."

"I would expect no less from a prisoner," the constable said.

"I object on the grounds that the sole reason for Eri's presence on this trip is his ability to protect us from harm. So, until we reach our destination, he will continue to do so, without interference."

"Then I must put a lead rope on his mount, to prevent him from escaping on the open road."

"That would be a wasted effort. Where could he possibly hide in this wind-scoured country?"

"Well, then, I will truss him up every night so that I may rest easy without fear of his slitting my throat while I sleep."

Kyle shook his head over the man's obstinacy. "Wolves and bandits will surely present more of a danger to you than Eri will. However, if keeping him bound at night will set your mind at ease, then so be it. I only hope you don't come to regret your decision."

Eri frowned, plainly displeased at the prospect of being tied up while she slept. Ordog scowled in obvious annoyance. Though Armand's reaction was more subtle, his clenched teeth and narrowed eyes still conveyed his disapproval of the constable's demand.

Their restrained yet evident censure prompted Kyle to give Eri a reassuring pat on the arm. "Don't worry," he whispered for her ears only. "Every time he binds you, one of us will let you loose."

She seemed less anxious after that, as did Ordog and Armand on seeing her relax.

When they had eaten their fill, they went out to the stable to saddle their horses. They rode down the main street, passing townsfolk going about their business early in the day.

They soon came to the crossroad, which was lined with shops and businesses. That was no surprise, for such a location was advantageous for tradesmen and crafters in that it gave them the best exposure to possible customers passing through town from any direction.

"There's the church," Brother Luke said, pointing to a small stone chapel set back from the road on the far corner of the street. He headed toward it, drawing the mule on the lead rope behind him.

Kyle and the others followed the friar around to the back of the chapel, where he dismounted in front of a one-room timber-plank house with a tiny garden patch beside it. He went up to the door and rapped lightly upon the hard wooden surface.

"May I help ye?" said the elderly man who opened

the door. With an expression of mild curiosity on his lined face, he glanced from the friar to the mule and back again.

"Are you the verger here?" Brother Luke said.

"I am." The man opened the door wide when he saw Kyle and the others. "Forgive me for making ye stand outside. We seldom get visitors here. Do come in for a bite to eat."

"Thank you for the offer, but we just broke our fast at the tavern," Brother Luke said. "I simply came to leave this mule with you." He related in brief the circumstances under which he acquired the animal. "So, it is now yours to use as you see fit."

The shine of unshed tears welled up in the old man's eyes. "This is an answer to my prayer," he said in a husky voice. "The old mare that Father Hugh rode for years only recently died, so your generous offer is greatly appreciated, now of all times. He won't have to beg a ride anymore to make the rounds in the county."

Brother Luke handed the lead rope to the old man. With a nod and a smile, he turned and trudged back to his horse, which he nimbly mounted.

They all gave the old man a parting wave before they rode across the grassy yard to the road.

They continued on their way for the rest of the morning. The sun was high overhead by the time they came to the market town of Thirsk, where they stopped to water the horses.

"It's a lonely haul from here to York," Constable Garvey said. "There's no more than a cluster of dwellings here and there along the road up ahead. We'd best buy food to take with us since we will likely be spending the night on the open moor."

After they ate the midday meal at an inn, they purchased provisions to last them through the evening and all the next day.

Sure enough, by the time dusk began to settle around them, there was not a dwelling to be seen in any direction. They turned off the road and looked for a place where they could build a fire.

While the others unsaddled the horses and set up camp, Kyle and Brother Luke foraged for dry sticks to make a fire. There was not that much deadwood to be had, so they pulled up a sufficient quantity of live shrubbery to last through the night.

"That was a nice thing you did for the verger," Kyle said as he walked beside the friar carrying a load of leafy brambles in his arms.

"We must share God's bounty with those in need," Brother Luke said. "Besides, the mule was only on loan to me. It really belongs to the church, and those who serve the church should benefit from the use of it."

"You're a good man, Brother Luke," Kyle said.

The friar seemed pleased at hearing such a compliment.

After a cold supper, they spread their blankets around the fire, from which rose billows of foul-smelling smoke from burning green shrubs. Despite the stench, they got as close as they could, not only because of hungry creatures prowling about, but because the temperature on the moor dropped considerably after the sun went down.

True to his word, Constable Garvey bound Eri hand and foot. He then reclined on his blanket with the other end of the rope wrapped around his hand. With his back to the blaze, he kept an eye on his prisoner until he nodded off.

When Kyle was sure the constable had fallen asleep, he motioned for Armand to remove the rope from Eri's wrists and ankles and retie the loose end around the base of a nearby shrub, which would offer resistance in case the constable tugged on the rope during the night to make sure his prisoner was still there.

Kyle woke several times during the night to toss additional sticks onto the flames to keep predators at bay. Thus, he was less than rested when he opened his eyes to a cold gray dawn.

In the early light, the moor looked more desolate and inhospitable than ever. The air was fresh, albeit tinged with smoke from the smoldering remains of burnt shrubs and brambles. The sleepers around the campfire huddled under their blankets in an effort to hoard the warmth from their own bodies.

Kyle rolled onto his side with the intention of going back to sleep when a movement on the far side of the campfire caught his eye. It was Eri, who had already risen from her blanket. He thought nothing of it until he noticed the strung bow she held in her hand.

He lifted his head as she fitted an arrow on the taut string and eased closer to one sleeper in particular.

Before he could cry out a warning, she drew back the string and released the arrow directly at the slumbering form.

Chapter 20

Now fully awake, Kyle leaped to his feet with a shout, which roused the others from their slumber. In three bounding steps, he crossed the short distance over to where Eri stood with the bow in her hand.

Constable Garvey sat bolt upright, apparently startled awake by the thrum of an arrow only inches from his head. "Ye missed," he said, glaring up at Eri. His voice sounded calm for a man who'd just had a near brush with death.

"Nay, I did not," Eri said. "See for yourself." She pointed at her chosen target.

The constable seemed reluctant to take his gaze off the imminent threat before him in the form of his prisoner. When he finally did glance to the side, he recoiled in horror, his eyes wide with alarm.

There beside him was a poisonous adder, pinned to the ground with Eri's arrow through its head. Its body still writhed in the macabre throes of death.

Kyle and the others gathered round to stare at the mortally wounded snake, murmuring to one another and nodding their heads. Apparently, the creature had sought a warm body to nestle against during the long cold night.

The constable scrambled to his feet. "Well, I'll be," he said, stepping back several paces to distance himself from the deadly serpent.

"It's a good thing for you that Eri didn't stay tied up last night," Kyle said.

"It is that," the constable said without thinking, his eyes fixed on the snake in fearful fascination, as if compelled to look yet repelled by what he saw.

"You do realize that if Eri wanted to kill you," Kyle said, "you would now be dead."

The constable cast a questioning glance in the deputy's direction. "What are ye getting at?"

"Clearly, the lad bears no malice toward you," Kyle said, "despite your insistence on pressing charges."

A mulish expression settled on the constable's face, as though he refused to admit he was wrong even if it was obvious that he could have been mistaken about the purpose of Eri's earlier actions.

Aware that the man's pride was at stake, Kyle proposed what he hoped would be a viable solution for all. "I will stand before the king within a matter of weeks to deliver important letters, on which the fate of both England and Scotland hang in the balance. I don't think His Majesty will be pleased to learn that someone tried to thwart those of us charged with delivering those missives. So, if I explain the situation to His Majesty, he might be willing to send a proclamation to Derlinton, expressing his appreciation for the constabulary's willingness to assist, rather than hinder, our mission." He fixed a piercing gaze on the constable. "What do you think?"

Constable Garvey pondered Kyle's words with a furrowed brow, as though weighing potential praise from the king of England against his reputation for the timely arrest and detainment of felons in his corner of

Yorkshire. Apparently, the prospect of gaining his sovereign's approval won out, for the shadow of doubt faded from his face. "The lad is free to go with ye. It is the least I can do for king and country."

Eri's relief was palpable, as was Armand and Ordog's, too.

"Now that the matter is settled," Kyle said, "there is no longer any need for you to travel to London."

It was the constable's turn to look relieved, though he tried not to show it. "None whatsoever," he said with certainty. He shook out his blanket, rolled it up, and tied it behind the cantle before saddling his mount.

"No need to rush off," Kyle said. "At least break your fast with us before you depart."

The constable mounted his horse. "Maybe some other time. I have a long ride ahead of me, and I want to get an early start." He met and held Kyle's gaze for a moment. "Ye won't forget what ye promised, will ye?"

"You have my word on it," Kyle said with a nod.

A brief smile flickered across the constable's face, softening his grim countenance for the first time in days. "Godspeed on your journey," he said, lifting his hand in a parting wave. He turned his horse's head to the north and set out up the road at a brisk pace. It wasn't long before he crested a rise and disappeared from sight.

"I thought we'd never be rid of the fellow," Reginald said.

"Nor I," Eri said. "And I had more reason to want him gone."

"At least ye could talk if ye wanted to," Reginald said.

"True," Eri said with an amiable smile. "But if I

had to choose between remaining silent for the rest of the journey or facing the gallows, I would gladly hold my tongue for the duration."

"I see what ye mean," Reginald said with a sage nod of his head.

They broke their fast on leftover cheese and stale bread. After saddling their horses, they mounted up and continued on their way to the south.

As the day wore on, storm clouds began to gather overhead. A brisk wind sprang up from the east, sending banks of heavy black clouds scudding westward. The old Roman road stretched out ahead of them through the barren moorland, etched like a white stripe against the dark landscape.

Soon, flurries of light rain fell from the leaden sky. Gentle showers that pattered on their heads and shoulders rapidly turned into a torrential downpour that lashed at them with a fury. A rising mist cut off all distances around them, forcing them to slow their pace. But for the stone pathway underfoot, they would have lost their bearings in such bleak surroundings.

After what seemed like half an eternity but was in actuality only three hours, the rain slowed to a steady drizzle. Soon, it stopped altogether. The air was still and smelled of damp earth. Though it was only midafternoon, the dreary weather had brought on a false dusk that hovered between darkness and light.

Rainwater gathered in glassy pools beside the road, reflecting the gray sky above. Runoff from escarpments and ridges formed angry little streams that tumbled into troughs and gullies, which was nature's way of draining excess water from higher ground.

****

Armand reined in his dappled gray mare to assess a possible impediment to their forward progress. There ahead of him, the road descended into a hollow and vanished under a torrential stream of roiling water over sixty feet wide. It was a flash flood—a common occurrence in vales and other low places on the moor after a heavy rain.

"It looks impassable to me," he said to the deputy, who halted the gelding beside him. "What do you think?"

"It looks that way to me, too," Kyle said with a nod.

"We should just go on across," Reginald said, stopping his mount between them. "It doesn't look that deep from here."

Ordog rode up to join them. "The water may not be deep, but you can be sure the current is powerful enough to drag your horse out from under you."

"It might behoove us to wait until the level goes down a bit," Armand said, his eyes on the churning water. "It might take a day or so, but we would have a better chance of making it across without mishap."

"There have already been too many delays," Reginald said. "I'm for crossing it now."

Eri drew alongside Armand's mare and reined in. "Why don't you go first then?" she said to Reginald. "If you make it to the other side, we'll follow you across."

"Cheeky brat," Reginald mumbled under his breath.

Kyle smiled. "You're the one in a hurry."

"I'll show ye how it's done." Reginald perched the letter pouch high on his left shoulder and tied it there before nudging his mount toward the flooded roadway.

The horse stepped daintily through the muddy foam that had gathered along the edge of the swirling torrent. As it walked into the swift current, tiny eddies formed first around its knees and then its flanks.

About twenty feet in, the valiant creature sank up to its neck, at which time it struck out vigorously with all four legs to keep its head above water while swimming forward.

Reginald clung to his mount's back, with only his head and upper shoulders visible above the surging water.

The force of the current carried both horse and rider several yards downstream. More than a few tense minutes later, the animal scrambled up onto the far bank, its head lowered and its sides heaving from the effort.

Reginald, thoroughly drenched and shivering from the cold, dismounted to let the horse catch its breath. He looked none too steady when he turned to wave at his companions waiting on the other side.

"Well, I reckon he proved it's safe to cross," Eri said, tilting her head at the sheriff across the way.

Ordog eyed the raging torrent, his brow furrowed with concern. "He only proved it's possible, not that it's safe."

"Be that as it may," Eri said, patting the shoulder of her mare. "This hardy creature should make it across just fine."

"I'll take you over, then," Ordog said.

"I really ought to take you across," Eri said, her eyes on the older man's pony. "Otherwise, you and that dwarf steed of yours would be swept away."

Ordog put his hands over the pony's ears. "Have a

care what you say, lest you hurt his feelings."

"I will take Eri across," Armand said.

"What makes you think you could do a better job than I can?" Ordog said, glaring at the younger man.

Armand kept silent, for anything he said would only anger the older man further.

"Uncle," Eri said. "You are right about crossing in pairs. It will be so much safer that way." Her acknowledgement of the older man's wisdom seemed to pacify him somewhat, for the scowl on his weathered face began to fade. "May I suggest that you go with Kyle Shaw? His warhorse is of a size to block the force of the current for your pony."

"If I go with Master Shaw," Ordog said, "that will leave you free to go with him." He cast a disparaging glance at Armand, as though to emphasize his point.

"Why should I not do so?" Eri said. "Our horses are of the same build and height, which makes us well suited for each other."

"What about me?" Brother Luke said, glancing from one to the other. "Who will take me across?"

"You will have the spare horse with you," Eri said. "Just make sure to stay on the downstream side of it."

The look of trepidation shadowed Brother Luke's face. "I wish I were as confident as you that it will work."

"You'll be fine," Eri said.

Her words seemed to reassure the friar, for he appeared less anxious after that.

"I suggest we tie the horses together to anchor one another," Armand said.

"Good idea." Kyle turned to Ordog. "What do you say?"

"Can't hurt," Ordog said noncommittally, as though reluctant to give credit where credit was due.

Armand took the reins from Eri's hand and tied them to his saddle, leaving a full yard between the horses. He would have preferred to shorten the distance, except for the fact that both creatures needed room to thrash their legs in order to stay afloat in the surging floodwater.

"Secure your gear with this," he said, passing to her a long thin strip of leather that he took from the travel bag tied to his saddle.

She affixed the arrows to the quiver, which she bound to her travel bag. She positioned both items high on her back and used the strung bow that she slung over her head and shoulders to hold them tightly in place.

"Ready?" he said.

She gathered two great handfuls of her horse's mane. "Aye."

"Whatever you do, hang on tight," he said. "A horse's will to survive is extremely strong, so the safest place is on its back."

"I'll do my best," she said.

"Let us go, then." He urged his mare forward, which in turn drew Eri's horse along a step behind.

As they approached the stream, it seemed to him that its width was not as great as when they'd first arrived. That gave him hope that the depth in the middle had also diminished somewhat.

As the two horses sloshed into the shallows, water swirled around their legs. It soon reached their bellies and inched on up to their shoulders. About midway across, both animals sank abruptly—an indication that their hooves no longer touched bottom. From then on, they struggled to keep their noble heads above the churning current.

Rushing water pummeled Armand's body, compelling him to hang on tighter to keep from being swept from the saddle. As with any risky venture, there was half a chance he may not make it across. Yet, his trepidation was not for himself alone; it was for Eri, too. Should he become separated from his mount, he was confident that he could make it to shore since he knew how to swim. Too late he realized he'd failed to ascertain if she could.

He cast a fleeting glance over his shoulder to check on her. From what he could see in that brief instant, she appeared to be holding up well enough. Like him, only her head was visible as she hunched over her steed's neck in an effort to remain astride.

Because the horses now floated freely, they began to drift downstream. The instant their hooves came in contact with solid ground, both animals lunged forward. It was only a matter of a minute before they climbed up out of the water close to where Reginald stood on the opposite bank.

As Armand slid from the mare's back, he released the pent-up breath that he'd been holding the whole time.

He reached up to help Eri from the saddle, grateful that they had made it safely to the other side. He almost forgot himself and hugged her when her feet touched solid ground. Reginald's looming presence reminded him to keep his distance. "Well, we did it," he said to her.

"We certainly did," she said, looking extremely relieved. "Still, let's not do that again for a while, if we can help it."

"Amen to that," he said with fervor. He lifted an arm to wave to those on the other side, signaling that all was well.

Kyle and Ordog then started forward.

On entering the stream, the gelding appeared oblivious to the water churning around its muscular body. It plodded onward, calmly and steadily.

The pony had the sense to stay close to the warhorse, instinctively using the larger animal's bulk to block the force of the current.

About halfway across, the pony lost its footing, for its legs were quite short. It swung out and away from the gelding's side. The only thing that kept the smaller creature from being swept downstream was the fact that its reins had been secured to the warhorse's saddle.

The gelding hauled the pony and its rider along. Evidently, the water had receded sufficiently to allow the huge animal to stay grounded all the way across. Not once did the warhorse founder or lose its footing.

Soon, the pony regained traction and could fend for itself. Before long, both animals clambered up out of the water and onto the visible portion of the road ahead.

Kyle and Ordog dismounted and set about checking their gear to make sure it was still secure. Armand, Eri, and Reginald, who had landed yards downstream, trudged over to join them with their mounts in tow.

Armand glanced up at the gloomy sky. "Darkness will soon overtake us. If we don't build a fire to dry our clothes, we could freeze to death out here before morning."

"Good luck on finding something dry enough to

burn," Reginald said.

"Everything is wet now, but sooner or later, it will dry out," Kyle said. "Better to have tinder on hand, than blunder about the moor at night trying to find it in the dark."

"I'll wager the food is ruined, too," Reginald said. With a sigh of resignation, he went over to help Kyle, Ordog, and Eri search for brambles and anything else that might burn.

Armand turned his attention to Brother Luke still waiting at the water's edge on the far side of the stream.

"Come on across," he shouted, his hands cupped around his mouth. In case the friar could not make out his words over the sound of rushing water, he beckoned to the man with the wave of an arm.

Brother Luke evidently got the message, for he lifted a hand in acknowledgment. For a long moment, however, he remained poised at the water's edge, as though reluctant to proceed. At length, he shook the reins and started forward, as if he finally mustered up the courage to cross. The riderless horse followed close behind on a lead rope.

All seemed to go well until the friar reached the middle of the stream, at which time his mount stumbled and lost its footing.

In the blink of an eye, the animal disappeared under the water, dragging its rider and the other horse down with it.

Brother Luke, who had either bailed from the saddle to save himself or had been swept off by the current, reappeared on his own several seconds later.

After a brief moment, both horses broke the surface with nostrils flared and eyes rolling. Now that their heads were up out of the water, they seemed to calm down enough to continue swimming toward the far side. Since they were bound together, where one led, the other followed.

In the meantime, the current carried Brother Luke farther downstream. He flailed his arms, struggling to stay afloat. His robes clearly hampered his movements and weighed him down. Once more, he vanished below the surface, only to reappear again, thrashing about and gasping for breath.

By that time, Armand had mounted his horse and was galloping beside the stream in an effort to outrace the hapless friar. Since the others were too far away to render assistance, he was now on his own.

Once he had a good lead, he turned the mare aside and plunged into the water. It took several precious seconds to reach the middle of the stream.

Meanwhile, the undertow sucked Brother Luke down for a third time. As the current swept him forward, the only thing to mark his passage was the billowing black robe inches below the surface.

Armand snatched at the passing garment. The moving fabric eluded his grasp, so that he tried again. This time, his fingers connected with the soft material. He closed his fist around a handful and hauled back on it until Brother Luke's head erupted from the water. He wheeled the mare around and started back the way he'd come, towing the friar, sputtering and coughing, along with him.

Only when he'd dragged the friar up onto solid ground did he release his grip on the man's clothing.

Brother Luke collapsed in a soggy heap on the damp earth. "Bless you," he said, breathing heavily from exertion. “I thought I was done for.”

“For a while there, I did, too.” Armand climbed down from the saddle and helped the friar to his feet. “Are you all right?”

“I think so.” Despite assurance of his own wellbeing, Brother Luke put a hand on Armand’s shoulder to support himself, as if afraid his knees might buckle under him. Although plainly relieved the ordeal was over, his face looked quite pale and he still seemed a bit shaken. “You saved my life,” he said with solemnity. “I am in your debt.”

Armand smiled. “Perhaps you can return the favor one day.”

“Holy Scripture teaches that we must give an eye for an eye, a tooth for a tooth, a life for a life,” Brother Luke said. “Should it ever fall within my power, I shall do no less for you. You have my word on it.”

Armand nodded his thanks. Little did he realize at that moment how prophetic the friar’s words would prove to be.

Chapter 21

Kyle walked up with an armful of sticks and twigs. “These are still pretty damp,” he said, depositing them at Ordog’s feet.

“They will have to do.” The older man removed a pair of flints from the pouch at his side and went down on one knee before the small pile. Holding one flint firmly in hand, he struck the other against it, sending a shower of sparks down on the tinder.

The others gathered around to watch, anticipation evident on their faces. Without a fire, they had no hope of drying their wet clothing before darkness set in.

Now that dusk had crept up on them, there was a definite chill in the wind. The air would only get colder as night descended upon the open moorland.

After repeated efforts, Ordog failed to coax even the tiniest flame to life from the moist twigs. He tucked the flints into his pouch and climbed to his feet. “It’s just too wet.”

“I told ye that early on,” Reginald said. “No use even trying again until the sun dries them out.”

“And what do you propose we do in the meantime?” Ordog said.

“I don’t know,” Reginald said. “Why don’t ye come up with an idea sometime? Why do I have to do all the thinking around here?”

While the two men bickered over who should do

what, Eri, who would normally have found their squabbling entertaining and perhaps even egged them on, now stood somewhat apart, frowning thoughtfully as she stared into the distance.

Curiosity prompted Kyle to walk over to ascertain what she found so captivating. “What do you see?”

“That,” she said, pointing to the south.

The overcast sky on the southern horizon reflected a faint glow that came from somewhere below it.

“What is it?” she said.

“Unless I miss my guess,” Kyle said, “that illumination is from the next town or village down the road. We couldn’t see it before because of the light of day.”

Armand ambled up to stand beside them. “Could that be York, I wonder? It cannot be that much farther ahead of us, considering how far we have already come through the moorland.”

At the mention of York, Ordog and Reginald abruptly broke off their heated discussion and hastened over to take a look.

“Is that truly York?” Reginald said, squinting into the distance. “Is it really that close?”

“I’m not sure if it’s York at all,” Kyle said. “As for how close it is, that’s a mite hard to judge at night. It could be one mile away or even five.”

“I’m for riding there now, whatever town it happens to be,” Reginald said.

“I agree,” Ordog said.

Kyle, Eri, and Armand turned to stare at the older man, for he’d never before given in to any of Reginald’s suggestions so quickly.

“It’s better than freezing to death out here on the

moor," Ordog said by way of justification.

"The sooner we leave, the better," Reginald said.

No one offered any objection, so they mounted their horses and headed south. They rode at a rapid pace, as though intent on outracing the onset of darkness.

In the event night should happen to overtake them, the moorland through which they traveled would be as black as pitch now that clouds covered the moon. Without light to guide their step, they would be riding blind, in which case they might miss a curve in the road and end up stuck in a bog.

As it turned out, luck was with them. It took less than half an hour to reach the outskirts of town, where thatch-roofed houses and wooden shops crowded together along a network of lanes and byways. Even in the gloom of early evening, men and women still moved about the streets.

Grateful for the imminent prospect of a hot supper and a dry bed, Kyle brought the gelding to a halt. "This indeed appears to be York," he said to the others who reined in beside him. "Keep a sharp eye out for an inn or a tavern."

"What makes ye say this is York?" Reginald said.

"Because of the size of it," Kyle said. "And we're nowhere near the city gates."

They stayed on the main road and stopped at the first inn they came across. There were no rooms available because of the horse fair that had been going on for the past two days. They found a second inn and a third, but they were turned away from both for the same reason: no vacancy.

"We are no better off here than we were out on the

moor." Reginald looked over at Kyle. "What do we do now?"

"I have a suggestion," Brother Luke said. By that simple statement, he claimed the undivided attention of every one of his companions.

"Let's hear it," Reginald said.

"We can go to Saint Nicholas's Hospital," Brother Luke said. "I am confident the canon there will give us food and lodging in exchange for a small donation."

"Are ye sure?" Reginald said.

"I am," Brother Luke said. "In my travels, I've heard good reports about the hospitals in and around York."

"Why Saint Nicholas's in particular?" Reginald said.

"Because it is located outside the city walls."

"Do you know how to get there?" Kyle said.

"I was told it's off the main road leading up to the gates of the city proper," Brother Luke said. "It can't be that hard to find."

They continued along the main road, which did in fact lead them to the city gates. However, there was no hospital anywhere in sight.

It wasn't until Eri asked a passerby for directions that they actually located the facility a half a mile away, at the end of a dirt lane that ran between rows of close-set wooden dwellings.

A ten-foot wall surrounded the hospital and its grounds, and a pair of large wooden gates set in two stone pillars marked the entryway.

Since the gates were wide open, they rode into the large courtyard beyond and halted before a sprawling one-story stone edifice. Yellow light from oil lanterns inside the building shone through mullioned windows set at intervals along the front wall. The illumination was sufficient for them to see the alleys on either side of the stone structure, which passageways were wide enough to drive a horse-drawn wagon around to the rear.

They waited outside in the courtyard while Brother Luke went into the hospital through the front entrance to speak with the canon.

The friar came out a few minutes later with a smile on his gaunt face. "We have permission to stay the night. They are a bit shorthanded, so we must look after the horses on our own. There is a pen in the rear where we can leave them."

They rode down the nearest alleyway to the back of the hospital and headed for the fenced yard on one side of the open area. Since there were more than two dozen goats already in the pen, they opened the gate with care to make sure none of the occupants escaped.

They stripped the saddles and bridles from their mounts and placed the gear along the top rail to dry. After tending to the horses, they went into the hospital through the rear door.

The canon met them in the vestibule with a lantern in his hand. He was a thin man of meager stature in a long brown robe and sandaled feet, gray of tonsure, direct of gaze, with a serene expression on his lined face.

"Come this way," he said as he escorted them through an arched doorway and down the corridor. "Brother Luke told me about the flooding on the road. Let's get you out of those damp clothes before you catch your death."

He opened the door to a rectangular room with ten unoccupied beds in it, half on one side and half on the other, all at right angles to the walls.

"This will be your room for the night," he continued. "You may leave your things in here. No one will disturb them."

He waved a hand at the apparel on the shelves against the wall beside the doorway. "You will find suitable robes and sandals here to bring with you to the lavatorium. When you are ready, I will take you there to wash up."

They rummaged through neatly folded brown robes to select those of suitable size. They did the same with the leather sandals on the two bottom shelves. Each article of clothing showed signs of wear by a former owner, yet it smelled clean, as if freshly washed.

When each of them had their choice of attire in hand, the canon led them into an inner courtyard enclosed on four sides by the hospital building.

They followed him up a covered walkway that faced the quadrangle and through one of several doors along the way.

The walls of the lavatorium were made of stone, as was the floor, which slanted ever so slightly toward the outer courtyard to allow water to drain through the narrow openings across the bottom of the wall.

A long shallow trough-like basin dominated the back wall. It was about waist high, so that those standing before it could wash themselves, and then dip water from the basin to rinse off. There were also tubs for washing clothes and drying racks to hang them on.

There was a well with a raised circular stone rim in the middle of the quadrangle where fresh water could be drawn to refill the basin and the washtubs.

The canon took a second oil lantern from the peg beside the door and lit it from the one he carried in his hand. “I shall prepare something for you to eat,” he said as he hung the lighted lantern back on the peg. “When you finish up here, go back the way you came and meet me in the dining room. You will find it to the left of the vestibule. We can talk then.”

He must have caught the troubled glance that Eri exchanged with Armand, for he beckoned to her. “Come with me, if you please.”

Without a word, Eri followed the canon from the lavatorium with her bundle under her arm.

Kyle and those with him then shed their damp clothing and proceeded to wash the dried mud and grit from their bodies and from their garments. The water, which had been sitting in the basin for most of the day, felt warm to the touch.

They dried off with squares of absorbent fabric provided for that purpose and hung their washed clothing on the wooden rack. After putting on the borrowed robes and sandals, they took the lantern to light their way down the covered walkway and on into the hospital building.

By the time they entered the small dining room, Eri was already seated at the table in a loose brown robe, her hair still damp from washing. Armand went over to sit on the bench beside her.

“What did the canon want with you?” he said.

“Nothing much,” she said. She turned to look directly at him. “He knows. When I explained why, he agreed it was best.”

“Good,” Armand said with a nod.

The moment Kyle and the others sat down, the canon came into the room bearing a platter of sliced mutton and small oblong loaves of bread. A lanky young man with sharp features wearing the white robe of a novice followed close on his heels, carrying six cups and a jug of ale.

The canon placed the platter on the table. “Please excuse this humble offering. It was all I could muster on short notice.”

“Not to worry,” Kyle said. “I am sure I speak for all of us when I say we are grateful for anything you put before us.”

His words brought on a round of murmurs of concurrence and nods of agreement.

The novice filled the cups and passed them out to Kyle and the others. The canon settled on the chair at the head of the table, while the novice placed the jug beside the platter of food before he withdrew and closed the door behind him.

“Help yourselves to as much as you want,” the canon said. “There is more where that came from.” He sat in silence while his guests ate their fill.

When they were done, the canon’s sharp blue eyes roved from one to the other until they came to rest on Ordog, possibly because he was the oldest.

“It has been my experience that no one ventures across the moor without good cause,” he said, eyeing the older man closely. He let the words hang in the air while he waited, mute and watchful, for a reaction to his statement.

“Kyle Shaw saved my life,” Ordog said, jerking his thumb in the direction of the deputy. “I am bound to him wherever he goes until that debt of honor is paid.

That is why I am here."

"That is as good an answer as I would ever want to hear," the canon said. "Still, I cannot help but wonder why you risked crossing the moorland in the first place. Was it perhaps due to extenuating circumstances?"

" 'Extenuating circumstances'?" Ordog said with a frown. "You mean like fleeing from the law?"

"That is not what I meant to imply," the canon said fervently. "Forgive me for even bringing it up. I have no right to meddle in your private affairs. As travelers in need, you are welcome to seek shelter here, no matter what your situation happens to be."

"Rest easy, Master Canon," Ordog said with laugh. "None of us are fugitives. In fact, those two"—here he waved a hand at Kyle and Reginald—"are men of law. They can better tell you what you want to know."

"That is true," Kyle said in response to the evident interest on the canon's face. "Reginald and I are couriers bound by oath to deliver sealed letters. I am not at liberty to divulge any more information than that."

Tension seemed to drain from the canon's body. "I understand," he said with a nod. "I only asked because of the patients in residence here. I would prefer that their solitude not be disrupted by intrigue of any kind. There has been too much of that in and about the city lately."

"Now that you mention patients," Kyle said, "I haven't seen a single one since we arrived."

"They are confined to the west wing," the canon said with a tight smile. He stood up and twitched his long robe into place. "You must be weary after your journey. When you are ready to retire, I will take you to your room. There are no rules or prohibitions in this hospital. The only thing I ask is that you steer clear of the west wing, lest you disturb the patients there. Most are terminal, you see. There is no hope of recovery for them. Peace and rest are what they need the most before they face the inevitable end."

"I'm sorry." Kyle glanced at the others, each of whom voiced their accord. His gaze then settled on the canon. "You have our word that we will respect your wishes."

They rose from the table and followed their host to the room he'd assigned to them earlier. He lit a tallow candle from his lantern and left it with them before he departed.

Ordog selected a bed in the corner for Eri and climbed into the next bed over from her, as though to isolate her from the others.

Kyle chose a bed close to the door, as did Armand. Both kept their daggers handy, just in case.

Reginald and Brother Luke didn't seem to care where they slept, for each of them chose the bed nearest to them.

Kyle blew out the candle. Within minutes, he sank into a dreamless sleep, oblivious to the sonorous snoring emanating from Ordog's corner of the room.

****

A bright intrusive light roused Armand from slumber the next day. His temples throbbed when he opened his eyes to sunlight beaming in through a row of unshuttered windows set high in the outer wall. It appeared to be about midmorning, judging from the angle of the rays that cast yellow rectangles on the smooth stone floor. He looked around for the others, but their beds were empty.

He felt a bit feverish. Still, it was long past time to start the new day. After stretching unaccountably aching joints, he got up and padded on bare feet to a small washstand near the doorway. He emptied the pitcher into the wooden bowl and splashed cool water in his face. With no drying cloth at hand, he used the sleeve of his borrowed robe to blot the moisture from his skin.

He slipped on his sandals and walked down the corridor to the dining room. On finding it empty, he went in search of the kitchen, which he located by following the tantalizing aroma of meat stew that hung in the air.

The kitchen was situated on the same side of the quadrangle as the lavatorium, and the door was open to let in fresh air and light.

Armand went inside, hoping to cajole a bite to eat from the cook, who, to his surprise, turned out to be the canon. "I see you are a man of many talents," he said, eyeing the large crock suspended over an open flame on the hearth. "It smells wonderful. Will it be ready any time soon?"

"It's ready now," the canon said, wiping the sweat from his forehead with a scrap of cloth. He ladled stewed capon with onions and turnips from the crock into a wooden bowl and handed it, along with a chunk of fresh bread, to his guest.

"Do you mind if I eat it here?" Armand said.

"Not at all," the canon said. "You can sit over there." He pointed to a low stool in the corner. "I'll be glad of your company while I make bread." He placed several scoops of barley flour into a sizeable bowl and poured in some water. He added a lump of leavening and set about stirring the mixture into a gummy mass with a wooden spoon.

"This is really tasty," Armand said after the first mouthful of stew. "Where did you learn to cook so well?"

"Trial and error, my son," the canon said. "The food here must appeal to the palate. Otherwise, the patients will not eat it. If they do not eat, they will not thrive. If they do not thrive, they will die before their time."

"I see." Armand continued to eat while the canon turned the sticky mixture onto a floured board on the work table against the wall, after which he sprinkled generous handfuls of loose barley flour over all exposed surfaces.

"I am surprised you did not go out with the others earlier this morning," the canon said as he kneaded the dough with deft fingers.

"I feel a bit under the weather today. That must be why I failed to hear them stirring about. Did they say where they were going?"

"To the horse fair," the canon said. "York's landed gentry hold it every summer in the field by the river. Your companions took the extra horse with them, to look for a buyer there, I imagine."

"I hope they get a good price for it," Armand said. "We can use the money."

"Who cannot use a few extra coins?" the canon said with a sigh. "This hospital depends on the patronage of the church for support. I am not complaining, mind you, but there are more times than not when expenses outweigh income." He shaped the dough into ovals the size of his fist and laid them out in neat rows on the large floured board. "Patients who come here have nowhere else to go. Plus, most are destitute, so they cannot be expected to pay for services rendered."

"I wish I could help," Armand said.

"I did not mention these things to burden your conscience," the canon said as he rinsed his hands in a wash bowl on the sideboard. "Forgive an old man for talking too much."

"Not to worry," Armand said. "My companions and I are not so churlish as to take advantage of your hospitality without compensating you accordingly."

"Whatever you are willing to give, I will accept," the canon said with a smile. "And gratefully, too."

Armand rose from the stool and smoothed the wrinkles from his brown robe with his hands. "I reckon I should change into my own clothes. They should be dry by now."

He had just turned to leave when Eri burst through the open doorway into the kitchen and stopped abruptly. His joy at seeing her suddenly transmuted into horror at the sight of her.

Her eyes were wide with alarm, and her breath came in gasps from the exertion of running. Besides the frantic expression on her face, her hands were covered in blood, as was the front of her shirt. She looked like she'd been in a knife fight and had come out on the losing end of it.

An iron fist tightened around his heart. "What happened?" he said, thoroughly shaken at the possibility that she'd been wounded. "Are you all right?"

"I searched all over for you," she cried, leaning on the doorjamb for support. "Come quickly. It's Master Reginald. He's hurt really bad."

Chapter 22

Armand, his throbbing head and aching joints now forgotten, followed Eri from the kitchen with the canon hard on his heels. The three of them hastened along the covered walkway, headed toward the south wing.

They cut through the hospital building and went out the rear door, entering the sunlit back yard just as Kyle, Ordog, and Brother Luke were lifting Reginald down from the gelding's rump.

Armand hurried over to help settle the injured man on a blanket that one of them had already spread out on the grass for that purpose.

Reginald's eyes were closed, and his face ashen, clearly from a loss of blood. He lay where he'd been placed on the ground, as still as death, except for the shallow rise and fall of his chest. A linen cloth had been wrapped tightly around his midsection over his tunic, with the knot off to one side. A dark red patch had blossomed on the pristine whiteness of the fabric where blood had seeped through it.

The canon knelt beside the prone body and pressed two fingers into the sheriff's neck on the left side of his throat. "He lives, but just barely. Take him inside."

Armand, Ordog, Kyle, and Brother Luke each took hold of a corner of the blanket. Together, they lifted him off the ground and carried him through the back door of the hospital.

Eri walked close behind them, a worried frown on her face and her eyes on the injured man.

"Put him in your room," the canon said over his shoulder as he headed in the other direction at a brisk pace. "I need to fetch medicaments."

The four of them trod down the corridor and into the room that had been assigned to them. Together they lifted the blanket high enough to clear the top of the nearest bed and gently laid their sad burden on top of it.

Two minutes later, the canon reappeared with a bulky leather bag under his arm and the sharp-featured novice a step behind him. "Fetch a bucket of water, a pan, clean rags, and a stool," he said to the novice, who departed at once to do as he was bidden.

Armand and the others gathered on the far side of the bed to watch in silence.

"Who wrapped this around him?" the canon said as he untied the knot on the linen cloth binding the wound.

"I did," Kyle said.

"You saved his life," the canon said. "He would have bled to death without it."

He laid back the edges of the linen cloth, exposing the blood-soaked tunic beneath. He removed a sheathed dagger from his medicament bag, withdrew the blade, and carefully cut the saturated garment from neck to waist to lay bare the sheriff's torso.

There were five slits in the skin, smooth-edged and rimmed with red, all located on the right side under the rib cage. Now that the binding cloth no longer pressed down on the wounds, blood began to ooze from each gash.

About that time, the novice returned with the requested items. He set the empty pan on the stool he'd brought with him and filled it with water from the bucket. He dropped in a rag, wrung out the excess moisture, and set about wiping the blood from around the wounds.

Meanwhile, the canon took a couple of corked phials from his bag. He shook a measured amount of powdered herbs from each one into a cup and mixed in a little water from the bucket. Using his fingers, he patted a thick layer of the herbal compound on each wound, after which he covered the affected area with a square of clean fabric. He drew the strip of linen cloth back across the sheriff's body and pulled it tight enough to stop the bleeding, at which time the novice stepped forward to tie the loose ends together.

The canon held his hands over the pan and nodded to the novice, who poured water from the bucket over them. "That is all that can be done for him," he said, drying his fingers on a clean rag.

"Will he live?" Ordog said, his brow furrowed with concern.

"Only time will tell," the canon said. "Of the five stab wounds, two are deep enough to imperil his life. He has lost a lot of blood. If he survives until morning, there's a good chance he will pull through. Of course, there is always the danger of fever setting in, or worse, gangrene. However, we can worry about that should it actually come to pass." He glanced from one to the other. "Have you any idea who did this to him?"

"It was that rascal we met on the road the other day," Eri said. "Viper," she added, her upper lip curled in scorn.

"So you say," Ordog said to her. "Yet you didn't actually see him do it."

"Nay, I did not," Eri said. "I saw him hanging about the stock yard, no doubt because he recognized the spare horse we brought there to sell, seeing as how it belonged to one of his cohorts."

"Is Viper left-handed?" the canon said.

"I'm not sure," Eri said. "Is it important?"

"The person who did this used his left hand to do the stabbing," the canon said, gazing thoughtfully at his patient. "All of the wounds, you see, are concentrated on the right side of your companion's body. Lucky for your friend, it was done in haste and with a skinning knife. If the attacker had used a longer blade, like a dagger, the consequences would have been far more serious."

"How can you be sure about the skinning knife?" Eri said.

"That kind of blade is designed to cut in one direction only. Thus, one edge is sharp, while the other is flat. That was the configuration of each wound."

Eri crossed her arms, her lips drawn tight in anger. "I still say this is Viper's handiwork. Even if he didn't do the deed himself, I would bet my saddle that one of his cohorts did it at his behest."

Armand looked down at the sheriff reclining on the bed, completely motionless, his breathing shallow and ragged, his face so pale that death seemed but a step away. A niggling thought groped its way into his conscious mind, something he'd heard in the Romany camp, rearing its insistent head relentlessly, until, in the next heartbeat, it came to the fore with blinding clarity. "I wonder if this is what Illiana meant when she said he would suffer tribulation in the flesh."

"That is entirely possible," Ordog said with a nod.

"As someone with the gift of sight, her predictions are rarely wrong."

Armand turned to Eri. "I was not at the fair this morning, so tell me everything that happened. Perhaps some detail will shed light on the identity of the perpetrator."

She cast a fleeting glance at Ordog, who gave her a nod of encouragement. After a brief silence, as though to compose her thoughts, she began to speak.

She'd ridden with the others to the horse fair, which encompassed most of a spacious field situated outside the walls on the south side of the city. The sun was bright, and the air warm. The sky above was blue, without a cloud in sight. The road was still muddy from the rain on the previous day, with pools of standing water in wagon wheel ruts along the way.

Like any marketplace, the fair grounds bustled with activity. Customers haggled with vendors over the price of goods. Peddlers with pushcarts filled with merchandise hawked their wares in the hope of a sale. Mongrel dogs fought over discarded morsels of food that fell to the ground. Children ran and played, adding shouts of glee to the din.

The open area at the center of the field had been reserved for the buying and selling of horses. Quite a number of rails and posts had been erected there for the purpose of showing off the noble creatures to be bought or sold.

Makeshift wooden booths erected by merchants to display their products had been built around the perimeter of the area assigned to the horses. Row upon row of those temporary stands and stalls radiated out from the center yard to take up a large portion of the field. A tent behind each booth served as temporary accommodations for vendors and tradesmen for the duration of the festivities.

As it was the third and final day of the fair, the pathways between certain popular booths were crammed with townsfolk and people from nearby villages. It was difficult to push through the crowd that had gathered there. She and those with her took a more circuitous but less congested route to the central area. The minute she tied the spare horse to one of several available posts, the purser came over to collect the fee for the use of the post.

Reginald paid the fee. The purser then gave him a receipt, which he tucked into his coin purse.

There were quite a few horses on display and as many prospective buyers making the rounds to examine each animal. It wasn't long before bargain hunters worked their way over to the spare horse they'd brought there to sell. Each professed interest, but none of them made an offer before moving on.

This process continued for half the morning. She had not yet broken her fast and neither had the others. Kyle, Ordog, and Brother Luke went off to buy something for all of them to eat.

Soon after the others had left, she spotted Viper the bandit across the way. There was no mistaking that bald head of his gleaming in the sunlight. She pointed him out to Reginald. By the time he looked in that direction, the fellow had vanished behind a row of booths.

She was afraid Viper would make trouble for them, especially if he caught them trying to sell a horse that belonged to one of his men. Reginald didn't seem worried at all, but she had a bad feeling about it. She suggested that the two of them take the horse and go look for their companions, after which they should all leave the fair grounds. The animal was sound and healthy, and they could always find a buyer elsewhere.

Unfortunately, Reginald had other ideas. He evidently saw the fair as the only opportunity they'd have to get a good price for the horse. He'd already paid the fee, and he was determined to stay there for as long as it took to sell it.

She insisted they would stand a better chance against Viper if the others were with them. He told her to go ahead and fetch them, that he'd be fine on his own.

She headed in the direction of the food carts. She knew she was getting close when the smell of fried pasties and roasted mutton grew stronger. Before long, she ran into Kyle, Ordog, and Brother Luke on their way back to the area reserved for horses. As they walked along, she told them about Viper and the danger that could possibly arise from his presence at the horse fair.

When she and those with her arrived at the central area, Reginald, along with his bay and the spare horse, were gone. She'd been away for less than a quarter of an hour, so it was surprising that Reginald had sold the horse in that short a period of time. However, if somebody had bought it, it would stand to reason that Reginald would seek out the purser in order to secure a bill of sale for the buyer.

She and the others set out for the purser's booth. On the way, they passed a cluster of people chattering excitedly and pointing at something on the ground between two stalls. She asked what was going on and was told that a man had been killed.

With a sinking feeling in the pit of her stomach, she squeezed through those gathered to take a look, as did Kyle, Ordog, and Brother Luke. Her heart nearly stopped at the sight of Reginald sprawled in the grass, motionless, with blood all over the front of his tunic.

Kyle went down on one knee to ascertain if Reginald was still alive. Apparently he was, for Kyle immediately pressed down on the affected area to stop the bleeding. He said he needed a narrow length of cloth to keep the bleeding in check. She tore a strip from the bottom of her shirt and hand it to him. He slipped one end under the sheriff's back, passed it around his body, and tied both edges together.

The constable in charge of the fair grounds arrived about that time and started asking questions. Kyle cut him off by insisting that Reginald be taken to Saint Nicholas's hospital for immediate treatment, otherwise he could die.

The constable gave Kyle an odd look before giving his consent, saying he would go to the hospital later to question Reginald about the incident.

With the constable's help, Ordog and Brother Luke lifted Reginald onto the gelding behind Kyle, after which they all rode from the fair grounds as quickly as they dared with such a seriously injured man.

"That's it," she said to Armand. "That's all I remember."

Armand pondered her words with objective detachment, looking for inconsistencies in the tale she'd related to him. There were none that he could readily find. "Does anybody have anything to add?" he said to the others gathered there.

Kyle, Ordog, and Brother Luke shook their heads.

Armand frowned in thought over something Eri had mentioned. “So Reginald’s horse is missing, too?” he said to her.

“Aye,” she said. “Along with the spare horse.”

Armand lifted a troubled gaze to Kyle’s face. “Master Reginald kept the courier pouch in his saddle roll. Does it not follow that whoever took his horse must now be in possession of those sealed letters?”

Chapter 23

Kyle scowled at the implication that important letters penned solely for the eyes of the king of England had fallen into the hands of a petty outlaw. Although the thought had occurred to him at the fair, he'd thrust it to the back of his mind. His first responsibility was to attend to Reginald's injuries. "All the more reason to find out who did this."

"I'm telling you, it was Viper," Eri said emphatically. "I'm sure of it."

"I concur that he's the most likely suspect so far," Kyle said. "However, there is no way he could have known about the letters in Reginald's saddle roll. I can see how he would have felt justified in taking the spare horse. Getting his hands on a second horse—Reginald's—at the same time would simply be an added bonus. I do not believe gaining possession of the letters was the main reason for the attack on Reginald. It is more likely that Reginald resisted when the man tried to take the spare horse by force, which resulted in Reginald being stabbed to prevent him from making a scene that would attract unwanted attention."

"What about the constable?" Armand said. "Should he be told about the letters?"

"Even if the constable tracked down Reginald's horse," Kyle said, "the thief will have already found and removed the letters from the saddle roll by that time. I don't hold out much hope of ever seeing them again."

"The patient needs to rest now." The canon turned to the young novice. "Brother James, stay here and watch over him. If he wakes up, let me know immediately. I will be in the dining hall with our guests." With a sweep of his hand, he made it plain that everyone else was to leave the room. "If you please," he said with a smile.

With a last glance at Reginald's pallid face, Kyle walked from the room. The others shuffled out into the corridor behind him.

They followed the canon to the dining room and seated themselves around the table.

"I shall be back in a moment," the canon said.

True to his word, he returned minutes later with a large container of stew. A stout monk of middle years in a brown robe trudged behind him, carrying a tray of wooden bowls and spoons, along with small loaves of freshly baked bread. The canon went around to each of his guests with the monk at his elbow, ladling stew into the bowl that was handed to him and setting it before each one. The monk then passed out bread and wooden spoons.

The canon set the container in the middle of the table and filled two more bowls, one for himself and the other for the monk. He sat down at the head of the table, while the monk settled in the chair on the opposite end. After a prayer of thanksgiving, they joined in eating the meal.

The canon paused between bites to gaze at Kyle. "I've been thinking about the letters that were lost. Can they be duplicated?"

“What do you mean?” Kyle said.

“If you know the contents of each letter, can you pen a similar one, along with an explanation of what became of the original?”

“I only know the gist of one of the letters,” Kyle said. “And there is no way I could rewrite it word for word. Otherwise, your idea would have been a good one.”

“What will you do now?” the canon said around a mouthful of bread.

“With your permission,” Kyle said, “I shall remain here another day, until I am sure Reginald is on the mend. I will then continue the journey without him and make it my business to deliver what I know of the message verbally.”

“So, the fact that the letters went missing is not a complete loss, then,” the canon said.

“It is with respect to the other letters, seeing as how I have no idea what they contain.”

“That is lamentable,” the canon said, his brow knitted in a frown. His countenance brightened, as though a thought struck him. “By the way, what do you think of our horse fair?”

“It is the largest I’ve ever seen,” Kyle said. “The profits must be enormous for the sponsors.”

“You would think with so much money at hand, both the church and the town council would be content with equal shares of the bounty.”

“Are they not?” Kyle said.

“Nay,” the canon said. “The church expects a larger percentage of the money since they own the land on which the fair is held. The problem is the town council puts on the fair and collects the tolls and tariffs, so the members feel entitled to a lion's share of the profits. I fear the constant squabbling between church and state may one day result in the cessation of our horse fair altogether."

"I doubt that seriously," Kyle said, "especially where there is easy money to be made."

"Therein lies another problem," the canon said. "It is the prospect of easy money that attracts the undesirable element of society. By operating beneath the eyeline of tradesmen and merchants, thieves and beggars and ladies of ill repute hope to acquire a portion of the wealth. Cutpurses and pickpockets take full advantage when there are large crowds and even larger purses to be had. What is worse, they linger in the city long after the fair is over, causing trouble for decent folk trying to earn an honest living."

"That would certainly account for Viper's presence and that of his band," Kyle said.

At that moment, a rotund white-robed novice entered the room and went over to speak to the canon. "Reverend Father, Constable Scanlon is out front," he said in a low voice. "He expressed a desire to speak with the wounded man who was brought here."

"Bring him around back to the vestibule," the canon said. "We shall meet him there."

The novice withdrew with a nod of ascent.

"He seems mighty eager to question Reginald," Kyle said. "I wonder what he will do when he discovers he came all this way for nothing."

"There is but one way to find out," the canon said, rising from his chair. "Come. Let us not keep him waiting."

Kyle and the others followed the canon to the

vestibule to await the constable's arrival.

Moments later, a tall skinny man in his midthirties with cropped ginger hair and a hatchet nose sauntered through the rear entryway. Resolute brown eyes in a ruddy face roved over those gathered there and came to rest on Kyle. "How fares the injured fellow?" he said in a broad Yorkshire accent.

"Not well at all," Kyle said. "He has not yet regained his wits."

"That's too bad," Constable Scanlon said. "I'd like to see him anyway." His gaze shifted to the canon. "If I may." He spoke the words with exaggerated politeness, yet the expression on his face left no doubt in anyone's mind that it was a demand, not a request.

"This way," the canon said with a tight smile. He swung around and started up the corridor.

"Ye don't seem to mind being at this hospital," the constable said to Kyle.

"Why should I?" Kyle said. "The canon has shown us nothing but kindness and generosity during our stay here. Besides that, Reginald would have died without his curative skills. With the canon's permission, I plan to remain here until my companion is out of danger."

"You really mean that, don't ye?" the constable said, incredulous.

"I do," Kyle said. "What of it?"

"Ye do know this is a leper hospital, right?" the constable said, eyeing him dubiously. "That's why the church built it outside the city walls."

Kyle stopped in his tracks, as did the others. His initial shock wore off as quickly as it had come, for he concluded that the canon was not the kind of man who would callously expose them to a dreaded disease for which there was no cure.

The canon paused, turning to face them. "This is indeed a hospital for lepers. Let me assure you, however, that there is no danger of contagion to you or anyone else who sets foot inside this facility. The poor unfortunates who come here for treatment remain isolated in the west wing. Only their caretakers venture there to tend to their daily needs."

A thought then struck Kyle that filled him with concern. "What of the lavatorium? Don't the lepers use it, too?"

"Nay," the canon said. "They have their own facility for washing, with separate accommodations for sleeping. They have their own dining room, as well as their own bowls and utensils. It is our practice to keep such patients apart from the general public, no matter the stage of their disease. Had there been the slightest chance of infection, I would have turned you away at the door."

The canon continued down the corridor to the room to which his guests had been assigned. "Master Reginald is in here," he said to the constable. He stood aside to let the man of law enter before him.

Constable Scanlon walked up to stand beside Reginald's bed. As he gazed down at the sleeping patient, his face reflected neither sympathy nor pity. "Who did this to ye?" he said, leaning close, as though hoping to evoke a response.

Reginald lay still and silent, without so much as the twitch of an eyelid to acknowledge that he'd heard what was spoken to him.

The constable turned to Kyle. "Did he say anything to ye about what happened to him?"

"Not a word," Kyle said. "We found him at the horse fair just as you see him. He's been like that ever since."

The constable glanced over at the canon. "What are his chances of pulling through?"

"Fair," the canon said. "If he is left in peace, that is."

The constable's thin lips twitched, as though to suppress a smile. "Is that yer way of telling me to leave him alone?"

"You may take it any way you wish," the canon said with a shrug of his narrow shoulders. "The fellow must have rest in order to recover. Unnecessary movement or any effort to rise will tear open his wounds, which could lead to complications."

The constable eyed Ordog and Eri with open suspicion. "What are those two doing here?" he said to Kyle.

"Why do you ask?" Kyle said.

"They're Romany," the constable said, as though no further explanation was necessary.

"So I've noticed," Kyle said. "What does that have to do with anything?"

"Did not the victim's steed go missing?" the constable said.

"It did," Kyle said, "as did the horse to be sold."

"Well, then," the constable said, letting the insinuation hang in the air between them.

"So you think they stole the horses?" Kyle said, tilting his head at Ordog and Eri.

"It has been known to happen," the constable said. "After all, they are Romany."

"They were with me the whole time," Kyle said. "I

would have noticed if they had taken the horses." He fixed an icy gaze on the man of law. "Are you done here now?"

The constable's ruddy complexion turned brick red, as though Kyle's dismissive words hit a nerve. "I'll let ye know when I'm done. Now, why don't ye tell me yer version of the incident?"

"My version goes something like this," Kyle said. "We took the spare horse to the fair to sell. About midmorning, we went to get something to eat. When we got back, Reginald was gone. We thought he'd sold the horse, so we headed for the purser's office. We were on the way there when we found Reginald in his present condition. You know the rest."

"How came ye by the spare horse?" the constable said.

"It was the spoils of a clash with Viper and his marauders," Kyle said. "It happened a few days ago on the North Road. I suspect Viper tried to take back the horse, and Reginald got in his way."

"That makes sense," the constable said. "However, your explanation strikes me as too perfect."

"What are you implying?" Kyle said.

"How do I know it was not you who stabbed Reginald because he would not hand over the horse to you and your Romany cohorts?"

"If that were so," Kyle said, "where are the missing horses? They are rather too large to hide just anywhere."

"Was that supposed to be witty?" the constable said. "Let's see if ye still find it amusing when I clap ye in irons and take ye to the county dungeon."

Ordog shook his head. "There must be something

in the water that causes the locals to act that way," he said to no one in particular.

The constable turned on him, his expression fierce. "What do ye mean by that?" he said, glaring.

"Never mind him," Kyle said. "Your accusations are unfounded and have no merit, especially in light of my connection with Sir Miles Aldensford, a knight of the realm in the service of Edward of England."

Shades of doubt and consternation crossed the constable's face at the mention of Aldensford, as though he were well aware of the power and authority associated with that noble family.

Kyle continued on, pressing his advantage by repeating word for word what Miles had told him. "I have in my possession proof of our acquaintance. Anyone of consequence in this county who sees it should recognize it." He reached into the pouch at his side and removed the bronze cloak pin with a tiny ram's head on each pronged end.

Constable Scanlon's eyes flared with recognition at the sight of it. Then, his demeanor changed in a blink. "How do I know ye did not steal that, too?" he said, his gaze narrowed and speculative.

Ordog rolled his eyes, as though in silent appeal to the heavens.

The canon stepped forward before Kyle could stop him. "This man who you accuse of theft," he said to the constable, "is a courier entrusted with carrying a message to the king of England."

Kyle groaned inside. Although the canon apparently meant well, the declaration had been made, and the harm done. It was too late now to take it back. His worst fear at that moment was for the constable to ask for proof. Sure enough, those were the next words that came out of the man's mouth.

"Then produce such a letter," the constable said, "and show me the wax seal on it. That is, if it does indeed exist."

Kyle muttered an expletive under his breath. He was back where he started, engaged in futile conversation with an overly suspicious man of law who was willing—no, eager—to toss him and his companions into the dungeon. "Unfortunately, Reginald had kept the letter pouch in his saddle roll."

"Don't tell me, let me guess," the constable said, holding up his hand. "The saddle roll just happened to be on the horse that was stolen."

"You may find it hard to believe," Kyle said, "but that is the truth."

"So ye say," the constable said, incredulity evident in the tone of his voice.

"What does the saddle roll look like?" Brother James said.

All eyes turned to the white-robed young novice perched on a stool beside Reginald's bed. No one had taken notice of him, for he'd sat in unobtrusive silence throughout the entire exchange.

"It's striped," Kyle said. "Tan and white, if I am not mistaken. Why do you ask?"

"Because I've seen it," Brother James said.

Kyle's breath stalled in his throat in anticipation. "Where?"

"Up there," Brother James said, pointing at the top of the shelved cabinet beside the door.

All eyes focused on the uppermost part of the cabinet. Only a small portion of the saddle roll was visible, yet it was enough to see the tan and white striping on it.

"I noticed it earlier in the day when ye brought Master Reginald in here," Brother James said. "I didn't think any more about it until ye mentioned it a moment ago."

The tight muscles in Kyle's shoulders began to relax. Now that the letters had been retrieved, he could refute the constable's accusations that he was a liar and a thief. More importantly, he could complete the task assigned to him and stand before the king of England with tangible proof of his mission in his hand. Otherwise, it would be difficult for a Scotsman to gain an audience before an English king with a verbal message alone, or worse, try to convince him of its credibility.

Since he was taller than Reginald who had put the saddle roll up there in the first place, it was no problem for him to reach up and take it down. A sense of gratification swept over him as his fingers closed around the pouch secreted within the fabric wrapping.

He unrolled the thin blanket, removed the pouch, and handed it to the constable. "The sealed letters are inside."

The constable opened the leather pouch and peered inside. "I find it odd that anyone would leave such important documents behind in a place like this." Without removing the letters, he picked through them with his index finger to look at the seal on each one. Apparently satisfied with what he saw, he closed the pouch and handed it back to Kyle.

"I can only guess why Reginald did it," Kyle said. "If you are that curious, perhaps you can ask him yourself when he regains consciousness."

"I plan to do just that." The constable gazed at each one in turn, including the canon and the young novice. "I shall return tomorrow to question him. He will either be awake or dead by then. I expect every one of ye to be here when I come back, in case I need to speak with ye."

"The patient might very well awaken on the morrow," the canon said. "His wounds are deep, however, so he will be in pain. He will likely need something to make him sleep, lest restless thrashing cause his wounds to reopen, which would be detrimental to him. I recommend giving him three more days. He will be in better shape to talk by then."

"All right," the constable said. "Three days it is." He turned on his heel and strode from the room without a backward glance.

Kyle and the others listened, mute and attentive, as the constable's footsteps faded down the corridor.

The canon was the first to break the silence. "What an unpleasant fellow. I thought he'd never leave."

"I was afraid he was going to say you stole the letters, too," Eri said to Kyle.

"I'm just glad he didn't insist on going to London with us to confirm that the letters are real," Kyle said.

"What is it with lawmen in this country?" Ordog said. "I didn't think it was possible, but he's worse than Constable Garvey."

"Reverend Father," Kyle said, turning to the canon. "I fear I must impose upon you once again when the constable comes back in three days."

"What would you like me to do?" the canon said.

"Reginald will likely be awake by that time, God

willing, and Constable Scanlon will put some pointed questions to him. Reginald should do well because he was in fact the victim of a vicious attack. However, if you will, kindly impress upon Reginald the necessity of whispering whatever he has to say, as though it was still too painful for him to speak out with his full voice."

"What shall I tell him if he asks me why?" the canon said.

"Reginald's Scottish accent will give him away, and as unpredictable as the constable is, there is a good possibility he could charge Reginald with being a rebel and place him under arrest."

"That is as good a reason as any," the canon said. "I shall make it my business to sit with him the entire time the constable is here to make sure he does not slip up."

"I would appreciate that," Kyle said. "If Reginald wakes up before midday tomorrow, I can tell him that myself. But if he does not come around by then, the task will fall to you. Either way, I must leave by noon at the latest. I had hoped to stay longer, but I cannot risk being detained by an overzealous man of law for unfounded conjectures." He glanced at the others. "I trust I speak for all of us."

They nodded their heads and murmured their accord.

"Where will you go?" the canon said.

"The less you know, the better," Kyle said. "If all goes well, I should pass back through here in a month or so. That should be sufficient time for Reginald's wounds to heal before we undertake the long ride home. I only hope Constable Scanlon can locate Reginald's horse and return it to him before then."

He dug in his pouch and removed the emerald pendant on a gold chain. "You gave this to me for my wife," he said to Ordog. "She would love it, but she doesn't need it like the Reverend Father does. Do you have any objection to my giving it to him?"

"It is yours to do with as you please," Ordog said. "And if it pleases you to give it to him, feel free to do so."

Kyle pressed the piece of jewelry into the canon's hand. "We've caused you trouble by showing up unannounced on your doorstep. Sell this bauble, as Ordog calls it, and use the money as you see fit."

The canon gazed down at the precious stone encased in gold nestled in his palm. "This will buy a lot of supplies that we need," he said, his voice thick with emotion. "I cannot thank you enough."

"You deserve no less for what you do at this hospital," Kyle said. To his companions, he said, "There is much to be done before we leave, so let us be about it."

They left the room and went down the corridor to the vestibule, where they walked out the rear door into the back yard. The late afternoon sun shone down on them as they cleaned their gear, brushed the horses, and made other preparations for the last leg of their journey to London.

Chapter 24

With the courier pouch safely ensconced in his saddle roll, Kyle rode out the main gate of Saint Nicholas's Hospital along with Ordog, Armand, Eri, and Brother Luke. The five of them headed for the southeast road that would take them to the port town of Hull. The sun at its zenith was bright and hot, typical for a midsummer day.

Kyle hated to leave Reginald, who had not yet stirred from a deep sleep—a condition which the canon assured him resulted from small intermittent doses of poppy juice to keep him immobilized for another day or two before he started moving about, which he was bound to do once he awoke.

On the positive side, Reginald's forehead was cool to the touch, his color better and his breathing regular, all signs he was on the mend. Consequently, Kyle had no problem committing him to the canon's care and keeping until his recovery was complete.

It took Kyle and those with him a couple of days to reach Hull. Once they arrived, they had to wait three more days until a southbound merchant vessel sailed into port. They lost another day while the crew offloaded the cargo and took on a new load, during which the purser had to match all the goods coming and going with the shipmaster's bills of lading.

On the fifth day of waiting in the port town, Kyle

and the others were notified early in the morning that they could board the ship with their mounts. The crew installed the horses in the cargo hold, cross-tying them to prevent a loss of footing, should the ship encounter choppy seas during the journey.

At long last, the merchant vessel pulled out of the harbor on the outgoing tide, only to meander down the east coast of England, docking at each major port of call along the way to pick up cargo or drop it off.

For the duration of the voyage, Kyle ate sparingly. The constant roll of the vessel made him queasy. It was worse when they were moored in port, where the ship bobbed up and down in place. He longed for the journey to end and often wished he'd taken the overland route to London, even though it would have taken more time to get there.

After ten days of harbor hopping, the ship rounded the headland and nosed into the Thames Estuary. At the master's command, the crew dropped anchor in the mouth of the inlet. The vessel drifted at the end of its massive chain for two hours while they waited for the tide to change. Soon, there was a noticeable shift in the direction of the water, and the ship began to swing about. The crew then weighed anchor, which enabled the incoming tidal waters to sweep the vessel up the river.

Kyle stood at the railing, gazing down at the spume slapping against the bow. After the clear blue depths of the North Sea, the river looked cloudy and brown. He also detected a foul smell coming up from the water. He turned to the ship's master beside him. "Will you sail all the way to London?"

"Nay," the master said. "The tide will take us only

as far as Gravesham. That is where we must turn back. A waterman can ferry ye upriver from there."

"How far is it to London?" Kyle said.

"About twenty-five miles," the master said. "Once ye set foot on the north bank, follow the road west."

As the tide carried the ship upstream, the river grew steadily narrower. After rounding two sharp bends, the weathered timber wharf at Gravesham hove into view.

Kyle shaded his eyes against the midmorning sun to look out over the cluster of houses and two large warehouses that comprised the sleepy village. Hardly anyone moved about the streets. Wherries and flatboats and barges lined both sides of a long pier leading to the sturdy wharf that extended fifty feet into the river. At that point the water was deep enough to accommodate keeled ships and merchant vessels laden with goods.

The master stood on the upper deck, his eyes trained on the wharf, as though mentally calculating the distance between it and the ship. "Drop anchor," he shouted suddenly, his tone brusque and urgent.

The deckhands stopped what they were doing and scrambled to do the master's bidding.

Once the huge iron anchor hit bottom, the entire vessel was now at the mercy of the current. The ship swung wide at the end of the chain, only to come to rest with a gentle thump against the wooden wharf.

"This is where ye disembark," the master said to Kyle in a matter-of-fact voice, as though the feat of docking the ship was no big deal. In reality, it took an expert to know when to release the anchor so as not to overshoot the wharf, or worse, slam so hard against it that the impact caused damage to both wharf and vessel.

Now that the ship had berthed, men and women from the village poured from their homes, scurrying about the streets like agitated ants. Ferrying passengers and transporting goods were their only means of earning a living, and they clearly took it seriously. They swarmed up the pier to receive the crates and kegs and barrels that the ship's crew lowered onto the wharf. Even the older children helped carry the stuff onto barges and flatboats tied along the pier.

Once the ship's cargo hold had been emptied of trade goods, the horses were then unloaded.

Kyle led the gelding down the long wooden pier. Ordog, Armand, Eri, and Brother Luke followed close behind him with their mounts in tow.

When he and the gelding stepped onto solid ground, Kyle could have sworn that his warhorse was as glad as he was to stand once again on dry land. With mincing steps at the end of its tether, the noble creature tossed its head and nudged him with its long nose.

Evidently the villagers' work was only half done. They now set about removing goods from the two warehouses and carrying them up the pier to the wharf, where they placed them into cargo nets for the crew to bring aboard the ship. Nobody stopped to rest. They were in a fight against time. The work had to be done before the tide changed. Otherwise, the ship would be stranded in the river for another six hours before it could make its way back to the estuary and out into the open sea beyond.

Kyle and those with him waited patiently while the villagers finished the task at hand. He then approached an able-bodied waterman in his fifties who appeared to be one of several supervisors overseeing the work.

"We would like to cross the river," he said to the waterman. "Can you arrange for someone to ferry us to the far side?"

The waterman scratched the salt and pepper stubble on his chin. "Well, now," he said, his brow furrowed in thought. "I could do that for ye. Where are ye bound?"

"London," Kyle said.

"For a small fee," the waterman said, "I could take ye all the way there by barge."

Kyle groaned inwardly at the thought of getting back on a boat. "I would prefer to go by land."

"That would take ye at least two days," the waterman said. "I could get ye there in hours."

Kyle turned to his companions. "What do you think?"

Ordog shrugged his shoulders. "Whatever you choose to do is all right with me."

"I will go along with whatever you decide," Armand said.

"Me, too," Eri said.

"I'm for taking the barge," Brother Luke said.

Although reluctant to board a watercraft of any kind, Kyle had to admit that it would save them more than a day of hard riding. "How much will it cost for you to ferry us to London?" he said to the waterman.

"Four pennies in the king's silver," the waterman said. "That covers the four of ye and yer horses. No charge for the holy man and his mount."

Kyle suppressed a sigh. "When can we leave?"

"As soon as ye pay the fare," the waterman said.

Kyle opened his coin purse and dug out four pennies, which he dropped in the waterman's waiting hand.

The waterman tucked the money into the pouch at his side. “Wait here,” he said over his shoulder as he started up the pier.

His barge was one of the last ones still tied to the pilings. The rest of the villagers had already set out up the river with their small vessels laden with goods.

The waterman stepped onto the wooden deck of his flat-bottomed boat, where three other men in off-white shirts belted at the waist over tan leggings were binding the crates to the deck with ropes.

“The cargo is secure,” said a muscular young man who gave the knot he’d just tied a final tug. “Shall we go?”

“Only after we get that lot on board,” the waterman said, tilting his head at Kyle and those with him.

“We’re full up,” the young man said. “Where do ye plan to put them?”

“Stack those crates a mite higher,” the waterman said. “That should clear a space for them.”

“Those horses could spell trouble we don’t need,” the young man said with a stubborn set to his jaw.

“They’ve already paid their way,” the waterman said, producing four silver coins.

The young man’s whole demeanor changed at the sight of the money. “Ye shoulda said that in the first place,” he said with an avaricious grin.

The waterman gave each of the three crewmen a coin and kept one for himself. He then untied the mooring line, after which he and his men used long poles to push away from the pier.

With coordination that came from long practice, the four of them—two on one side and two on the other—maneuvered the barge until the blunt front end slid onto the sandy shore.

The barge was too high to bring the horses on board. Two of the men produced a narrow ten-foot ramp to bridge the gap between deck and shore.

The wooden ramp looked sturdy enough to support the weight of a horse. In addition, it had cross strips every twelve inches to prevent boots and hooves from slipping during wet weather conditions.

The waterman signaled for Kyle and those with him to approach. "Let's get ye loaded up," he said, jumping down into knee-deep water to hold the access ramp steady.

Kyle went first, leading the gelding up the incline and onto the barge. Because there was no cargo hold on a flatboat due to its shallow draft, the horses would have to remain on the deck. For that reason, he looked for a place to stand where he and his mount would be out of the crewmen's way.

"That's a big warhorse ye have there," the waterman said. "Take him to the far end and make sure he stays centered. A sudden shift of his weight to one side or the other will upset the balance of the load and dump us all in the river."

Kyle did as he was bidden. There were no railings at either end of the barge for convenience of loading and unloading cargo. Consequently, he tied the reins to the rope binding a heavy crate to the barrel next to it. He placed a hand on the horse's bridle to keep the creature from moving around.

One after the other, Ordog, Armand, Eri, and Brother Luke urged their mounts up the ramp and onto the deck. They followed the waterman's directions to position the horses—two on one side and two on the other—to distribute their weight evenly on the barge. Once they'd lashed the reins to ropes binding the cargo in the middle, they, too, kept a hand on their horses' bridles.

It was unnecessary to pivot the barge since there was no difference between bow and stern. After stowing the narrow ramp on board, the waterman and his crew simply pushed off from shore with their poles and started up the river. Each one worked in harmony with the others, like a well-ordered team.

Going against the flow was no easy task, which was why they stayed close to the shoreline, where the current was not as strong.

There was nothing for Kyle and the others to do for the next few hours except watch the scenery go by.

The river had an unpleasant smell. They soon got used to it, after which it was hardly noticeable. Flat empty marshland on either side gave way to higher ground with rutted lanes and thatch-roofed dwellings. The farther up the river they traveled, the more houses and barns and garden plots there were to be seen.

It was early afternoon when the waterman and his crew stopped to rest for a quarter of an hour. They ate a light meal of bread and smoked fish, which they shared with Kyle and those with him. When they finished eating, the waterman passed around a jug of mead, of which they all partook.

After taking a swig of the sweet brew, Kyle handed the jug back to the waterman. "What is London like?"

The waterman plugged the open mouth of the jug with a cork and set it aside. "Where are ye from?"

"A small town up north." Kyle did not think it

necessary to elaborate on how far north. Nor did he consider it prudent to mention the name of the Scottish town for obvious reasons.

"A small town, ye say?"

"Aye," Kyle said.

"Well, now," the waterman said, brushing crumbs from his lips with the back of his hand. "Prepare yerself for a shock. London is nothing like anything ye have ever seen before."

"Can you be more specific?"

"The streets are narrow and crowded. Too many folks live inside the city walls. Space is limited. Houses rise three and four stories in the air. The upper floors hang over the street in such a way that sunlight never reaches the ground. The air is foul from garbage thrown in the streets and offal from chamber pots emptied into the gutters. Shall I go on?"

"Nay," Kyle said, holding up his hand. "I've heard enough to get an idea of what to expect."

"Do ye still want to go there?"

"Aye," Kyle said.

"Why?"

"The call of duty."

"If ye must, then what can ye do, eh?" the waterman said with sympathy. "I like open spaces myself, where I can feel the wind in my face and smell fresh air." He picked up his pole and signaled to his men. "Up and at 'em, lads."

The other three men retrieved their poles and positioned themselves at their respective stations. On the waterman's command, they resumed poling in tandem. Arm and shoulder muscles rippled under homespun shirts stained with sweat.

They continued poling their way up the River Thames as it snaked its way inland. In among the many twists and turns was an occasional straight stretch, where the river became wider and shallower. That was not necessarily an advantage for anyone who navigated the waters because of the silt deposits that accumulated in the shallows. Those mounds of sediment presented a hazard to all watercraft. Even flat-bottomed boats with a low draft had been known to run aground on them.

Then, there were places where the river grew narrower and the water flowed more swiftly. That was common in crooks and bends, of which there were many along the length of the river's course.

When the horses were first loaded onto the barge, the waterman had been especially particular about their placement on deck. The significance of that became all too clear when they encountered an unusually sharp bend in the river.

Upon entering the turn, the barge tilted slightly as the force of the water pushed against the port side of the hull. The starboard side scraped along the high bank that had been cut out by the current over the years. Then, the fore corner got hung up on protruding roots in the mud wall. Without warning, the port side dipped lower, and the now-stalled barge began to take on water.

"Put yer backs into it, lads," the waterman bellowed to his crewmen. "Ye there with the horses," he shouted over his shoulder to Kyle and the others. "Keep yer mounts as steady as ye can." The urgency in his voice bordered on panic.

In desperation, Kyle clung to the gelding's bridle, uttering nonsensical words in a soothing tone to keep the horse calm while the deck underfoot tilted wildly. Being a heavy-shanked muscular animal, the warhorse could easily have flung him aside with a single toss of its head. All the same, it had been trained to obey its master, especially under distressing circumstances, like those common to a field of battle.

Despite flared nostrils and rolling eyes, the gelding remained stationary, its legs braced to contend with the unnatural angle of the deck, its ears pricked to the sound of its master's voice.

Meanwhile, the waterman and his crew poled frantically to dislodge the corner of the barge from the tangled roots. Once they pushed free of the undercut portion of the mud bank, the barge leveled out and ceased taking on water. They rounded the bend without further mishap, after which everyone on board heaved an audible sigh of relief.

Two of the crewmen set about bailing the excess water from the floor of the boat with wooden pails kept handy for that purpose.

Had the horses not been placed just so on the deck, the imbalance of their weight would have caused the barge to capsize and dump the load. Not only would the cargo be lost, but there was also the possibility that those on board might drown in the treacherous current.

Kyle tacitly acknowledged the waterman's wisdom and experience by doing his best thereafter to keep the gelding from shifting around, as did his companions with their horses, in the interest of maintaining the stability of the load.

Before long, Kyle caught sight of the walled city of London in the distance. His anticipation grew as each stroke of the pole brought him closer to completing the task that had been assigned to him, which was delivering Sir Percy's letters to the king of England. Once he fulfilled that duty, he could return home to his family whom he longed to see after so many weeks apart.

He wondered how Joneta was faring and how much his infant son and his toddler stepson had grown in his absence. He'd left them in good hands before his departure. Yet it troubled him that they were still in Ayrshire, where growing enmity between Scottish folk and English soldiers might culminate in open hostility at any time. He dared not dwell on such disturbing thoughts. There was nothing he could do about it at the moment, and that bothered him the most.

In the course of his musings, the poisoning of Sir Guy de Forz came to mind as it often did, unbidden yet not necessarily unwelcome. Since he and Reginald had to leave in the middle of their investigation, he wondered whether the English marshal from the local garrison had made any progress on the case in their absence, or if he and the sheriff would have to pick up where they'd left off upon their return to Ayr.

Another matter for consideration was the sudden demise of Sir Kenneth de Forz, Sir Guy's brother. Sir Kenneth's retainers had claimed devilry was the cause of their master's death. Still, there had to be a more realistic down-to-earth explanation for it. Although Penrith was out of his jurisdiction, he would make it his business to pass through there on the way home. Perhaps by then, the local constabulary would have determined how Sir Kenneth had actually died and why there were no visible marks on his body.

By that time, the walled city loomed just ahead of

him. The late afternoon breeze coiled softly around him, bringing with it the foul odor of a castle midden.

Earlier in the journey, when he had first approached Newcastle, he'd been impressed with the height of its walls. The fortifications encircling London were much more formidable than those surrounding that northern city on the River Tyne. These walls appeared to be twice as high and were likely twice as thick, as well.

There were also landmarks—the Tower of London being one of them—that he recognized, not from personal experience, but from tales related to him by acquaintances who had visited the city.

The Tower jutted up over the eastern wall, its crenellations stark against pink and orange clouds in the western sky. Political prisoners were often relegated to a stay of indeterminate length on the upper floors, until either executed or pardoned, based on the severity of their crimes against the crown. There were also a handful of detainees who languished in confinement there because of the threat they posed to the throne of England. Their fate depended on the mood of the monarch who had imprisoned them and the extent of civil unrest taking place at the time.

Another thing he'd heard about the Tower was that the lower floors had served as the royal residence for past kings. Edward of England had lived there for years with his queen. After her death eight years ago, he chose to reside elsewhere, although he was known to return on occasion to spend a week or two in the royal suite.

That being the case, the king may not even be in London at the moment. Thus, he—Kyle—would have to make discreet inquiries to ascertain the king's whereabouts before applying for an audience to deliver the letters.

"Make ready to dock," the waterman said in a loud voice.

That roused Kyle from his reverie. "Can we enter the city there?"

"Nay," the waterman said. "The postern gate is reserved for the king's troops only. Common folk like us go in through Aldgate. It's just up the road. Ye can't miss it."

The waterman and his crew drew abreast of a long wharf made of stone, where other boats already moored there were being loaded or unloaded. With the skill of long practice, they maneuvered the flatboat into an empty slot. Two of the crewmen jumped onto the stone landing and tied ropes, both fore and aft, around sturdy wooden bollards to secure the barge.

Half a dozen men descended from horse-drawn wagons parked nearby and came over to help the waterman and his crew offload the cargo. The men carried the goods back to their wagons and stacked it on the wooden beds.

With the crewmen otherwise engaged, Kyle and his companions were left to unload the horses on their own. Since the water was high due to a recent rain, the deck of the barge was nearly level with the edge of the wharf, with only a narrow gap between them. That made it easy for them to lead their mounts straight off the flatboat and onto the landing. Once they stood on solid ground, they gathered together in the shadow of the Tower wall a dozen yards from the bank of the Thames.

"I reckon this is where we go our separate ways," Kyle said.

"Aye, it is." Brother Luke swung up into the saddle and gazed at each one in turn. "I am grateful that you let me ride along with you. I doubt I would have made it this far as quickly on my own. God bless and goodbye." With a parting wave, he turned his horse and set out at a trot up the inland road that ran beside the east wall of the city.

Kyle cast a questioning glance at Ordog.

"I'm going with you," Ordog said.

"And I'm going with him," Eri said, tilting her head at Armand.

"So you say," Ordog said with a frown.

"Aye, I do," she said, folding her arms and jutting a stubborn chin in his direction.

"If the two of you keep this up, it will be dark by the time you sort it out," Armand said. "Why don't we go to the nearest tavern and eat what might be our last meal together. You can then discuss who goes with whom at your leisure."

"Great idea," Kyle said. "I'm for it." That was as good an excuse as any to spend a little more time with his traveling companions. He'd grown fond of them over the last few weeks. Plus, it would afford him an opportunity to listen to the prattle of local folks who frequented the public house. If luck was with him, he might even overhear something that could prove to be useful during his stay in the city.

Chapter 25

About midmorning on the day after their arrival in London, a guardsman escorted Kyle, Ordog, and Eri through the arched entryway of the White Tower. They walked into the large vestibule beyond, where guards stood at attention on either side of interior doors that led to other parts of the castle.

The guardsman set out for a doorway on the far side of the vestibule. Kyle and those with him followed close behind him. The clump of their boots on polished flagstones echoed with each step. High above them, enormous wooden beams vanished into the shadowy recesses of the vaulted ceiling.

The visit to the tavern the night before had been advantageous in that Kyle had learned that Edward of England was now in residence in one of the outbuildings within the Tower of London enclave. The occasion for the king's rare visit was the impending Feast of the Assumption on August fifteenth, which was just two days away. Prior to her death, Edward's first wife had faithfully attended High Mass at Saint Michael Paternoster on that day to commemorate Mary, the mother of Jesus.

As they crossed the floor, Kyle and Ordog gaped in awe at the splendor of their surroundings, craning their necks to take in artfully embroidered tapestries hanging on the walls, as well as numerous shields on display reflecting the heraldic coats of arms of noble families.

On the other hand, Eri trailed behind them with downcast eyes, her expression glum and her step slow. The evident cause of her somber mood was Armand's sudden departure after supper on the prior evening.

Ordog had refused to let her go out by herself to look for Armand, nor did he offer to join her in the search. His reason was a practical one. Neither of them knew their way around London or its environs. Thus, there was a good chance they might end up blundering into the dodgier sections of the city and needlessly exposing themselves to danger.

When they reached the doorway on the other side of the vestibule, the guardsman led them into a long corridor of hewn stone with an arched ceiling. Illumination came from lighted oil lanterns suspended from brackets affixed at intervals to both side walls.

They passed several closed doors along the way. After turning a corner, the guardsman opened the door at the end of the corridor and walked into the chamber beyond.

Kyle stepped into the room, squinting against the sunlight that poured in through the mullioned windows on the east wall. After the gloom of the corridor, the chamber seemed bright by comparison.

"Give yer name to the clerk and wait yer turn," the guardsman said. With a slight bow, he turned on his heel and withdrew from the room, closing the door behind him.

There were a dozen men in the room. They stood around in groups of two and three, talking in low voices. All were dressed in fine clothing cut in the latest style, ranging from midnight blue to dark red. Some wore velvet garments with slashed sleeves underlain with a contrasting color. Others had on short fitted tunics made of embroidered linen. Each wore matching hose to complete his ensemble. Their swords looked more ornamental than serviceable, with hilts studded with precious stones and narrow blades sheathed in silver scabbards.

The clerk was easy to spot among those gathered there. He wore a plain black cotte over black hose with a black skullcap on his head. He looked like a raven hunched over a sheet of paper vellum, perched on a stool at a tiny desk against the far wall beside a pair of ornate doors.

A couple of guards on either side of the doorway, which evidently led to the royal receiving chamber, stood at attention with their halberds grounded, their eyes forward and their faces impassive.

Kyle had taken care to make himself presentable in anticipation of appearing before the king of England. He'd even polished his boots for the occasion. Despite that, he was no match for the fashionable occupants of the room. His belted brown linen tunic was plain and unadorned, as were the sheathed dirk at his waist and the sword at his hip.

He walked across the room, ignoring disdainful glances cast his way by Englishmen who seemed more concerned about a fellow's appearance than his character. He now knew firsthand how Ordog and Eri must have felt when people treated them with contempt merely because they were Romany.

When he reached the clerk's desk, he stood there for a moment while the man made an entry on the paper vellum before him. Although he would have to wait his turn behind the men already in the room, he felt a distinct thrill that the end of his mission was so near at hand.

"What can I do for ye?" the clerk said, glancing up at the tall muscular man with pale blue eyes and windblown hair the color of a lion's mane. His dark eyes lingered briefly on the white seam of a scar that ran from temple to jaw on the otherwise handsome face of the fellow towering over him.

"I've come to see Edward of England," Kyle said. "Sir Henry Percy, Castellan of Ayr and Warden of Galloway, charged me with delivering these letters"—here he held up the leather courier pouch—"to the king."

"I'll see that His Majesty gets them," the clerk said, extending his hand, palm up.

"I was instructed to deliver the letters personally," Kyle said. "I am to wait for an answer, if there is one."

The clerk dipped the point of the quill into a tiny pot filled with black liquid. "Yer name?" he said, his pen now loaded with ink and ready to use.

"Kyle Shaw, deputy to the sheriff of Ayrshire."

Three Englishmen within earshot turned to stare at him. Their faces reflected contempt, which none of them bothered to conceal.

"Ayrshire, as in Scotland?" the clerk said with a frown.

"Aye," Kyle said with a nod.

The clerk hesitated for several heartbeats, his quill pen poised over the vellum. He apparently reached a decision, for he proceeded to write Kyle's name below the others on the list. He then thrust the quill into the holder at the edge of his desk and rose to his feet. "Wait until yer name is called," he said as he rounded the corner of his desk. He hastened over to the ornate doors and opened them wide enough to slip inside the receiving chamber.

Kyle took that as a dismissal. As he gazed around the room, he noticed Ordog standing by himself, looking very much like he—Kyle—felt: a drab sparrow in a room full of peacocks. He walked over to join the older man. "Where's Eri?"

Ordog tilted his head to indicate her location across the way.

Eri, who had been wandering aimlessly around the large room, ambled up to the ornate double doors. She paused to peer through the narrow gap that remained after the clerk had failed to close the doors completely behind him. She was apparently close enough to hear what was being said within the royal receiving chamber, yet far enough away to seem like she was only there by chance.

While standing before the doors, she brushed imaginary specks of lint from her shirt sleeves, clearly listening to those within without appearing to do so. Suddenly, her countenance changed in a blink from utter boredom to intense interest. She turned away from the doorway to scan the room.

Kyle, who had been looking her way, caught her eye.

The instant she saw him, she started toward him at a brisk pace. On the way, she skirted clusters of men chatting and laughing together.

She halted in front of Kyle and Ordog. "We need to leave," she said to them, her voice urgent and low. "Now!"

"Why?" Kyle said. "We just got here."

Ordog stared at her in bewilderment.

"Someone in there ordered your arrest," she said to Kyle, jerking a thumb over her shoulder to indicate the receiving chamber. "They fear you might be a rebel sent to threaten the king."

Kyle shook his head over how quickly the purpose of his presence had been grossly misconstrued. It came as no surprise, though, for the mindset of most Englishmen was that all Scots were rebels on the verge of revolt. He glanced in the direction of the receiving chamber in time to see the clerk step through the ornate doors.

The clerk said something to one of the guards, who lifted his gaze to scrutinize the occupants of the waiting room.

"It's time to go," Kyle said.

The doorway leading to the corridor was only a couple of steps away. The three of them hastened from the room and shut the door behind them.

"What do we do now?" Ordog said. "Even if we run, they will surely catch us. They know their way around this castle better than we do."

Kyle started down the corridor. On turning the corner, he came to the first door. He put his hand on the latch and pushed it open. The room was small with no place to hide. He closed the door and continued down the corridor. He tried the second door and then the third, but neither room was suitable. On opening the fourth door, he saw what might be a meeting room. He stepped inside with Ordog and Eri hard on his heels.

There was a huge fireplace on one wall and a large table in the center of the room with carved wooden chairs around it. Three sizeable wooden storage cabinets with shelves filled with scrolls occupied most of the space along a side wall.

"They are only looking for me, so I will hide," he said. "You two can sit at the table." He told them what to say if someone came into the room and wanted to know why they were there.

He climbed into a nook where the guards were least likely to find him. After a short wait, sure enough, somebody barged into the room. He could not see who it was, but from the harsh timbre of the man's voice, he surmised it was one of the castle guards tasked with his arrest.

"What are you doing in this room?" the intruder demanded.

"Sir Miles Aldensford bade us to wait for him here," Ordog said calmly.

"What would he want with the likes of you?" the intruder said, his tone demeaning.

"Perhaps you should ask him that," Ordog said, unruffled. "He is the one who arranged this meeting."

After a tense moment of silence, the intruder left the room with a huff of contempt and slammed the door behind him.

"He's gone," Ordog said. "You can come out now."

"Let's give it a few more minutes, just in case," Kyle said from his place of concealment. True, it was tiring to remain where he'd hidden. Yet, that was nothing compared to being chained to a wall in an English prison with an iron collar around his neck and manacles on his wrists.

After what he deemed a sufficient time for the

guards to move along to another part of the castle, he climbed down from his precarious perch. He'd been up inside the flue, straddling the fireplace below, with his feet propped on the narrow lip of stone that ran around the inside of the chimney. He was glad it was still summer. Otherwise, there would be a blaze in the fireplace, which would have rendered the chimney useless as a place to hide.

His hands were black with soot from touching the inner walls of the chimney flue. Any effort he made to dust the streaks of grime from his clothing only made them worse. "Shall we go?" he said with a sweep of a sooty hand toward the doorway.

Ordog opened the door and stuck his head out far enough to glance up and down the corridor. "All clear."

Kyle led the way out of the meeting room and into the corridor. He trudged back the way he'd come earlier, his ears stretched for any sign of pursuit. He and those with him nearly made it to the vestibule where they'd first entered the Tower when he heard the sound of hurried footsteps coming up behind him.

Chapter 26

Kyle glanced over his shoulder to see who was approaching from the rear. Despite the subdued light from oil lanterns in the narrow corridor, there was still sufficient illumination for him to discern that it was not an armed guardsman in hot pursuit, much to his relief.

Rather, it was one of the Englishmen who had been in the waiting room. He was the stout fellow in a forest green cotte with a jaunty cap and fitted hose of the same hue.

Without a word, Eri turned on her heel and headed back up the narrow passageway. She hastened past the stout man and appeared to continue on her way.

When the stout man came within ten feet of Kyle and Ordog, he stopped in his tracks. "You! Traitor!" he said, his voice sharp with alarm. He opened his mouth, as though to shout.

In the next instant—much to Kyle's surprise—the stout man closed his mouth and simply stood there, mute and unmoving, as if rooted to the stone floor.

Kyle exchanged a questioning glance with Ordog. On taking a closer look, only then did he notice the steel blade pressed against the side of the stout man's throat. It was Eri's, of course, which explained the reason for her ploy to get behind the man.

"Let's get him out of the hallway," Kyle said, "lest someone else come along." He strode over to the nearest door and pushed it open. After determining there was no one in the room, he turned back to his companions. "In here," he said, motioning for them to enter.

Eri steered the now-compliant man through the open doorway with Ordog behind her.

Kyle cast a last glance up and down the corridor before slipping inside and closing the door behind him.

He paused just inside the doorway and gazed around the room, taking in the accoutrements contained therein. On hindsight, he was unsure if this was the ideal place to hide. They had apparently stepped into an armory.

The late morning sun beamed in through a small window in the back wall, shedding light on axes and lances and crossbows of various sizes and configurations affixed to the wall on the left. Half a dozen racks displaying metal suits of armor with chain mail coifs stood against the wall on the right under the crimson and gold pennant of England. Six highly polished Norman helmets gleamed in the light of day on a table in the center of the room. Six pairs of mesh gauntlets lay in a row on the same table.

Ordog tore a strip of cloth from the hem of his shirt and used it to gag their prisoner. "This should keep him quiet, in case he had any notion of crying out for help."

"Good thinking," Kyle said with a nod of approval.

"So what shall we do with him?" Ordog said, tilting his head at their captive.

"He is our means for safe passage out of here," Kyle said. To the stout man, he said, "Take off your clothes."

The man's expression changed from intense

concern to abject horror. His eyes widened as he shook his head with vigor.

"I would hate to befoul such a nice garment with your blood," Kyle said in a menacing tone. "So either you do it, or I will do it for you."

"I'll be glad to give you a hand," Eri said, eyeing the captive in a meaningful way while using the tip of her dagger to clean under her fingernails.

"Why take his clothing?" Ordog said. "We can just tie him up and leave him here until somebody finds him."

"The guards are looking for a fair-haired Scotsman in a brown tunic," Kyle said.

"But they won't even notice a tall man dressed in green clothing," Eri said with a knowing grin.

"Precisely." Kyle turned to the stout man and leveled a piercing gaze at him. "Well?"

With great reluctance, the man removed his cap and his sword belt, after which he began peeling off his clothes, one piece at a time. At last, he stood before them wearing nothing more than a pair of black leather boots and a flimsy off-white linen undershirt that reached the middle of his thighs.

Eri picked up the garments and handed them to Kyle. She then turned her back to him and walked over to where the crossbows hung on the wall. She stood there, looking at each one in turn, as though inspecting the mechanism to see how it worked.

Kyle shed his tunic and donned the forest green cotte, tucking the courier pouch inside the front of the garment. The fabric was tight across his broad shoulders, and the sleeves were too short. He then pulled on the hose, which rode low on his hips due to the length of his legs. He raked back his hair with his fingers and twisted it into a tight knot, which he stuffed under the cap that he placed on his head.

Other than being uncomfortable in the ill-fitting outfit, at least he looked presentable. That is, if he didn't have to run or sit or breathe too deeply.

Ordog tore another couple of strips from the bottom of his shirt. With Eri's help, he bound the captive's hands and feet to keep him immobilized while they made their escape.

"The guards will likely be on the lookout for my two Romany accomplices," Kyle said. To Ordog, he said, "How about putting on my tunic to throw them off your trail?"

Ordog removed his belt and slipped the brown tunic over his head. Since he was shorter than Kyle, the garment hung down to his ankles, which hid the baggy pants beneath. He slung the belt around his waist and buckled it. "What about you?" he said to Eri.

"There is no more clothing to be had," she said. "I'll be fine."

"I beg to differ," Kyle said, his gaze on the stout man sitting on the floor, gagged and bound both hand and foot. To Ordog, he said, "Help me take off his shirt, will you?"

The two of them removed the article of clothing with an effort and laid a couple of gauntlets across his lap for the sake of modesty, not for his but for Eri's.

Eri put on the linen shirt and tied it at the waist with a leftover strip of cloth from Ordog's shirt. The garment was rather voluminous for her slender frame, yet it served the purpose of concealing the clothes that identified her as Romany.

"Just so you know," Kyle said to the captive, "I am only borrowing your clothes. You can fetch them from the nearest church, which is where I will leave them. And by the way, I'm not a rebel."

"Are we just going to abandon him here?" Eri said. "What if nobody finds him in time? He could starve to death."

"With all the weapons at hand," Kyle said, "I am certain he will free himself in no time at all. The problem is whether we can depart from the castle grounds before he alerts the guards and sends them after us."

"We'd better get a move on, then." Ordog opened the door and looked into the corridor. "Let's go."

They filed from the room and hurried up the corridor to the door that led to the vestibule.

Kyle halted with his hand on the latch. "Eri, you go first. Walk slowly, as though you have all the time in the world. When you get outside, go around to where we left the horses. Ride from the grounds without haste. Do not look back. Once you pass under the last archway, go to the nearest church and wait for us there. We'll find you."

Eri nodded her head, her jaw set and her lips pressed together in determination.

Kyle opened the door and stepped aside.

She took a deep breath and walked through the doorway.

Kyle pulled the door partially closed, leaving a two-inch crack through which he watched her amble across the flagstones to the outlet on the far side of the vestibule.

The guards beside the entryway hardly spared her a

glance as she passed under the stone archway on the way outside.

"You're next," Kyle said to Ordog.

The older man ran a finger under the collar of his shirt beneath the brown tunic, as though the fabric had suddenly grown too tight around his neck. Beads of sweat formed on his forehead, and two vertical lines appeared between his dark eyebrows. He drew in a shaky breath and let it out in a soft hiss before stepping through the doorway into the vestibule.

By way of the gap between the door and the wooden jamb, Kyle watched Ordog walk over to the outlet across the room and vanish through the arched entryway without mishap.

Now, it was his turn. With freedom a mere twenty paces away, what could possibly go wrong?

He filled his lungs with air and stepped into the vestibule, headed toward the outlet. As he sauntered across the floor, he kept his head down and his cap pulled low. That would not entirely conceal his face, but it did make it harder to see.

On the way, he kept a furtive eye on the guardsmen on either side of the outlet. His only hope was that they were looking for a man in a brown tunic with a scar on his face.

He was a couple of steps from the arched outlet when one of the guards said something to him. He stopped in his tracks, every muscle in his body coiled like a tight spring, ready for fight or flight. "Did you say something to me?" he said without turning his head.

"Aye, m'lord," the guard on the left said. "Ye dropped something. I am not at liberty to leave my post to retrieve it for ye."

He lifted a hand to his brow on the pretext of adjusting the cap on his head, where in reality the gesture was meant to cover the scarred side of his face as he turned to see what he'd dropped.

About ten feet behind him, a scrap of white linen with lacy edges lay crumpled on the floor in a tiny heap. Rather than leave it, which was his first inclination, he decided it would be more convincing to retrieve such a fine article.

He turned on his heel and started toward the lacy handkerchief. He'd taken four steps when the door on the far side of the vestibule flew open.

The stout man burst through the doorway with the crimson and yellow pennant from the weapons room wrapped about his waist. He skidded to a stop on the smooth flagstone floor, causing the loose ends of the silky banner to flap against his bare thighs. "Stop that varlet," he shouted. He pointed directly at Kyle with one hand, while holding the pennant in place with the other hand. "He's a thief."

Thinking quickly, Kyle extended his arm and pointed at the stout man. "That's him," he said in a loud voice. "That's the man who stole my coin purse." He glanced over his shoulder at the guardsmen on either side of the entryway, both of whom gazed back at him with bewilderment on their faces. "Don't just stand there," he said to them. "Arrest the villain before he runs away."

The two guardsmen looked from Kyle attired in splendid finery to the wild-eyed man with a colorful banner swaddling the lower half of his naked body. They apparently decided which of the two had committed a crime. With a nod to each other, they trotted toward the stout man with their halberds leveled at his chest.

"Not me, you fools," the stout man snarled as they drew near. "Him!" He jabbed a blunt finger in Kyle's direction. "He's the culprit."

By that time, Kyle had swung around and sprinted out the entryway into radiant light from the sun at its zenith. With his eyes narrowed against the glare, he hurried down the stone stairs and ran around the side of the Tower building where he'd left the gelding tied to the rail. He loosened the reins with a sharp tug and leaped into the saddle.

The gelding responded to the urgent prodding of his heels against its ribs and broke into a canter.

The fact that he'd fled the scene must have persuaded the guardsmen of his guilt. He could hear their shouts behind him as they rushed through the entryway into the inner courtyard.

"Shut the gate," bellowed one of the guardsmen to his comrades on the castle wall.

Kyle leaned low over the gelding's neck, urging the horse to a faster pace. With the furious pounding of galloping hooves in his ears, he hurtled up the sloped ramp that led to the arched outlet of the gatehouse ahead.

With the exception of Traitor's Gate, which was accessible only by boat from the River Thames, this was the first of eight arched gateways that he must pass under in order to get clear of the castle grounds. Such were the stringent defensive measures that had been employed to protect the kings and queens of England and their noble families.

Three soldiers on the wall above the first stone

archway scurried over to a huge wooden winch. Thick heavy chains clanked and whined in protest as the trio put their backs into cranking the handle to lower the portcullis.

Metal scraped against metal as the massive iron-barred gate with sharp spikes along the bottom descended slowly. Kyle held his breath as the gelding raced toward the ever-decreasing opening, hoping against hope that he could make it through before it was too late.

Then, by some miracle of timing, he swept under the pointed iron teeth of the portcullis with barely an inch to spare.

That took him into a long dark tunnel adjoining the archway. The beat of hooves on cobblestones echoed off the confining walls and low ceiling. About halfway along, he hauled back on the reins to slow the gelding's pace.

When he came out the other end of the tunnel, he laid the reins on his mount's neck to make a sharp right turn. Otherwise, both horse and rider would end up at the iron grating that barred the way to the river at Traitor's Gate.

He halted his mount under the next archway and removed his cloak from his saddle roll. He slung the dark red garment over his shoulders and took off the cap, which he tucked under his belt. If the soldiers were looking for a man in green, they would be hard-pressed to find him now.

Iron-shod hooves rang against stone as Kyle urged the gelding into a trot down the length of a long narrow street-like courtyard with walls on either side. He did his best to blend in with townsfolk there who were either coming or going. Some were headed for the inner bailey with wagons loaded with foodstuff and other salable products. Those on the way out drove empty wagons, apparently having delivered their goods. All were engaged in the business of supplying the amenities necessary to manage a fully staffed castle and extant manor houses located on the Tower grounds.

At the end of the long courtyard, Kyle rode under another arched outlet before entering a short tunnel with a watchtower over it. None of the soldiers on the crenellated tower above him challenged his passage, so he continued on to a narrow causeway that took him across a moat that was nearly eighty feet wide.

Water from the river fed the moat that encircled the Tower of London and the grounds around it. A dyke-like embankment of earth bordered the outer rim of the moat, adding yet another layer of defense for the protection of those of royal blood who lived inside the walls.

Kyle rode through another short tunnel with a watchtower over it smaller than the one before it. That brought him to a short ramp, which led to a tiny half-moon bailey surrounded by water. A hard right took him through three successive arched gateways before he finally ended up on dry land well outside the castle walls.

Although he was no longer on Tower grounds, he was still within range of both crossbow and long bow. Those were the weapons of choice by soldiers posted along the wall because of the distant reach of either weapon in the hands of a skilled archer. With that in mind, he nudged the gelding into a canter along the grassy verge and turned left at the first street he came across, thus ensuring that he was no longer an easy target.

He slowed the gelding to a walk after spotting a small stone church nestled among humble dwellings built of wood that huddled together on either side of the street.

The street he'd chosen was the one closest to both the river and the castle grounds. It also led directly into the city, which was why it bustled with activity. Pony-drawn wagons and dog carts traveling in either direction jostled one another as they passed each other on the narrow lane.

Urchins with grubby faces and ragged clothing ran between the wagons, raising shouts of anger from the drivers. Men in threadbare garments loitered in groups of three and four along the street. Women washed clothes in wooden tubs in front of their houses or they swept their walkways with straw brooms or sat on low stools in the shadow of jutting eaves with their babies on their laps.

In addition to the shabby occupants of even shabbier houses, the foul smell of the river and the stench of offal hung in the air. That brought the waterman's description of London to mind. He could only imagine what the rest of the city was like if it was this bad on the outer edge where there were fewer residents. His only consolation was that he would leave this place as quickly as he'd come once he took care of the business at hand.

He turned into the diminutive church yard, where Eri and Ordog were sitting on the grass in the shade of a tree.

"What took you so long?" Ordog said, rising to his

feet. There was no mistaking the worried expression on his weathered face. “I thought something happened to you.”

“I ran into a bit of trouble,” Kyle said as he brought his mount to a halt. “I really need to get out of these clothes as soon as possible.”

Eri got up and dusted the grass from the seat of her pants. “Does your haste have anything to do with the trouble you ran into?”

“It certainly does,” Kyle said, swinging down from the saddle.

Ordog removed his belt and slipped the brown tunic over his head.

Kyle took his tunic from the older man. He removed the courier pouch from where he had hidden it in his cotte and placed it on the saddle while he changed into his own clothes as quickly and as modestly as he could, using the horses to block the view of prying eyes.

In the meantime, Eri removed the off-white linen undershirt.

Kyle secured the letter pouch in his saddle roll before folding each piece of the borrowed green clothing, including the cap, and wrapping them in the undershirt. He then walked around to the back of the church and knocked at the rectory door.

A short man of middle years in a loose black robe opened the door. “May I help you, brother?”

“Are you the verger?” Kyle said.

“I am.”

“A man will come by here either later today or tomorrow to collect this from you.” Kyle handed over the bundle with a silver penny on top of it. “Please convey my thanks to him for the use of it."

The verger's eyes lit up at the sight of the coin. "Will do," he said as he took the bundle. "What do I say if he asks who gave this to me?"

"He already knows," Kyle said dryly.

"All right, then, you can count on me to do as you ask," the verger said with a smile before he closed the door.

"Well, then," Ordog said. "Where do we go from here?"

"We're in London now," Kyle said. "There should be shops aplenty where we can purchase finery to wear."

"Has the use of one fine garment given you a taste for luxury?" Ordog said.

"Of course not," Kyle said with a shake of his head.

"Then why do we need fancy clothes?" Ordog said. "Is what we have on not sufficient?"

"Not if we want to blend in with English gentry," Kyle said.

"We tried that already," Ordog said. "It didn't work out so well."

"It will this time," Kyle said. "On August fifteenth—that's the day after tomorrow—the king will attend Mass at Saint Michael Paternoster. That is where we shall deliver Sir Percy's letters to him."

"We tried that already, too," Ordog said.

"Only this time we won't fail," Kyle said with determination.

Chapter 27

The day had finally arrived: August fifteenth, the Feast of the Assumption. Kyle, Ordog, and Eri left their mounts in the tavern stable and walked up the street in the midmorning sun, on their way to Paternoster Lane.

Kyle tugged on the hem of the maroon linen tunic that barely reached the top of his thighs. Fitted leggings of the same color accentuated the muscles in his legs. To complete his ensemble, he wore a soft maroon cap, the peak of which hung low over one ear. If the need arose, he could shift the droopy end forward slightly to conceal the scar on his face.

His only adornment was the sheathed dirk attached to the leather belt around his waist. He'd left his sword in the room at the public house, lest he be denied entry to the church for bearing a weapon. To alter his appearance, he'd cut his shoulder-length tresses, leaving a cropped cap of tawny hair on his head, most of which was hidden under his cap. Instead of carrying the courier pouch in his hand, he'd tucked it inside the front of his tunic.

Ordog looked imposing in a russet velvet cotte with matching hose. Puffy slashed sleeves showed a flash of yellow from shoulder to wrist. He, too, wore his dagger on his belt and had trimmed his hair and his mustache for the occasion.

Of the three of them, Eri's transformation was the

most remarkable. She had on a powder blue chemise under a fitted dark blue kirtle. A sheathed dagger hung from a delicate chain attached to the light blue sash around her slender waist. There wasn't much she could do with short hair, so she'd covered her dark curls with a thin white gauzy wimple secured to her head by a narrow silver circlet. She'd exchanged her leather boots for delicate white slippers that peeked out from under her skirts with every step she took. Now in her true form as a woman, her stunning appearance brought stares of appreciation from males and looks of envy from females whom she passed on her way to the church.

When the three of them came to Paternoster Lane, they continued on to the church, where they turned right to enter the grounds. They cut across the open yard, walking through summer grass still damp with morning dew.

Saint Michael Paternoster, so named for the street on which it was located, was a large red brick church with pale yellow sandstone trim that set off the round-headed windows and square-headed doorways.

A square stone bell tower over three stories high dominated the right front portion of the edifice. Under the gable on the front wall, there was a huge circular window. Below that was an enclosed porch-like entrance hall, which extended from the tower on the right to the left edge of the church building.

The gray slate roof was peaked along the center with sloping sides, except for the part where the tower wall adjoined the roof. That portion was flat, like a catwalk that served as a lookout over the graveyard below. The elevated walkway on the roof was rarely used because it was accessible only through a narrow door on the top floor of the tower. For the safety of those who did go up there, it had around it a marble balustrade that ran the length of the building.

The only blight to the pristine beauty of the church was the scaffolding that jutted up past the roof at the back of the building. Although unsightly, the structure was necessary for the masons to complete the work of enlarging the vestry at the rear.

The graveyard lay to the right of the church building, with lichen-covered headstones protruding at various angles from hallowed ground. A statue of Michael the Archangel stood on a sandstone pedestal directly below the catwalk, facing the burial grounds like a lone sentinel keeping watch over the dead. The life-sized statue was fashioned from black marble. Its right arm was extended over its head, and its right hand held a long bronze sword pointing skyward, as though ready to battle the great dragon for the souls in its care.

Kyle and his companions fell in step with well-dressed lords and ladies on their way into the church. They kept a cautious eye on the guardsmen who were lined up on either side of the walkway as a security precaution during the king's annual visit.

The three of them followed the crowd through the front entryway of the church and into the cool gloom of the vestibule.

As Kyle walked across the smooth slate floor, he detected the fragrance of incense that emanated from the small chapel on his left. The narrow door on the right side of the vestibule led to the stairwell in the bell tower.

He, Ordog, and Eri continued on through the

arched opening just ahead to gain access to the spacious nave, where the heavy scent of beeswax candles hung in the air. The three of them took up a position behind those who had arrived before them.

He glanced around him, aware that he stood out among the men of average height gathered there. In an effort to make himself less conspicuous, he squeezed through the press of bodies to stand beside a tall man in a red velvet cotte with gold trim. Ordog and Eri moved forward to take up a position behind him.

A surfeit of windows along both sides illuminated the interior of the church. Reflected light from white plastered walls made the nave seem even brighter. On the vaulted ceiling overhead, exposed timber beams ran from one side wall to the other, like giant ribs. An embroidered white cloth covered the rectangular granite altar at the front. The door beside the confessional on the left side of the chancel led to the vestry behind the altar.

Above the archway at the back of the church connecting the vestibule to the nave, statues of saints stood side by side on a narrow ledge under the circular window. The ledge was railed for the safety of the cleaners and accessible only through a small door in the bell tower wall.

Unlike a cathedral that had reserved seating along the side walls for nobles and their families, Saint Michael's had no such permanent accommodations. Since the king visited the church but once a year on the Feast of the Assumption, the rector hired carpenters prior to that to build a raised platform complete with cushioned chairs on which the king and his son could sit during that particular commemorative occasion.

Every year, the king bestowed a generous donation on the rector for the upkeep of Saint Michael's.

The crowd in the nave grew steadily larger as the hour drew closer for High Mass to begin. Before long, the tramp of boots on the slate floor of the vestibule signaled the arrival of the king in the midst of a small troop of elite soldiers.

The hum of voices trailed away as the sixty-year-old reigning monarch entered the nave with his entourage trailing after him. Heads turned on craning necks to catch a glimpse of him resplendent in royal attire.

Edward of England stood straight and tall, looking every inch a king. At a height of six feet two inches, he towered head and shoulders above the royal guardsmen who surrounded him. Instead of a crown, he wore a gold circlet studded with precious stones. There was a sharp intelligence in the wide-set blue eyes that stared straight ahead. White streaks had invaded the dark blond curls on his head. His reddish-blond beard—neatly clipped and veined with gray—encircled a narrow implacable mouth, which was a legacy of his Angevin forebears who were noted for their mercurial behavior, violent tempers, and a propensity to great cruelty.

The crown prince, who walked beside the king, looked younger than his fourteen years. Edward the Second was thin and tall with curly blond hair like his father in his youth. The resemblance ended there, however, for his face was round and his lips full, with soft brown eyes beneath a broad forehead. Unlike his father who exuded confidence, the young man looked ill at ease at being the center of attention, as reflected by the nervous habit of gnawing his bottom lip.

Edward the King mounted the stairs of the waist-high platform with his son a step behind him.

The instant their sovereign sat down, the royal guard closed ranks in front of the platform and stood facing outward with hands resting on the hilts of their swords. They alone were allowed to bear arms inside the church.

The nobles who had accompanied the king shuffled into position among those already gathered in the nave. Sir Miles Aldensford stood among the newcomers, looking dapper in a midnight blue cotte trimmed with silver cord.

A hush fell over the entire assembly at the tinkling of a tiny bell coming from the back of the church.

The crowd in the nave parted to let a small procession pass through their midst.

Three young altar boys in long white robes headed the column. The first youth rang the little bell intermittently. The second held aloft a long-shafted gold processional cross. The third carried a short staff with a brass censer suspended from the end on a fine chain. The sweet odor of smoldering incense wafted up from the perforated holder that swung gently with each step.

Four acolytes in white vestments over black cassocks came next, one after the other. Each bore a lighted candle in his hand.

An elderly priest stooped with age came after them, his pace slow and deliberate. The pale green chasuble that he wore over a long white linen tunic had a large gold cross embroidered on both front and back.

A dozen hooded monks brought up the rear, with

their heads bowed and hands tucked into the sleeves of their long black robes. Their sandals slapped against the soles of their feet as they walked.

The procession moved on to the chancel up front.

The monks gathered in the choir section on the right, standing shoulder to shoulder in two rows facing the altar. They pushed back their hoods in unison to reveal tonsured heads.

The elderly priest approached the altar in the center, while the acolytes and the altar boys dispersed to their designated stations on either side of him.

Prompted by a nod from the chief acolyte, the altar boy with the little bell rang it loudly for several seconds to signal the start of High Mass.

In a melodious tenor that reached every corner of the nave, the old priest lifted his voice in praise before the golden monstrance situated in the middle of the altar. He continued in a singsong voice as he conducted the service in Latin. The monks in the choir chanted a response to his every utterance in the same language.

With High Mass now underway, Kyle let his mind wander over the best way to deliver Sir Percy's letters to the king. Despite alterations to his appearance, he was still recognizable by his height and coloring, not to mention the scar on his face. As they had already discussed, if he or even Ordog tried to approach the king without invitation, their motives for doing so would immediately become suspect by the royal guard, whose sole duty was to protect the king at all cost, which included their lives, if necessary.

So, at this juncture, the only person who might have a decent chance of passing the letters along to the king would be Eri. Edward of England was said to have an eye for beauty. In feminine attire, Eri certainly fit that description. The most opportune moment for her to do it would be during communion, which was the only time during High Mass that the king would be on his own.

The three of them would then leave the church as quickly and as inconspicuously as possible. In the interim, they must remain alert and watchful of those around them, trying not to draw undue attention to themselves.

During one of his frequent glances around the nave, Kyle caught a glimpse of a man with blond streaks in his long brown hair. The fellow reminded him of Armand, except for the clothes he wore—a high-collared white brocade cotte threaded with gold that glinted in the light coming in through the church windows. Armand could never afford such finery. Before he could get a better look at the man, he lost sight of him in the crowd.

At the appointed time during the service, the old priest turned away from the altar and approached the pulpit, where he mounted a short stairway to speak to the assembly.

Kyle groaned inwardly, for he'd heard that this priest was known for long-winded sermons and fiery denunciations.

The old priest planted both hands on either side of a huge open Bible atop the oaken pulpit. Before expounding on the gospel from the scriptures, he launched into a flowery speech thanking the king and the nobles assembled there for coming to Saint Michael's to celebrate the Feast of the Assumption.

While the priest droned on, Kyle continued his

musings about delivering the letters, after which he and his companions could start the journey home.

Without warning, a heavy hand clamped down on his shoulder, jerking him back to the present. He spun around, only to stare into a pair of cold gray eyes.

The eyes belonged to the somber-faced guardsman who had chased him during his hasty departure from the Tower of London. A cohort of his stood beside him, looking equally grim.

"Well, well," the guardsman said in a low voice, ostensibly out of respect for the sanctity of the church. "Look what we have here."

Kyle caught Ordog's eye over the guardsman's shoulder and tilted his head ever so slightly, indicating that he should stay out of sight. It would not do for Ordog or Eri to get caught, too. He was also quick to notice that neither guardsman carried a weapon, a circumstance that might make it easier for him to escape their grasp.

Each of the guardsmen latched onto an arm to keep him from taking flight through the crowd. Before they could hustle him outside, the bell in the tower began to toll—a slow repeated bong that echoed from the rafters above.

The priest fell silent in the middle of a sentence, his brows drawn and lips pressed together in disapproval. He glared in the direction of the bell tower at the rear of the church, as though hoping to catch a glimpse of the scoundrel who dared interrupt his discourse.

The tolling of the bell ceased as abruptly as it had begun. Seconds later, a stentorian voice sounded forth from the back of the church. "Debase ye not the sovereign line, those born to reign by right divine, else face ye must the grievous bane, who cannot be by mortal slain."

Kyle looked to the rear of the nave in search of the speaker. He'd recognized in the voice some echo from far and away. The words, too, were hauntingly familiar, as though he'd heard them before, and not that long ago, either.

Everyone in the nave turned to look behind them, some in puzzlement and others out of curiosity.

"Look, there," cried a lady in the crowd, pointing up at the circular window at the back of the church.

A hooded man with a lighted candle in his hand stood among the row of statues on the ledge above the vestibule, silhouetted against the light coming in through the window. It was impossible to identify him by either size or shape, for he kept himself half hidden behind one of the statues.

Those assembled began to whisper to one another and mill about. The murmur of voices soon escalated to a low hum.

The hooded man extended his arm at full stretch with an accusatory finger pointed toward the platform where the king and the crown prince sat on cushioned chairs. "You are guilty," he said in a thunderous tone, "before the God of Heaven, who sees all and knows all."

The resounding denunciation brought the buzz of conversation to an abrupt end. The entire assembly stood rooted in a silence so intense that not even the usual coughing or shuffling of feet broke the hush.

"There is a price to pay for violating God's law," the hooded man said in an ominous tone that reached every ear in the nave. "And pay you must, for you cannot hide from God's justice. You shall answer in full measure, for your iniquitous deeds have brought shame to the house of Plantagenet."

He lifted the candle and held it aloft. "Your eternal life is in peril, yet you have shown no sign of repentance. Therefore, you are here and now separated from the precious body and blood of Christ and from the society of all Christians. You are excluded from all sacraments and shall be cast without mercy into outer darkness. You are judged as one of the damned with the devil and his fallen angels and all reprobates."

He turned the candle upside down and let it go. It hit the slate floor below with a thud, extinguishing the flame in the process. "Thus, you are anathema and shall henceforth be declared excommunicated."

In one swift movement, he produced a cocked crossbow from behind the statue and aimed the steel bolt directly at those seated on the platform.

Chapter 28

What happened next took place in the space of a single heartbeat.

"Look out!" cried someone near the platform in a shrill voice.

The sight of the crossbow galvanized the king into action, as though compelled by the instinct to survive under duress from years of experience on the field of battle. He flung himself from his chair, drawing with him his son, whose arm he grasped and whom he pulled none-too-gently off the padded seat. Both of them landed on hands and knees on the wooden surface.

A split second later, a steel bolt thudded at an angle into the cushioned back of the crown prince's chair, exactly where he'd leaned against it.

"Protect the king," bellowed the captain of the royal guard.

Edward of England placed a hand on the rim of the platform to steady himself as he hopped nimbly to the floor three feet below. His elite guards swarmed around him, forming a solid wall with their bodies.

The rasp of steel against metal scabbards filled the air as the royal guards drew forth their swords. The gesture was more perfunctory than practical, for a thirty-inch steel blade was no match against a well-aimed bolt from a crossbow.

In that same instant, the crown prince scrambled to

the edge of the platform and jumped down to the slate floor.

The lords and ladies closest to the wooden structure were exposed to the greatest danger, so it was understandable that they retreated in haste to distance themselves from it. Unfortunately, the measures they took to protect themselves left the crown prince standing alone and in the line of sight from the shooter.

The moment the steel bolt hit the cushioned chair, the two guardsmen had relaxed their grip on Kyle's arms, evidently distracted by the more imminent threat to the royal family.

Kyle yanked free of their grasp and set out with bounding steps toward where the crown prince stood motionless, frozen in shock, his mouth agape and eyes flared in panic.

It might take five or six seconds for the hooded man to fire another shot. He would first have to cock the mechanism, set a bolt in the furrow, fit the grooved end against the taut string, and then take careful aim at a target some eighty feet away.

The thought flashed through Kyle's mind that it would take a mite longer than that to cover the twenty odd feet between him and the crown prince because of the people blocking his path. But try he must.

In the event he reached the young man in time, the plan was to thrust him out of sight behind the far edge of the platform. At that moment, the penalty of death meted out to anyone laying hands on a royal personage was the farthest thing from his mind.

An unanticipated delay of several seconds on the hooded man's part enabled Kyle to approach the crown prince and interpose his broad back between him and the villain on the ledge. He could only hope the man's inability to see either target would be enough to dissuade him from firing a second bolt. Still, he braced his legs for impact, just in case.

Before he could even glance over his shoulder at the shooter, something slammed into his back, knocking him forward into the crown prince. He took the young man down with him as he fell, turning his body slightly to the left to break the fall with his own shoulder. He hit the slate floor hard enough to jar the soft cap loose from his head.

For several heartbeats, he lay there without moving, puzzled that he felt no searing pain from the bolt in his back. He turned his head and lifted his gaze to the ledge at the rear of the nave in time to see the hooded man vanish through the small door in the tower wall.

When he lowered his gaze, his heart jumped upward to lodge in his throat, choking him so that he couldn't breathe. There was Ordog, sprawled at his feet with a steel bolt sticking out of his upper back.

At the sight of the older man lying face down on cold slate, a desolate cry of anguish erupted from his mouth—an inhuman sound, even to his own ears.

Over the past few weeks of their acquaintance, he'd grown fond of Ordog, treating him like the older brother he'd never had. It hurt him sorely to lose such a dear friend.

A slight movement under his body reminded him that he still had the crown prince pinned to the floor. He sat up, which enabled the young man to clamber to his feet.

The crown prince stared down at Ordog in horror,

as though he grasped that, except for Heaven's grace and that fair-haired man seated on the floor, he could have been the one lying there, bleeding. "Is—is he dead?" he said in an appalled stammer.

Before Kyle could reach out to check Ordog's condition, Eri burst through a ring of onlookers beginning to gather around the fallen man.

Her skirts spread out around her as she dropped to her knees, her countenance grim. She pressed two fingers into the left side of Ordog's neck. "He lives," she said, sagging with evident relief. A cursory inspection of the position of the bolt jutting from the center of an ever-widening dark wet stain seemed to satisfy her. "The wound is serious but not fatal."

By that time, Armand had appeared at her elbow, seemingly out of nowhere, looking quite handsome in a white and gold brocade cotte over white hose.

Subtle emotions played across Eri's face at the sight of him standing beside her. "You're here," she said, gazing up at him.

"I've been here the whole time," Armand said, laying a gentle hand on her shoulder. "What can I do to help?"

Her dark eyes narrowed and glittered brightly for a moment. "You can find the rogue who did this and bring him to justice."

In the meantime, the king had broken through the royal guard to check on his son. He seemed vastly relieved that the young man had suffered no harm during his trying experience.

"How dare that brigand shed blood in the house of God," the old priest declared in a forceful tone from the pulpit, his body rigid with indignation. He turned to descend the stairs, his expression stricken and dismayed, as though acutely distressed that a blessed service had turned into a chaotic event. In his haste, he missed the last step and nearly fell, except for a nearby acolyte who reached out to catch him.

The acolyte retained a grip on the old priest's arm as he helped him walk across the chancel. The other acolytes followed them through the doorway beside the confessional and into the vestry beyond. The altar boys and the monks from the choir trudged from the chancel and set out in single file across the nave, bound for the vestibule in the rear.

Now that High Mass had been cut short, most of the congregation turned to leave, heading toward the back of the nave. They spoke in hushed tones as they shuffled along.

"Give way," shouted a man from the vestibule. "Let the guardsmen through."

"He fled into the tower," someone said in a loud voice.

The sound of fists hammering on a wooden surface reverberated off the high ceiling of the nave.

"The door is stuck," said another man.

"It's not stuck," somebody said in reply. "It's barred from the inside."

"We've got the rascal trapped on the roof," cried still another man. "The only way down is through the tower stairwell."

Kyle gazed up at Armand. "There is another way down."

Armand looked confused for a split second before his face cleared. "Of course," he said, his amber eyes bright with understanding. "The scaffold!"

Kyle got to his feet, but he made no effort to move. "I can't leave him like this," he said, frowning down at Ordog.

"I'll take care of him," Eri said. "Go, before that villain gets away."

Kyle and Armand turned and sprinted without hindrance toward the front of the nave, for there was hardly anyone now left in that part of the church.

They sailed over the low rail that separated the chancel from the public nave and headed for the doorway beside the confessional.

Together they burst into the vestry, where the old priest had begun the ceremonial divesting of his priestly robes with the assistance of the acolytes.

"Sorry," Kyle and Armand said in unison.

They hastened across the small room and climbed out the large hole from floor to ceiling that the masons had made in the far wall to enlarge the chamber.

Once outside, Kyle halted briefly at the foot of the scaffolding propped against the back of the church building. "We're just in time," he said to Armand, pointing up at the hooded man who had climbed halfway down the wooden structure with the crossbow slung across his back.

To make matters worse, the man also had a sword strapped to his hip—another circumstance which, besides their lack of protective armor, put Kyle and Armand at a disadvantage, since the two of them carried no weapons other than a dagger and a slightly longer dirk.

"Another minute's delay," Armand said, "and he would have been long gone."

The hooded man undoubtedly saw Kyle and

Armand, too, for he immediately reversed direction and started climbing back toward the church roof.

Kyle and Armand scaled the sixty-foot wooden scaffold as swiftly as they dared, for the structure swayed and wobbled as a result of their frantic efforts to climb to the top.

Kyle reached the roof first. He edged an eye over the rim to ascertain whether their adversary was lying in wait for them with his weapon cocked and ready.

He was half right about that, for the hooded man had paused in flight to cock the crossbow, after which he quickly fitted a bolt into the groove.

Kyle scrambled up onto the catwalk—the flat part of the roof—with Armand hard on his heels. Rather than charging the hooded man outright, they inched away from each other to make it more difficult for the man to cover both of them at the same time.

That ploy didn't seem to faze the shooter at all. He simply swung the cocked crossbow from one to the other, aiming at each of them in turn.

Shouts from the ground forty feet below drew the attention of the three on the catwalk. A crowd had gathered in the graveyard, apparently to watch the goings-on up on the church roof.

Over a dozen guardsmen stood among those gathered in the church yard. Several had crossbows cocked and ready to shoot. None of them released a bolt, possibly because they had trouble getting a clear shot at the would-be assassin.

A couple of guardsmen broke away from their cohorts and circled around to the back of the church building, likely with the intent of mounting the scaffold.

"Why are you doing this?' Kyle said to the hooded

man.

"Because it is God's will."

The voice sounded terribly familiar.

Kyle squinted against the glare of the late morning sun to peer into the shadowed recesses of the hood. "Brother Luke?" he said, more surprised than alarmed.

"Aye," he said, pushing back the black fabric to reveal a gaunt face and bluish-gray eyes burning with a fanatical zeal.

"You fired upon the king," Kyle said. "God's will or not, that is a treasonous offense punishable by death."

"I wasn't aiming at the king."

"Then who—" Armand said.

"Who else could it be but the crown prince," Kyle interjected grimly. "The lad must have been his real target all along."

"But why?" Armand said, clearly baffled.

"Aye," Kyle said, turning to the friar. "Tell us why."

"His illicit proclivities have brought disgrace and dishonor upon the royal family," Brother Luke said.

"What sort of 'illicit proclivities'?" Armand said.

"He took on a male lover," the friar said with his upper lip curled in contempt. "He lay down with him as he would with a woman."

"I've heard those rumors, too," Armand said. "It sounded like idle gossip to me."

"You are gravely mistaken," the friar said. "On more than one occasion, his lover bragged about his immoral exploits with the prince."

"There are others who have such leanings," Armand said. "Will you do away with them, too?"

"That is outside the scope of my mission," Brother Luke said. "Those born to reign by divine right have a responsibility to the kingly line. It must be kept pure and clean, without defilement."

"What about noblemen who are guilty of murder?" Armand said. "Are they not also reprehensible in the eyes of God?"

"They are, indeed," Brother Luke said with smug satisfaction.

Kyle stared at the friar. It was the expression on the man's face, not what he'd said, that triggered a distant memory at the back of his mind. In a flash of enlightenment, it occurred to him that he might, in fact, have already witnessed the abolition of undesirables from the kingly line without being aware of the reason for it at the time. "Did you have a hand in the sudden demise of Sir Guy de Forz?"

Brother Luke gave him a cryptic smile without saying a word.

Kyle recalled John the apothecary's assessment of the cause of Sir Guy's death. "You used mandrake, didn't you?" he said, watching the friar closely for a reaction. "You put it in his wine so that he wouldn't notice the taste."

At the mention of that particular poison, Brother Luke's left eye twitched involuntarily. He seemed totally unaware that he had just given himself away.

But Kyle had caught it and now pressed him for more information. "Who did Sir Guy supposedly kill to bring such a fate upon himself?"

For a long moment, Brother Luke stared at him in silence. "I am surprised you have to ask," he said at last.

"Are you referring to Sir Charles de Forz?" Kyle said. "Witnesses have already confirmed that he died from a stray arrow while hunting."

"His death was no accident," Brother Luke said with conviction.

"Sir Guy was not on the scene at the time," Kyle said. "Are you implying that he paid someone to kill his brother?"

When the friar made no reply, he continued with a speculative theory that might not be speculation after all. "With his elder brother out of the way, Sir Guy would be one step closer to the throne. I suppose an overly ambitious man from the House of Lancaster might consider that a valid reason for fratricide."

"A man with his brother's blood on his hands has no right to rule," Brother Luke said.

Kyle's thoughts turned naturally to the third and youngest de Forz brother. "And Sir Kenneth? Is his death also your handiwork?"

"He dabbled in the black arts," Brother Luke said with righteous zeal. "There is no place for him in the kingly line."

"Seeing as how there were no marks of violence on him," Kyle said, "how did you manage to pull it off?"

Once again, Brother Luke gave no response.

"His death had nothing to do with the witch's curse, did it?" Kyle said without expectation of an answer. "I'll wager you did the deed while I was ill, which is why I failed to notice your absence from the Romany camp. His tent with those colorful stripes would have been easy to spot in the forest. You could have entered through the slit in the canvas that the Romany boy had made upon his escape. Once inside, you may well have held a pillow over his face until he quit breathing. That would be easy to do if he was drunk or even slumbering deeply. Whatever the case, you murdered a helpless man in his sleep."

"It wasn't murder," Brother Luke said. "He was purged from the sovereign line. It was a right and just fate for those of his ilk who cater to demons."

"By my reckoning, you are guilty of homicide on two counts," Kyle said. "Brother Luke, I hereby place you under arrest for the unlawful killing of Sir Guy de Forz and Sir Kenneth de Forz. You are also charged with the attempted murder of the crown prince. Drop your weapon and surrender yourself into my custody to face the king's justice." He took a step forward.

He stopped abruptly when the friar swung the cocked crossbow from where it had been trained on Armand, only to aim it directly at his chest.

"I cannot comply with your demand," Brother Luke said, backing up a pace.

"Do you deny that you are answerable to a court of law for your crimes?" Kyle said, keeping a wary eye on the friar in anticipation of his next move.

"I answer only to God," Brother Luke said with impassioned fervor.

The sudden clatter of the two guardsmen climbing onto the slate roof from the scaffolding caused Brother Luke to focus his attention in that direction for a split second.

Armand, who was closer than Kyle, lunged forward in an attempt to snatch the crossbow from the friar's grasp.

Brother Luke swung the crossbow toward Armand and released the bolt at nearly point-blank range.

Chapter 29

"Don't!" Kyle cried.

His shout came too late, both to prevent Armand from taking an unnecessary risk and to stop Brother Luke from releasing the bolt. He watched in dismay as Armand crumpled like a rag doll onto the slate roof.

Because Armand's back was turned to him, Kyle could not see where he'd been hit. From where he stood, it looked like a shot to the gut.

Such an injury may not seem like a mortal wound. However, it would surely lead to a slow and painful death over the next few days. If luck was on Armand's side, he would succumb sooner.

With balled fists and clenched jaw, Kyle started toward Brother Luke, intent on accosting him before he had a chance to reload the crossbow. The whisper of drawn steel brought him to an abrupt halt. "Do you plan to kill everyone in your path?" he said, his gaze on the sword blade leveled at his chest.

"Only those foolish enough to interfere," Brother Luke said.

Armand pushed himself upright to a sitting position with a groan of pain. He shifted his body, as though to find a more comfortable position on the hard slates.

The slight movement drew Kyle's eye, prompting him to glance in that direction. Relief rushed through him at the sight of the bolt sticking out of Armand's upper thigh. The wound, although painful, would not be fatal if attended to in time. Of course, the metal tip might have lodged in the bone—a circumstance that could lead to serious complications later.

Armand removed his belt and slung the leather strip around his thigh above the injury and pulled it tight. Blood still seeped from the wound, but the flow had slowed considerably. He made no attempt to remove the bolt, given that the wooden shaft plugged the hole in his punctured flesh.

"You could have easily killed him," Kyle said, tilting his head at Armand. "Yet you only winged him. Why is that?"

"I owed him for saving me from drowning during our journey." Brother Luke took a step back. "Now, we are even."

"So, what's next?" Kyle said.

"That is entirely up to you," Brother Luke said, backing up another pace.

It was clear to Kyle that the friar meant to work his way toward the door in the bell tower that adjoined the flat part of the roof. With the two guardsmen barring the way to the scaffold, the tower stairwell was the only other way to the ground.

Even though Brother Luke took but one measured step at a time, he still made progress, seeing as how from where he now stood, he was nearly halfway to his goal.

Kyle hoped to keep his adversary occupied with small talk until he got close enough to physically take him down. He would have to time his assault with the utmost care to keep the man from whirling around and fleeing before he was ready to pounce.

"I cannot let you go free," he said, matching his stride to the friar's unhurried pace. "I am bound by law to take you into custody. You killed two men and attempted to take the life of another. Do you really think you will actually escape the executioner's axe?"

"That fate will never befall me," Brother Luke said. "I cannot be by mortal slain. So says the prophecy. Hence, no man who raises a hand against me will prevail."

"Are you that confident?"

"I am foreordained to succeed," Brother Luke said with a feverish light in his eyes. "Otherwise, I would never have undertaken this mission." Without warning, he hurled the uncocked crossbow at Kyle's head before he spun around and started toward the bell tower. His rapid pace faltered after the first few steps, for the long skirts of his robe severely hampered the movement of his legs.

Kyle dodged the crossbow, even as he lunged forward to catch the loose folds of the friar's robe with his hand. The instant his fingers closed around the black fabric, he yanked back on it, effectively arresting the man's flight.

Now that he'd been jerked to an abrupt halt, Brother Luke immediately swung his sword in a wide horizontal stroke at Kyle's bare neck.

Kyle ducked in time to avoid the blow. He released his grip on the friar's garment and took a brisk step back. Once out of the reach of the longer weapon, he stood erect and drew his dirk—a fourteen-inch blade that was no match for thirty inches of steel. Yet it was better than nothing at all.

He and Brother Luke began to circle one another,

each looking for an opening to strike. Because he had the shorter weapon, he would have to muster all the skill he possessed for defense and, should the opportunity present itself, for offense. His secondary motive for shifting around was to insinuate himself between the friar and the tower in order to block the only other path to freedom.

Since he was now facing in the direction of the scaffolding, he could see the two guardsmen moving stealthily toward the friar, ostensibly to take him by surprise from behind. They were still too far away to be of any immediate assistance.

Brother Luke clutched the hilt with his right hand and pointed the blade at Kyle with his right arm extended to the limit. At first glance, it appeared as though he lacked the experience necessary to wield such a weapon. "It's been years since I've held a sword," he said, as though he'd read Kyle's mind.

"Were you any good at it back then?" Kyle said, his eyes on the wavering steel tip.

"You tell me." Brother Luke shifted his weight to his left leg and slid his right foot back slightly to retain his balance. He grasped the hilt with both hands and went into a defensive crouch to guard his chest, the sword poised to strike.

Kyle looked at Brother Luke with new eyes. The friar had clearly assumed the stance of a skilled swordsman. The next few minutes would test his adversary's capability, as well as his own.

From the grim expression on the man's face, they were now engaged in a fight to the death, with no quarter asked and no quarter given.

Brother Luke leaned to the right as he swung the

sword in a vertical circle, finishing with a swift downward chop to Kyle's head.

Kyle nimbly stepped to the left and raised his dirk, deflecting the stroke with a metallic clang. He went into a slight crouch to protect his body, his blade held ready against the friar's next move. His foe was quick on his feet. In order to survive he must remain vigilant.

Brother Luke lunged with the blade leveled at Kyle's chest, seemingly intent upon coming up under his guard.

Steel bit into steel as Kyle batted aside the tip of the sword with his dirk.

Brother Luke recovered immediately and executed a slanting backhanded stroke at Kyle's midsection.

Kyle leaned back, but not far enough. The sharp point of the blade slashed through the thin fabric of his maroon tunic and burned a diagonal trail across his torso until it struck the packet of letters beneath.

Ignoring the searing pain, he stepped back to avoid another overhead swing aimed at his head. The tip of the sword came so close to his face, he heard the whoosh of the blade and felt the breeze as it passed. Sweat beaded on his forehead and ran down the sides of his face, both from the heat of the sun on the hot slate roof and from the effort of defending himself.

Brother Luke pressed his advantage against his wounded opponent by swinging back the blade to strike yet again.

Kyle flung up his arm to block the blow with his dirk.

Metal scraped against metal as the longer sword slid down the shorter blade, only to stop abruptly as one hilt guard met the other.

With their weapons locked together, they glared at each other over crossed blades, eye to eye, teeth clenched, muscles strained to the limit as each tried to prevail over the other.

A rush of warmth down his belly reminded Kyle that he was losing blood at a rapid rate. He felt a burning sensation across his chest, yet the pain was tolerable, likely because of the surge in his veins from a compelling and primitive instinct to survive.

Rather than wait for his strength to wane, he relaxed his arm to throw off his opponent. With a quick sidestep and a twist of his wrist, he wrenched his dirk free from the friar's hilt guard.

The unexpected ploy caught Brother Luke by surprise. He stumbled forward. To catch his balance, he grabbed the balustrade that ran the length of the catwalk. Old weathered mortar adjoining the marble rail to the waist-high post beneath it crumbled under his weight.

The rail gave way unexpectedly. The friar threw out his arms, flailing the air to catch his balance. His expression was that of surprised disbelief.

Kyle instinctively reached out his hand to catch hold of the man's flapping robe. Blatant relief washed through him that he was too far away to do so. He surely would have been dragged over the edge had he succeeded, never to see his beloved family again.

Brother Luke was now leaning out past the verge at an impossible angle, his eyes wide with terror. All pretense of bravado was gone.

He disappeared in a blink. Yet his scream rent the air for a long terrible moment.

Then, there was silence, so final, so absolute.

Kyle fell to his knees with a grunt of pain and leaned forward to peer over the edge of the roof.

By that time, the two guardsmen had drawn near. They, too, dropped to their knees to look down.

Forty feet below, Brother Luke lay with his mouth agape and sightless eyes staring up at nothing, his body skewered on the long bronze blade in the upraised hand of Saint Michael the Archangel.

Chapter 30

Armand looked over at the nearest guardsman. "I fear that my companion might bleed to death should his wound be left unattended for too long," he said with a grimace from the insistent throbbing pain in his thigh. "Though I am better off than he, I still cannot walk under my own power. Will you be so kind as to fetch help to carry us off this roof?"

With a nod, that guardsman hurried away toward the tower to do as he was bidden.

Armand eyed the bolt sticking out of his thigh, noting that the angle of protrusion was problematic. Should he try to remove it on his own, he might cause himself more harm than good. He used his dagger to cut a large opening in his bloodstained legging to expose the area around the wound. "What is your name?" he said to the other guardsman.

"Higgins."

"Well, Higgins," Armand said. "Can you give me a hand here?"

"What do you need me to do?"

"Pull out this bolt."

Higgins hesitated for only an instant before he went down on one knee at Armand's side. He wrapped his fingers around the shaft and looked him in the eye. "Ready?"

At Armand's nod, Higgins yanked the slender

missile from where it was lodged in the red swollen flesh.

Armand grunted through clenched teeth at the sudden excruciating pain that radiated from his upper thigh throughout his whole body. Blood seeped from the open wound and dribbled to the slate roof beneath him. With his mouth compressed against the agonizing ache at the site of the wound, he nodded his thanks. It was all he could manage at that moment.

When the sharp pain subsided somewhat, he loosened the belt high on his leg and slid it down a couple of inches to cover the puncture in his leg. With gritted teeth, he tightened the leather strap to stem the flow of blood. The wound still hurt immensely, but at least now he could move his leg without an unbearable stabbing sensation in his thigh muscles.

"Help me up," he said, extending a hand to Higgins, who hauled him to his feet.

Once he stood upright on his good leg, he slung his arm across the man's shoulders and hobbled over to where Kyle sat near the edge of the roof with his right hand pressed against the wound on his chest. "Hang on, *mon ami*," he said as he lowered himself onto the slates with a grunt. "Help will soon be here."

"Good to know," Kyle said, his face ashen and his breathing ragged. Blood seeped through his fingers and ran down his wrist to stain the cuff of his sleeve. He removed from his tunic the courier pouch drenched with blood and handed it to his companion. "Just in case," he added grimly.

About that time, Eri burst through the tower doorway. She ran over to where Armand and Kyle sat near the gap in the balustrade railing.

On seeing blood on Armand's thigh and the tightened belt around it, she nodded her head in approval. "Can you manage for now?"

"I think so," Armand said through clenched teeth.

Evidently reassured, she turned her full attention to Kyle. After assessing his condition in a single glance, she set about tearing a narrow strip of fabric from the hem of her skirt. She then wrapped the long cloth tightly around his chest and tied the ends together. "This should hold you until I can attend to your wound properly."

"How is Ordog?" Armand and Kyle said in unison.

"As well as can be expected," she said.

"Is he going to die?" Kyle said.

"He will eventually," she said. "But not today. And neither will you, if I can help it." She glanced from one to the other. "This is going to be a busy afternoon," she added with a sigh.

At that moment, five guardsmen spilled through the tower doorway and strode up the catwalk. Four of them spread a blanket beside Kyle, after which they lifted him bodily and laid him on the woven cloth. Each of the four grasped a corner and lifted the blanket in unison, after which they proceeded to carry him away. They would likely have trouble negotiating the tower stairs, but it was better than making a gravely wounded man walk down on his own.

Eri looked unsure whether to stay with Armand or follow the deputy.

"Go with him to make sure he's settled properly," Armand said. "If the king is still on the grounds, perhaps you can pass this along to him." He handed to her the courier pouch stained with blood. The slash in the leather from the friar's sword did not seem to affect the letters contained therein.

She received it with a frown. "I hope whatever is in here is worth the trouble it caused." She turned away and hurried after the departing guardsmen.

Higgins and the remaining man helped Armand to his feet and supported him on either side. Together, they made their way over to the tower door and down the winding staircase with Armand hobbling from one step to the next. Slotted openings in the outer walls let in sufficient illumination to light their way to the bottom.

"Where is the fellow who was wounded in church?" Armand said as they passed through the open doorway on the ground floor and into the church vestibule.

"The man of whom you speak has been installed in the rectory behind the church," said the other guardsman. "We have been ordered to take you and your companion there as well. Master Camdale, who is the king's own physician, will attend to the three of you."

"How gracious of Master Camdale," Armand said. Evidently, Kyle and Ordog's effort to defend the crown prince did not go unnoticed.

"Gracious or not," the guardsman said, "he had little choice in the matter."

"How so?" Armand said.

"His Majesty himself ordered him to see to your wounds."

"Well, well," Armand said skeptically. He could only hope the king's physician knew more about the art of healing than bloodletting with a sharp knife or the application of leeches. Both were popular methods of treating ills and ailments of every kind, including broken bones and troublesome teeth. Of the two, he hated leeches the most. Just the thought of those little black slug-like creatures on his body made his skin crawl.

Except for a trio of armed soldiers standing in the vestibule with their hands on the hilts of their swords, the church appeared to be empty.

Armand and the two guardsmen continued on through the front door of the church and around to the side of the building, where a large crowd had gathered in the graveyard.

Even the king and his son were there, surrounded as usual by the royal guard.

The old priest was present as well, along with the acolytes and the altar boys.

Those assembled spoke in hushed tones as they beheld the friar's body impaled on Saint Michael the Archangel's upraised sword.

Rivulets of blood had trickled down the length of the black marble statue, only to puddle on the square sandstone base beneath the sculpted feet.

As Armand approached the grisly scene, he slowed his pace. "Hold up a moment," he said to the guardsmen, who complied without objection to his request.

The sight of bright red blood on the pale stone pedestal reminded him that there was more to the prophecy than a warning to those who debased or defiled the sovereign line.

There was also a word of caution directed at the so-called grievous bane, in this case Brother Luke, who had appointed himself in that role. Unfortunately, the friar had failed to consider the last stanza of the prophecy. "Lest stain he will the base of stone, with blood from wounds that be his own." He spoke the words in a low voice, more for his own elucidation, rather than for the guardsmen to hear.

"What did you say?" Higgins said, turning his head to gaze at him.

"It's from the prophecy," Armand said. "The first part of it goes like this: 'Debase ye not the sovereign line, those born to reign by right divine, else face ye must the grievous bane, who cannot be by mortal slain.' " He fixed his gaze on the bloodstained pedestal. "The last line says: 'Lest stain he will the base of stone, with blood from wounds that be his own.' "

"What does it mean?" Higgins said.

"It means there was always the possibility that the self-appointed bane could fail in his lofty calling to keep the royal line pure and clean. To his detriment, the friar evidently assumed he was above failing in his mission, and thus in no danger of receiving corporeal punishment for his deeds."

Higgins eyed the impaled body. "It appears God had other ideas about the fellow's fate," he said dryly.

"Amen to that," Armand said with gravity.

Meanwhile, the old priest had stepped forward to stand before the statue. He turned to face the crowd, his hands raised for quiet with his black cassock billowing in the breeze. His sharp voice cut through the muted murmuring of the assembly. "This misguided soul committed heinous deeds that warranted the penalty of death. He has now paid for those sins with his life." He bowed his head and made the sign of the cross. "May

God have mercy on his soul." To the acolytes, he said, "Fetch a winding sheet and a bucket of water. In spite of his failings, he was still a man of the cloth."

The chief acolyte and one altar boy withdrew in haste, only to return minutes later. The chief acolyte had a folded length of fabric under his arm, which he spread out at the base of the statue. The altar boy carried a pail of water and a scrub brush, which he set on the ground nearby.

With the help of a couple of soldiers, the acolytes removed the friar's body from off the upraised sword.

"Clean it as best you can," the priest said to the altar boys, indicating the bloodstains with a wave of his hand.

The oldest of the three boys sloshed water on the black marble figure and used the brush to scrub off the blood. Try as he might, he could not remove from the porous sandstone base the scarlet stains that would serve as a reminder of the fearful event that had taken place that day.

Before long, the crowd began to drift away. The king and his entourage mounted their horses and headed back to the royal palace. With the priest leading the way, the acolytes carried Brother Luke's body around to the rectory to be laid out properly.

The excitement was over, but the event would not be forgotten. For those who had witnessed it, it would be a tale to tell and retell for years to come.

The insistent throb in Armand's thigh reminded him that he'd lingered too long and that his wound was in sore need of attention. He and the two guardsmen continued on their way around the back of the church to the rectory.

Once inside the stone building that housed the priests and the resident acolytes, the three of them were directed to a large room with four beds in it, all perpendicular to the wall.

Ordog lay on his side in the first bed. His upper torso was bare, except for a white bandage wrapped around his chest and one shoulder. His breathing was deep and rhythmic. The fact that he failed to stir or even blink at the sound of voices in the room likely meant he'd been drugged to keep him from moving about during the initial stage of healing.

Kyle occupied the second bed. He reposed on his back, silent and unnaturally still. The front of his tunic was laid open to expose the angry red gash across his chest. His breathing was regular and even, despite his pallid complexion. It was clear that he, too, had been drugged prior to Eri's ministering to him.

She bent over his upper torso, plying a threaded needle in order to truss the gaping flesh. The apron she wore over her finery kept the blood from staining the fabric beneath. Her head was bare, for she had earlier removed the wimple and circlet.

Master Camdale, the king's physician, was there, too, with his medicament pouch in his hand. He was a stout man in his midforties, clad in black with a face set in a perpetual frown. He stood beside Eri, looking on with interest as she worked.

Armand hobbled over to the third bed and eased himself onto the soft edge. "Thanks for your help," he said to the guardsmen before they withdrew. He then watched as Eri deftly sewed together the edges of the slashed skin on the deputy's chest.

When she finished, she cut the thread with her

dagger and straightened her back to survey her handiwork—a long neat row of stitches. She dribbled a bit of honey along the site of the wound before she covered it with a clean rectangle of linen cloth. "That should do for now. I will check it again in the morning to see how it looks."

"Where did you learn that technique?" Master Camdale said. He seemed intrigued.

"There have always been healers among my people," she said. "Knowledge of herbs and simples has been handed down for generations."

"Are you a healer, then?" Master Camdale said.

"Nay," she said. "I picked this up on my own by watching it done many times."

"Ah," Master Camdale said, visibly impressed. "When will you remove the thread?"

"In seven days," she said. "That is how long it will take for the flesh to knit together. If the stitches are taken out too soon, there is a possibility that any strain on the wound may cause it to split open again."

"Quite so," Master Camdale said with a nod, looking even more impressed than before.

She walked over to where Armand perched on the edge of his bed. "Let's have a look at you."

Armand loosened the belt around his upper leg. Blood began to flow freely from the neat round hole in the center of a small mound of bruised and swollen flesh on his thigh.

Eri washed away the blood, both crusted and fresh, from around the wound and blotted it dry before applying a dab of honey on the affected area. She wrapped a strip of linen around his upper leg, pulled it tight, and tied the ends together. "Stay off your feet for the next few days."

Armand used both hands to lift his affected leg onto the bed with care. He then leaned back against the wall, his good leg slung over the edge of the bed with his foot touching the floor. "No worries about that. It hurts too much to move about."

Master Camdale dug in his medicament pouch and removed a small corked phial. "Two drops of this in a mug of ale will dull the pain," he said to Armand.

"What is it?" Armand said.

"Juice extracted from crushed poppy seeds," Master Camdale said.

Armand glanced at Eri. Only after her nod of approval did he take the tiny phial from the physician's hand.

"Mistress Eri," Master Camdale said. "I am curious as to why you used honey on their wounds."

"Unbeknownst to many," she said, "honey contains healing properties. I don't know how it works exactly, but it has proven quite effective in the past. In addition, it keeps the cloth from sticking to the wound, which makes it easier to remove the soiled bandage to replace it with a new one."

"Interesting," Master Camdale said. "These men cannot fail to recover under your care."

"I hope for a full recovery for each of them," she said. "However, that may not happen on its own. I plan to come here every day to check on their progress."

"I will see you in the morning, then," Master Camdale said with a courtly bow.

She escorted him across the room. "Thank you for your assistance," she said as he walked through the doorway.

Master Camdale stepped out into the corridor and turned to face her. "Nay, my dear lady. Thank *you*. This has been a most enlightening experience." With a slight inclination of his head, he went on his way.

She stood in the open doorway with her back to the room for a long moment.

"May we talk?" Armand said to her.

She swung around to face him. "I'm listening."

"Will you come nearer so I don't have to shout to be heard across the room?"

"As you wish," she said, her manner cool and aloof. She approached the foot of his bed and stood there with her fingers laced together at her waist.

"You must have thought me callous for leaving without a word the other day," he said.

She remained silent, as though waiting for him to continue. The fact that she didn't rant or rail at him gave him hope that she might be inclined to hear him out.

"I began this journey with a purpose," he said. "As you may be aware, I have connections with the Knights Templar. I am not a member of the Order. I do concur, however, with their doctrines and beliefs. That is why, when the need arose, I willingly offered my services to carry out a holy mission for the church."

"Go on," she said.

"I was tasked with the responsibility of delivering a sacred relic to Saint Paul's Cathedral in London. That is where I went when I left you at the tavern. I must confess that, at the time, I fully intended to go on my way alone."

"Yet you came here instead," she said. "Why?"

"While I was preparing for the journey home,

something became very clear to me."

"What was it?"

"That I missed you terribly," he said.

A smile tugged at the corners of her mouth. "And?" she said softly.

"When I first met you," he said, "I felt a strong attraction for you. Because I thought you were a man, I made an effort to resist your charms. However, the better I got to know you, the less your gender mattered to me. I fell in love with *who* you were, not *what* you were. Nonetheless, I will admit that when I stumbled upon the fact that you were a woman, I was quite ecstatic."

She held his gaze as she walked around to the side of the bed.

He reached for her hand and held it between both of his own. "I have never loved anyone like I love you. I thought I was content to live my life alone, with no companion to care for or who cared for me. After I met you, my outlook changed, apparently without my being aware of it. While I was away from you for the past two days, you've been in my thoughts the whole time. I wondered how you were doing, what you were thinking, how you were feeling. Your absence left a hole in my heart only you can fill."

"What do you plan to do about it?" she said after a brief silence.

"That is up to you," he said. "I took you for granted, and that was a mistake. Can you find it in your heart to give me a chance to make it up to you?"

She gazed at him in silence, which this time was longer and deeper than before.

"I will gladly fall to my knees, if that will move

you."

"That would be foolhardy," she said gently, "for it would surely tear open your wound."

"What do you say, then?" he said. "Will you forgive me?"

He slid his injured leg off the edge of the bed, ready to follow through with his threat to kneel. The sudden movement caused a blotch of bright red to blossom on the white bandage over the site of his wound. He clenched his teeth with an indrawn breath against the sharp pain that pierced his injured thigh.

"All right, you win," she said, eyeing the fresh blood staining the linen cloth that bound his wound. "I forgive you."

He sagged with relief, although the act of lifting his leg back onto the bed made his pain more acute. When he'd settled himself as comfortably as he could with a throbbing ache in his upper thigh, he took her hand in his and brought it to his lips. "It was not my intent to burden you with my confession. I will understand if you do not feel the same way about me."

"And if I do?" she said.

He gave her a blank look, unsure he'd heard her correctly. "Are you saying that you like me?"

"Nay," she said with a shake of her head.

"Oh," he said, not bothering to hide his disappointment.

"I love you," she said.

A smile spread over his face. "It is amazing how those three simple words just made my heart overflow with joy."

"The question is," she said, "are you willing to take responsibility for me?"

"Of course I am," he said.

"As far as marriage?" she said.

"Well, uh," he said, at a loss for words. He wasn't opposed to marriage. He just wasn't sure he was ready for it.

"I see," she said. "I suppose this is not the time to tell you that we are already handfasted."

"How?" he said, taken by surprise. "When?"

"Remember the time I fell ill in my home camp?" she said.

"I do," he said.

"You may recall that we ate from the same bowl. We even exchanged gifts."

"Aye," he said. "What of it?"

"I asked if you liked my gift, and you said you did. I asked if you liked me, and you said you do. All was done in accord with Romany custom. The witness who was present at the time will attest to that."

"Your uncle, of course," he said. "That explains his less-than-friendly attitude toward me." He glanced down at the plaited leather bracelet around his wrist. "Why did you not tell me about this sooner?"

"I was afraid you would run away if you knew I'd tricked you into marriage."

"So you admit you tricked me," he said, lifting his gaze.

"I do," she said, clearly not sorry at all.

He heaved a heavy and troubled sigh.

"Is it that hard for you to accept?" she said.

"I, um," he said, his manner hesitant as he searched for the right words to express his sentiments.

It was her turn to sigh. "I take it you find a union with me burdensome." Without waiting for his reply, she continued, "I suppose that means we are not meant to be. In light of that, I release you from the ties that bind us together. There, it's done. You are free."

"Would you throw me away so easily?" he said.

"I have no use for a reluctant husband," she said.

"Who says I am reluctant?" he said. "At any rate, your declaration of annulment is invalid."

"How so?"

"There is no witness to confirm it. Is that not a requirement, in accord with Romany custom? So, whether you like it or not, we are still wed." He reached out and pulled her down to sit on the edge of the bed facing him. "Shall I claim my marriage due here and now to prove it?"

A worried frown clouded her features. "Perhaps it would be more advisable to wait until we are alone," she said, glancing pointedly at their wounded companions.

"To tell you the truth," he said with a sheepish grin, "I am in too much pain at the moment to carry out my threat. Perhaps we can do this later. Much later."

She remained mute, but she looked greatly relieved.

He gazed at her, enthralled by her delicate beauty. "Have I told you how lovely you are?"

His declaration brought a deep rose flush to her olive countenance. "Not even once," she said, meeting his gaze.

"You can expect to hear it every day from now on," he said.

She bestowed a dazzling smile upon him that caused his heartbeat to quicken noticeably. They sat in silence, gazing at one another for a long moment.

"Oh, before I forget," she said at length. "While I was going through the church yard earlier, I was able to deliver the courier packet to the king."

"That will surely take a load off Master Kyle's mind," he said. "Once he learns his duty is done, it will be hard to keep him from heading back home."

"According to Master Camdale," she said, "we are to remain here for a full month. Then, when the three of you are hale and hearty once again, you are obliged to appear before the king."

"I wonder what Edward of England has in store for us," he said, musing aloud. "I have heard that he is an unpredictable fellow."

"There is but one way to find out," she said, "and that is to wait and see."

Chapter 31

Kyle, Ordog, Armand, and Eri stood in an anteroom where over a dozen other men and women waited their turn to see the king of England. After about two hours, a palace guardsman finally called out Kyle's name.

He and Ordog followed the guardsman through the doorway into an opulent and lavishly decorated chamber. Armand limped in behind them, leaning heavily on his cane. Eri walked beside him with a possessive hand on his arm.

Highly polished black and white marble tiles on the floor reflected the morning light that came through five tall mullioned windows along a side wall.

At the far end of the large room, Edward of England sat on a raised dais in an ornately carved chair gilded with gold. He looked regal in a white brocade robe encrusted with rubies that glimmered with each move he made. Instead of a circlet on his head, he wore a gold crown with a precious stone set on each of its four points.

There were ten other men in the room. Three were servants in attendance to the king, recognizable by their plain clothing. The rest appeared to be men of high rank and position who served in an advisory capacity, identifiable as such by the finery they wore.

To the left of the throne, a clerk clad in black sat at

a tiny desk with quill pen in hand, recording the events of the day, while Sir Miles Aldensford stood on the king's right, unobtrusive in a midnight blue cotte with hose to match.

Although it had been a month complete since he'd sustained his injury, Kyle walked with care. Any sudden movement resulted in a painful pulling sensation in the long scar across his chest. Because of the nature of his wound, it would take more time and much exercise to return to normal activities. If not for Armand and Eri's timely intervention, he might have bled to death on the church roof. Then, instead of his returning to his family, they might have only received word of his demise. He dared not dwell on that because the thought pained him more than did the actual damage to his body.

In anticipation of their appearance before the king, he and his companions had been supplied with fashionable attire, which garments had been personally measured, fitted, and sewn by the royal tailor. Their other finery had been befouled beyond repair and thus discarded as unusable.

The guardsman stopped five paces from the dais and bowed to the king before he withdrew without a word.

Kyle, Ordog, and Armand came to a halt and gave the English monarch a courtly bow, while Eri curtseyed gracefully. When they stood upright once again, they waited respectfully for the king to speak.

"Are you well?" Edward said, looking from one to the other.

"Aye, Your Majesty," they said in unison.

"Good, good," Edward said.

Although the king inquired after their health, Kyle got the distinct impression that the man cared not a whit about their welfare, that his inquiry was but a perfunctory gesture required by polite society.

Edward fixed his gaze on Kyle. "I am not unacquainted with your role in preventing harm to my son that day in Saint Michael's church. As you may have surmised, that is why I have called you here today."

"It is my duty to protect you and your son, sire," Kyle said.

Edward's eyes then settled on Ordog. "And you?" he said, his eyebrow cocked in curiosity. "I have been informed that you are of Romany descent. Neither you nor your people owe allegiance to me. Yet you acted with courage in defense of someone who is not of your kind."

"It is true that I am Romany," Ordog said. "Still, we camp on English soil. That makes us indebted to Your Majesty to a large degree. However, in this instance, my actions were not prompted by loyalty to the crown as much as by a more personal reason." He placed a hand on Kyle's shoulder. "I owe this man my life. When the opportunity presented itself in the church, I was bound by honor to return the favor to him."

The king looked impressed at Ordog's declaration. "Would that all of my subjects were like you!" he declared with fervor.

Kyle and those with him waited in silence for the king to continue.

"Kyle Shaw, deputy to the sheriff of Ayrshire," the king said. "Approach the throne."

Kyle stepped forward as bidden, halting one step short of the low platform. He nodded a greeting to Sir Miles Aldensford, who smiled at him from where he stood beside the throne.

"Aldensford speaks very highly of you," Edward said. "Too bad he was not in attendance on the day you first attempted to deliver the courier pouch to me in the Tower. His counsel as to the purpose of your visit would have allayed the unfortunate misunderstanding that later ensued."

Even though Kyle agreed wholeheartedly, he kept his opinion to himself about how quick the English were to jump to an erroneous conclusion that all those of Scottish descent were rebels against the crown of England. Now that he was in the king's favor, it would not do to harp on a regrettable incident that could not be undone.

Edward rose to his feet and held out his right hand to Sir Miles, who drew his sword and placed the hilt in the king's palm.

"For meritorious service to the crown at the risk of your life," the king said. "Kneel, Kyle Shaw."

Kyle went down on one knee on the tiled floor, his gaze fixed on a blood red ruby fastened to the front of the king's robe.

The king tapped the blade first on Kyle's right shoulder and then on his left shoulder. "Rise, Sir Kyle Shaw, knight of the realm."

Kyle got to his feet and bowed to the king. "You are gracious, Your Majesty. May I always be worthy of the honor bestowed upon me this day." Rather than taking up a position beside his companions, he remained where he stood at the foot of the dais.

Edward handed the sword back to Sir Miles and resumed his seat on the cushioned chair. When he looked up, he seemed surprised that Kyle had not yet moved from before the throne. "Is there something you wish to say?" he said with mild interest.

"There is, sire," Kyle said. "May I ask Your Majesty to grant me a boon?" The king was not the kind of man to give anything away without receiving something in return. In this instance, he hoped the man would make an exception. Otherwise, he would have to give Derlinton a wide berth on the way home.

"You may ask it," Edward said. "However, I cannot guarantee I will grant it until I first hear what it is."

"It is but a small favor," Kyle said. "Yet it will mean the world to the recipient. On the way here, we encountered a Constable Garvey of Yorkshire who was instrumental in clearing the way for us to pass safely through his province. If it is at all possible, I request that a commendation be sent to him in the form of a letter, expressing Your Majesty's appreciation for Constable Garvey's unstinting service to the crown. I will be glad to deliver it to him personally when we pass through Derlinton."

Edward glanced aside at his clerk, who nodded his head. "Consider it done," he said, turning back to Kyle.

"Thank you, sire."

"I understand that you are anxious to go home," Edward said. "When do you plan to depart?"

"In two days' time."

"I will have the letter of commendation delivered to you at the rectory in the morning. I shall send with it a courier pouch containing a communication to Sir

Percy, which I trust you will deliver immediately upon your return to Ayr."

"You may count on me to do so," Kyle said with a courtly bow. After stepping back a couple of paces, he turned to join his companions, at which time he could not help but notice the disapproval on the faces of all seven of the king's advisors.

He and those with him bowed to the king one more time before taking their leave.

Once they had stepped out of the royal chamber and into the anteroom, they heaved a collective sigh of relief.

Ordog ran a finger under the stiff collar around his neck. "I'm glad that's over. Now I can shed these fancy garments and get back into my own clothes. I don't know how the English can stand to wear them all day long."

"My sentiments exactly," Eri said with fervor. She looked down at her voluminous skirts. "It is nearly impossible to run or ride in this attire."

Ordog clapped Kyle on the back "Well, how does it feel to be *Sir* Kyle Shaw?" he said with emphasis on the newly bestowed title.

"It will take some getting used to," Kyle said, "though I reckon I'll manage."

"Perhaps now," Armand said, "the English will not be so quick to brand you as an insurgent against the crown."

"I think not," Kyle said in a low tone meant for their ears only. "Judging from the blatant censure on the faces of those noblemen in court today—Sir Miles Aldensford being the exception, of course—I doubt if it will make any difference to them. Don't let Edward of

England's amiable demeanor fool you. He is no better than they are. He has on numerous occasions made it abundantly clear that he considers Scotland and the Scottish folk who live there as shite on his boot. Perhaps now you understand why I can't wait to leave this place."

"I, too, am anxious to depart." Armand glanced from Eri to Ordog and back again. "Perhaps we can all ride together until we reach the camp."

Ordog cocked a skeptical eyebrow. "How long do you intend to keep up this farce?"

"Which farce is that?" Armand apparently knew full well what the older man meant, for his lips twitched to suppress a smile as he spoke.

"As I am sure you are aware, there can be no marriage without the consent of both parties," Ordog said.

"I am glad you brought that up," Armand said. "Let us discuss it outside, away from the prying eyes and ears of strangers."

The four of them made their way out the antechamber and down the corridor to the vestibule. Once they had passed through the arched entryway, they strolled across the green lawn toward the stable, where they had left their horses.

Ordog halted halfway across the open area, as did the others.

"What is it you have to say?" the older man said, turning to confront Armand.

"That my heart is set on Eri and no other will do," Armand said as he grasped her hand. "She feels the same about me. You can ask her yourself if you doubt my word."

"It's true, Uncle," she said with a nod. "I love him dearly and will have no other."

Ordog frowned at Armand. "Do you accept this woman, body and soul, as your wife, to protect and cherish all the days of your life, forsaking all others?"

"I do, of my own free will," Armand said.

Ordog's frowning gaze shifted to Eri. "And you?" he said to her. "Do you accept this man, body and soul, as your husband, to honor and respect all the days of your life, forsaking all others?"

She looked at Armand with the unmistakable warmth of a lover. "I do, of my own free will."

"Then I acknowledge the union between you." Ordog said. "May the goddess bless your household with peace, and may you find joy in each other." The frown faded from his brow, only to return a moment later. "Where will you live?"

"Armand and I already discussed that," Eri said. "We plan to stay in the camp."

"In our own tent, of course," Armand said.

Ordog looked relieved to hear it.

"Don't you fret, Uncle," she said. "I don't intend to leave you on your own. I will see to it that you eat what is good for you and take your medicaments on time so that you may live a long life."

"Sweet child," Ordog said to her. "You are too dear to me to lose to a lesser man."

Armand seemed surprised that the older man spoke so highly of him after treating him like a pariah ever since they'd left the Romany camp. "Why, thank you, Uncle. You may be sure that Eri will want for nothing under my care."

Ordog narrowed his eyes at Armand. "I'll be

watching you, boy," he said with unsmiling countenance. "If you ever make her cry…" He left the sentence unfinished, but the implication was clear.

"Stop it, Uncle," she said, glaring at the older man. "You'll scare him away."

Armand squeezed her hand. "It will take more than that to run me off. I am afraid you are stuck with me, whether you like it or not."

"I'm glad to hear it," she said, giving him a radiant smile, "because I feel the same way."

Chapter 32

Epilogue

October, 1298

Kyle rode into the outskirts of the port town of Ayr on the west coast of the Scottish lowlands. The legs and belly of his warhorse were crusted with mud from rutted roads made worse by seasonal showers.

The sun was high overhead, yet there was a cool nip in the autumn air. Leaves on deciduous trees lining the streets were tinged with golds and reds in anticipation of the coming winter.

On their way north from London, Kyle, Ordog, Armand, and Eri had stopped at Saint Nicholas's Hospital near York to fetch Reginald Crawford. By that time, the sheriff had fully recovered from his wounds. Because the assailant had been left-handed, the blade had missed vital organs, which accounted for his recovering at all. Had the attacker been right-handed and the blade longer, death would likely have ensued from such an assault.

While Reginald had been abed at the hospital, Constable Scanlon had tracked down the outlaws who had stolen the sheriff's horse. The constable not only recovered the rawboned bay, saddle and all, but he also managed to capture three of Viper's men who were responsible for both the theft and the attack on the sheriff. Unfortunately, the leader of the bandits had fled before he could be apprehended.

Kyle's only lament was that Constable Scanlon, for his dogged pursuit of justice, deserved a commendation from the king but didn't get it, whereas the mulish and obstinate Constable Garvey, who actually received the commendation, had done nothing to deserve it.

After a brief stop in Durham to visit the cathedral there, the five of them had continued on to the Romany camp nestled in the forest of the Tyne Valley. Kyle and Reginald then parted from there laden with food for their journey. They also received a warm invitation from Ordog, Armand, and Eri to visit the camp, should they ever pass that way again.

He and Reginald had pressed on to Carlyle, where they'd heard reports of a large troop of English soldiers passing through the vicinity weeks earlier. That news confirmed what Sir Miles Aldensford had told him during his recuperation in London about Edward of England dispatching over a hundred men to fortify Ayr Garrison, apparently in compliance with Sir Percy's request.

Now that Kyle was back in Ayr, nothing could dampen his high spirits, bone weary and saddle sore though he was after such a long journey.

Nevertheless, as he glanced around him, it struck him that not all was as he'd left it upon his departure months ago. There were fewer townsfolk in the streets going about their business in the middle of the day. Some of the homes in the poorer section looked abandoned. That troubled him because there was always a housing shortage in that part of town. Other dwellings had been burned to the ground, which disturbed him even more because it indicated that mischief had been afoot during his absence. Still, he was extremely glad to be home.

His elation was short-lived, however, due to the sudden appearance of four heavily armed English soldiers who rode from a side street to intercept him and Reginald.

"Captain Pilcher," said one of the soldiers. "What shall we do with these rebels?"

Captain Pilcher was a stout man of middle years with heavy jowls that bulged from under a Norman helmet. His shrewd black eyes raked Kyle and Reginald from head to toe, taking in their unkempt and begrimed appearance. "Let us first see what they are about," he said to his subordinate. To Reginald, he said, "State your business here."

"I am the sheriff of Ayrshire. Reginald Crawford, at yer service."

Captain Pilcher seemed to take Reginald's announcement in stride. "I see." His gaze shifted to Kyle. "And you?"

"I serve as deputy to the sheriff of Ayrshire. Sir Kyle Shaw, at your service."

"A knight of the realm, are you?" Captain Pilcher said. He looked impressed.

"I am indeed," Kyle said. Judging from the hostile expressions on the faces of the other three soldiers, he hoped his status—albeit newly acquired—would forestall any mistaken impression they might harbor that he and Reginald sided with the rebels.

"Have you been on the road long?" Captain Pilcher said.

"It has taken us several weeks to travel from the south of England."

"Where are you bound?"

"Ayr Garrison," Kyle said.

Captain Pilcher exchanged a cryptic glance with his fellow soldiers. "Then you have not yet heard."

"Heard what?" Kyle and Reginald said in unison.

"Scottish rebels burned the garrison to the ground."

Kyle and Reginald glanced at each other in disbelief.

"How did it happen?" Reginald said.

"When did it happen?" Kyle said.

"About a month ago," Captain Pilcher said. "The rebels staged a raid in the middle of the night. This town has been under marshal law ever since."

The sheriff stared at Captain Pilcher in pensive silence, as though unsure what to say.

"What provoked the raid?" Kyle said, aware the answer might be couched in half-truths or outright lies. After all, the captain and his men were English soldiers, and as such, they would incriminate themselves if they admitted to inciting the insurrection.

"The usual discontent among the populace, I suppose," Captain Pilcher said.

The captain's blasé attitude signaled the end of the conversation for Kyle, for the man was clearly biased against Scottish folk. "What of Sir Percy?" he said, abruptly changing the subject. "Was he injured during the raid?"

"Not to my knowledge."

"Where is he now?"

"Why do you ask?"

"I have letters to deliver to him."

"I'll take them," Captain Pilcher said, holding out a gloved hand.

"The king of England has instructed me to deliver these letters personally," Kyle said.

"As you wish," Captain Pilcher said. "Come with me." To his men, he said, "Keep watch until I return."

Kyle and Reginald nudged their mounts forward to follow Captain Pilcher down Harbour Street.

Along the way, Kyle noticed the sullen faces of burghers and townsfolk who happened to be out and about. There was also an unusual concentration of English soldiers patrolling the streets, either on foot or on horseback.

Before long, they came to a manor house with a high stone wall around it.

Captain Pilcher led the way through the open gates, passing a handful of soldiers guarding the entryway. He continued on to the large stone dwelling set well back on the property. On drawing abreast of the front door, he brought his horse to a halt. "You will find Sir Percy inside." Without another word, he turned his mount and rode back toward the street.

Kyle and Reginald swung down from the saddle and tied the reins to a wooden rail adjacent to the entryway, where an English soldier stood at attention.

As the two of them drew near, the soldier opened the door and stepped aside to let them enter the house.

A man whom Kyle recognized as Nicholas the clerk rose from a desk just inside the doorway.

"Welcome back," Nicholas said to both of them in a Cornish accent. His gaze dropped to the courier pouch in Kyle's hand. "I take it you are here to see Sir Percy."

"Aye," Kyle said.

"Follow me." Nicholas swung around and started across the main hall. "I'm sure by now you've heard what happened to the garrison," he said, glancing over his shoulder.

"I did," Kyle said with a nod. "Burned to the ground, did it?"

"Just like you predicted before you left," Nicholas said. "Every last piece of timber went up in flames, including the gates and the drawbridge. The blaze lit up the night sky for hours. It was truly a sight to behold."

"I'm sure it was," Kyle said, conjuring up a mental image of the conflagration that consumed the old timber castle, the stable, the sheriff's office, and everything else made of wood inside the curtain walls.

"Were there many casualties?" Kyle said.

"Not as numerous as you would suppose," Nicholas said. "Sir Percy was away at the time, and most of the soldiers were out on patrol. Some of those still inside the garrison escaped through the midden in the seaward wall. Others saddled the horses that remained in the stable and raced them across the drawbridge before the fire made it impassable."

"Since my old office is gone," Reginald said, "have I been assigned a new one?"

"Aye," Nicholas said. "This manor now serves as headquarters for Sir Percy and displaced officers like you. A small troop has been garrisoned here, although the majority of soldiers have been billeted in other large houses around town."

"So where is my office?" Reginald said.

"I shall take you there in a moment." Nicholas turned into a dimly lit corridor and knocked on the first door. When a voice from within bade him enter, he opened the door and announced the deputy.

Kyle went inside as Nicholas continued on down the corridor with the sheriff trailing behind him.

Sir Percy sat at a rectangular oak desk in the center of a small room. Bright light from the mullioned window behind him cast his face in shadow. "So you have returned at last," he said, looking up from writing on a sheet of vellum paper. "I was beginning to think you weren't coming back."

"I ran into a bit of trouble while in London."

"What kind of trouble?"

"The kind that involved thirty inches of steel. The wound I sustained forced me to delay my return."

"I see," Sir Percy said, giving Kyle a frowning glance from head to toe. "Are you now fit for service?"

"I have yet to put it to the test, m'lord." Kyle handed over the courier packet.

Sir Percy opened the leather pouch and took out a letter with the royal seal on it. He broke the rigid red wax and unfolded the vellum. As he read, the frown faded from his brow.

"Good news, m'lord?" Kyle said.

"The best I could hope for," Sir Percy said. "His Majesty plans to send additional troops to fortify all Scottish castles large enough to pose a threat to the crown. That should deter the rabble from further rebellion."

It was Kyle's turn to frown, for that boded ill for his countrymen. Over the past ten years, oppression and mistreatment at the hands of English soldiers had served as the catalyst for civil unrest among the Scottish populace. An influx of English troops would only make a bad situation worse.

Kyle removed from inside his tunic the small leather cinch purse that Sir Percy had given him for expenses. “This is what is left from the journey,” he said, laying the purse on the desk. “If you have no more need of me, m’lord…” he added, hoping to be dismissed so that he may seek out his family.

“His Majesty writes that you have been knighted as a peer of the realm for saving the crown prince’s life,” Sir Percy said, clearly ignoring the hint. He looked up at the deputy. “I hope you appreciate the extent of the privilege that has been bestowed upon you.”

“I do, m’lord,” Kyle said.

“Well, then,” Sir Percy said. “I will expect your full cooperation in ferreting out the perpetrators of this latest revolt and actively quashing the next uprising, should there be one, as is your sworn duty.”

“As a deputy in the service of the king, I will uphold the law to the best of my ability,” Kyle said. “Now, if there is nothing further, I shall take my leave.” Without waiting for a reply, he turned on his heel and strode toward the doorway.

On entering the corridor, he retraced his steps to the main hall and crossed the floor to the clerk’s desk. He sat on the hard wooden bench beside it with his back against the wall to await the man’s return.

Before long, Nicholas ambled over and sat on the stool behind his desk. “I take it you are here to collect your pay,” he said with a knowing glance.

“You read my mind,” Kyle said.

Nicholas took one of the scrolls from the rack on the edge of his desk and unrolled it to peruse the writing on it. After making a notation on the scroll with a quill pen, he wrote a number on a small piece of paper vellum and signed it at the bottom with a flourish. “Take this to the paymaster,” he said, handing it to the deputy. “His office is up the stairs and to the left. I think you will be pleased with the amount.”

Kyle glanced at the figures on the scrap of paper. “I am,” he said, getting to his feet. “Thanks.”

“What do you plan to do now?” Nicholas said.

“I shall fetch my family,” Kyle said. “After that, I’m going home to sleep in my own bed at long last.”

“I meant about the most recent rising,” Nicholas said. “Arresting your own countrymen could get mighty tricky for someone in your situation.”

“That’s for sure,” Kyle said grimly. “The truth is, I haven’t had time to give it much thought.”

“May I make a suggestion?”

“Of course,” Kyle said. “I’m all ears.”

“Take your family and leave this place,” Nicholas said in a low voice, his tone urgent. “You said it yourself before you left. Things will only get worse in this part of the country, especially up north, which seems to spawn pockets of resistance. As a deputy, you will be caught in the middle of warring factions no matter what side prevails.”

“You forget that I am bound by oath to uphold English law,” Kyle said.

“Turn in your resignation prior to your departure,” Nicholas said. “I will withhold it from Sir Percy until you have had time to board a ship. Five days should do it. You told me once that you served under the king of France. Why not do it again? If not for yourself, then do it for the sake of those whom you love.”

Kyle’s eyes narrowed in speculation at the clerk’s suggestion. It was certainly worthy of thought, given the dark days looming on the horizon.

"Should you decide to heed my warning," Nicholas said, "tell no one lest a loose tongue or careless speech give you away before you can pack up and leave." The slightest of smiles touched his lips. "In case you are wondering why I am helping you, it is because I liked you from the moment I'd met you. And I liked you even better after you suggested months ago that I send my family back to Cornwall to keep them safe from the strife and dissention that broke out here shortly thereafter. This is my way of repaying you for that."

"You're a good man, Nicholas," Kyle said. "Too bad there aren't more Englishmen like you. The world would be a better place because of it."

****

Kyle braced his legs on the wooden deck of the Scottish merchant vessel, his eyes on a distant strip of land dead ahead on the eastern horizon. Cold wind swept across the choppy waters of the North Sea, tugging at his dark red cloak and ruffling the cropped tawny hair on his head.

Joneta stood beside him with their infant son in her arms. Both she and the baby were bundled against the cold.

John Logan was there on deck, too. He had decided to accompany them on the trip across the sea for reasons of his own, the most obvious being the safety of his wife, Colina. She stood beside him with one hand on the wooden rail and the other holding Kyle's toddler stepson Bruce propped on her hip. John would have no problem earning a living in France or anywhere else. As a skilled apothecary, he would be welcomed no matter where he went.

When Kyle had discussed the idea of leaving Scotland with Joneta, she'd objected to running out on her countrymen in their hour of need. Yet she realized there was little chance that her children and those of other Scottish women would thrive under the current unfavorable living conditions.

Once she'd learned of her husband's purpose for going to France, she wholeheartedly supported his decision. No matter how long it took, he would persist until he'd convinced King Philip IV to send the promised aid to Scotland, which would enable his countrymen to stand firm against English domination. Scottish folk did not mind being subjects of Edward of England. They did, however, have a problem with the abuses heaped upon them by English nobles and English justiciars who meted out biased justice in favor of their own kind.

Kyle knew that the day would come when he would go back to Scotland to join his countrymen in their fight for independence. When that time came, he hoped to return with a large number of French soldiers whose sole aim was to help the Scots throw off the English yoke. Until then, he would live on foreign soil and watch his children grow up.

In the meantime, he would seek employment with the provost marshal of the French king's army, to solve crimes and bring felons to justice. After all, that was what he did as a man of law.

A word about the author…

E. R. Dillon was born in New Orleans and still lives in Louisiana. Her acquaintance with certain aspects of the law comes from working for civil and criminal attorneys for many years. As a medieval history buff and a fan of mysteries, she incorporates both elements into her stories.

For author's website, visit:

http://www.erdillon.com

Thank you for purchasing
this publication of The Wild Rose Press, Inc.

For questions or more information
contact us at
info@thewildrosepress.com.

The Wild Rose Press, Inc.
www.thewildrosepress.com

www.ingramcontent.com/pod-product-compliance
Lightning Source LLC
Chambersburg PA
CBHW061327050726
47504CB00013B/707
* 9 7 8 1 5 0 9 2 3 9 0 1 6 *